Screwed

by

Mike Owens

Screwed

Contact Information: info@thewildrosepress.com

Cover Art by *Diana Carlile*

The Wild Rose Press, Inc.
PO Box 708
Adams Basin, NY 14410-0708

Visit us at www.thewilderroses.com

Publishing History
First Scarlet Rose Edition, 2017
Print ISBN 978-1-5092-1664-2
Digital ISBN 978-1-5092-1665-9

Published in the United States of America

She'll take the money…and run.

"Take a good look, kid." Gloria lifted her glasses. Her left eye was swollen almost shut and colored a dark blue.

"Jesus, who did this?" Sharon asked.

"In our business we don't name names. Remember that."

"Shouldn't you tell the police?"

Gloria started a laugh that came out as a snort. "That's the last thing I would do. They know me there, and they know how I make my living. If I went to the police station crying over a black eye they'd laugh right in my face."

"It's not right," Sharon said.

"Your ideas about right and wrong are mixed up. Once you get the whore label stuck on you nobody cares what happens to you, unless you get your throat cut and you bleed out in a public place."

Sharon shook her head. "I can't believe what I'm hearing."

Dedication

To Marilyn and Molly…different species, same heart.

Author Acknowledgments

Many thanks to writers at the East Beach Writers Guild and the Hampton Roads Writers. It takes a village, after all. To Melanie Billings, my editor at The Wild Rose Press, thanks seem hardly sufficient, but here it is. Thanks to Jim Healy for helpful discussions and suggesting the title for this book.

Chapter One

"Fifty bucks if you'll show 'em to us, honey. Come on, take it off." A sheen of sweat gleamed on the face of the man waving the bill in one hand and a half-smoked cigar in the other. Was it really a fifty? She'd have to get closer to tell, and Sharon, now down to a wisp of a bra and a flesh-colored thong, didn't want to get too close. She'd seen what happened when one of the other dancers reached into the front row to retrieve a handful of cash, and it sure wasn't worth fifty bucks, not even five hundred.

The music was getting louder, and the bass beat reverberated through the stage. Damn Lennie. The sleaze ball manager turned up the volume, egging the crowd on. Sharon danced to the other side of the platform and edged around a foamy puddle that she hoped was beer. If things really got crazy, which way would she run?

Now the chant rose from the back of the room and spread like a tidal flood. "Take it off. Take it off."

The man in the front row slapped the bill down on the stage. "Come and get it, darlin'. I ain't gonna wait all night." He covered the bill with his hand.

Adding up numbers helped her block out the sound, the smells, and the hands that grabbed for her every time she got close to the edge of the stage. If the man really had a fifty, that would put her just over three hundred dollars for the night, even after she slipped a few bucks to Rodney, their three-hundred-pound bouncer, and Lennie took his thirty percent. She undulated back to the center of the stage, arms waving above her head.

The chant drowned out the music. "Take it off. Take it off."

The moneyman flashed his cash then belched out a blue cloud of cigar smoke that made her head spin. She took a few steps back to catch her breath.

"A goddam little tease, ain't you?" The man held his bill up high.

Yep, fifty bucks.

Sharon inhaled deeply and reached behind her back to unclasp her bra. She turned her back to the audience and started a slow shimmy. The noise behind her dropped off to a whisper. They were going to get what they wanted.

She turned, flimsy bra dangling from one hand with her left arm folded across her breasts. There's a first time for everything, she said to herself. It was bound to happen sooner or later. With the extra fifty bucks she could cover fall semester tuition and then some. She dropped her arm to her side, and the crowd roared its approval. Now, how to retrieve the fifty?

The sweaty man held the bill between his thumb and forefinger. When Sharon reached for it, he jerked it away. "You ain't finished yet, sweetheart." He pointed to her thong.

"But you said..." Sharon stopped herself mid-sentence. *Never argue with the customers, even when they behave like pigs.* She covered her breasts with her arms.

"I know damned well what I said." He began waving the bill again. "And when you take that thing off, I want it."

The man standing next to Mr. Fifty Bucks guffawed and pounded him on the back. Something foamy—beer?—gushed out of his nose.

To hell with this. No way she was going to get completely naked. She turned, just enough to catch Lennie's gestures. He made a stripping motion at his waist with his right hand and drew his left forefinger across his throat. Clear enough. Either take it all off or lose the job. And she couldn't lose the job. All the local positions that paid anything at all were taken up by other students. She could make more in a weekend of stripping than she'd make in a month bagging groceries.

Sharon walked back to center stage. She began a little strut toward the waving fifty. Now other hands clutched other bills. They looked like fronds waving on a coral reef. All that money for a filmy strip of fabric that hid nothing at all. She couldn't see the denominations, but with any luck at all, this might be her biggest night yet.

She turned her back to the audience again and ran her thumbs along the elastic band of the thong. The chant swelled behind her. She couldn't make out the words and didn't want to. She leaned forward, her ass pointed skyward, and slowly peeled the thong down over her thighs.

"Spread 'em, honey."

She did. They'd get their money's worth, so long as she got hers, too. She stepped out of the thong and straightened up, twirling her last remaining garment on her forefinger.

"Turn around, honey. Let's see it."

She lowered her eyelids enough to make all the faces in the crowd go out of focus. Then she walked toward the waving sea of bills, plucked the first few from waving hands, careful to jump back when one of them grabbed for her legs. Mr. Fifty Bucks waited.

"I want that panty thing you're wearing."

What the hell. She could replace it for a couple of bucks. She flipped it to the man and reached for the fifty. He was a lot quicker than he looked. He grabbed her arm and pulled her off the stage into the sea of hands. They were all over her. Her blonde wig was gone in an instant. Fingers invaded every orifice. One bastard even forced his thumb into her mouth. When she clamped down, he jerked it out and slapped her hard across the face. "Rodney," she screamed.

The giant bouncer loped across the stage and jumped into the crowd. He lifted her up and sat her back on the platform. She dashed behind the curtain. Her breasts ached from the groping. Her fifty bucks, along with the other money she'd collected, was long gone.

****

Monday morning and a quiz in her accounting class awaited, not her first choice of how to start a day. A long morning soak in a hot tub took away some of the aches and pains of the Saturday night mauling, but her body was covered with so many fingertip-sized bruises that she looked like a polka dot doll. Long sleeves this week for sure.

"You look wasted." Brad Gilmore, a classmate, slid into the desk beside her. "Big party weekend?"

"No, no. I just had some trouble sleeping." Sharon pulled pencils from her bag and lined them up beside her notebook.

"Hey, is that a black eye?" Brad leaned in close. Others nearby apparently overheard his question, and the girl on Sharon's left peered in at her.

"I fell, okay?"

"No need to get huffy." Brad leaned back in his seat. "Think you've got enough pencils there? I mean, it's only a quiz. Nobody's asking you to write a book or anything."

"Knock it off, Brad. I've got a splitting headache, and you're just making it worse."

"Okay, okay. Excuse me for trying to be friendly." He turned away from her and in a mock whisper, loud enough to be heard several rows away, said, "Anybody got a Midol?"

"Damn you." Sharon gathered up her notes and pencils and headed for the door.

"I was right," Brad said. "I knew it."

She almost collided with the graduate assistant, Herb Collins, who walked in with copies of the exam under his arm.

"Ms. Saluda, leaving so soon?"

"No, sir. I was just going for a drink of water."

"Don't be long. We'll start the exam at ten sharp."

"Yes, sir."

Sharon slipped back in the rear door of the auditorium and took a seat in the last row.

"Do not break the seal on your exam until I tell you to." Collins paced back and forth in front of the class. His flannel shirt was worn at the elbows and apparently hadn't been ironed since the semester began. "You'll have forty-five minutes to complete the test. If you have to leave the room for any reason, bring your test booklet to the front and leave it with me until you return. Any questions? You may begin."

Sharon flew through the first three pages before the flashbacks started—hands squeezing her breasts, hands prying her legs open, fingers penetrating her. Then came the nausea. She ran her hand across her brow—moist, sticky. Concentrate. Halfway through. She bit her lip and stared at the page, trying to focus. But the numbers blurred, ran together as if she spilled water on her paper. She dug her nails into her palms, tried deep breathing with her eyes closed. Nothing worked.

"Time's up. Pass your test booklets to the right."

What? No. Where had the time gone? She'd only finished half of it. Had she blacked out?

The student to her left nudged her with his elbow then handed her a stack of completed exams to pass along. She added hers then handed them off.

****

The summons from the head of the business administration department, her major field of study, came much quicker than she'd expected. The same afternoon after she botched the exam she found herself seated in front of the department head flanked by the graduate assistant.

"Would you care to explain this, Ms. Saluda?" He held up her exam booklet. "You completed the first half of the exam perfectly, I might add, but left the last half blank."

"I wasn't feeling well." Sharon stared down at her hands, unable to meet his gaze.

"Mr. Collins mentioned you weren't looking quite

yourself, but all you had to do was speak up, and some arrangements could have been made."

"I'm sorry, sir. I have no excuse."

"I hate to see you fail this exam, Ms. Saluda. So far all your work has been excellent, and I particularly want to see one of our best business majors do well."

She shrugged. What could she do? There was no way she could tell them what really happened.

The head man folded his hands on top of Sharon's exam booklet. "This is most unusual and something I would not ordinarily condone, but Mr. Collins has convinced me that a make-up exam might be in order."

Could this be real? A second chance? Sharon smiled at Collins. "That would be most generous of you, sir. I'd greatly appreciate another try at it."

"I'll ask you to keep this strictly confidential, Ms. Saluda. If word ever got out I allowed make-up tests, I'd never hear the end of it. I'd be up to my ears in requests."

"Thank you, sir. I understand."

"Very well. Set up a time with Mr. Collins. I suggest you take this test in his office for the sake of privacy."

****

In the expanded closet that served as his office, Herb Collins shoved aside a stack of folders, then balanced three thick textbooks on top of the pile. "There," he said, patting the small cleared area on the table. "Will that be enough room?"

"That's just fine, Mr. Collins." She had to take a deep breath to slip between the table edge and the chair, but she wasn't about to complain. Not now. Second chances were too few and far between.

"I thought you could just take the last half of the exam over. Does thirty minutes sound okay?"

Sharon nodded.

Collins laid her original exam booklet on the table. "Why don't you just start where you left off?"

"Okay," she said. "And Mr. Collins, I really appreciate your going to bat for me. I won't let you down."

"I know you won't. You're an excellent student. You do feel better now, don't you?"

"Much, thanks."

Collins glanced at his watch, then left.

Sharon was able to clear her mind with a few deep breaths. She still had plenty of reminders from her ordeal; her breasts were bruised and tender where some bastard had tried to twist off her nipples. She'd taped gauze pads over them because even the light abrasion from her bra caused unbearable pain, and going braless was not an option, not with breasts like hers. When she crossed her legs, it felt like something had been shoved inside her and left there.

After Rodney carried her backstage and covered her with a sheet, Lennie walked into the dressing area and tossed several wet twenties on the floor beside her where they landed with a soft splat. "Sorry 'bout that, but you really got 'em riled up."

"You're saying it was my fault? Where's the rest of my money?"

"I ain't sayin' nothin'. You're responsible for your cash. You lose it, it's gone." He looked her over and smirked. "You looked good out there. You ever want some real work, come and see me."

Accounting test. Sharon slapped her forehead.

Concentrate. Her watch lay beside the exam booklet. Five minutes gone already. Then all the work she'd put in preparing for the exam kicked in. She cruised through the last half of the test with time to spare.

As she waited for Collins to return, she looked around his office. So this was the life of a graduate assistant. Not much to show for years of hard work. She saw only two possibilities; either he loved the work or he wasn't worth a damn doing anything else. She quickly dismissed possibility number two. For no obvious reason, Collins struck her as someone who could do whatever he set his mind to. Confidence, that was it. He radiated a quiet confidence. What she wouldn't give for a few spoonfuls of that about now.

Collins tapped gently on the door before he entered. "Everything work out?"

"Much better." She handed him the completed exam.

He flipped through the last pages of the booklet. "This is more like it." He smiled at her.

Warmth started in Sharon's fingers and toes, then quickly spread inward. She enjoyed the sensation for a moment until the scene from the previous night exploded in her brain once again. The thought of any man's hands on her body made her skin crawl. "I have to go." She rushed through the open door.

****

The photos turned up on her computer the following Tuesday. There she stood on stage, naked as the day she came into the world except for her blonde wig and shoes, both of which she lost shortly afterward. Her thong hung limply from her left hand. At least she wasn't smiling, not that anyone was looking at her face.

The site was named, Lennie's Social Club, but at least her identity wasn't. Great. Now she was famous. But even if her name wasn't public domain, her body certainly was. The e-mail addresses on the distribution list took up almost a third of a page, so her fame would spread far and wide in no time.

Just before she'd been jerked from the stage, she recalled the flash of several cameras. Lennie promised there would be no cameras allowed inside, but he made no attempt to enforce his own rules, especially when the customers carrying them could pay for drinks.

Sharon returned to her bedroom and crawled back under the blanket. It was her bedroom for now, but for how long? Rent would come due next week. If she wanted to continue eating regularly and sleeping indoors, she had to have a job. But there was no chance she could find employment to cover her bills in time. She pulled the blanket over her head.

When she left the strip club, Lennie's last words to her were, "You wanna make some real money, you let me know. I'll take good care of you." There was no mystery about his offer. Lennie ran a string of prostitutes from the strip club, girls who couldn't quite cut it on the dance floor. Sharon had talked with a couple of them. The money was good for Lennie. They'd all started out just like Sharon found herself now, desperate. Prostitution was just something to pay the bills until they found something better, but most of them never did. The job market for ex-hookers was nonexistent. And now Lennie wanted her to join his little troupe. Not likely. If she paid Lennie a visit, it would be to break one or both of his legs.

Another sleepless night. The accounting exam was

over and done with, but she had other problems, like keeping a roof over her head. Sharon threw a pillow at the ringing phone but missed. Who'd be calling her at eight in the morning? Then again, who else?

"Good morning, Sunshine. How's our family scholar?"

"Hi, Mom. I'm fine." *Yeah, destitute, but otherwise fine.*

"Did I wake you?"

"No, no. I must have just dozed off. I put in kind of a late night."

"Oh, honey. You work so hard. You should take some time off, enjoy yourself. You're only young once."

"I will, Mom. Right after mid-terms."

"I was hoping you could come home for a visit. We'd love to see you."

"I'd love to see you, too. It's just, you know, things are hectic right now." *Hectic? Try desperate.*

"Well, you know our door is always open for you. Do you need anything?"

"No. I'm fine, Mom. Really." *Well, maybe a few thousand bucks.* But she would dump her studies altogether before she'd ask her mother for money.

"Your father sends his love. I still can't get him to come to the phone. I wonder if the house ever caught on fire, would he even call the fire department."

"He's never going to change, Mom." Sharon tuned out her mother's update of recent family history. The phone cord reached just inside her tiny kitchen, so she began making coffee.

"Sharon?"

"Yes, Mom."

"I thought I'd lost you. You didn't answer. I said that nice boy, Steven Wright, asked about you. He's got a good job at the Burger Barn, assistant manager."

"I remember him." A tall, shy kid who could barely look her in the eye, that is until he got her alone in his truck. She had to elbow him in the throat to keep him from tearing her blouse off.

"He wants you to call him when you're home."

"Maybe I will. Mom, I have to run. I'll be late for class."

Pisgah College, a small liberal arts institution, was home to just over eight thousand students. The college with its brick buildings and sharp white trim sat at the southern tip of the Pisgah National Forest in the southeastern corner of the Blue Ridge Mountain range. Its founder, a Mr. Horace Blackwell, made his money from a string of furniture stores, and the endowment he established, while sufficient in 1938, fell short by 1998. The school had no choice but to squeeze the students by a raise in tuition prices, putting Sharon and others on very thin ice.

Mr. Blackwell had little input into the curriculum at Pisgah, aside from establishing a strong business program, some working knowledge of which he considered one of the keys to success as his students entered the real world. Business wasn't Sharon's first choice, and she had, in fact, changed majors three times before she landed in business administration. Being an English major was fun, but it didn't require a crystal ball to look into the future and see the poor job prospects it would likely attract.

Aside from the business program at Pisgah, there wasn't much to write home about. The school boasted a

European gymnastics instructor who had developed a widely known program for young female hopefuls, some of whom received special attention that had nothing to do with prowess on uneven parallel bars. Fall football weekends were loud but inconsequential, because the team hadn't had a winning record in recent memory. None of that mattered, not really. The beauty of the setting, solid brick buildings with ivy-covered walls, all nestled in a valley where the fall colors were beginning to come on strong, more than made up for extracurricular features. Mr. Blackwell would, no doubt, have been very proud.

Her first fall term there in 1996, started off well with a scholarship to supplement her own savings. After only three weeks on campus, she contracted a virulent case of mononucleosis that left her bed-ridden. She had to return home, because she was able to do little of her daily care. The short trip from bed to bathroom left her exhausted.

Still weak, she decided to return for the spring semester, but discovered that through an administrative glitch her scholarship funds had been awarded to another student. A very downtrodden Sharon returned home to a job in a local furniture factory.

Her work in sales went well from the start, and she began to stash away a few dollars, with hope of more to come. This plan ran off the rails when her boss, a persistent ass-pincher, assaulted her after hours on one of the beds in the showroom. Winning the battle with her assailant was a hollow victory; she lost her job.

She rejoined the academic community at Pisgah in the fall of 1998, as a twenty-three-year-old freshman. Every activity she undertook required a consideration of what it cost and what she had to spend.

Right from the start, she fought a losing battle. She might have made it if she'd been able to keep her job at Lennie's, but that job was history. She had about six weeks to come up with some major bucks or her career as an independent, full-time student was over.

The job openings in her day-old newspaper looked bleak. She'd seen all of them before, dead-end minimum wage positions. Nothing like what she'd made stripping.

She drained her coffee cup and poured another. She made damned good money taking off her clothes during the six weeks she worked at Lennie's. And for a while, she had complete control of a room full of men, a real power trip. But Lennie ran the only place in town where she could strut her stuff, and she wasn't going back there, ever.

Several of the other dancers were students, and more than once, she'd recognized university faculty members in the audience. Even if it wasn't included in the college catalogue, the flesh trade was very much alive and well at Pisgah College. If others were making good money from carnal pleasures, why couldn't she? There was certainly an abundance of nubile young flesh on campus. Wouldn't it be neat if she could open up her own club, just match up supply and demand?

Coeds and college faculty, a cliché but otherwise a perfect match. Most of the girls she knew had been propositioned by their teachers at one time or another, at least, that's what they claimed. Some of them even said they'd considered it, but of course, most of the faculty guys were married, so it was a trade-off, a little sex for a better grade.

Student hookers, yeah, it sounded crazy, like the title of a cheap porn flick. It sounded even crazier that afternoon at lunch when she suggested it, in a joking fashion, to a few of her friends. The laughter from their table drew stares from their neighbors.

The conversation had taken a weird turn when one of her classmates described in detail the offer from her math professor...a passing grade for a little weekend trip with him to his cabin in the mountains. And the deck was stacked, the professor held all the good cards. Wasn't that always the way? That's when Sharon suggested her crazy alternative, one that allowed her classmate to maintain control and get the grade or anything else she wanted.

The idea sounded a little less crazy that evening when she got calls from two of her friends. If she was serious, maybe they could get together just to talk. By the end of the week five girls had called her. If she added herself to the roster, she had six. Was that enough? Too many?

One of Lennie's "employees" told her he usually ran twelve to fifteen girls in his stable, as he called it. Of course, they weren't always available for business. Sometimes the customers roughed them up, and they took time off for bruises and black eyes to go away. Surely college faculty would be gentler. They'd have to be.

She spent most of Saturday night pacing around her apartment while two opposing voices waged war in her head. One kept telling her how impossible the whole idea was. What would she do if her parents ever found out? Wouldn't it make a lovely headline? "Student Kicked out of School for Running Prostitution

Ring." Her mother would die of shame.

By Monday morning, she was exhausted, but she had a plan. Since it was her idea, she'd have to assume the role of manager. All she had to go on was her own limited business experience, and that probably wouldn't be enough to get the job done. But if a jerk like Lennie could do it, why couldn't she?

On Tuesday, Gloria Parker, one of Lennie's girls that Sharon had met soon after she began stripping for Lennie, agreed to meet her for a late lunch. Gloria had been a promising student herself before two kids and a husband who ran off with a dental hygienist slapped her with the hard realities of life. Now prostitution was the only way she could make ends meet and make time for her kids.

"What do you want to know about all this stuff for?" Gloria pulled off bits of a grilled cheese sandwich and ate it piece by piece. Sharon had given her a list of sexual positions that she'd gathered from several books.

"I'm writing an article, for class." Sharon saw this one coming and had her answer ready.

"I thought you were a business major."

"I am, but I have to take a creative writing course. You know, the liberal arts thing. Just wanted to get my facts straight."

"That's reasonable, I guess." Gloria waved at the waitress, then pointed to her empty coffee cup.

"I don't know exactly how to ask this." Sharon faltered. "How do you decide what you'll do and what you won't do?"

Gloria looked at her long and hard. "Damn, girl, if I didn't know better I'd swear you were going into business for yourself."

"No, no. It's just information for my article."

"You sure?" Gloria winked.

"Absolutely. Stripping was hard enough. I'm a small town girl, remember?"

"Aren't we all?" Gloria pulled Sharon's notebook across the table and wrote down several entries. She pushed the notebook back to Sharon. "Most of the girls do these."

Sharon ran her finger down the list. "What's this?"

Gloria took the notebook and scratched though the line in question. "If you don't know what it is, don't even think about doing it."

"And this one, I mean, is that possible?"

"Just barely. I wouldn't recommend it unless you're taking a yoga class."

"I just need to know, for my paper."

"Paper my ass. You're planning something, right? You'd better be careful. Lennie would kill you if he ever found out." Gloria wrote in a few more lines. "No matter what, don't ever do any of this shit. People get hurt doing it."

"I don't even know what it is."

"Stay away from it. If they ask for it, say no."

Sharon leaned across the table and whispered, "How much?"

Gloria wrote dollar amounts by each of the entries. "I gotta go pick up my kid, but let me leave you with a little friendly advice. Don't do this. There are safer ways to make money."

"It's just for a class article."

"Yeah, right."

Sharon read over the list of sexual acts and fees Gloria left her. This was her business plan, all of it. Not much, but she'd have to go with what she had. The more advice she asked for, the more suspicion she'd raise.

Her conversation with Gloria proved difficult enough, but formatting her pitch to her prospective hostesses kept Sharon awake for two nights in a row. To begin with, she decided to call them hostesses; she still couldn't get her head around the idea that she was recruiting some of her classmates for prostitution. The very word caused her head to spin.

But what really knocked her flat on her butt was when she delivered that pitch. Seven of them, five junior students and two seniors including Sharon, gathered round a table in the north corner of the school cafeteria. And there she presented her proposal for the small group to join the world's oldest profession, foregoing all sense of decency and respectability, immersing themselves in sin…becoming whores.

Now, considering the strong affiliation of Pisgah College with the Baptist Church, her words should have been followed by a thunderclap and disintegration of the ceiling, allowing fire and brimstone to rain down upon them. It didn't happen.

"You're serious, aren't you?" Maggie Kirkland, a slightly plump junior psychology major asked. "Not just joking around?"

"No joke," Sharon said. "This way we keep control. We call the shots, and we get paid for it, simple fee for service."

She took a deep breath, then several more. Would they laugh in her face? Would they rat her out to the school administration and applaud as she was run out of town?

Maggie stared her down for a long moment, apparently wondering if Sharon would burst into laughter, just a big joke after all. But no laughter, just Sharon's stone face.

Instead, the guffaw came from Maggie. "Shit, girl, sign me up."

From that moment, the only course available for Sharon was forward.

Thursday, she emptied out her meager savings account and made a deposit on a small, furnished house at the end of a tree-lined avenue about a half mile east of the campus. The little cottage sat back off the street and had parking in the rear.

The arrangement of space inside the house—four bedrooms, each with a private bath and a small closet, but no kitchen—fit her purposes perfectly. The real estate agent said it was used to provide overnight lodging for transient faculty.

The front room of the house faced the street. The large open area with built-in bookcases taking up two walls held four plush leather-clad chairs, a bit worn, but each with its own end table. A comfy area, a place where a stressed academician, tired of the daily grind of complaining students and time-consuming committees could sit comfortably, have a brandy, read a book, smoke a cigar, choose a girl and exit by the back door, no questions asked. Certainly worth the price of admission.

Now Sharon had three pieces of the puzzle, she had a place of business, a sketchy business plan and the girls, her hostesses. She lacked only the clients, and their money. Her target audience would be male faculty members at or above the assistant professor level.

Graduate students and instructors would not be able to afford her services, and undergraduates would pose too many problems, loud, drunken behavior among them. She could provide an atmosphere where senior faculty members would feel comfortable and safe from prying eyes. The mission would appear entirely academic, and if, during their time there they desired an invigorating romp in the sack with one of her young lovelies, no problem. They would pay handsomely for the privilege.

She needed no reminder that, in spite of its harmless appearance, the business conducted here would be strictly illegal. At all times she and her girls would have to be scrupulously discrete, and the entire operation would have to remain under the radar. There could be no paper trail, no letters, or statements that might be intercepted by secretaries or female faculty, and especially not by wives. The clients would be expected to abide by a code of silence, because exposure would bring everything crashing down, including academic careers.

Chapter Two

Early Wednesday evening she had all the girls over for a planning session.

"We need more chairs," Brenda Barrow, a winsome redhead said

"I was thinking a couple of love seats," Sharon said, "in case somebody wants to cuddle up, just get acquainted."

"You don't mean we'll be fucking in the parlor." Maggie Kirkland laughed as she spoke, but from the look on her face she wouldn't mind doing just that.

"Not unless you really want to," Sharon said. "I want smaller chairs alongside the big stuffed seats, someplace for us to sit in case the guys need a little encouragement."

She led them into the bedroom area. "Four bedrooms," she said. "I don't know whether we'll need all of them or, whether we can use one for storage and stuff. We'll just have to wait and see, you know, how busy we are."

"New sheets, new towels and stuff. We'll need that for sure." Brenda wandered into one of the bathrooms. "Are we going to have a maid, or do we clean up ourselves?"

"Once we buy the new stuff we'll need we'll be cutting it pretty close, so I think we should clean up after ourselves, at least at first. We're going to need a phone, too. Maybe a little desk to put out front in the corner," Sharon said.

"Not bad, really," Maggie said. "Not like we'll be spending a lot of time here, and I don't figure the guys will notice much while they're around."

"Oh, and condoms, I almost forgot," Sharon said. "Since we'll be buying them in bulk, I guess I should get them somewhere out of town. Don't want to start anybody wondering about what we're doing here."

"A whole lot of fucking going on," Maggie said, complete with her usual cackle.

They reconvened in the sitting area out front. "So, how do we get the professors here?" Brenda asked. "We can't very well run an ad in the school paper."

"That's a tricky part," Sharon said. She told them about her thoughts on clientele, associate professors and above.

"Yeah, I can go for that. So, what's the grand plan?"

"I've given this a lot of thought, and I'll be the first to admit that I can't come up with a perfect plan for getting them here. We know it has to be quiet, discrete, or they'll run like scared rabbits. We all know a few teachers that look at us that certain way, like they'd like to drag us off and do us in the bushes. I can think of three right now, and it wouldn't take much encouragement to set them off.

"Now, if each of us can come up with a few casual contacts, two or three, and cozy up to them over the next few weeks, I think that will be a good first step. That will give us around fifteen to twenty possible clients. I have no idea how many of them will actually show up. If any of you have a better idea, let's hear it."

"How cozy are you thinking?" Maggie said. "My psychology professor never misses a chance to rub up against me. All I have to do is put my hand between his legs, and he'll follow me anywhere."

"That's the general idea," Sharon said. "Just little stuff, smile at them, pat them on the arm. I'll bet most of these guys are just dying for a little physical contact, so it shouldn't take much."

"And when they grab my ass?"

"Pretend you like it. Just giggle, don't scream."

"I'm still not sure how we actually get them here," Brenda said.

"A reception, I thought," Sharon said. I've made up little business cards with the address and phone number. Once you've got them warmed up, tell them there will be a small reception, just a few professors and some of the female students."

"That's all? You think they'll get the message?"

"If we've done the job on them, they'll crawl over here if they have to. We'll have wine and cheese, keep the lights down low, soft music, all that crap," Sharon said.

"What about the money? Will we be fucking at the reception?" Maggie asked.

"Not actually fucking, but everything else. We'll just have to see how it goes. If they want some action right off, then maybe we'll have to accommodate them. We'll get a few glasses of wine into them, then a little hugging, some kissing, really get them lathered up. Then we'll hit them up for the money. See what you think of this." She passed around sheets with anticipated revenue, expenses and such.

"One thousand dollars a month? Do you really

think they'll come up with that kind of money?"

"When we show them what we're offering, I think they'll be glad to hand it over. Look, if they were getting what they wanted at home, they wouldn't be coming onto us. This way they'll be getting what they want, when they want it, in a nice private place. There's just no other way for them to get it, not with girls like you.

"And for that thousand bucks, they get unlimited access. If they want to come every evening, that's okay, but I'll guarantee none of them will. They have to go home sometime."

"I can't believe it," Brenda said, "but I think we're going into business."

Sharon spent the next two weeks gathering items for the house, sheets, towels, etc. She had a phone installed under her own name. She also had business cards printed with the house address and phone number, but no other information.

Opening day, Saturday, November 5. The reception would run from five to seven o'clock. The girls all came in early. They dressed in regular student attire, except the skirts were a bit shorter, and the sweaters a bit tighter, all in line with the fantasy, sex with a young coed. There was a lot of nervous giggling, but otherwise they all seemed ready for business.

"What if nobody comes?" Brenda asked.

No sooner had she asked the question than they heard the knock on the front door. The professor who knocked was one of Sharon's own, a math professor from the year before.

"Am I the only one?" he asked.

Sharon took his arm and led him inside. "You win

the prize. You're number one." She kissed him on the cheek.

There quickly followed more knocks and more entrances until the room was mostly full of coeds and slightly awkward professors. The issue at hand, a satisfying sexual encounter, was never mentioned, but always present. Sharon made sure that wine glasses were always full, and very soon the unease dissolved in alcohol.

She was very proud of her girls. They mingled, flirted, permitted a few caresses, but stopped short of hands beneath sweaters or up skirts. Now the tension became purely sexual. Sharon switched the soft music she'd had on earlier for something with rhythm and a beat, something like Lennie might play at the strip club, without the volume.

It was time to close the sale. Sharon rang a soft gong and on cue, the girls slipped out of the room.

"Gentlemen," she said. "I'm sorry there's not seating for all. Usually the room won't be nearly so full, so if you return, and we hope you will, you can be assured of comfortable seating, among other pleasures. We want your time here at the Faculty Club to be relaxing and pleasurable. Always, your visits will be kept in the strictest confidence.

"I'm sure you've all guessed that we aim to provide more than a place to drink wine and read the newspaper. Here is a sample of our offering."

Again, the soft gong, this time followed by the girls entering from the hallway leading into the bedrooms. They'd made a quick change from their regular clothes into lingerie, some only modestly revealing, some barely there at all. The room went deathly quiet as the six coeds strolled like pixies among the men, caressing a cheek here, grasping an arm there, but always moving. Then they all skipped to the side and stood waiting in a corner of the room.

"I think our plan is clear enough." Sharon hadn't yet had time to change from her street clothes. "I know that some of you will not wish to partake of our offering, and I thank you for coming."

Three men went to the front door, but two returned after a couple of minutes.

"I assume those of you remaining would like to know more about our operation. As with all good things, our girls come at a price, and that price is one thousand dollars a month, payable in cash. For that sum, you will have free access to our young ladies five nights a week from the hours of seven to nine o'clock. As I said before, all encounters here are conducted in complete confidentiality.

"Those of you who wish to sample our offering may do so tonight, free of charge. If you wish to continue to visit the Faculty Club, and I hope most of you will, payment is due in cash at the first of each month. Anyone who signs up will be given a number code, and that is the only way you'll be identified. As I said, your presence here will be kept in strict confidentiality. Are there any questions?" Sharon asked.

"Where do I sign up?" The questioner was a tall, gaunt individual with a straggly beard. Sharon had seen him on campus but didn't know his department

"I want the little redhead," he said, pointing to Brenda.

Her pale complexion failed to hide her blush,

which probably made her all the more alluring for her suitor. She took his arm and led him away.

All it took was one man to break the ice, then the others followed. For a while, Sharon felt like a traffic cop at rush hour, trying to match up girls and horny professors. The last man in line looked a bit young to be senior faculty.

"Any preference among the girls?" she asked.

"Yeah, I want you."

She took a deep breath and smiled at her first client. *Well, I'm now officially a whore.*

"Hi, I'm Sharon." She extended her hand. God, what was she thinking? No names.

But he returned the gesture. His grip was firm, dry. "Bob," he said.

"Shall we go back?" She turned and headed for the bedroom. Maybe some small talk would have been in order, but she had no idea what to say. The moment of truth, the actual transaction, was something she hadn't discussed with Gloria. Now she was on her own. She sat on the bed. "Could you tell me what you have in mind, anything special?"

He shuffled from one foot to the other so fast he looked like he was running in place. "Just regular, I guess. But…" He pointed at her clothing.

Shit. She still had on her skirt and sweater. "I'll change. Won't be a minute."

She put on a sheer red negligee with matching bra and thong. She checked herself out in the bathroom mirror. The outfit added a crimson blush to her skin but concealed nothing.

There had been that moment of panic the week before when she'd gone through her closet looking for something sexy. All of her regular sleepwear was heavy-duty flannel, the kind of stuff that could repel small caliber bullets. She'd have to buy something. Red or black? Short or long? See-through? Not that it mattered anyway, she'd just be taking it off.

She made a quick trip out to the only shop in Pisgah that might sell such items. Reba's Intimate Apparel sat in the corner of the only shopping mall in the area. Her own ideas of intimate were apparently a few decades out of date. Her stripping outfits were altogether basic, now she had to pick something to wear up close and personal.

The matronly clerk who followed her around seemed totally out of place among such sheer, next-to-nothing apparel. Sharon didn't feel much better herself. For instance, she got stuck in the maze of panties. The item she was examining seemed to have one opening too many. The clerk intervened.

"They're crotchless," she said.

"Crotchless, oh, yeah," Sharon said trying to sound more confident than she felt.

"Right, do I have to draw you a picture?" the clerk asked.

Sharon tossed them back onto the counter. She bought two outfits and prayed her mother never saw either of them.

Now she was about to take her new bedroom wear for a test drive. Bob or Tom or whoever he was waited beside the bed. He'd removed his jacket but otherwise was still fully clothed. He apparently liked what he saw.

With great effort, she managed to put one foot in front of the other, enough to get her to the bed. She would never dare get this close to customers at

Lennie's. Except for that disastrous night when she'd been dragged into the audience, she'd always managed to keep them at arm's length. Now touching was the order of the day. She patted the spot beside her. "Shall we?"

Bob loosened his belt and dropped his trousers. The sight of her practically naked must have inspired him. He began to show signs of life. He made no attempt to remove her negligee so she took it off herself, slowly. She made a little show of it. One thing she knew about was stripping.

Later, when she thought back on the actual event, it seemed like a bad first date—awkward, fumbling, and over quickly. As she lay there waiting for him to dress, she wondered how she'd ever be able to ask full price for such a brief encounter. But if he was disappointed, it certainly didn't show.

"Can...can I see you again?" he asked.

"Of course. If you have a pen, I'll give you my cell phone number and you can call me directly." Only when she handed him the card with her number did she remember she was still stark naked. "Can you find your way out?"

"Sure."

"Next time, if you want, you can park in back."

There it was, money for sex. She was now officially a whore. Trouble was, it was a damned sight easier than she'd anticipated. Where was all the guilt, shame? She'd performed a service and been paid for it. Just like years before. Maybe Gloria was right after all; when all was said and done, it was just business. Still, stripping, now whoring, made for a dicey employment history. She couldn't very well include either of those occupations on any future job application.

The last customer left shortly past eight. Sharon directed him out the side door in the back. She had turned off the front porch light earlier, discretion, always discretion.

They all gathered in the front parlor, Sharon and her girls, because she did consider them her girls, she felt responsible for them. They'd each cleaned up after their last encounter and were once again in the clothes they'd worn over earlier. Just a bunch of innocent coeds, nothing at all suspicious.

"Everybody okay?" Sharon asked.

"Oh, yeah," Maggie Kirkland said. "I'm ready to go again."

The others seemed more subdued, a few giggles, most looked down at the floor. Doubtless, the realization, that permanent change in status, was setting in. Becoming comfortable with the idea of prostitution would take some time, and unlike the Kirkland twins, for some of them it would never become comfortable at all.

"If there are any issues, or if any of you just want to talk, I'm always available. I know this is a big step, but look on the bright side...we'll be making money, and for once, we'll be in control. That ought to mean something."

Sharon made up a schedule for the weeks to come. Most evenings she would be there too, better not to leave things to chance. She knew that much.

****

For an operation that was illegal, immoral and frowned upon by almost every level of society, the Faculty Club ran smoothly, more due to luck than careful strategic planning. But since when were brothel owners known as great planners? The choice of clientele was a big plus; faculty types tended to be well-behaved and easily managed. They might possess academic credentials that were recognized all over the country, but here at the Faculty Club she was in charge. So, yeah, a late-middle-aged professor with an academic reputation to protect and carnal desires to fulfill, the perfect client.

Even so, she lived in dread of that possible moment when campus police would break down their front door and haul them off to jail. She dreamed about it, and the dreams were nightmares. All of them, Sharon and her whole crew marched off campus while the entire community shouted insults and threw rotten fruit. And they would be followed by all of their unfortunate faculty patrons. Yeah, a frigging nightmare.

But their luck held, and the Faculty Club prospered.

Her social life, never a prominent part of her campus activity, was put on hold for the time being. Except for prostitution, she was living like a nun. She couldn't risk getting attached to another undergraduate, and she was too busy anyway. The graduate assistant, Herb Collins, who had gone to bat for her when she'd had that disastrous day with the accounting exam, was very friendly, but so far, nothing had developed. Her first client at the Faculty Club, Bob, had returned several times and always asked for her specifically. With a little coaching, he had become a far more proficient and satisfying lover. Now, instead of squeezing her breasts as if he were testing fruit for freshness, he stroked, he caressed. And when her nipples popped up to say hello, as they always did, he grinned and lapped away at them like a thirsty puppy at a water dish.

But she had no illusions about forming real relationships with any of the men she serviced, Bob included. Gloria specifically warned against this, every whore's dream, that prince charming would come and take her away from the life of shame. Only it never came true.

Chapter Three

The Christmas holiday was their first real break. The Faculty Club was closed as was most of the campus.

"I really needed some time off," Brenda Barrow said. She and Sharon were walking between classes, just before the campus emptied out for the Christmas holiday. Sharon spent more time with Brenda than with any of the other girls.

"It's going okay, though?" Sharon asked.

"Better than I expected. Sometimes I even enjoy it a little." She giggled briefly. "God, I never thought I'd say that."

"Just a job," Sharon said. "Just a job."

"Are you going home for the holidays?" Brenda asked.

"Unless I can come up with a good excuse." She'd begged off Thanksgiving, said she was afraid her mononucleosis might be coming back, so maybe she should just rest in her room on campus.

"You can rest here," her mother said. "We'd really love to see you."

But Sharon prevailed. Now all she had to do was come up with a way to make her Christmas stay as brief as possible.

"I'm sorry, Mom, but I have a part-time job, and they would only give me Christmas Eve and Christmas

Day off, and I really need the money. I had to replace the brakes on my car, and that took most of what I was saving up for my tuition payment."

"I just wish we could see more of you."

"I know, but school won't last forever," Sharon said. Of course, she would stretch it out as long as possible, then hunt for a job far, far away from her hometown of Jacob's Bluff.

January brought a snowstorm, plugging up streets on campus and reducing mobility to very basic forms, sleds, cross-country skis, and such. It also reduced traffic at the Faculty Club, and no traffic meant no revenue. Except for her weekly trysts with Bob, Sharon conducted no business there. She'd never considered prostitution as seasonal work, but the weather had a definite impact on their income. This was okay with her, because it gave her more time to prepare for semester finals. And she was certain that things would pick up when the weather improved.

But the streets were barely cleared when a second snowstorm bottled them up again. For the month of January, they made just enough money to meet expenses.

****

Sharon convened the first quarterly meeting of the Faculty Club on a Sunday morning in early February. There was a threat of more snow flurries, but no accumulation was expected. She'd bought a round oak table at a garage sale and had it moved to their little house. It was a tight fit for all seven of them, but they managed to crowd around.

"I've copied all our financial records for each of you. I don't need to mention if these documents were ever leaked out we'd all be toast." Sharon passed around the copies. Each had CONFIDENTIAL in bold red letters at the top. "With the holidays and the weather, things have been slow lately, but spring isn't that far off, and we should be busy again."

"Gosh, we're still making a little money." Brenda Barrow smiled at the figures. "You've done a great job keeping expenses down, Sharon."

"It's a bare bones operation," Sharon said. "Unless we decide to expand I'd like to keep it that way."

"Hah! Look at that." Maggie Kirkland elbowed her twin sister, Donna. "I beat you out. I beat everybody."

"Can we give her a whore-of-the-month award or something, just to shut her up?" Donna asked.

"Whore-of-the-month? I'm aiming for whore-of-the-year." Maggie laughed and clapped her hands.

"Low profile, ladies we're technically illegal, remember?" Sharon said. "I'm glad you enjoy your work, but we have to stay under the radar." How could it be they were all chatting so casually about whoring? They were all smart ladies, college undergrads, they knew the risks they ran. But for the Kirkland sisters it all seemed like a big joke. Okay so long as they didn't go in for any public displays. The fact that prostitution had survived so long as human history had been recorded didn't make it any less objectionable.

"I want to suggest something," Sharon said. "Since we're here every night now, I think we need someone up front, here in the parlor, sort of a receptionist. And she could provide backup in case there are more guys than we can handle."

"Every night?"

"It would only be one night per week, per person,

since there are seven of us now. It shouldn't be busy at all. Whoever is here could use it as a little study hall for the evening. Then, before we close up for the night, check everything, make sure the place is tidy, clean linens, things like that."

"So, it's a combination of receptionist, hall monitor, and maid." Donna Kirkland didn't look all that convinced.

"Could we just try it for a couple of weeks?" Sharon asked. "We're gonna start having mix-ups with the schedule if we don't do something. If this doesn't work, we can try something else."

Her receptionist idea paid off the next week when, on Thursday evening, two girls reported for duty followed by five guys looking to get laid, but they only had four beds. Brenda Barrow, who sat at the reception table that evening, headed off a potentially touchy situation with a deft bit of rescheduling and participation herself.

When Sharon heard of her plan's successful application, she toasted herself with a glass of orange juice. Maybe business administration was her niche after all. Her biggest successes so far had come in areas that weren't exactly mainstream. First stripping, now running a brothel, and only the latter required organizational skills, but she'd made a go of it.

Best of all, she was making money. She bought new clothes. On evenings when she wasn't working, she went out to eat, at real sit-down restaurants. More than once that was in the company of her now-favorite graduate assistant, Herb Collins. But from a promising start, their budding romance had failed to develop as she'd hoped. Their dates became less and less frequent, and even when they were together, he seemed to be elsewhere, distracted. Sharon wasn't used to losing guys.

She thought once or twice about luring him into one of the private dance studios in the Performing Arts Department and doing her strip routine for him. If that didn't have him running around the room like a rabid dog, she could declare him officially dead.

She went so far as to get a room key from one of the other students, but she never followed through. She wanted him to like her for who she was, not just an exquisite set of tits and an ass to die for. She wanted to be valued as more than the sum of her parts, although those same parts had brought her great success as a stripper and a hooker.

****

On her nights at the registration desk Sharon settled in with her books. With all her extracurricular activities, profitable as they were, she'd gotten behind in her class work, and she needed the time to catch up. She'd just gotten immersed in her economics text when Brenda Barrow walked in, dressed to kill.

"Wow, look at you," Sharon said. "What's the occasion?"

"One of my guys, he's gotten to be a regular."

"And he's coming tonight?"

"Right. Seven o'clock." Brenda pulled a chair up to the table. "Have you met any nice guys here?"

"Well, most of them seem pretty nice. That's the advantage of sticking to the college faculty. They're a clean-cut bunch," Sharon said.

"Some of them are a little kinky, though."

"Not violent, I hope. If there's ever any rough stuff

you let me know immediately."

"Oh, no. When they ask me to do something I don't want to, I just refuse, and that's the end of it. I've never had anybody try to force me or anything like that."

"Just remember, if anybody ever gets out of hand, yell. We'll take care of it."

"I still don't figure that." Brenda brushed off the sleeve of her dress. "I mean, there's just us girls. We might not be able to overpower the guy."

"We won't have to. We'll hit him where it hurts the most."

"In his balls?"

"Worse than that. We threaten him with exposure. Tell him there are video cameras in the rooms, and we'll take the tapes to the cops." It was a bluff at best. A whore with a tape claiming sexual abuse? No way. On the other hand, reputations were precious, and for all the clients knew, she held the power to destroy them.

"Damn. I didn't know about any cameras." Brenda looked around the room.

"That's because there aren't any. But the guy won't know that." Sharon winked at her classmate.

"You are the devious one. You know, of all the people I can think of, you'd be the last one I'd think would be doing something like this. How on earth did you get started?"

Sharon drew a large dollar sign on a sheet of paper. "Basic necessity. I needed money for rent, tuition, books, food, you name it. Everything came due at once. I had to come up with money or drop out and move back home. Frankly, I'd rather die."

"But how did you pick this? There must be other

things you could have done."

"It seemed like the best way to make money fast. I couldn't very well rob banks, and everything else paid minimum wage," Sharon said.

"I don't think I could have cooked up a scheme like this, not in a million years."

"Think about it. Half the time the professors are hitting on the female students anyway. They always have the upper hand; they control our grades. This arrangement just shifts the power around. We have the upper hand here. They still get what they want, but on our terms, and they have to pay for it."

Brenda moved her chair closer to the table. "It was so hard the first time. I went home afterward and cried all night. I usually call my mom when I'm really down, but I couldn't. I hope she never finds out about this."

"No reason she should. And don't you start crying now, not with this special guy coming over."

"You never told me whether you were seeing anybody."

"There's a guy in the math department. We've been going out for about a month."

"Is he a, a customer?"

"No, no, just a regular guy."

"So he doesn't know about…"

Sharon shook her head.

"Well, I'm going back to tidy up. When my guy comes, just send him on back." Brenda grabbed her oversized handbag and headed off.

Sharon twisted around trying to find a comfortable position in an uncomfortable chair. She'd just gotten back into her economics text when the front door opened.

"I'm here to see Brenda. Oh, my God, Sharon. What are you doing here?"

Sharon looked up into the startled eyes of Herb Collins.

Before she could say anything Brenda sauntered in wearing a transparent green negligee. Little Brenda, who was too shy to shower with the rest of the girls after gym class, now walked right into the parlor naked except for the shimmering cloud of green. "I thought I heard voices." She walked over and kissed Herb on the cheek. "Ready if you are." She took his arm and led him into the back.

Sharon sat alone for a moment. Herb, her new best friend. Now she knew why the relationship had withered. He was hooking up with a prostitute. Wait a minute, though. That prostitute was her friend and colleague, and she was just doing what Sharon herself did several nights a week. No, it wasn't the prostitute angle. She'd thought she had an exclusive on Herb Collins. Now she knew why he was always so patient, why he never pressed her for sex. He was getting all he needed right under her nose, from one of her own girls. She couldn't handle this. She gathered up her books and headed for the door.

Back at her apartment, she poured herself a glass of chilled Pinot Grigio then watched while the mist formed on the outside of the glass. This was bound to happen; sooner or later she'd run into a familiar face at the Faculty Club. It would happen to all the girls. The whole campus community numbered about twelve thousand and just over twenty percent were faculty. Yeah, sooner or later.

But now she had to deal with the fall out. Herb

taught a small discussion group she would attend in the morning. How would she face him? It seemed very unlikely that he'd tell anyone about the incident at the Faculty Club; it wouldn't do his professional standing any good to be associated with a whorehouse.

She sipped her wine. What was that line she remembered from the movie about the mob, how it wasn't personal, just business? She really liked Herb, but her feelings for him came in second place. Business came first. Business paid the rent, paid for tuition, bought new clothes. Herb made her feel good, but he'd never pay her bills. He barely did that for himself.

Sharon poured herself a second glass. Tomorrow morning she'd walk into his class with her head held high, look him straight in the eye, smile, and take her seat in the front row. It was business, nothing more, nothing less.

Without the reinforcement of her wine glass, she felt less than courageous the next morning. In fact, she dreaded seeing Herb Collins at all. Knowing that he was probably no more enthusiastic about seeing her didn't help. So, their first meeting after the encounter at the Faculty Club proved awkward, in spite of her plans to keep it quite professional. She found herself looking at the floor, the ceiling, out the window, anywhere to avoid meeting his gaze. Instead of her usual active participation in their group sessions, she added almost nothing to the discussion, a fact not missed by her classmates.

"You okay?" one of them asked her in the hallway later.

"Headache," she said.

On the subject of Herb Collins, there was some

lingering resentment that she'd been cut out so easily by her friend, Brenda. Of course, she had to admit, Brenda in her transparent negligee could set off fire alarms

Just business, she kept telling herself, just business. Speaking of business, now that she was running one, shortcomings in her own expertise were showing up more and more frequently. She had gotten by so far on her strong organizational skills, but if her group's activities became more complex, she would need a better grasp of the business aspects.

She maintained a separate record for identification purposes. Who knew when such a thing might come in handy? But she never entered the girls' names in the ledger. She noted each of them by an assigned number, so that anyone who managed to lay hands on the book would have only numbers to go by, just an expense sheet with nothing to identify the players or what they did.

As she pored over the entries in her book she understood that things were about to get out of hand. Her own amateurish management style was sufficient during the early days of the venture, but now business was booming. Instead of just two girls available for duty on any given night now there were usually three, sometimes four. The four available bedrooms were in constant use from around seven to nine.

If the current trends continued, and there was no reason to think they wouldn't, she would be forced to expand. With an expansion would come a new set of problems and opportunities. Either she relocated to a larger space, or split their activities between two locations.

Her first thought, putting some limitations on the number of visitors, had been met with a mini-revolt by her girls. In fact, the Kirkland sisters had begun an expansion on their own. They had taken it upon themselves to enlist a new member without even consulting her or any of the other girls.

The new recruit, a baby-faced freshman English major named Chloe, exuded an air of childlike innocence that must have made her irresistible, because her name appeared in Sharon's appointment book four to five nights each week, often more than once.

Chloe was from Binghamton, NY, and Sharon had strong misgivings about bringing a freshman into their group, but it became apparent soon enough that Chloe was no novice when it came to sex games. "Satisfaction guaranteed," she always said about herself, and from the number of clients who requested her services she made good on that promise.

One thing Sharon found bothersome about young Chloe was that, while she and the rest of the girls performed services out of financial need, Chloe had no such motivation. Her father was a prominent orthopedic surgeon and her mother, a bank vice-president, so she never lacked for money. She drove a new BMW convertible that she always parked by the curb in front of the house. "Sends the right kind of message," she said.

"Why?" Sharon asked her one evening, as Chloe's latest client walked toward the door wearing a facial expression that could only be described as pure bliss.

"Why what?"

"Why do you do this?" Indeed, why would any female prostitute herself but for money?

"Because I like it. Tell you the truth, I'd do it for nothing. In fact, if you ever want to get together, do something weird, let me know. I'll do you for free." With that, she winked at Sharon and walked away.

Not likely, Sharon thought, not very damned likely.

She set strict limits on her own sessions at the Faculty Club, never more than three times per week. That proved just enough to keep her checking account flush, but more would cut into her study time. Unlike the other girls, she always referred to her sessions as appointments, never as tricks. And unlike Chloe, in particular, she did it for the money, always the money.

Chapter Four

The fear of exposure always lurked in the recesses of her mind. On campus, she made herself as unobtrusive as possible. She kept her hair pinned up in an unattractive, old-fashioned bun, wore no makeup at all. While most of the other coeds who wore jeans opted for skin-tight apparel, Sharon wore at least two sizes larger than necessary.

In her sessions at the Faculty Club, she donned another persona altogether, very heavy on the makeup, garish red lipstick, enough eye shadow that her eyes appeared sunk in their orbits. Often she topped this off with a blonde wig. She completed the package with the scantiest, most transparent bedroom wear. To the original red and black outfits, she'd bought for her first session, she added several others, including one short white gown so transparent that it seemed not there at all.

On her last shopping trip, she ran into the same saleslady who sold her those earlier outfits.

"What on earth is going on over at that school?" the portly woman wanted to know as she followed Sharon through the adults only section of ladies' bedroom wear. "Used to be, this sort of stuff hung around gathering dust. Now I can't keep it on the racks. You girls are buying it right out of the box. And a Baptist school at that."

The saleslady took a long look at Sharon who was doing her best to look mousy.

"You certainly don't look like the type to buy this stuff."

"Actually it's for a friend," Sharon said. "You're right, I could never wear anything like this."

****

Early April, with spring break just a couple of weeks away, Sharon called a meeting of her group. Would they close up shop for spring break, or would it be business as usual? The Kirkland sisters announced that they were heading for St. Petersburg, Florida, and taking Chloe along with them.

"I'll be going to Lynchburg," Brenda Barrow said. She blushed as she spoke.

"With Herb?" Sharon asked.

Brenda nodded. "To meet his parents."

"Wow, that's serious." Sharon's feigned enthusiasm stuck in her throat.

"I think maybe it is." Brenda blushed even more furiously.

Sharon thought back to that evening when she had first learned that Herb was seeing Brenda, how Brenda had waltzed right into the parlor practically naked to greet Herb. She hadn't blushed at all then.

"I'll probably be going out of town for a few days myself," Sharon said. "So I guess we ought to close the place down for a few days. No trouble starting up again." They had already gone through a similar situation with the Christmas holidays when, since the campus was pretty much deserted, the Faculty Club closed up as well.

She had contemplated a real spring break road trip

for herself. A few days of fun in the Florida sun sounded very good indeed, much better than holidays with her family, enduring her mother's endless innuendos about marriage and grandchildren. The woman was in loop mode when it came to grandchildren. She just couldn't let it go.

Up until now, Sharon had endured those inquisitions in silence, but the solution lay right in front of her. What if she blurted out, "Mom, I'm a hooker now. You really want to talk about grandchildren?" End of conversation.

But she needed a real excuse, some viable reason for not making the trek back to Jacob's Bluff. Along came Bob. They had just finished their Thursday night tryst, one that left her altogether satisfied and Bob, lying naked beside her, panting like a longhaired dog on a hot day. After their sessions, they usually chatted for a few moments before she had to tidy up the room for its next occupants. She brought along a robe to cover herself now. In the sort of hybrid relationship they had drifted into, she was part whore, part girlfriend, and although nudity was an expected aspect of the whore part, not so with a girlfriend. Some degree of modesty, even if it was a total sham, seemed called for.

"So, any plans for spring break?" Bob asked. He rolled himself up onto his elbow and although she was covered, he remained completely nude.

"Haven't thought much about it," she said. For sure, those thoughts had not included Bob. And she wasn't sure it was such a good idea anyway. If he persisted, she could cover her tracks by using her usual trip to see her parents as an excuse. That could work both ways. This would be her time, hers only. She had earned it.

****

There might be locations more severely afflicted with spring fever than a college campus, but they would be hard to find. Almost overnight, the landscape turned from brown to green and all shades in between. Birds, bees and all those other creatures that crawl or fly appeared right on schedule. That same force of nature swept right through the students as well. How they dressed (brighter) how they walked (faster), how they talked (louder) were all pushed up a notch by the promise of spring. That's what it was, still a promise, because temperatures were yet far from balmy.

Sharon was no more immune to these changes than any of the others. She spent a bit more time on her appearance before going out. She brushed out her hair, which had grown to shoulder length, and added a light touch of lipstick. Last year's skirts still fit, a bit more snugly than before, but no matter. She had only one class before lunch, and she planned to cut it anyway.

Sharon rummaged through her closet and was not pleased with what she found. She'd bought most of her clothes during those lean times, when she counted every penny. Now she had some extra cash. Time to upgrade the wardrobe, and shoes, definitely. She'd been trudging around campus in a pair of grubby sneakers long enough. What good was having money if you couldn't spend it?

She parked in front of the diner where she was meeting her friend Gloria for lunch. Gloria sat by the window and must have seen her drive up.

"New car?" she asked.

"My old one died," Sharon said. The Toyota she

now drove was four years old but looked new. She seldom parked it on campus. This was one extravagance that would attract attention for certain.

"Business must be good," Gloria said.

"I guess. Say, what's with the dark glasses?"

"I'm sensitive to these fluorescent lights."

"Sensitive my ass, you've got a black eye," Sharon said. The area of Gloria's left eye not covered by the glasses was swollen and discolored. She had apparently tried to cover the discoloration with makeup, but the swelling was not so easily concealed.

"I ran into a door."

"Come on, Gloria, somebody punched you."

"Take a good look, kid." Gloria lifted her glasses. Her left eye was swollen almost shut and colored a dark blue.

"Jesus, who did this?" Sharon asked.

"In our business we don't name names. Remember that."

"Shouldn't you tell the police?"

Gloria started a laugh that came out as a snort. "That's the last thing I would do. They know me there, and they know how I make my living. If I went to the police station crying over a black eye they'd laugh right in my face."

"It's not right," Sharon said.

"Your ideas about right and wrong are mixed up. Once you get the whore label stuck on you nobody cares what happens to you, unless you get your throat cut and you bleed out in a public place."

Sharon shook her head. "I can't believe what I'm hearing."

Their waitress, a girl Sharon recognized from an

economics class the year before, arrived. "Can I get you ladies something to drink?"

"Coffee for me, and a grilled cheese sandwich," Gloria said.

"I'll have the same." Sharon kept her head down, hoping the girl wouldn't recognize her.

"Ashamed to be seen with me?" Gloria asked.

"Just trying to keep a low profile."

"Still think you're too smart to get caught, huh? Let me tell you something. This business we're in, it's a very small world. Something happens, people notice."

"I don't follow you," Sharon said.

"Don't play dumb, kid. We're both in the same line of work now, and if I know it, other people know it, too. How many girls you got now?"

"Eight."

"Eight? Holy shit. Who runs your house?"

"I do."

"You? What do you know about running a whorehouse?"

"It all seemed pretty simple at first. You do what the customer wants, and they pay you for it."

"Who handles your security?"

"We don't have anybody."

Gloria lifted her glasses again, revealing her swollen eye. "Take a good look at this. You know how many times some jerk has used me as a punching bag?"

Sharon shook her head.

"You been at this for what, five months now, and none of your girls have been knocked around?"

Sharon sat mute. She hoped all along that since her clientele was made up of college faculty they would behave properly. So far, that assumption held true, but seeing Gloria's damaged eye she began to wonder, and worry.

"I don't want to see you get hurt, that's all. You've been damned lucky, but you keep doing what you're doing and sooner or later, you or your girls are going to get roughed up. You remember our little friend, Lennie? He knows about you, and believe me, he's meaner than any snake you'll ever come across."

"I'll call the cops on him."

Gloria laughed again, that harsh, grunting sound without a hint of happiness in it. "I just can't seem to get through to you. You are no longer a member of polite society. Whores are a separate social class. Like I said before, unless somebody cuts your throat, nobody will bat an eye. Whatever bad happens to you, you had it coming. That's how they all think."

Gloria signaled the waitress for more coffee. "You gonna eat your sandwich? I hate to see food go to waste."

Sharon pushed her grilled cheese sandwich across to Gloria. This discussion of workplace violence, even if that workplace was a whorehouse, took her appetite away.

"You're a smart girl, but you're stubborn, too. That's a bad combination." Gloria reached across and took Sharon's hand.

"You're not gonna quit, are you? In spite of what I said."

"No, it's my business. I built it myself. Besides, I need the money."

"I'll do what I can to look after you. I mean, if Lennie starts planning anything I'll try to let you know. But for God's sake, keep my name out of it. The bastard would kill me if he ever found out."

****

"Mom's not feeling well," Sharon said. "I should go home and check on her."

"I understand," he said. "Some other time."

As appealing as a few days of fun in the sun might be, she wasn't ready to make that kind of commitment with Bob, so she begged off the spring break trip. He didn't seem too disappointed. For all she knew, he had backup plans for himself anyway.

****

Her hometown of Jacob's Bluff was just over two hundred miles from the university. There was no bluff, and no one claimed to know about any former resident named Jacob. Like so many small southern towns, the founder had left a name but little else. Two interstate highways bisected the route she now traveled, but both headed away from the direction she wanted to go. The absence of any connection to a major highway system had stunted the growth of Jacob's Bluff, keeping its small town flavor intact. An unofficial motto remained visible on a tattered banner that still hung across Main Street. "If we don't have it, you probably don't need it."

The long, slow bus ride back to Jacob's Bluff gave her time to think, and it also saved having to explain her new car. But the bus made so many stops, that the trip took forever. The day before she left the campus she called home to tell her mother about her change of plans. No problem. One thing about going home, you really didn't need a reason to show up. Of course, that didn't mean every visit would be sunshine and roses.

The only hitch in the conversation came when she asked to speak to her father. She and her mother had avoided any discussion about the decline in his faculties, as if failing to acknowledge it meant it didn't exist. But she wanted some clue as to what she might expect when she got there.

"I'll try," her mother had said. "You know how he is about telephones."

After several minutes she heard his voice faintly. "Sharon?"

She could easily envision him standing there holding the phone in front of his face, scowling at it as if he expected something to leap out at him.

"Dad, put the receiver next to your ear so you can hear me."

"I can hear you fine."

"Well, I can barely hear you. Speak into the mouthpiece so you won't have to yell."

"What?"

"Never mind. Let me talk to Mom."

Sharon intended to talk to her father about the .22 caliber pistol he gave her for her twelfth birthday. The present caused a family rift that persisted until Sharon left for college. She left the gun at home then, but had every intention of retrieving it now. She had business assets to protect, as well as the personal safety of her girls at the Faculty Club. And if, as Gloria had warned, she could not count on police protection, she would take matters into her own hands. If Gloria was right about Lennie's violent tendencies, a little firepower might come in handy.

Her mother had been outraged at the gift. "The very idea, giving that girl a gun."

Sharon was delighted. They celebrated her birthday on a Friday, and by Sunday afternoon she had already shot up an entire box of shells and was begging for more.

Soon she was rummaging through the garbage searching for bottles, tin cans, anything she could shoot holes in. Her dad laid down strict rules about targets; the neighborhood cats were strictly off limits.

"Even Thomas?" Sharon had asked.

"Especially Thomas."

The big gray tomcat that lived next door had pretty well cleared the area of song birds, and she would like nothing better than to put an end to his reign of terror. She'd seen her dad chucking stones at the cat a number of times, but that only had a short term effect. "How about I just wing him?" she asked.

"You shoot that cat, and I have to take your gun away for good."

But it wasn't so much that she hated Thomas, which she did, rather, she wanted to shoot at a moving target. Stationary objects provided no challenge as her marksmanship improved. So, soon she had her dad tossing tin cans into the air for her, and she seldom missed. Those afternoons with her dad, him tossing, her shooting were among her fondest memories. Some other memories were less pleasant.

The fun ended when they had to go back inside for dinner, where her mother still sulked.

"Not fitting, a girl shooting like that." If she said so once, she said it a hundred times.

Sharon never could figure out her mother's opposition to the gun. What harm could it do? When Sharon left for college, she wrapped the pistol in an oiled rag and had her father stash it high on a shelf above his workbench in the basement. If her mother ever got her hands on it, it was gone for sure.

****

The bus was crowded, hot and smelled like an overflowing laundry hamper. Most of the foul aroma seemed to emanate from the toilet in the back of the bus, and although Sharon's bladder practically screamed at her for the final hour of the trip, she did not venture back there. So she sat, legs crossed tightly, trying to think of anything but how badly she wanted to pee.

The bus station in Jacob's Bluff was a station in name only. The driver stopped in front of the Texaco station next to the red brick post office to let off passengers. Sharon was one of the few to disembark; most were headed farther along. No reason to get off in the middle of nowhere.

She spotted her parents parked just to the side of the parking lot. The old family Ford Fairlane looked to be still in mint condition, the kind of car collectors would love to get their hands on. Sharon slid her bag into the back seat. "Gotta run to the bathroom, Mom."

"Can't you wait until you get home?"

"No way."

A few moments later, she climbed into the back seat, much more comfortable than she'd been for the past three hours. "You didn't both have to come for me," she said.

"Your father is getting a bit forgetful," her mother said. Her eyebrows arched upward, the usual sign that there was more afoot than she was saying.

Her father forgetful? Senile? He seemed way too young for anything like that, but for certain, things were changing with him. He didn't say a word when she got into the car. She wanted to ask whether he'd seen a doctor, but that question would have to wait until he was back home tucked into his recliner, out of earshot.

A most unsettling scenario was forming in Sharon's head, in spite of her strongest efforts to dismiss it. What if her father was indeed showing signs of early onset dementia? An ominous possibility, worse because she'd seen it all before.

Her grandfather had lived with them when she was a young girl. She remembered the questions she'd asked her mother. "Why won't Grandpa Ray talk anymore? Why do you have to feed him? Why does he wet his pants?" He was acting like a baby, but when she said so to her mother, she got a vicious whack on the backside.

She remembered the heated discussions behind closed doors, her mother and father yelling. Then, one day when she got home from school, Grandpa Ray was nowhere to be found. "Where's Grandpa Ray?" she asked her mother.

"We had to put him in a place where they could take better care of him," her mother said. She spoke quietly, as if it were some big family secret.

Two weeks later, she went with her parents to visit Grandpa Ray.

"What kind of place is this?" she asked as they drove up. She had been to a hospital a few times before, once with a broken arm after she'd fallen off her bike, and another for a tonsillectomy, but this didn't look anything like she remembered. The yard outside the main building was fenced, and there were old people standing around outside, not doing anything, just standing.

"It's like a hospital for people like your grandfather."

"Do they go home when they get well?"

"Sometimes."

"It stinks in here," Sharon said once they were inside. "Don't they ever flush the toilets?" That was exactly how it smelled to her…like unflushed toilets.

Grandpa Ray's room was at the end of the hall, but he wasn't there. "He's in the day room," a nurse's aide told them.

Perhaps the shock would have been less if they only had Grandpa Ray to contend with. But here was a room full of vacant stares, stains on gowns where bits of breakfast had fallen out of slack jaws and dribbled down the front. Her grandfather sat in a wheelchair by a window, tied in the chair by a strap around his waist.

The three of them approached together. Sharon held out a small bouquet of violets she had picked that morning. But Grandpa Ray sat mute, as if unaware they were even in the room.

"Is he mad at me?" Sharon asked. "I mean, he won't even talk to me."

Sharon watched as both her parents tried, without success, to engage her grandfather in conversation. After a while they gave up and left. Her mother was crying, and her father's face was blank, unreadable.

"Guess he's mad at everybody," young Sharon said.

Two weeks later, on a rainy Friday afternoon, their small family attended Grandpa Ray's funeral.

So, early in her life Sharon had learned about dementia. She didn't know what to call it back then, but she knew how it looked and how it smelled. Now she feared she was seeing it once again, and the worst was yet to come.

That night she slept in her old bed in her old room again. Her mother maintained the room exactly as it had been when Sharon was there, apparently expecting her to come home someday and take up her role as dutiful daughter.

Chapter Five

The next morning her mother announced that she needed to go grocery shopping and asked if Sharon would watch her father until she returned.

"When did you start driving, Mom?" Sharon asked.

"Just to the store and back. I can't depend on your father anymore. We'll talk more when I get back. He shouldn't be any trouble this morning. After breakfast, he goes to sleep in his recliner. I'll be back before he wakes up."

"How can he sleep with the TV so loud?"

Her mother pointed to her ear and shook her head.

****

Sharon crept downstairs to the basement where her father's workshop took one entire corner. She ran her fingertips over dusty tools that he would never use again. Perhaps, she thought, the greatest thief of all was time.

She reached up to the top shelf where years before she had stashed the pistol her father had given her. It still lay there, wrapped in its oiled cloth, and beside it a box of shells. Sharon cradled the weapon in her palm. She loved the weight of it, and it was small enough to fit easily into her purse.

A little target practice seemed in order. Her father slept upstairs by the blaring TV, so if she walked a short distance away from the house it seemed most unlikely that he could hear the gunshots. She collected a few tin cans from the garbage bin in the kitchen, then headed out back.

The back yard was almost two hundred feet deep ending in an embankment that reached just over ten feet in height. She placed her targets along the base of this bank. After a few near misses, she began to make contact. She took a few steps back, then a few more, still putting holes in the cans with almost every shot. She laughed with the pure joy of it.

"What the hell are you doing with my gun?" Her father bellowed across the yard.

She whirled around as he lurched toward her like some zombie character from a movie set.

"You stole my gun." He was almost upon her.

"No, this is mine. You gave it to me."

He lunged for her. He was still strong but not at all agile. When Sharon ducked aside, he sprawled on the lawn.

"Dad, stop it, please." She kept just out of his reach. There was no way she was going to give him a loaded firearm. Who knew what he might do?

"Sharon, what have you done?" Her mother's voice, high-pitched and nearly hysterical. She was halfway across the yard, running toward them.

"I was just shooting at cans, then Dad came after me."

"She stole my gun." He was still on his hands and knees, crawling after her.

"Sharon, go inside right now. I'll take care of him. Oh, Lord, what will the neighbors think?"

Sharon did just that. She went straight to her room and started packing. By the time her mother and father came back inside, she had her bag beside the front door and had called for a cab to take her back to the bus depot.

She bought her return ticket from Nina Brown, who did double duty running the post office and selling bus tickets as well. Travelers were responsible for handling their own bags.

"You just got in yesterday," Nina said. "Going back so soon?"

"Yeah, I got some things I have to get finished at school."

"Plan on coming back after you graduate? I know your mom expects you to. She can barely keep up with your dad now. Poor woman is going to need some help soon."

"We'll work something out," Sharon said.

In terms of physical discomfort, the return trip was a great improvement. There were fewer passengers on board, so Sharon had a bit of leg room. More important, she'd begun this trip with an empty bladder, sparing herself some of the agony she'd experienced the day before. Even the bus driver was in a cooperative mood. He took a more direct route back, shaving a full hour off the ride.

No doubt her mother would be calling for help. There was no way she would be able to take care of him by herself. But whatever plan of care she came up with, Sharon wanted no part of it. She was going to be a bad daughter. She owed no debt to her father. Nothing he had ever done *for* her could make up for what he had done *to* her.

****

Her apartment was only a couple of blocks from

where she got off the bus, but she decided a walk around the campus might help clear some of the demons she'd been battling for the past few hours. The image of her own father lurching toward her with eyes that no longer seemed to recognize her as his own flesh and blood terrified her and broke her heart at the same time.

Most of the students had left for the spring break holiday, leaving the campus almost deserted. The solitude was just what she needed. She strolled along, her bag over her shoulder. For the moment, the entire place was hers and hers alone.

The university campus was like a second home, and with things gone all crazy in Jacob's Bluff, she desperately needed a place to belong. The sense of belonging as she wandered about had become so important to her.

And in a way, creation of the Faculty Club formed a new family for her. Strange that she considered them as such, not associates, not employees, certainly not whores, but as her family. Not a family in the traditional sense, of course, but a group for whom she had developed an almost motherly affection. With this affection came a strong sense of responsibility for her small group. She had recruited them. She made up their schedules, kept track of their finances. She settled their little disputes.

After her discussion with Gloria, she now had to consider her responsibility for their safety as well as her own. Theirs was a house of cards, more exactly a house of ill repute. It was vulnerable in ways that an ordinary household was not. But how could she protect them? Yeah, she had her pistol now, but would that be enough?

She changed course and looped behind the chemistry building, a rather squat structure with most of its laboratory space below ground level. From there it was only a few blocks to her apartment, all uphill, but she didn't mind the walk.

The unit she'd moved into three months before was a block of four apartments on a side street lined with mature maple trees just beginning to leaf out. Hers was an end unit with parking right out front. Having two bedrooms, a rather luxurious bathroom and a kitchen with stainless steel appliances was a serious upgrade from her previous lodgings.

She tossed her bag on the bed. The few things she had to unpack could wait until later. The pistol in her purse was another matter. She stashed it in a shoebox, and then pushed it deep into the bottom corner of her closet. For sure she'd need a more secure home for it, but the shoebox would do for now.

She drove down the little main street where most of the shops were located. Most of them catered to student needs—food, clothing, and alcohol. She drove a little farther out and stopped in front of a small building composed of concrete blocks painted dark green. The sign over the door said Carl's Electronics.

"Surveillance cameras?" she asked the clerk behind the counter.

"What you got in mind?" Small grease spots dotted the sweatshirt that the skinny clerk wore. They might well have come from his hair, which looked as if it hadn't been washed in months, or longer.

"Something small, easy to conceal, with a manual control. And I want to be able to download the photos into a computer."

He grinned. "This is all legal, right?"

"Oh, sure." She grinned right back at him, as if cameras could be legal in an illegal business. "We've had a bit of trouble with intruders, and I want to get a look at who's coming and going."

"Intruders? You tell the cops?"

"They're the ones who suggested the camera."

"So, this is like, for a store or something?"

"No, it's a private residence. Just some girls from school. You do the installation, right?"

"You bet. Let me show you what we got."

The next morning shortly past eleven she met the clerk, Carl Jr., at the Faculty Club where he installed the camera in a concealed spot at the edge of a bookshelf. In spite of his rather unassuming appearance, Carl Jr. knew his stuff when it came to surveillance items. Before he left, they gave the camera a test run, and the first image recorded on Sharon's new system was Carl Jr. himself entering the front door.

The system was, of course, an insurance policy. Now with her log of client names and dates of service, she had visual confirmation to back up her written entries. She could meet any threat from the university with ammunition of her own. Using her information would be a nuclear option, destroying everyone connected to the Faculty Club. Surely the threat alone would suffice.

Lennie would probably require a different kind of ammunition; he really had no reputation to destroy— but she had plenty of that, too.

****

Sunday morning, one of those beautiful spring days

when just drawing breath was enough to make for a good day, Sharon indulged in one of her guilty pleasures—coffee and a donut at the little bistro beside an upscale clothing store on the main drag. Normally besieged by students, the holiday break had thinned the crowd, so she found a corner booth, one bathed in morning sunlight, all to herself.

She was savoring that first delicious bite of her donut when Bob walked through the door of the shop. Outside of their weekly sessions at the Faculty Club, they had no contact, certainly nothing out in the open like this. In what could have been a very awkward moment, he smiled, she smiled, then waved him over.

"Care to join me?" she said. "Unless you'd rather not. I mean, I'll understand."

"Are you kidding? This is great." He slid into the booth across from her.

"So you didn't go away after all?" she said.

"Nah, it was kind of a last minute thing. And since you couldn't go, it really didn't seem worth it. How's your mom doing?"

"Mom?" Yeah, that was the excuse she'd given for not joining him. "She's okay. Actually my dad is the problem now." She tapped the side of her head with her forefinger. "He's starting to lose it. Don't know what's going on with that."

"Some kind of dementia?" he asked. "You should get him checked out medically. There are a lot of different causes of dementia, and some of them are treatable."

"That's what I told my mom. It's just impossible to get him to a doctor." She was quite mindful of the fact that she was talking about a man she had effectively shut out of her life for reasons she would probably never share with Bob or anyone else.

They sat there bathed in the warm spring sunlight streaming through a storefront window that needed washing—two friends, a chance meeting, a casual chat. A closer observer might have guessed that casual wasn't quite the right word. Such an observer might have picked up on the subtle electricity that passed between the two, the body language that was more expectant than relaxed.

Certainly Sharon felt it. She felt her usual reserve melting away. She leaned forward until her body pressed against the edge of the table. "I don't even know where you're from," she said. In all the months she'd been seeing him professionally, all those small details with which she might construct a solid image of him had never been filled in. Now she found she wanted more of it.

"Here and there," he said. He looked down as he spoke, something she attributed to shyness. "I was born in Michigan, but we moved around a lot."

She waited in vain for him to fill in the obvious gaps; why had they moved around? Military families moved a lot, she knew, but if this were the case surely he would tell her. But when no answer was forthcoming, she tried another question. "How long have you been on the faculty here?

"Just finishing up my fourth year," he said, again with downcast gaze.

"Then we arrived here about the same time," she said. "I started my freshman year four years ago. Some coincidence, huh?"

"Yeah." He twisted in his seat. "Say, that place

where you and the other girls, you know, is it open today?"

"What do you mean?"

"Could we go there, you and me?" he asked.

"I guess, if that's what you want." She felt as if she'd been punched in the gut. She wanted to chat; he wanted to fuck. So much for her quiet Sunday morning.

She drove the half mile to the Faculty Club with Bob following behind in a BMW convertible, quite similar to the one Chloe sported around town. She didn't want to be doing this. Why on earth had she ever agreed to it?

The house felt stuffy after being closed up for five days. She opened the two windows in the parlor area, then did the same in the bedroom off the hallway to the right. She checked to make sure the sheets were clean, then looked into the bathroom—soap, towels, washcloths—everything that might be needed after a tryst.

She walked back out into the parlor where Bob stood waiting by the desk. "Well, I'm ready, I guess."

"You remember that little black number you wore our first night?" he asked.

She nodded.

"Could you put it on for me?"

"Now?"

"Yeah." He was practically drooling.

All the girls kept their evening costumes in a large closet at the end of the hall. As she usually did, Sharon marveled at the outfits arrayed there. All were variations on a theme—skimpy and transparent. Who would wear such apparel? It wasn't really a question. She knew exactly who donned these filmy bits of practically nothing. She wore them herself, and she was going to do it again, right now.

She pulled the sheer black gown from its hanger, the one Bob had requested. The miniscule bra and underpants hung from the hook of the hanger. She left the bra but took the underpants with her. Why? She had no good answer. She wouldn't be wearing them for long.

She changed in the bathroom, shocked to find herself barely dressed as she was in the middle of a Sunday morning.

When she walked back into the bedroom Bob was waiting for her by the bed. He had stripped down to his undershorts, and the bulge at his crotch indicated he was ready for her.

She did a little pirouette. Some of her clients liked it, some didn't seem to care. It was either that or jump straight into bed. Usually with Bob there was a little cuddle time, hugs, a few kisses before they got right down to the act itself. But this morning his manner was different. He showed no interest in their usual intimacies.

"Take it off," he said.

"But I just put it on, like you wanted."

"Take it off." It wasn't a request, more like a command, and not gently put.

So she did. She had just hooked her thumbs into the elastic band of her panties when she paused. "Everything?" she asked.

"Everything."

She was by now well-schooled in the variety of sexual practices preferred by her clients. Most, since there was no requirement that they please their partner, bypassed any sort of foreplay altogether and went right to it. The upside of such encounters was that they were usually brief. A bit of bouncing around, then a shudder, and it was over and done with. The downside was that these were rather rough experiences. There was no hint of any emotional connection. Often she felt as if she could be replaced by some inanimate humanoid form, and the guy wouldn't know the difference, or care.

Then there were those unusual guys like Bob who, up until now, seemed to care about her feelings. These rare individuals enjoyed their time with her and wanted her to enjoy it as well, or so it seemed.

But what had become of her Bob, her gentle, caring Bob this Sunday morning? Bob who was so eager to please, but this time after a few thrusts and a grunt, climbed off her with no more ceremony than if he were dismounting a horse.

She covered herself with the sheet as he walked into the bathroom carrying his clothes under his arm. She was still sitting there, all glazed and confused when he returned a few minutes later.

When he pulled out his wallet, reality returned like a slap in the face.

Chapter Six

Even though final exams lurked in the near future, getting back into the rhythm of her class schedule was a relief for Sharon. This was familiar, this was known territory, and after the hornet's nest she'd left behind with her father, the routine of the university campus was a welcome respite.

The issues with her father were far from settled. As his dementia worsened, his need for care would increase. She knew her mother would be calling, asking her to drop everything and come back home, like any good daughter should.

With the likelihood of being asked to care for him in a most intimate way, how would she respond? How could she? No, this story was far from over, and hovering over it all was the history she shared with her father, a history she alone would acknowledge.

The home stretch of the year between spring break and final exams always seemed to fly by. Already four weeks had zipped past, and she couldn't figure where the time had gone. The Faculty Club, helped along by the improved weather, was more active than ever. Sharon took a quick survey of their books, and this last quarter was shaping up as their busiest ever.

Thursday night she had already serviced two customers by nine o'clock. The first almost killed her. Sharon couldn't recall ever having seen a man shaped like her first appointment of the evening, a very round mass of flesh onto which were attached two arms and two legs, and somewhere on the surface, a penis.

He'd already made several visits to the Faculty Club, and the girls who wound up as his bedmates gave frightening accounts of being pinned beneath his suffocating bulk. Chloe alone had escaped the crushing part; she put him on the bottom while she climbed on top.

Sharon was not so fortunate. With no preliminaries of any sort, he mounted her straightaway, up and down, up and down, and she was sure that either the bed frame would collapse or she would be crushed to death or possibly both. Before any of this happened, their vital parts found one another and he entered her. Each thrust pressed the air from her lungs, and a gasp in between was all she could manage.

Then it was over. He rolled off of her, pulled on his pants, which was all he'd taken off, and left.

Once her head stopped spinning and her breathing returned to normal, she checked herself for broken body parts. Everything seemed intact, so she hurried to the bathroom to rid herself of the lingering stench of him. Next time around, she would arrange for him to visit one of the Kirkland twins. They were by far the sturdiest of all her girls and might even enjoy such an encounter.

By the time she had herself back in order, the sheets changed, and the room all neat and tidy, her second guy had arrived. At least he was thin, cadaverous, even. But there was nothing moribund about his personality. His eyes had a merry twinkle, and he laughed frequently, even after he was completely nude.

But it wasn't his demeanor or his physique that caught her eye, rather it was the member hanging between his legs. She'd never seen one so long. The expression, "hung like a horse," came to mind, but she'd never believed it until now. And she wasn't even sure whether he was fully aroused. What if the damned thing got bigger?

Mr. Happy Face must have known the fear and surprise he caused, because his smile widened. "Do you do anal?" he asked.

"Absolutely not."

What a night. She'd barely escaped death by suffocation with the first guy only to be threatened with internal injury by the man with the elongated penis. Later, she lay on her back wondering how anyone survived very long in this business. The Kirkland twins for this guy next time, for sure.

The tap on her door would be her third, Bob. And he'd brought a friend. She hadn't seen him in over three weeks, and now this. Was he expecting a threesome?

"Hey, Sharon, this is my friend Lou," he said.

She was suddenly aware of her near nudity. The filmy black negligee concealed nothing.

"I was hoping you'd be wearing that one," Bob said through a broad grin.

The man Bob introduced as Lou moved up alongside Bob wearing an even broader grin. He was a couple of inches shorter than Bob, but of a much heavier build. He had broad shoulders and a neck so short and thick that his head appeared to sit directly on his shoulders. "Wow, great tits," he said. He made groping movements with his big, hairy hands.

"Bob, I don't do threesomes. You know that." She fetched her robe from the back of the bathroom door and covered herself.

"No threesome," Bob said. "Just Lou. I want to watch."

"What? No way. I want you to leave."

"I'll pay double."

"No."

"How about one of the other girls?"

"No. Go, Bob. Go now, and take your friend with you."

Lou took a half step toward her. She'd never felt so helpless before. If they forced her, what could she do? She wouldn't scream. That would draw unwanted attention to the house, and would definitely be bad for business. And she couldn't very well cry rape. Raping a whore in a whorehouse probably wasn't a crime. Gloria told her as much.

After what seemed an eternity of staring, Bob and his friend left. She would have been okay with taking care of Bob, but more than one guy at a time was out of the question.

At least she knew now where she stood with him. Any questions she might have had were answered by his latest request. To Bob she was a whore, nothing else. Her fantasies about a developing relationship were dashed to pieces.

"Just business," she told herself. She pulled the robe tightly around her.

Sharon found her slippers, then walked out to the front desk. Brenda was on triage duty that night. "No more for me," she told Brenda. I've had enough for one night.

"I'm sorry to hear that." Brenda looked at her closely. "Anything I can do for you?"

"No, I think I'll go back to my apartment. Hey, who's that?" A tall man in a blue blazer stood by the door. He had his back turned. When he took a step, she got a profile view. Stunning. Unless the other side of his face was deformed, this had to be the best looking man she'd seen in a long time, maybe ever.

"New guy," Brenda said. "Really cute. I was just going to send him back to you. Too bad you're not feeling well."

"Is he faculty? I've never seen him before," Sharon said.

"I don't know for sure, but that is one fine looking man."

He turned toward them. Still stunning, only more so. Then he left.

****

"Damn, damn, damn." Who in God's name would be calling her at eight o'clock on a Saturday morning? But then, who else? Her mother, of course.

Her whole body ached as she reached for the phone. The night before had been one of frenzied activity at the Club. It was supposed to be Sharon's night off, but neither of the Kirkland sisters showed up, so she went into the pit for the second night in a row. Two nights straight of being plunged and plowed until the only area of her body with any feeling left lay between her legs. Why couldn't that area go numb like everything else? She'd slept with a pillow between her legs, trying to keep the abraded surfaces from touching.

She took several deep breaths before she answered the phone.

"I was beginning to think I wasn't going to reach you," her mother said.

"Good morning, Mom."

"I need you here."

This wasn't the usual whiney voice her mother used when she wanted something, more like a command.

"What's wrong?" Sharon asked.

"Like you didn't know. You left a big mess here, got your father all stirred up. He's been impossible since you left."

"You're blaming me for his condition?" This was not the conversation she wanted to have, and not the time she wanted to have it.

"Come home and mess everything up and then just leave. You can't do that, Sharon. I can't manage him by myself."

"I have classes, Mom. If you want to hire a nurse I can help pay for that."

"Your father doesn't like strange people in the house. It only makes him worse."

"Why don't you call Aunt Dorothy? She's not that far away, and Dad always liked her."

"Stop beating around the bush, Sharon. He's your father, and he needs you. He was always there for you. Now it's your turn to be there for him."

Adding to her substantial physical discomfort, Sharon's stomach began to roil, and nausea made a steady climb upward. "Mom, I have to go. I'm feeling sick."

"If it wasn't for that young man you sent out I don't know how I would have made it through the week."

"Young man? What young man?"

"Your friend Bob. I wasn't sure about him at first, but he said you two were classmates, and you were very close. He was so nice. Just pitched right in with your dad like he'd known him forever. But that doesn't mean you can just turn your back on him when he needs you so much."

Bob? Bob had gone to her house? How did he even know where she lived, or where she used to live? What was he up to?

The nausea reached its target. "Mom, I'm sick." Sharon hung up the phone and bolted for the bathroom, just in time.

****

After her economics class, Sharon headed across campus to a little stand that sold fresh fruit. Eleven o'clock was too early for lunch, and she wanted an apple to hold her over until the noon meal. As usual, she would eat her lunch alone. House rules, on which all had agreed, discouraged socializing among the girls outside the house. The risk of anyone making connections, seeing the girls together, were small, but real. Why take chances? Of course, the Kirkland sisters were the exception. They seemed to spend all their spare time together.

That's why Sharon was so surprised when she felt someone grab her elbow—Brenda. "Hi," she said. Okay, it was against the rules, but she liked Brenda. "What's up?"

"You've got to see this." Brenda handed her a copy of *The Tattler*, the campus newspaper. On the bottom half of the front page, she saw described in lurid detail the downfall of a professor of political science who had impregnated one of his students. His protests that the sex was consensual had gotten him nowhere.

The professor's fate was sealed in a statement by the dean. The rather pompous and portly academic who sported a walrus mustache proclaimed, "Any faculty member who engages in sexual relations with a student, consensual or not, shall be dismissed immediately."

"I know that professor," Brenda said. "I had a class with him, spring semester last year. He's not a bad guy, and he's a great teacher."

"Good or bad, he's history now," Sharon said.

"Poor guy, his whole career shot to hell all because he couldn't keep it in his pants. Now if he'd come to the house we could have saved him all that trouble. We could have given him what he wanted, and he would still have a job."

"You make it sound like we're providing a public service," Sharon said.

"In a way, we are, don't you think? We get money, and they get sex. Everybody leaves happy."

"So long as nobody finds out," Sharon said. Obviously the dean had come down with both feet on the poor professor's neck, and would do so with anyone else caught in a sexual relationship with a student. This was her ace in the hole, maybe. With her ledger and the recordings from her video camera she could incriminate between fifteen and twenty per cent of the faculty, enough to bring the institution to its knees, not to mention the scandal. Of course, she hoped she would never have to use her evidence, but if they ever pushed her into a corner they would be very sorry.

"I just hope it doesn't hurt our business," Sharon said.

But nothing the dean had said or done made even a small dent in the activity at the Faculty Club. A couple of weeks later, when Sharon was going over the books, visits from their clientele still showed a steady climb. If it continued on like this, they were going to need a bigger house and more girls.

No, Sharon wasn't worried about the business. That was doing better than she'd expected. But she was worried about Bob, the creep. The thought of him showing up at her parents' house gave her chills, even on a warm day. For that matter, who was he? What was his angle? Even though he claimed to have started classes four years before, she was sure she'd never seen him on campus. She had checked the yearbook for each of the four years, but no Bob.

With luck, maybe he wouldn't come back, not after she had chased him away last time. Just as well, the things he had asked her to do still stung, made her feel cheap. Reminding herself that it was all about business and that she was providing a service and being paid for it didn't help that much.

Which brought up another question. Where did Bob get the money to pay for his visits to the Faculty Club? Was he even faculty? She went back through her ledger and found that he had dropped thousands of dollars over the past year. Even more than she expected, since she found that he'd been seeing some of the other girls as well.

Just business, she kept telling herself, just business. But her old friend Bob would bear watching, for sure.

****

"That guy was hung like you wouldn't believe. I felt like I should be paying him," Maggie Kirkland said to her sister.

"Next time, I get him, okay?" Donna said laughing.

"I think I remember this guy," Chloe said. "Skinny little fart, nice smile, huge dick."

"Has to be him," Maggie said. "Like a Louisville Slugger. He could rent that thing out."

"Definitely my kind of guy," Chloe said.

Sharon winced. She remembered. This same guy, the skinny one with the baseball bat between his legs had left her feeling as if she'd been blasted out by a fire hose. If Chloe and the Kirklands liked him, he was all theirs.

But today was about business. A late Sunday morning in early May, she called a meeting in the house. They opened all the windows to air the place out.

"Getting a bit ripe in here." Brenda wrinkled her nose as she walked in.

"We can leave the windows open most of the day," Sharon said. "I brought my books so I can hang out here and study."

"The mattress covers need changing," Maggie said. "The one in back smells like my cat's litter box."

"I bought new ones," Sharon said. "We can put them on right after we finish the business meeting." She passed out copies of the ledger sheet covering the last three months.

"Hey, you've upgraded. This looks like a real business report," Brenda said.

"Yeah, I'm taking accounting this semester. And like I said before, ladies, keep these in a very safe place. Better still, burn them."

"Wow, we're making money," Maggie said. "I

never dreamed this could be so profitable."

"Which brings us to the summer," Sharon said. "Do we stay open for business, or do we close down until the fall semester? Am I the only one who will be staying on campus?" She had already calculated her expenses for the extra year she would need to complete her business degree, and she had enough in the bank to cover those costs, and more. Still, since she had started the whole operation, she felt obligated to continue if the girls wanted to.

"Keep in mind," she said, "the longer we continue, the greater the risk. We've been lucky so far, but nobody knows how long that will hold out."

"Me, I feel like I've discovered a new career. I was born for this." Maggie Kirkland concluded her declaration with a horse laugh, joined by her sister.

"Me too," Donna said, in between guffaws.

After a discussion that went on for much longer than necessary, they agreed to shut down for the summer and to start up again with the fall semester. Sharon, being the only full time summer student, would keep an eye on the house. They would need to recruit at least two new girls for the next session, and all agreed to defer that action until after the semester started.

After the others left, Sharon settled in to study. With all the windows open, she was all too aware of the spring afternoon in full force outside. By late afternoon, the numbers on the pages became a blur, and she put her head down on the desk for a short nap.

She must not have heard him come in, but she certainly heard him when he kicked the desk. Lennie.

"Wakey, wakey," he said. "Sleeping on the job with the front door unlocked, not very smart. Anybody could walk right in."

"What do you want, Lennie?"

"Hey, that's no way to greet an old friend. I thought you'd be glad to see me, since we're like colleagues, you know."

"We're not colleagues, and I want you to get the hell out of here."

Lennie ignored her, walked around the room like he was taking inventory. "Nice little place you got here. They tell me you're doing right well for yourself, so far."

"Get out. I mean it."

"You know, I was real disappointed, the way you left, and then you start up here and don't even ask me."

"I don't need your permission."

"Still, I could be a real help to you."

"Lennie, I've had it with you. All I want is for you to disappear, right now."

"See, there you go being unfriendly again. Maybe you haven't had any problems yet, but this business we're in, it can get rocky sometimes." He pushed the lamp off the end table by the window and watched it crash to the floor. "See what I mean?"

"You bastard. You owe me thirty dollars for that lamp."

"And if I don't pay, what are you going to do? Call the cops? I don't think so. The last people you want sniffing around here is cops. All the more reason we should think about some kind of agreement, so we can look out for each other."

"No agreement." She slipped the little .22 caliber handgun out of her purse and pointed it at Lennie. "Now, I want my thirty dollars, then you're leaving."

Lennie walked slowly toward the desk, a big confident grin on his face. "I'll bet you've never even fired that little thing before."

"Wrong. I practice all the time. I can shoot the balls off of squirrels when I really try, so yours should be no problem at all." She lowered the barrel so that it pointed directly at his crotch. "Now, thirty dollars, then get the hell out of here, or so help me God, I'll make a soprano out of you."

He took out his wallet and tossed three bills on the desk. "This don't end here. You and me, we got unfinished business."

"Out."

Chapter Seven

"Brenda, it's me, Sharon, my lab project ran longer than I expected, so I'm going to be a few minutes late. Can you stall them for me?" Evening business hours at the Faculty Club started at seven sharp. Sharon was forever nagging the other girls about being on time, and this meant setting a proper example by being on time herself, but not tonight.

"Don't rush," Brenda said. "You only have one guy tonight, and he won't be here until nine."

"Just one? What's going on? That never happened before."

"Remember that hunk you saw last week, the really sharp looking guy, you know, tall, dark and handsome? He came in just before seven, said he wanted you all to himself, but he wouldn't be here until nine. Asked for you by name. Paid up front for the whole evening."

"The entire evening, just me?"

"I hope it's okay. I went ahead and set everything up for you. I mean, he's gorgeous. I'm not sure, I might have been drooling when he left. For sure, I was wet in other places."

"Did we ever decide, is he faculty?"

"I don't think so. He looks too fine to be an academic. If he taught here every girl on campus would be fighting to get in his classes," Brenda said.

"I guess I'll see you around nine." This would be a

first. Most of the other girls had their favorites, but one guy for the entire evening, that was new. She remembered him very well, and very often.

She got to the house with thirty minutes to spare. She donned her favorite black negligee and waited. While she waited, she paced, wearing a shallow furrow in the carpet.

He entered her room without knocking. The door was only about six feet from her bed, and he seemed to float across the distance. She froze. Just looking at him was enough to stop any girl in her tracks, but he wasn't coming for any girl, he was coming for her.

"Sharon." He said her name like he was tasting it, tasting her. He stopped about four feet from her. His gaze traveled slowly down her body, every contour, every crevasse, she felt it. He caressed her with his eyes.

"Yes," he said softly. "Please, turn around."

A simple enough request, but could she do it without falling? From the waist down, she was losing control. Putting one foot in front of the other would require careful planning. And turning around? Her head was already spinning. There was a better than even chance that she would topple, but she had to try. It's what he wanted, and she would do almost anything to please him.

He'd only been in her room for a minute or so, and already he possessed her. Her breathing, the beating of her heart, all under his control, his command.

She turned slowly, not for effect, although it couldn't hurt, but because doing it quickly would probably wind up with her sprawled on the floor.

Midway through her turn, he inhaled sharply.

"Yes," he said again. "You are beautiful."

When she started to undress he said, "No, let me do it." He seemed to take forever, not like she was wearing much to begin with. By the time he slipped down her transparent panties, she was almost foaming at the mouth.

He insisted on keeping on the overhead light while he circled around her. First he closed her eyelids with soft pressure from his fingertips. Then he touched her, and touched her, and touched her. Sometimes with just a single finger, light wispy caresses that made her gasp. He kept on until she said "Please." Then he did it some more.

When he took her shoulders and guided her back onto the bed she was breathing through clenched teeth, trying not to cry out.

Sometime, she wasn't sure when, he'd slipped off his jacket. Otherwise, he was fully clothed. Where was this going? Then she knew. He began a slow descent starting with her breasts. He caught a nipple between his teeth, bit down, causing her to gasp. Then to the other side, where she expected the same brief slash of pain, but instead he suckled gently, holding the nipple between his lips. He trailed kisses across her thorax, her abdomen. She knew just where he was headed, and she wanted him to hurry. The anticipation was almost painful. So slow, so damned slow. Each place his tongue touched burst into flame. He must have known, yet he would not relent.

By the time he'd reached her center, all the flames coalesced, and she was completely ablaze. He parted her with his fingertips, and when he probed with his tongue she convulsed. There was no helping it. Her circuits were overloaded, and something had to give.

This was crazy, upside down and backward. This was her room, her bed, her show, her body, but now they were all his. Whether she'd surrendered it all to him or whether he'd simply taken it, the result was the same, ownership had changed.

And through it all, she moaned like an animal, and he would not stop.

Had she blacked out? She felt as if she were regaining consciousness, without being sure when or where she might have lost it.

"Sharon, my name is Connor Shaw." He was sitting beside her on the bed, holding her hand. When she tried to raise up on her elbows, he pushed her back down gently.

"No, stay just as you are. This is how I want to remember you." Then he kissed the tip of her nose and left. In all her time at the Faculty Club, this was the first time she wanted a man to stay with her. She almost asked him to.

He would remember her, that's what he'd said. And she remembered him, too, and each time she did she felt his touch all over again. Days after he'd left, the places he'd touched still prickled at the memory. One particularly vivid recollection had forced her to walk out in the middle of her accounting class. Hers had to be the first orgasm ever in accounting.

And he was coming back, for her.

Since she wouldn't be due at the Faculty Club for almost two hours, Sharon decided on a nice hot bath, although a cold shower might have been more appropriate. Ever since she'd learned that Connor Shaw would be there again tonight for her, just for her, her emotional state had vacillated like the changing colors in a kaleidoscope. She'd bounced between exhilaration and panic and all stages in between. And the hot bath didn't help at all. Hot water coursing around her body only heightened her anticipation of things to come.

She had already taken the bottle of pinot noir off the rack when she decided against it. She really had no idea what might happen that evening, but she had best remain sharp in case things ran off the rails. On second thought, one glass couldn't hurt.

At quarter to nine, she entered the Faculty Club through the side door. He wasn't there yet. Chloe was at the reception desk, poring over a textbook. "Wow, you look great," she said.

"I just cleaned up a bit," Sharon said. In fact, she had spent every minute of the almost two hours past preparing for this moment.

Chloe sniffed the air. "Smells like you did more than just clean up. What is that you're wearing?"

"Chanel, something. I can't remember."

"Whatever, you smell delicious. Some guy is going to get his money's worth for sure."

Money, the word blew all Sharon's fantasies away like so much dust. The reality, she was selling herself for a price, stared her in the face once again.

"I'll be in back. Just send him through when he comes in."

"I'll beep you when he gets here," Chloe said. "I can't wait to get a look at this guy. You're sort of his own private property now, huh?"

"No, nothing like that. Whatever the customer wants, that's what we do."

Sharon sat on the bed. How should she prepare?

What would he want? Usually this part of her preparation required no thought at all. The only requirements for her apparel were that it be revealing and easily removed.

The chime from the intercom was followed immediately by a soft knock at her door. *He's here.* Two very deep breaths, and she opened the door.

She'd forgotten how tall he was. The little crinkles that formed at the edges of his eyes when he smiled, the eyes themselves, so gray and penetrating. He'd dressed just as before, a blue blazer, striped shirt and gray flannel slacks, standard academic garb, but he was much too hot to be a professor.

"May I come in?"

"Oh, sure, yes, of course." She stumbled over the carpet. She might have fallen had he not caught her arm. Idiot, she said to herself. *Idiot, idiot, idiot.* Like it was her first time, and she didn't know what to do next.

"Are you all right?"

She nodded. She didn't remember his voice, because their previous encounter had been almost wordless. That time had been about touching, caressing, about giving and receiving pleasure. And how much pleasure could one body provide to another? Far more than she'd ever imagined.

"You look very nice." His voice was just as soft as his voice had been. He caressed her with words.

She sat, fully dressed, wearing the same clothes she had arrived in. "I wasn't sure what to do, I mean, what you would want me to wear."

"What you have on is quite lovely." He pulled a chair alongside. "I hope I didn't upset your schedule, taking up your entire evening."

"No problem," she said. "This works out just fine for me." But what worked out, exactly? She knew what she wanted, but he'd paid for her entire evening, so he would be calling the shots.

He placed a white box on the bed beside her. How had she not noticed it before?

"I brought a couple of outfits that I'd like you to try on."

Sharon took the box into the bathroom to change. She trembled a bit as she opened it. What would she find inside? This would be the first solid clue about his intentions.

The box contained two short gowns, both of which appeared finely made. The stitching in both was practically invisible, as were the garments themselves. One, at least, was opaque. Held up against the light it became transparent, but otherwise it would be an alternative to going back out completely nude, which was how the second gown left her. She rubbed the gown against her face. It was like rubbing against a cloud.

Sharon folded her clothes into a pile that she left on the toilet seat. She slipped the very slightly opaque gown over her head. Neither outfit came with a bra or panties.

He had moved his chair up against the wall. "Walk back and forth a few times, slowly."

Any thoughts she had about the gown providing concealment disappeared with her first few steps. Even the movement of walking slowly caused the garment to cling to her body as it had been applied with a spray bottle. She couldn't have felt more naked wearing nothing at all.

After she'd made a few trips back and forth across the room, he said, "Very good. Now the other."

The second gown, while obviously constructed of a far superior substance, she couldn't really call it fabric, than her own regular gowns, was still just a variation on a familiar theme, transparent. Still, she did what he asked, paraded about until he told her to stop.

"Please, put your clothes back on. I'd like to talk a bit," he said.

Sharon returned to the bathroom, stripped off the gown, then put her own clothes on again. The entire little fashion show lasted, what, ten to fifteen minutes? What next? This wasn't at all what she'd expected. She remembered, her body remembered, the ecstasy of his last visit. That's what she wanted now. She wanted to get laid, penetrated by Connor Shaw. She wanted to feel him deep inside her while they rocked together to a rhythm so primitive that it made no sound.

When she entered the room, he was still sitting there, waiting for her. She handed the white box with the two outfits she'd worn to him, but he refused it.

"Keep them. They're for you, for us."

She sat on the bed and placed the box beside her. She couldn't have felt more at a loss if she'd been suddenly dropped into a strange city where she didn't speak the language.

"I have a proposal for you," he said. "I don't want your answer tonight. I'd like you to think about it for a few days."

She said nothing. Indeed, what could she say? *I'm on such a losing streak.* First her budding romance with Herb Collins had ended abruptly when he chose one of the other working girls. Then her fling with Bob, promising but never passionate, took a crazy turn. Now this. Her session the week before with this splendid specimen of manhood had been the most enjoyable she could remember. That one hour raised her hopes for how much pleasure she might expect if only she found the right guy. Now this *right guy* was about to go all weird on her. Whatever he had in mind was sure to be freaky, and her answer was sure to be *No*.

"Please, listen carefully. I would like to purchase exclusive rights to your…services."

Services, he stumbled over the word as if seeking something more suitable. "I will cover all your regular fees, and then some. You will be well compensated, I promise you."

Sharon squirmed. Suddenly the bed, where she had spent so many unsatisfying hours, was more uncomfortable than usual. She wanted to be someplace else, anywhere else.

"As I said, I don't want your answer tonight. I'm sure you'll have many questions. With your permission, I will reserve your evening next Thursday, and we can continue our discussion then."

With that, he got up and left, without even touching her. And she wanted to be touched, very much, preferably without first being paraded about like a prize piece of livestock at a county fair. But he was gone without laying a finger on her, or in her. *Damn.*

Chloe was stuffing her papers into her book bag when Sharon walked out. "How'd it go?" she asked. "Your guy looked pleased as punch when he left, and he reserved you for all of next Thursday again. Oh, I never did get his name."

"Me either," Sharon said. She lied, of course, but

she wanted to keep his identity to herself, for the time being.

"I guess we'll have to call him Mister Mysterious until we know better."

"Are the other rooms cleaned up?" Sharon asked.

"Yeah, the Kirkland twins were here, and they all tidied up before they left. Sometimes Maggie says she did when she really didn't, but I checked, and her room was neat as a pin. That just leaves yours."

"No problem," Sharon said. "I took care of it."

"That didn't take long."

"Not much to do." Indeed, there was nothing to do, nothing at all. The bed, that essential piece of furniture in any whorehouse, had nary a wrinkle.

"Then I guess we're ready to go," Chloe said.

Sharon had insisted that the girls never leave the house alone, for safety's sake.

"You still haven't told me what a great time you had with Mr. Mysterious," Chloe said.

"It was okay, you know."

"Just okay? I mean, he seems to want you all to himself."

"Yeah, I don't know how long that's going to last." Indeed, her misgivings were piling up at a rapid rate, creating a sizable mound of doubt. She was in no mood to become anyone's private property at the moment, perhaps not ever.

After making sure that Chloe reached her BMW in safety, Sharon drove back to her apartment. As usual, she drove past her assigned space, making sure there were no unsavory types about. She always carried her handgun along, and although the .22 caliber cartridges lacked the punch to take down a determined pursuer, they could prove quite annoying if aimed well, and her aim was flawless.

The blue Datsun, with the dent in the driver's side door, she had seen that car before. She drove past it, slow enough that she could memorize the license plate. She had moved the handgun from her purse to her lap, just in case.

The front seat of the Datsun appeared to be empty, but on closer inspection, she detected a shapeless mound, as if someone had slumped down in the seat trying not to be seen.

The smart move would be to drive away fast, but Sharon felt she'd been manipulated enough for one night. Time for her to start calling the shots. She slipped the handgun into the pocket of her jacket, got out and walked over to the parked Datsun. When she rapped on the window, Bob rose up into a sitting position, rubbing his eyes.

He rolled down the window. "Sharon, I was waiting for you. Must have fallen asleep."

"What the hell are you up to?"

He looked bewildered. "Nothing, I just wanted to talk, get things straight between us."

She took a step back. "Bob, you need to understand this, there is no us. There's nothing to get straight between us. I don't want you visiting my family again, and I don't want you following me around."

"Sharon." He started to get out of the car.

"No. Stay where you are. I want you to leave now, and don't come back."

He mumbled something that she couldn't make out. The only part of his statement that came out clearly was "You'll be sorry."

Under other circumstances, this would be a clear signal for her to contact the police, but her own situation was a bit delicate. Bob knew too much. Why had he switched cars? The Datsun was a long way down from the BMW she'd seen him drive before. The man was too full of inconsistencies for her taste.

****

Her Friday luncheon with Gloria had become a regular thing. They met each week at a small diner just off campus.

"No dark glasses this week," Sharon said.

"You mean no black eyes to hide."

"I'm glad. I hate to think of guys punching on you."

"Just part of the business," Gloria said. "And there are other places they can hit you, places that don't show, but they hurt just as bad."

"I guess we've been lucky so far. None of us have been beaten up," Sharon said.

"You serve a better clientele than I do. Some guys don't think they've got their money's worth without smacking the girl around."

Mary, their usual waitress, stepped up to the table. "Same thing today, ladies?"

This meant a house salad for Sharon and a grilled cheese sandwich for Gloria.

"Someday we're going to change the order," Gloria said. "Just to mess you up."

"Be right back." Mary grinned and left.

"Something I want your opinion on," Sharon said. She told Gloria about Mr. Mysterious and his proposal, and that he wanted her decision next week.

"And you don't even know his name?"

Sharon shook her head. She felt bad about holding out on Gloria, but still wanted to preserve Connor Shaw's secrecy.

"You already know what I'm going to say. It's all about Gloria's three rules for hookers. Rule one, never get kinky. No matter what they ask for, stick with the basics. Otherwise you could get hurt, bad. If your Mr. Mysterious, or whatever, wants to get weird, tell him to bugger off.

"Rule number two is, never get attached. Guys will get stuck on you, that's natural. But if you get hooked on one of your clients, you'll only get your heart broken, and that hurts worse than a black eye.

"Rule number three is, keep it in the house, no outside parties, no special events. Your house is the only place where you're covered. You start picking up outside gigs, the guys can do anything they want to you. Don't let it happen."

"Yeah," Sharon said. "Pretty sound advice all around."

Mary brought their orders. "Anything else?" she asked.

"Nope."

"Enjoy."

"Sweet kid," Gloria said. "Too bad she's running her ass off for minimum wages plus tips."

"Not enough to pay the bills, that's for sure." Still, that seemed to be the basic transaction that made the world go around—buying and selling. The only difference lay in the details, otherwise, all the same.

"So, you clear about all this now? It's all about keeping your risks as low as possible."

Sharon nodded.

"When do you see Mr. Wonderful again?"
"Next week. I'll let you know."

Chapter Eight

"These are for you, Sharon."

Long-stemmed red roses. That about did it. That voice, the way he said her name, like she was the only woman in the world, not just in the room. That same voice swept Gloria's warnings right off the table. Anything he wanted, whenever, wherever, anything at all.

She had questions, but she couldn't remember. "I didn't know how to dress," she said.

"You're lovely just as you are."

That same dress she'd spent almost three hours shopping for. Now it was all worth it, every minute.

"Do you have a passport?" he asked.

She shook her head. What a rube, not even a passport.

"You should get one."

She nodded. When had she become mute?

"I'll give you a few details, about myself and what I'll ask of you. I am a corporate attorney, and I'm vice-president of a large firm. My work often involves international travel. That's why I asked about the passport.

"You will, no doubt, have wondered why I put this proposal to you. I work long hours, but that doesn't mean I don't have the needs of any other man. I do. What I lack is the time to devote to all the foolishness usually required to fulfill those needs. I want someone who will be available at the time and place of my choosing. I don't need to add that the person would be attractive and educated, someone like yourself."

So far, he had supplied not only the answers, but the questions as well.

"I suppose I might come off as a controlling SOB, and that's not far off the mark. I want what I want, when and where I want it. And I'm ready and willing to pay for the service. If you accept my offer, you will receive two thousand dollars a week."

"Where, I mean, where would we do it?"

"At my home. My man, Clark, will pick you up at your apartment and take you back home again after."

"You know where I live?"

"Yes. I also know that you are very fond of a certain California pinot noir. Your new dress is size six. I've done my homework."

She searched for questions. Before she'd had so many, now her mind was blank. "How long?" she asked.

"Either of us can terminate the agreement at any time. There is a document that we both will sign agreeing never to disclose the details of the agreement or the name of the other party."

"When would we start?"

"Now. That lovely new dress, take it off."

****

"Are you out of your mind?" Gloria glared across the table at Sharon. "You didn't listen to a word I said last week, did you? I might as well have been talking to the wall. You're hopeless."

"You're probably right. Believe me, I didn't plan

for it to work out this way."

"You're taking too many chances here. I just don't want you to get hurt. If you were a man I'd say you were thinking with your dick, but since you don't have one of those you must be using something else, certainly not your brain."

"Maybe I wasn't thinking too straight." Maybe she wasn't thinking at all. That's what the man, Connor Shaw did to her, turned her brains to oatmeal. No, she wasn't thinking, she was too busy feeling, experiencing the most intense pleasure she had ever known, the kind of pleasure that had her breathing through her eyelids.

As if he had a sensory map of her body, he hit all the right places, sometimes a light touch, sometimes more forceful pressure. She kept trying to guess where he would go next, and she was always wrong, and she was always delighted wherever he wound up. His damned voice, caressing her one moment, penetrating her the next. How in hell could someone penetrate her with just words?

"What about the other girls?" Gloria asked. "Are you just going to walk out on them?"

"I talked to Brenda. She wasn't too happy about me leaving, but since we'll be closed down for the summer it shouldn't make that much difference." She still had guilt pangs about leaving the Faculty Club. It was her baby, after all, so she couldn't just walk away. At the very least, she would continue to help with the administrative details through the summer, but her body, that now belonged to Connor Shaw.

"Sharon, girl, what am I going to do with you?" Gloria shook her head slowly, like a concerned parent might.

****

"Sharon, please, I can't handle this by myself."

"You don't have to, Mom. There are home nursing services that can help you. I'll pay for it. All you have to do is make the call."

"Your father won't allow strangers in the house. You know that. You're his only daughter, Sharon. All those years he took care of you, that must count for something."

"Yeah, he took care of me, all right."

"What do you mean by that?"

"You know exactly what I mean, Mom. Sexual abuse, for years. That counts for something, let me tell you." Child abuse, the nuclear option, guaranteed to shred any and all family ties, which was the reason she tried to keep it shut away, out of sight, but never out of mind.

"How dare you say that about your father? That never happened, and you know it."

"Oh, it happened, over and over again. Do you know what that does to a child, being abused by her own father? And you knew about it and did nothing to stop it."

"I won't listen to this trash. You better pray to God for forgiveness, such lies."

"I've already prayed, Mom. When I was a little girl, I prayed for God to make my father stop hurting me. But God didn't help much then, and I'm not going to waste my time with Him now."

"That's blasphemy, Sharon, pure and simple. I won't listen to it. I don't know what they've done to you at that college, but they've messed you up something awful. And your father and I will get along fine without you." She hung up.

****

She began having nightmares during her freshman year. Halfway through her sophomore year they became a nightly event. In early December, on a cold day with skies that threatened snow, a sleep-deprived, desperate, and somewhat haggard Sharon went to the university counseling service. Actually, she went twice. The first time she climbed the short staircase, then turned around and left. Only a particularly frightening nightmare brought her back.

The next time, she was shown into the office of Anna Baldwin, Ph.D. A fifty-ish psychologist with dark brown eyes and an odd way of tilting her head to the left when she looked at you. "Yes?" she asked.

Sharon, seated in a cozy chair on the other side of Dr. Baldwin's messy desk said, "I'm having nightmares."

"For how long?"

"I remember having some in high school, then more my freshman year here. But this year they've gotten much worse."

"How do you mean?"

"They come almost every night. I can't sleep. Some nights I'm afraid to go to bed."

"What are they like?"

Sharon clammed up. Talking about the horrors she experienced each night might unleash them right there. Then she might see more clearly the figure that haunted her dreams. She might see who it was. She already knew. Even in his current state of incapacity and dementia, her father still had the power to terrify her.

"Are you afraid?" Dr. Baldwin asked.

Sharon nodded.

"Nothing can harm you here. Nightmares are so frightening because they occur in darkness, when we're all alone. You're not alone now. I promise."

She took a long look at Dr. Baldwin. So far, she had only told her mother about her secret, and that had ended badly, with her mother slapping her and calling her a liar and worse. What if Dr. Baldwin responded the same way? What could she do then? "Maybe I shouldn't have come here," she said.

"These nightmares must be very frightening for you. Sometimes talking about them can make them less scary."

"Or worse," Sharon said. "What if it only makes them worse?"

"I don't think that will happen. In fact, I can assure you, it will not."

Sharon started to get up, then sat down again. She took a deep breath, then another. "There's someone in my dreams."

"Always the same person?"

Sharon nodded again. Speaking out loud seemed to require so much effort.

"And you recognize the person?"

"My father." There, she'd said it. No backing out now. She would have to go all the way. "When I was nine years old my father began abusing me."

Sharon hadn't taken off her coat. Now she pulled it tightly around her as if to ward off any evil that might be lurking about. The wall clock showed the passage of only three minutes, but to Sharon time seemed to have stopped altogether.

"How long did this go on?" Dr. Baldwin's voice

was unchanged, no suggestion of surprise, no disapproval, no doubt.

"Just over two years, no, longer."

"Did you tell anyone?"

"My mother."

"What happened?"

"She called me a liar and slapped me."

"Did you ever go to her for help again?"

"Later that same year, but she got all angry with me again, said whatever happened was my own fault."

"Ah, yes, blame the victim. Sooner or later that always seems to happen in abuse cases."

"You've seen other people like me?"

"Many, so very many. You probably thought you were the only girl ever molested by her father, didn't you?"

How would she know? It was not a secret that one shared, except with a therapist. The deep shame of it all required that it be kept shut away. Even becoming angry about it, and she had been angry, oh yes, did not remove the blot. Shame and guilt carried the day, and also the nights.

"You said the abuse stopped when you were eleven or so. Did he just stop, or was it something you did?"

"I wedged a chair under the doorknob so he couldn't get in."

"How did he react to that?"

"He started drinking. He would stand outside my door and beg and plead. I know my mother heard him, but she never lifted a finger."

It wasn't until their third weekly session that Sharon told Dr. Baldwin what she considered her darkest secret. "Sometimes I let him. If there was something I really wanted, new clothes, a new bike, something like that. I'd make him promise to buy it for me if I let him do it."

"You traded sex to get things you wanted?"

"Uh huh. I know that sounds awful*." I've been a hooker since I was twelve years old. Still am. What do you think of that?*

"How do you feel about it? That's what's important."

"At the time, it didn't seem like such a big deal. He got what he wanted, and I got what I wanted."

When the nightmares stopped, her visits to Dr. Baldwin stopped, too. Baldwin urged her to continue, but Sharon knew, at some fundamental level, that all the therapy in the world could never recreate her warped childhood. That was set in stone. It would always be a part of her.

"Thanks, Dad," she said as she left the building that held Dr. Baldwin's office for the last time. "You fucked me up in more ways than I can count."

****

Early Tuesday evening would be her first session with Connor Shaw at his home, and Sharon's anxiety level was pinging off the ceiling.

"Clark will pick you up at your apartment at eight o'clock." That's all she knew for sure.

"Relax." If she'd said it once she'd said it a hundred times. Nothing happening here that she hadn't done before, many times.

But the lie wouldn't stick. Yeah, she had used her body as a means to an end on any number of occasions. This was different. This time she had sold herself, body and soul, as well.

It was an open-ended arrangement; she could get out at any time. But could she really? Once you'd sold yourself as she had done, could you ever truly get that self back again? "Relax." She said it once more.

She spent way over her monthly clothing allowance, a lot of it on new underwear. This was all part of the mystery; what did he like, what didn't he? She stuffed a few extra items in her purse, a change of underwear, new, a toothbrush, and deodorant.

At precisely eight o'clock, a Lincoln Town Car, black with tinted windows, pulled into the parking lot in front of her apartment. The man she guessed must be Clark got out and waited by the car. Sharon did her usual deep breathing exercise, then headed out.

When Connor mentioned Clark, the man he would sent to fetch her, Sharon expected a driver, not the taciturn, almost fearsome individual who stood by the limo holding her door open.

"You must be Mr. Clark?" she asked when she was alongside him.

"Just Clark."

She couldn't help making comparisons between Connor and this man, Clark. Connor, she thought, was a couple of inches taller, but Clark was broader in the shoulders. Connor's face was handsome—GQ handsome—and very expressive. There was no doubting his pleasure when he saw her.

From Clark she got nothing. His face was completely unreadable. If she touched him, which she certainly would not do, she would not be surprised to find him firm and unyielding, like marble.

Would it have killed him to give her a kind word, a smile? But she got none of that from Clark. The questions she put to him got a monotone yes or no, nothing more. And the few questions she asked about Connor Shaw got no answer at all.

She had a momentary sexual fantasy about him. While Connor seemed all about giving and receiving pleasure, an encounter with Clark might be a more primitive event, even savage. A fearful thought. If he ever came to the Faculty Club, she would hide under the bed.

Maybe he just didn't like the idea of call girls in the first place. Probably a lot of people would disapprove of her planned activity, but Connor Shaw hadn't asked other people. He chose her. Women who might cast disapproving looks at her would likely change their tune in a heartbeat when they got a look at the handsome Mr. Shaw. To no avail. Tonight he was hers, and she was his.

There must have been others before her. For certain, the uptick in Connor Shaw's sexual appetite was not a recent event. He was far too skilled and practiced a lover. No, she was one in a long line of women he had bedded. Not the first and certainly not the last.

At eight-twenty, Clark pulled into an underground garage. Sharon didn't get a look at the building above.

He parked the car, opened her door and said, "Follow me."

They took the elevator to the top, four floors up. Clark led her down a short hallway, then unlocked the door they would enter. He led her through a living room with the largest floor-to-ceiling window she had ever seen.

She began to wonder about the extent of Clark's

role. Would she be expected to undress in front of him? No way in hell.

He opened another door. "Wait here."

The same floor-to-ceiling window formed one wall of the bedroom where Clark left her. A huge bed, larger than king-sized, filled the center of the room, but there was still plenty of space for a dressing area and a bar off to the left. She gradually became aware of a subtle scent...lavender. A woman's touch, for sure. No man would ever anoint his bedroom with lavender.

By the time she'd finished touring the bathroom—the largest and most lavish she'd ever seen—Sharon realized she could easily fit her entire apartment in this bedroom space.

She walked over to the wall of windows, pressed her nose so close to the glass that her breath condensed on the surface. It was too dark to pick out details from the area below, but she guessed it to be a dense woodland stretching almost to the horizon. A quarter moon had risen early and cast enough light to reflect off a river that she didn't know existed.

With a little time to kill, she decided to explore the room more thoroughly. Wonder if he had cameras installed? If so, they would likely be those tiny affairs used by professionals, cameras so small that unless you held it in your hand you'd never detect it. The guy who had installed the cameras at the Faculty Club tried to sell her a couple of those, but they would have destroyed her budget. So if Connor Shaw had a few, or even a lot of those tiny devices, she would never be able to find them in a room so large.

She rummaged through the drawers of his dresser, the nightstands and his closet, turned up nothing remarkable, except that persistent faint scent of lavender. Who was the woman who put it there?

The iron hooks with dangling chains above the bed that she might have expected weren't there, no visible restraints of any sort, nothing kinky. Gloria might be glad to hear that, if Sharon ever told her. Aside from the extreme luxury of it all, this seemed to be a very ordinary bedroom.

She wasn't aware he'd entered the room until she saw his reflection in the glass.

"Sharon." As before, the way he said her name made her knees weak.

"I'm so glad you're here. I've been thinking about you all day." He kissed her, a light kiss, not much pressure, then drew back but only a little so that their lips were almost touching.

Again with the wobbly knees. Much more of this and she would have to sit down.

"A glass of wine?"

He brought over two glasses. "This isn't your favorite pinot. It's one from my cellar. I hope you like it."

The single bottle probably cost more than an entire case of her usual, she guessed. So far, so good. She felt more like a real guest than hired help.

This was a new look for him, at least one she hadn't seen before, black silk shirt with an open collar, black slacks. It suited him nicely, adding yet another layer of intrigue to this mysterious man with a non-verbal driver who appeared capable of nearly anything, but carrying on a conversation.

Had he dressed as she was accustomed to seeing him, blue blazer, striped tie and gray flannel slacks, his college professor appearance would have blended well with her own apparel. She had chosen a skirt and sweater set, just purchased two days earlier, that any co-ed on her way to meet with her professor might wear. Naughty professor, naughty co-ed.

"I have to step out for a few minutes," he said. "Why don't you finish your wine while I'm gone?"

"Should I get undressed?"

He looked at her, and she could feel his gaze slipping across her body, and wherever it stopped...her breasts, her pelvic area...got pleasantly warm.

"No. I'll do that."

Oh God, he was going to undress her. She'd had lots of practice stripping off her own clothes during the past year, so it shouldn't be such a big deal, but it was. She could already feel his hands moving across her body, slowly undoing buttons, zippers, unsnapping her bra, rolling down her panties. The warmth between her thighs grew warmer, much warmer. Move, release, she had to do something, otherwise she might be thrashing around on the floor by the time he returned.

About fifteen minutes later, he returned. He dimmed the lights, but the bedroom remained relatively bright.

"Don't worry about the window," he said. We can see out, but no one can see in."

No problem, she'd already forgotten about it. Besides, she didn't care, not at this point. If he wanted to strip her in the street, she would probably go for it.

Gloria, her mentor, had been right—keep it in the house. By moving outside her safe zone, Sharon had assumed a new level of risk. But instead of dampening her attraction, the risk was electric. It coursed through her, danced along her skin. She was ready. Connor Shaw, bring it on.

He pulled her cashmere sweater over her head. When her face emerged she found him gazing into her eyes. So, this was a man who liked eye contact. Something new. Her clients at the Faculty Club seldom if ever made eye contact. They might look at any other part of her body, but never her eyes.

Connor Shaw was obviously different. Not only was he going to get into her pants, he might just get into her head, into her soul.

"Now, close your eyes," he said, a whisper that, had his lip not been right next to her ear she could not have heard.

She couldn't remember losing her skirt, her underwear, or how it all came to be a part of the pile that eventually included his shirt and slacks. No matter, the important fact was that now they were both the way they had come into the world—totally bare.

He ran his hands down the center of her back, then cupped her buttocks, pressing her into him. His erection pushed against her abdomen. Yes, she wanted it, but she wouldn't get it, not yet. He lifted her and carried her to the oversized bed. When he started on her, it was with his lips.

He seemed to be everywhere at once—an earlobe, the base of her neck, a nipple, the soft down that covered the center of her lower abdomen, almost invisible but he found it, and lower still, yes. His head nestled between her thighs, he opened her with his thumbs. His tongue flicked her rising clitoris, and a groan rose in her throat that she couldn't stop.

What was he doing down there? Nipping, sucking,

a quick burst of air, and each time a wave of delight flowed outward all the way to her fingertips, her toes. Yes, he had discovered the center of her universe, and he was the conductor, for now.

But, dammit, she should be doing something. She was being paid, after all. Someday she would make him moan and cry out the way he was forcing her to, someday but not today. At the moment, she was not capable of doing anything of the sort. She could still move her arms and legs, but the movement was random, without purpose, certainly lacking in the fine point discrimination with which he was manipulating her sensory system.

When he entered her, it was almost a relief, a reprieve from the rapid vacillation between ecstasy and torment, where he moved her so quickly that she couldn't tell one from the other, and didn't care. Now she was over the edge, and they were falling together. They reached climax together, and for a moment locked onto one another, stretching the time out, losing nothing, sharing everything. She heard him moan. Yeah, she had gotten to him after all.

And then it was over. He lay facing her, his hand cupping her left breast, tweaking an erect nipple with his thumb. "How are you?" he asked.

"Never better." It was true, what she said, but about as witty as cat food. She was being paid to please, to entertain, but this required a clear head, and after making love with Connor Shaw her head was anything but clear. This man could choose any woman he wanted, so she'd better sharpen up a bit, or Clark would be parking the limo at someone else's door.

****

One thing she had learned about men, keeping them interested required variety. Without it, they would simply look elsewhere, or as crazy Bob had done, start requesting kinky variations in the sexual act. Her best bet would be to arrange any variations herself, but how would she manage that with a partner who was in control so completely?

Her partner, her employer, provided an answer before she could respond. As she was gathering up her things to head to the bathroom, Connor, watching her from the bed, said, "You were a dancer before."

"Well, a stripper, actually." It was a part of her life she hoped to keep in the past, hidden. A false hope, because he seemed to know everything about her, and apparently her blonde wig hadn't fooled him at all.

"I attended some of your performances, several of them."

"Oh."

"Perhaps sometime you'll dance for me."

"Sure." She shuddered at the thought of Connor sitting in the audience watching her cavort at Lennie's. But he must have been somewhat impressed, because he'd pursued her and was paying her a hell of a lot more than she'd ever made stripping. And if he wanted a repeat performance that's just what he'd get.

When she came out of the bathroom, he was gone. Now she had to find Clark, or he had to find her. She walked into the living room where he stood facing the window, waiting. He would know everything she'd just done. Her status in the world seemed to drop several notches.

Without a word, without even looking at her, he crossed the room, and she followed.

They got back to her apartment shortly after ten. She gave up on trying to engage Clark in conversation, so the ride was silent. When he stopped to let her out, she discovered that the door handles in the rear seat were inoperable. She had to wait for Clark to open the door for her. Cute, she thought, real cute.

Chapter Nine

She'd been gone only two hours or so, but her own apartment looked very good just now. She had lots to process and needed a glass of wine to help things along. The phone rang before she picked up the bottle.

"Sharon, it's Brenda, we've got a problem, a big problem."

"Where are you?" Sharon asked. The Faculty Club should be closed by now.

"I'm here, at the house. We've had some trouble."

"You need me to come over?"

"Yeah, definitely."

Brenda was there alone. Her normally fair complexion was about two shades paler. She'd locked the front door, but Sharon still disapproved; there should always be at least two girls there, or none at all.

"A guy came in around nine. A real sleazy looking character. And he had two other guys with him. They looked rough, scary. He was looking for you. Said he was a friend of yours. I told him you weren't here anymore."

"Did he say his name?"

"Yeah, Lennie. And then he wanted to know who was running the place with you gone. I told him that was none of his business. I threatened to call the cops, but he just laughed.

"Then he said something about being our new

manager. And I said, 'Like hell you are.' All three of them crowded around the desk. I was scared to death."

"God, I'm sorry, Brenda. I've had trouble with that bastard before, but I never dreamed he would come back here."

"There's more," Brenda said. "Chloe was in back cleaning up, and she came out while they were here. One of the big guys said something like, 'Well, there's two of them. That's enough to go around if we take turns.' Then he walked up to Chloe.

"She pulled a switchblade out of her purse. 'I'll gut you like a pig.' That's what she said.

"Then Lennie said he didn't want blood everywhere, how it was bad for business. He said he would be back. What are we going to do?"

"Chloe carries a switchblade?"

"Yeah, a big one. And she looked like she knew how to handle it."

"I never would have dreamed it. Look, I'm so sorry about all this. It's my mess, and I'll take care of it."

"How? They were big guys, and Lennie looks mean as a snake."

"My problem, not yours. I'll fix it." She spoke with much more confidence than she felt.

But how? She went to bed without a clue about how to handle Lennie, and woke up the same way. When the phone rang just past seven, she thought it had to be her mother. Not so. She knew that voice immediately.

"You had a spot of trouble last night," said Connor Shaw.

"How on earth did you find out about that?"

"Don't worry about a thing. Clark will take care of

it."

"But there were three of them."

He laughed. "You don't know Clark very well."

The following evening, Sharon dropped by the house, not knowing what to expect. Christine, whom Sharon knew least well of all the girls, was at the desk. "Coming back to work?" she asked when Sharon walked in.

"No, just wanted to make sure things were going well."

"Do you think those guys will come back? Brenda was petrified."

"I hope we've seen the last of them." What would she do if they showed up? She had no real plan. She still had her little handgun in her purse, but a shootout would close the Faculty Club permanently, and the aftermath would be very unpleasant.

Lennie and his goons didn't show that night or the next. Sharon learned nothing new about him until her Friday luncheon with Gloria.

"I saw Lennie in the parking lot at the club yesterday," Gloria said. "He looked like he'd been hit by a truck, broken arm, face all puffy. Somebody really did a number on him. You wouldn't happen to know anything about that, would you?"

"Not me," Sharon said. "Last time I beat somebody up was the kid next door when he pulled the head off one of my dolls."

"I wonder who got him," Gloria said. The look on her face suggested that she didn't buy Sharon's innocent act.

"He's got lots of enemies, and like you said, that's just part of the business."

"You stopped working, I hear," Gloria said.

"Yeah, word gets around pretty quick."

"I hope you're not doing anything foolish with that new guy."

"More foolish than running a whorehouse?"

"You know what I mean," Gloria said. "I just hope you'll tell me if you are. It's too easy to get into trouble, and sometimes you don't see it coming."

Sharon shoved lettuce leaves around her salad plate. "I can't say anything right now. I just can't."

"Will you at least be careful? Will you do this for me?"

She placed her hand over Gloria's and gave it a squeeze. "I will, and thanks."

Sharon wasn't sure which of the bits of news she'd heard over the past couple of days—Lennie's mishap or learning that Chloe carried a switchblade impressed her most. But more impressive than either of these was the realization of the extent to which Connor Shaw now directed her life. Not only did he know so very much about her (her dress size, for heaven's sake), but he apparently was ready, willing and able to put that information to use.

As much as she liked having someone on her side, particularly when it came to thugs like Lennie, she'd never asked for that help. He'd taken it upon himself to smash Lennie.

And then there was that guided missile, Clark, who Connor could send anywhere he chose, and heaven help whoever was in his sights.

Sharon got a firsthand look at Clark's handiwork the following Saturday morning. She was heading into Bullock's Drug Store for the stack of newspapers that would make up her weekend reading, just as Lennie was coming out carrying what looked to be a bag of medications. Gloria's brief description had hardly done justice to the ruin wrought upon that poor man.

"Lennie, oh my God." A wave of remorse smacked her in the face. No way did he deserve what had been done to him. The parts she could see—the battered face, the right arm in cast—were bad enough, but his bent posture indicated similar damage had been done to his torso.

When he saw her he backed into the magazine rack. "Please, I didn't mean nothing before."

"Wait, you think I had something to do with this?" Her remorse was in high gear now. Sure, she had threatened to shoot off his balls, but she'd made that threat to scare him away.

"I'm sorry," he said. "I won't bother you no more, ever." He scuttled past her like a bird with a broken wing.

"No," she said. "It wasn't me." The poor bastard. He didn't deserve this. Nobody deserved this.

She caught up with him easily enough. He couldn't walk very fast. "Lennie, what can I do? How can I help you?"

"Just let me be. You've done enough." He hobbled off.

He left her standing there on the sidewalk, the freedom of a spring weekend bustling all around her, tears streaming down her face. Damn Clark, damn him to hell. But Lennie was right, wasn't he? He'd gotten his ass kicked because of her.

****

Sharon had just returned from breakfast when the

phone rang. Most of her calls of late had been bad news in one form or another, so she didn't pick up until after the sixth ring.

"This is Lynne Cartwright. Is this Sharon?"

"Yes, Lynne, is it really you?" A high school classmate, they'd been friends but drifted apart their senior year when Lynne became the full-time girlfriend of a guy who'd graduated the year before.

"Sure, I'm married now, and my official name is Johnson, but I didn't think you'd know that. It's been five years or more since we talked."

"At least that," Sharon said. "What's up with you?"

"Married, two kids. I stay at home now. The kids and a house to keep clean were just too much, so I quit my job. Wasn't much of a job anyway. I know you're wondering why I called; it's your dad. He died late yesterday."

"Oh, my God." Sharon grabbed for a chair. "What happened?"

"Your mom said it was a stroke. He's gone downhill over the past couple of weeks, so this didn't come as a big surprise."

"I'll get back there as quick as I can. How's Mom?"

"She's okay, but there's a problem. I guess you two had a big fight when you were here last, and she's been telling everybody about it. Says she doesn't have a daughter anymore."

"I knew she was angry, but I didn't expect anything like this. Was she even going to let me know?"

"I didn't think so. That's why I called. She's rented out your room, so if you come, you can stay with me. I live two houses up, where the Masons used to live."

"Thanks, Lynne, but I don't want to be any trouble."

"You won't be, not at all. Besides, there's not a decent hotel in the whole town."

"I'll be there sometime this afternoon."

"Okay, the funeral is tomorrow, but things might be pretty tense with your mom. I don't know about the other neighbors. I expect she's got them all riled up too."

How are you supposed to feel when your father dies? As her father's illness worsened, Sharon had asked herself this question many times. It had even come up during her earlier sessions with Dr. Baldwin. Would the bad memories, the years of abuse, die with him?

Dr. Baldwin hadn't given her an answer, but Sharon knew nonetheless. The memories were hard-wired into her psyche. Only her own death would put an end to them.

She thought about not going, just blowing the whole thing off. They could certainly have funeral without her. And if her presence was going to be disruptive, why bother? *Honor thy father*, when that same father had dishonored her in the most despicable way hardly seemed like a fair exchange. All those teen years when her classmates had whispered and giggled about the mysteries of the sexual act, those weren't mysteries to Sharon. By then she was a veteran when it came to sexual intercourse, thanks to her own father.

As she drove down Route 20 toward her hometown, she wondered what finally tipped the scales; why was she going back to what might become a maelstrom? Not for the sake of that man who left her damaged goods. And not to support her mother who lived in a bubble of denial.

****

She slowed as she drove past the house where she grew up, where cars filled the driveway and spilled out onto both sides of the street. This was no longer a welcoming place for her, and she resisted a strong impulse to simply keep on driving.

The former Mason residence, two houses down, where her friend, Lynne, now lived, looked much more promising. Two children that she guessed to be four and five years of age, chased an overweight golden retriever around the front yard.

Lynne must have been on the lookout for her, because she came out as soon as Sharon pulled into the driveway.

Her old friend looked to be about twenty pounds heavier than when Sharon had last seen her. From her wide smile, domestic life apparently agreed with her.

"Sharon, gosh, you look great."

The embrace was hearty, genuine.

"These are my little ones," Lynne said. "Josie is five, and Ronnie is four."

"Four and a half." Ronnie corrected her.

"Okay, four and a half. And the fuzzy one with the long tail is Sebastian. Boys, say hello to my friend, Sharon."

"Where do you live?" Josie asked.

"I live in Pisgah. I go to school there."

"Why do you still have to go to school?" Josie again. His expression suggested he thought anyone who had to attend school for such a long time must be a bit on the dumb side.

"Sharon goes to college," Lynne said. "That's where smart people go to school, and if you guys make good grades, you'll go to college too."

"Why don't you go to college, Mommy?" Josie asked.

"Because I have two little boys who run me ragged." She turned to Sharon. "These two will keep asking questions for the rest of the afternoon. Let's go inside for some grown-up talk. Did you bring a bag?"

Sharon couldn't remember how the Mason house had looked in times past, but now it looked like a happy place. There was the usual disorder, inevitable with two small boys and one large dog afoot, but the walls and almost every flat surface was filled with family photos, beaming smiles in every one.

"I've made up our guest room for you. You'll have to keep the door closed to keep the kids and dog out, but I've opened up all the windows to air the place out."

"Lynne, I can't thank you enough for taking me in."

"No problem at all. It'll be fun to catch up. Been so long since I've seen you. While you get situated I'll make some coffee."

The bedroom was small, cozy. This was exactly how Sharon remembered rooms from the other homes she used to visit on this same street. She had to remind herself that there was a time when small rooms were the norm, unlike Connor Shaw's massive sleeping quarters. She hung her dark suit, her *funeral* suit, in the closet, alongside an assortment of winter coats and jackets.

"Umm, that smells good," she said as she walked into the kitchen where Lynne was pouring coffee.

"So, they'll have a viewing tomorrow around noon, then the funeral service at three o'clock," Lynne said.

"What's the rush, I wonder."

"I don't know. That's just the way your mother wanted it."

Sharon sipped her coffee, stared down into the dark, steaming liquid as if hoping she might find some answers in the depth of the cup. "I don't know what to do," she said. "Mom didn't even call me to tell me he was gone, so I guess she's still pretty pissed at me."

"That's putting it mildly. I went over this morning, and she was into her, I don't know what to call it, her *Blessed Christian Martyr* routine. My mom used to do the same thing. You know, where you tell everybody what a rotten time you've had, and how you've sacrificed so much for some ungrateful so-and-so. She was laying it on pretty thick."

"In that case, I'll just go to the funeral, skip the preliminaries. Maybe she will have gotten most of it out of her system by then." Maybe, but not likely. Her mom wasn't one to forget or forgive a grudge.

Sharon stayed in her room the next morning while Lynne bundled two boys and a dog over to her sister's house for the day.

"The viewing is at Smith's Funeral Home, in case you change your mind," Lynne said. "And the funeral service is at First Methodist, three o'clock."

"I'll go in my own car," Sharon said. "No need for Mom to know I'm staying with you, in case she's still in a bad mood."

Lynne laughed. "Sad, but true. You know, I still can't get over how great you look. I mean, half the models in these so-called glamour magazines don't look nearly as sharp as you."

"Thanks, but I don't expect my mom to care one way or the other."

"I'd give anything to have your figure, but two pregnancies really did a number on me. I never could lose the weight."

Sharon linked arms with her friend. "You've got something better. You have a happy home. I knew that the moment I walked in the door."

"Bless you." Lynne kissed her on the cheek. "But I still wish I had your figure."

Three o'clock and Sharon found a parking place just up the street from the burial tent. She thought about lurking on the outskirts of the crowd, staying out of sight, but no, she was family. She'd come this far, and there was no point in stopping now.

Her mother sat in a chair beside the open grave. As Sharon approached, a low murmur rumbled through the crowd. Unfriendly faces turned toward her.

She was a few paces from her mother's chair when she lurched to her feet. "Sharon, no." Her voice must have carried all the way out to the street.

"No what?"

"Your father made his wishes clear he did not want you at his funeral. Neither do I."

"You're throwing me out of the funeral?"

"Please, go and leave us in peace."

Being struck in the head by a baseball bat would have been a minor event compared to the shock she felt when she heard her mother's admonition. She turned around on feet that she could not feel, and carefully placed one foot in front of the other. With her head held high, she looked straight ahead and walked out. She bit her lower lip until she tasted blood, but she would not cry. No one would see her cry.

Before she began her retreat, she glimpsed a familiar face seated alongside her mother Bob Hastings. Sonofabitch. He'd looked right through her.

She'd gone just a short distance when she felt Lynne's arm around her.

"That was the damnedest thing I've ever seen," Lynne said.

"Careful, you might not want to be seen with me. I'm toxic."

"Anybody that doesn't like it can go straight to hell, and that, excuse me for saying so, includes your own dear mother."

****

She drove straight back to the campus that night. This had to be a first, getting thrown out of a funeral. It took the better part of a bottle of wine before she could get to sleep. The next morning, she called Dr. Baldwin's office and set up an appointment. Due to a cancellation, she got in that same afternoon.

The office and the therapist were just as Sharon remembered them. No change at all.

"Sharon, it's good to see you again. It's been, what, almost a year."

"I think you're right. Thanks for seeing me so soon."

Dr. Baldwin smiled. "How are things going for you?"

Sharon told her about the last confrontation with her mother, her father's death, then the awful scene at the funeral.

"Really? She turned you away at the funeral? I

don't believe I've heard that one before."

"Yeah, I think she turned the whole town against me. She made it sound like she was just following Dad's wishes, but it was all her. Dad was so out of it I doubt he knew his own name, much less who he wanted or didn't want at his funeral."

"I won't ask how that made you feel. I can imagine," Dr. Baldwin said. "You said you had a big disagreement with your mother, still, this sounds extreme."

"In a way I can understand it. Branding me as the bad guy in front of everyone sort of reinforces her own denial. Now she'll never have to answer for sexual abuse charges against Dad, or her own failure to stop it when I asked her to. She's closed the door on all of that, for herself at least."

"But not for you. Let's talk about that."

They talked, but Sharon had no great expectations. She had not come here seeking a cure, but she had to talk to someone. At most Dr. Baldwin's counsel would provide a Band-Aid, something to cover the hurt until time could take away the sting. She would only be able to do more if Sharon were willing to provide more information about her current activities, which she would not do.

Just as on her earlier visit, Dr. Baldwin urged Sharon to set up a series of appointments, so they could get deeper into the hurt that she'd suffered. But Sharon begged off. Not only did she not want Dr. Baldwin to know all of her secrets, she wasn't so sure that she wanted them out in the open herself.

That left one glaring question. What was Bob Hastings doing at the funeral? Just a concerned bystander? A friend of the family? None of the above. Bob would bear watching, and if he caused trouble she had a guided missile named Clark she just might send in his direction.

Chapter Ten

When she got home that evening, she found a single message on her answering machine. "Next time, dance for me." She was expecting this. Okay, if the man wanted a dance she would give him one, a dance that would set his hair on fire.

The mechanical aspects of the dance might be similar to those she'd done before, in front of the howling mobs at Lennie's, but that's where the comparison ended. She'd never performed for just one guy. This one would be personal, very personal.

With Connor it would be different. Ah, there was that treacherous word...different. Was the situation truly unlike her previous experiences, or did she simply hope that was the case? Was he so detached that he could give her the most intense physical pleasure she had ever known and still feel no real passion for her as a human being?

Was this, as she'd told herself so often, *just business*? Was he doing for her the same thing she did for the other men she had serviced? She had pondered this question before, and each time the answer came up a resounding NO. The experience with Connor was just too intense. He would have to be an android, some form of pleasure-giving robot to raise her to such heights of ecstasy with no emotional component.

Still, most of what she knew about him she'd

learned in his bedroom, and for now, that would have to do.

****

Dance night, per Connor's instructions, would be Thursday. Other than time and place, he'd provided no details, so the particulars would be up to her. He'd already caught a few of her performances at Lennie's club. Those exhibitions were quite basic; start out wearing little and get down to nothing, or nearly nothing as quickly as possible.

That was Lennie's own formula, apparently based on his experience and his knowledge of his clientele. The crowds he drew weren't interested in a slow tease. They wanted bare skin, the sooner the better.

With Connor, this would be her first real chance to run the show, to be in control, if only temporarily. Those times when they'd been together he had drawn out her rapture to and past the point where she was begging him, and the admission that she had reached that sharp edge between ecstasy and anguish seemed to be just what he was aiming for. He kept her there in limbo, sometimes pushing her beyond until she cried out, sometimes drawing back until she moaned with delight. When it came to pleasure, the man was a magician.

And that's what she would be tonight, a magician, a temptress. And she knew how to do it with style and grace. A few years back, before she began her labors at Lennie's flesh pit, she studied some of the strippers of old, the techniques they used to heighten anticipation, how they always promised more than they gave.

So, if Connor was expecting her to bounce out in a thong and a transparent bra, he'd best think again.

129

Yeah, she would get down to the barest basics, but first she would make him sweat a bit.

Now, what to wear? The old time strippers worked with layers upon layers of filmy fabric. You take one off and there's another underneath, then another, then another. But that wasn't her style, and probably wasn't Connor's either. Besides, she didn't want to spend all evening pulling off layers. She wanted to leave plenty of time for him to reward her hard work. At Lennie's, by the time she got naked, the show was pretty much over. But tonight that's where the real fun would begin.

She bought a business suit, a gray flannel affair with a tastefully muted pinstripe. To that, she added a powder blue silk blouse with lots of buttons. She wanted buttons, zippers, anything to prolong the process, anything to make him squirm. A chemise? Sure, why not? Nude stockings with a black lacy garter belt, a new black bra and panty set, and a new pair of navy blue heels.

She winced when she tallied up the costs of her shopping spree, a hell of a lot to spend on something she'd be taking off not long after she'd put it on. A couple of accessories, a leather brief case and a pair of gold-rimmed clear glasses, and she was almost ready for battle.

She did her hair up into a bun, a bit severe but not too much so. Besides, Connor loved her hair, loved running his fingers through it, tugging at it just enough to make her protest, and tonight he wouldn't wait very long before releasing it and letting it flow over her shoulders. She preened in front of her bedroom mirror. She looked positively corporate, the kind of woman Connor passed in the hallway every day. No doubt he had bedded a number of them, but none of them would have danced for him the way she was going to dance.

The implacable Clark picked her up at eight sharp. She made no attempt at conversation. By now she knew better. As usual, he unlocked doors and led her straight to the bedroom. This time, instead of waiting for Connor, he was waiting for her. He sat in a chair by the bed, a glass of red wine in his hand. He looked her up and down. "Yes," he said softly.

When the music started, it would be her show. Until then it was his. He seemed to flow through the space that separated them. He placed his open palm beneath her chin, tilted her head back and kissed her. She wanted him to tear her new suit right off her, no waiting around. The bastard had made her go all wet before she'd touched the first button.

All her planning, all her preparation shot to hell with one kiss. Now she would be lucky if she could walk across the room and kick off her shoes.

"Something to drink?" he asked.

"Not yet." A drink might help her relax, but it might just as well make her faint dead away. One fucking kiss. It just wasn't fair.

"Would you like to dance now?"

At first she thought he meant the two of them together, but no, just her. This was her show. This was her job.

He'd set up lamps on either side of the window that made up one entire wall of the bedroom. This space would be her stage. He'd told her before that no one outside could see through the tinted glass, but how could she know this for sure? How could she know she wasn't putting on a show for anyone passing by?

"I wasn't sure what music you'd like. If you'd prefer something else…"

She recognized the composer, Vivaldi, a part of his Four Seasons work. But Vivaldi? In the annals of stripping, had anyone ever disrobed to Vivaldi? At first she thought he was joking, but this was no joke. The light from the lamp shone on his face, on his big grin. He was testing her, challenging her.

Okay, boss, you want Vivaldi in the nude, you got it.

She pulled a ladder-backed chair into her small space. Then she began, a long, slow tug on a zipper, buttons being undone one by one, no rush. She loosened her hair, let it fall to her shoulders.

When she looked over at her audience of one, his wine glass was empty, and he was pouring another.

Taking off a suit was no great mystery. There was only one way in and one way out, but she stretched out the process, making it into a real production. By the time those garments were lying on the bed, Connor Shaw had loosened his tie, and his wine glass was almost empty again. She could see the sheen on his forehead.

She'd chosen a blouse with lots of buttons. She took her time, teasing him. Halfway through, she sat on the chair to release the snaps on her garter belt. Then, with her leg sticking straight up in the air, she slowly peeled off a stocking, then the other. For a stripper, it was standard operating procedure, but it worked every time.

He refilled his glass.

By the time she was down to bra and underpants, he had taken off his own clothes. His erection pointed straight at the ceiling, and he was pulling on a condom. Yeah, he was ready, but she wasn't, not yet. She undulated around the chair, paying him no mind whatever. She dropped a strap off her shoulder, then another.

She had her back to him, but she saw his reflection in the window as he stormed at her, picked her up and threw her onto the bed. No gentle caresses this time. He ripped off her underpants, forced her legs apart, the shoved into her like a man who hadn't seen a naked woman in a long, long time.

A few quick thrusts, an explosion, and it was over. He lay on her, his breath coming in short gasps.

I got you this time, Mr. Connor Shaw. I got you. Game, set and match to Sharon. She began to give him a bit of what he always gave her, light kisses around his neck, over his chest. A nipple tugged with her teeth. Then down to the abdomen, kissing caressing. By the time she got as far south as she intended to go, he was moaning, and he was erect once again. This time was slower. She was on top. She controlled the rhythm, everything. When they came together, they both laughed out loud.

****

Friday afternoon, after she had just dropped her book bag on the sofa, her doorbell rang. A young man wearing a dark suit handed her a small package.

"Please, sign here," he said.

"What? I didn't order anything."

He smiled and handed her a pen.

She sat at her kitchen table and peeled off the white wrapping. Cartier. She had a package from Cartier.

Inside, nestled on a white velvet backing, lay a

diamond necklace, a large stone in the middle flanked on either side by three smaller stones, all held together by a glittering gold chain. There was no card, but she knew who had sent it. Diamonds from Connor Shaw, straight from Cartier. A hell of a lot better than the tips she'd sweated for at Lennie's.

****

Often now, well, most of the time now, it seemed that her feet barely touched the ground. The world in which she walked and worked had lost some of its gravitational pull. Might she not, unless she held onto something sturdy, simply float away?

As if the window through which she gazed had suddenly been wiped clean, images were sharper, colors more dazzling. Surely there had never been a spring season so vivid as this one. Everything around her seemed to be in a state of sustained celebration, plants bursting forth in color, birds singing their fool heads off, an absolute riot.

Equal to, if not surpassing the jubilee outside, was the unleashed spirit careening inside her. It required conscious effort to keep from singing out loud. No more the quiet, mousy, try-not-to-be-noticed Sharon scurrying between classes with her head down and her shoulders hunched. Now she sashayed along in a new spring frock that she had bought for the sole reason that the colors screamed at her from the store window. Too much? How could anything be too much today?

Gloria looked at her over the rim of her coffee cup. "Good heavens. What did you do, win the lottery?"

"Maybe. Hey, I was thinking, we might have lunch outside, like a little picnic."

"Hold on, girl, I don't do picnics. Haven't for

years."

"All the more reason you should get outside today, out of this stuffy little diner."

"What's gotten into you, Sharon? Spring fever? No, it's more than that. So, let's hear it."

"Let's just stick with the spring fever idea, okay?"

"What's the big secret? You've been acting weird for a couple of weeks now, and today you've gone completely round the bend."

"It's this guy. I can't say more than that."

"That's what you said last time. Pisses me off the way you're holding out on me. Next thing, you'll be getting married, and I won't know anything until I read about it in the newspaper."

"No marriage plans. Absolutely not, I promise." She found it very difficult to place an end point on happiness. Sure, she knew where and when it began, but not where it would likely end. Did it have to end at all? Logical Sharon knew the answer to that, but logical Sharon wasn't leading the way, not just now. Logical Sharon was floating on the breeze, about three feet off the ground.

Gloria tugged away small bits of her napkin until all that remained was a small mound of shredded white paper.

"Come on, Gloria, be happy for me."

"I am happy for you. I was just thinking about Lennie. The few times I've seen him lately he was moping around like a whipped dog. Somebody really put the fear of God in him. Just tell me, please, that whatever is so great in your life right now is not connected with what happened to Lennie, and I'll be satisfied."

Lennie. She had forgotten all about Lennie. All too easily she had let herself go, let herself get swept along by the euphoria that was Connor Shaw. For the moment she was living in an alternate universe, a universe where troubles such as those Lennie caused simply didn't exist. "No connection," she said. There was no room in her world for poor Lennie.

Of course, it wasn't a permanent solution. Bliss didn't last; it couldn't. Reality was certain to rear its ugly head soon enough, but until then she was going to enjoy the ride. Just along for the ride, and what a ride it was.

****

Monday afternoon when she returned to her apartment, there was another message on her answering machine. "Dinner tomorrow at seven. Dress sharp."

That now familiar mix of elation and anxiety bubbled up inside her. Dress sharp. That could mean almost anything, and she didn't want to get it wrong. How many "unforced errors" did a girl get with Connor Shaw? She didn't want to find out.

Her closet was stuffed with new clothes, and most of her purchases had been made with a purpose—to please Connor Shaw. They were chosen with an eye toward both style and function. Easy on, easy off was almost as important as looking good for someone in her situation, because she never knew whether she would still have her clothes on at the end of the evening, most often she did not.

She had three dresses suitable for eveningwear; before, she had none at all. Each was cut low enough in front to call attention to what she considered her foremost assets. Her breasts had earned her a tidy sum in tips when she worked at Lennie's, so she knew what they were worth. Each outfit could be doffed by tugging at a single zipper, fulfilling her second requirement— easy on, easy off.

She would, of course, top off the outfit with the diamond necklace Connor had given her. A stunning necklace dangling above a stunning set of breasts, how could she go wrong?

Tuesday evening at seven sharp, Clark rang her doorbell. He escorted her out to the limo and opened the door for her. To anyone watching, as she was sure her neighbors were, this sort of scenario could mean one thing and one thing only. She had been hired for the evening, not cheaply, but hired all the same. Let them watch. If they knew where she was going, who was waiting for her, any woman in the building would trade places with her in a heartbeat.

Clark delivered her to a rather plain white structure, understated in almost every way. Dense forest flanked both sides, and there were no other buildings to be seen. There was no sign to indicate that this was a restaurant at all. She jumped just a bit when the white-gloved attendant opened the door for her.

The inside contrasted starkly with the unassuming exterior, dark paneling throughout, paintings of quaint country scenes, portraits of lords and ladies, most nude from the waist up, some below as well. So like an exclusive men's club, which it was, hidden away out here in the wilderness.

Connor materialized at her side. As usual, she hadn't seen or heard him arrive; he just appeared. He held her hands while he took his usual survey, looking her up and down. Apparently, he liked what he saw.

Then he kissed her, and she was his, top to bottom, inside and out, body and soul, she was his, the same routine every time, she responded like a trained pet, and she didn't mind at all.

A man wearing a tuxedo appeared as silently as Connor had done. Didn't anyone make any noise in this place?

"If *Monsieur* will follow me."

The man in the tuxedo opened a door and stepped aside to let them enter. Six people sat at a round table. The three men, immaculately dressed, appearing to be in their fifties, stood when they entered. Sharon realized, perhaps for the first time, she could actually smell money. She smelled it now.

As impressive as the men were, the women sitting at the table were stunning. Sharon uttered a short gasp as she took in the view—two gorgeous blondes and a ravishing redhead. These were women you only saw in fashion magazines. Their jewelry alone would fill a small display case. Ah, yes, the smell of money.

She paid more attention as Connor introduced the women. The two blondes were called Alicia and Claudia, although Sharon couldn't remember which was which. The redhead was Crystal. Any concerns Sharon might have had about displaying too much cleavage were immediately quelled. The mounds of milky white flesh arrayed across the table made her feel almost inadequate in comparison.

The group dynamics became apparent quickly enough. Although the men were senior to Connor in years, he was clearly top dog at this table. He led the conversation, chose the topics, set the pace. He steered the conversation away from Sharon, allowing her to ease her way into the group.

The women smiled, spoke only when addressed directly. At first, Sharon thought this was because they had nothing meaningful to say. They couldn't possibly be so beautiful and intelligent as well, but they were.

Redheaded Crystal spoke in a clipped British accent that Sharon found totally intimidating. Alicia, one of the blondes when Sharon finally figured out which was which, spoke in a soft southern drawl, words coming forth at less than half Crystal's rapid delivery. Her drawl was slow and syrupy, but her content was not.

From the bits and pieces Sharon gleaned from their conversation, these women could hold their own on just about any topic that might arise, all the while providing a view guaranteed to dazzle any man with eyesight.

Over the course of the dinner, Sharon watched, and she studied the performance of her female companions. For her it was like a small classroom exercise, a course for courtesans. They never set the topic of discussion. Instead, whether sports, auto racing, business, they added small bits to the conversation, like spice to a dinner course. Yes, these ladies were pros, expensive pros, but worth every penny.

As if on cue, after the waiters had cleared their salad plates, the three women rose as one.

"We ladies are going to excuse ourselves for a few minutes. Sharon, why don't you join us?"

As soon as the ladies' room door closed, all three gathered around Sharon.

"So, you got the grand prize," Alicia said. "How did you manage that?"

"What prize?" Sharon asked.

All three laughed.

"You're the coy one, aren't you?" Crystal said. "Our Connor, he's the grand prize, and you have him, for tonight, anyway."

"He always had a taste for the younger crowd," Claudia said. "I guess we old ladies are just out of luck."

"We'll find out soon enough," said Crystal.

"What do you mean?" Sharon asked.

"How they pair us off."

"I don't understand."

Crystal took Sharon's hands. "Honey, you can't possibly be as clueless as you make out. Why do you think we all left the table together? It's to give them a chance to decide who gets whom for the evening."

****

This time the box was bigger than before, but the same young man in the same dark suit delivered it. He didn't ask her to sign for the package, just the standard "Have a nice day," and he was gone.

This box was almost two feet in length, some super sexy outfit he'd chosen for her, she guessed. But inside, she found a white leather jacket. The texture was so soft and creamy that she wondered how it might taste.

The fit, of course, was perfect. Why not? He knew everything about her right down to her shoe size, so picking out a suitable jacket couldn't have posed too great a problem. And she guessed, as well, that he had feminine assistance. That faint but persistent aroma of lavender in his bedroom could only have come from the gentler sex.

She paraded back and forth in front of the mirror in her bedroom. This garment, so soft that she felt she could push her fingertip right through it, was far more luxurious than anything else she owned. Even the new outfits she'd bought recently suffered by comparison.

But the face that stared back at her from the mirror didn't look entirely pleased. Sure, she liked presents, especially the type she was receiving now. Still there was that little furrow between her eyebrows, the one that said she needed to know more.

What did these lavish gifts mean? That was the question behind the furrow. Was this just standard operating procedure for her benefactor? Did he send expensive gifts to all his girlfriends? If bliss had a downside, this must be it, torturing herself with questions when she already knew the answer. Only, she wanted a different answer.

She could have no illusions about being his one and only. No man could be so skilled at pleasing a woman without extensive experience. And he must have learned his sexual pleasure techniques the same way she'd earned hers—practice, and lots of it, with many different partners. There was no other way.

But if these gifts had some special meaning, and if, by chance, she was truly special to him, this is what she wanted to know.

The brief conversation with the other women at the dinner the night before had proven very upsetting. For all she knew, she would be raffled off at the end of the meal as an after dinner treat for any one of the four men there. She was, in fact, preparing herself for that possibility.

But Connor gave her no cause for concern. After coffee and brandy, he led her outside. He cradled her face in his hands.

"Thank you for being so lovely tonight."

"This certainly helped." She fingered the diamond necklace.

"Just a trinket," he said. "We'll have to make sure that you're properly outfitted with baubles and such."

He ended the evening with a long kiss, one of those kisses that, at the end of which she was barely able to stand, and she would have done anything he asked, anything.

Clark drove her back to her apartment. She was grateful for his silence. Conversation might break the spell she was under, and she wanted to stay inside that golden bubble for as long as possible.

Chapter Eleven

Wednesday morning Sharon sprained her ankle. She'd had to park in one of the auxiliary lots almost a half mile from her classroom building, and she was rushing to make up the extra distance. The walkways were still wet after an overnight rain, and when she had to stop abruptly to avoid a couple of students chatting beside a bench, both of her feet slipped from beneath her.

Although she sustained a number of bumps and bruises, her left ankle suffered most of the damage. She didn't realize the severity of her injury until she tried to stand and found that it wouldn't even come close to supporting her weight.

If standing was out, walking would be impossible. For certain, she would miss her class, but for the moment, that was the least of her problems. She was almost two hundred yards from her auto, much too far to crawl, assuming she would even be able to drive if she got there. To top things off, the rain from the night before had begun to creep back in. What else could go wrong?

"Here, let me help you over to the bench. Do you think you might have broken anything?"

Ordinarily, a friendly voice in time of need, the supporting arm around her waist, would have been most welcome, except that both of these gestures came from

Bob Hastings.

"I'm okay, really," she said. It was a hollow protest; she was helpless.

"No way," he said. "You can't even stand up." He shouldered her book bag and helped her over to the stone bench.

"I'll get my car and drive you over to the infirmary. Here, you'd better take my umbrella. It's starting to rain again."

Before she could object, he was gone at a trot, her book bag still slung over his shoulder.

****

"Your X-rays are negative, so it's just a sprain, but a bad one." The infirmary doctor slipped a rigid plastic boot lined with soft foam over her damaged ankle. The apparatus closed with Velcro straps.

The infirmary was been packed when they got there, students coughing, students limping, and some, no doubt, just suffering from a bad hangover. She had to wait almost an hour to be seen. All the while, Bob waited at her side, no complaints.

Sharon stared down at the bulky boot. "I won't be able to drive with this."

"Certainly not," the doctor said. "In fact, it's going to be a week to ten days before you'll even be able to bear full weight on the ankle. Until then you'll have to use a crutch."

She hung her head. "Oh, no." *What now?* Small town living had one great advantage, when things went all to hell, usually the neighbors rallied round. They pitched in with those things that otherwise would not, could not get done. Part of this came from a sense of caring, part of it to ensure that when their own time of need arose, they could count on assistance for themselves.

Sharon had no such network. The interpersonal ties of her college campus were too flimsy to stand up under stress. If she made demands on her friends, they would simply disappear. But then, assistance sometimes came from unexpected places.

"You're going to need help," Bob said. "I'll drive you back home, and I'll get somebody to drive your car back. Then we can sit down and go over your class schedule. I'll make sure that you get there and back every day."

"No," Sharon said. "I can't ask you to do this. It's too much."

"No problem," Bob said. "And you didn't ask, I volunteered." And this from a guy she'd scratched off her friends list and reassigned to the weird and not-to-be-trusted column.

"Most people would be grateful for this kind of assistance," the doctor said as he prepared to leave.

"I am grateful, I really and truly am. But it's too much to ask of you."

"Like I said before, you didn't ask. Now, if you're ready to go, I'll drive you back to your apartment. You've had enough excitement for one day."

Sharon had had nightmares before, some so severe that they drove her into counseling, but even those paled in comparison to the nightmare of her current predicament—being dependent on Bob Hastings.

She wasn't comfortable having anyone in her private space. Of course, with Connor it was different. With him she had no space, private or otherwise. It all belonged to him. She was there at his pleasure. If suddenly he had a change of heart, saw someone he fancied more than her, she would be cast out into nothingness.

With Bob Hastings, she felt as if she had been invaded. Next to Lennie, she could think of no one she'd less like to cozy up to than Bob. The fates had played a nasty trick on her, very nasty indeed.

Bob drove her back to her apartment, held the umbrella while she hobbled inside. He stayed only a few minutes.

"This is my cell phone number, my office number, and my home number. If you need anything, anything at all, call me any time." Then he was gone. True to his word, her own car was parked outside her apartment early that afternoon.

The following day she had only one class, economics, at eleven o'clock. Bob called early that morning and asked what time he should pick her up.

"I really hate putting you to all this trouble," she said, and she really meant it.

"I don't mind," he said.

At ten to eleven, he was waiting in front of her apartment.

So far all the fears she had about being in close proximity to Bob had amounted to nothing at all. He made no demands on her. When he dropped her off at her apartment, he helped her to the door but went no farther. The weirdness that she had anticipated and dreaded never surfaced. Had she misjudged him? Was he an okay guy after all?

After he left, she clomped around the kitchen, cursing the heavy boot with every step. Cooking on one leg presented a challenge. The only thing she felt safe doing was opening a can of tomato soup, and thank God, the wine bottle was still manageable.

She had just polished off one bowl of soup and two glasses of wine when the doorbell rang. Bob? Had he come back? Damn, and just when things were going well between them.

But it wasn't Bob at her door; it was Clark.

"Good afternoon," he said. "May I come in?"

For Clark, who never had more than one or two words for her, this was an outburst. She stepped aside to let him enter.

He carried a cardboard box about the size of a shoebox under his arm. Another gift from Connor? Damn, she was already responding like Pavlov's dog, salivating in the hope of a new treat.

"I'm sorry about your injury. Is it very painful?"

"It's getting better." She lied, but he didn't have to know that.

"Mr. Shaw is concerned about you."

"How did he find out?"

"I told him. He would like you to move into his house until your injury heals. You'll have your own private room, of course, and I'm available to take you anywhere you wish to go, whenever you like."

Had she not braced herself against a chair she probably would have fallen. How on earth did Clark know about her fall? This was too much, and way too soon. "Thanks, but really, I'm fine here."

"Of course, but Mr. Shaw would like you close by. He'll have his own doctor look in on you."

"But I'm not ready. I'm not packed or anything."

"Mr. Shaw has taken care of all that. Everything you'll need is already in your room."

"Someone might call here, my mother, a friend."

He opened the box. "I have an answering machine here. It will only take a minute for me to attach it to your phone. You'll need to record a brief message of your own. Then you can call back here anytime to retrieve your messages."

"I have a friend who's been driving me to class. He'll worry if I just up and disappear."

"I'll take care of that."

"What do you mean?"

"I'll explain everything to him."

Yeah, like you explained everything to poor Lennie. "Promise me you won't hurt him."

"Certainly not." He looked as if she'd slapped him in the face.

A confused and conflicted Sharon followed Clark out to the limo, clunking along on her crutches. He carried her textbooks and notes in her book bag. All she could manage was her purse and her jacket. She hadn't even visited the bathroom to gather up her toiletries, Clark assured her for the fourth or fifth time that her private room was completely outfitted.

She sat in the back seat and looked out at azaleas and other blooming shrubs, but the elation that such sights usually gave her was lacking. Her world wasn't under her own control at the moment. She had so many questions, questions about Clark, about Bob Hastings and about Connor Shaw himself. She still figured Clark had done the job on her old nemesis, Lennie. For sure he seemed capable of violence, but having the ability and using it were not necessarily the same. Still, if not Clark, who?

Connor Shaw, the man who showered good things

upon her at the most unexpected times, what was his angle? Did he even have an angle?

By the time Clark pulled into the underground garage, she had resolved her internal arguments with the old adage, "Actions speak louder than words." Connor Shaw's actions said he deeply cared about her, even though he never expressed the same in words.

On this occasion, Clark led her farther down the hallway, past the bedroom where she usually entertained his boss. He slowed his pace so she could keep up with him, crutches being a particularly slow mode of travel. Beside the door where he finally stopped stood a tall, slender woman that Sharon guessed to be in her mid-thirties. Blonde hair swept up into a stylish bun, green eyes, another beautiful female. Connor seemed to have an endless supply of them

"This is Ms. Spenser," Clark said. "Mr. Shaw's personal assistant."

"Ms. Saluda." The woman extended her hand. "I've been looking forward to meeting you. I'm so sorry about your poor foot." She helped Sharon struggle out of her coat, another activity that crutches impeded.

When Ms. Spenser helped her out of her coat, Sharon caught a faint scent of lavender. Ah, a mystery solved. Now she understood the presence of that subtle fragrance in Connor's bedroom.

Clark placed Sharon's book bag on a desk by the far wall, nodded, then left.

The room into which Ms. Spenser led her was almost as large as Sharon's entire apartment, and she hadn't even seen the bathroom yet.

Ms. Spenser appeared open to conversation, so Sharon seized what she thought was an opportunity to learn more about Connor Shaw. "How long have you worked for Mr. Shaw?"

"It will be six years next month."

"So, I guess you know him quite well then."

Her smile broadened. "Well enough to know that he prefers his private life kept private. If you need anything just dial zero. My office is in the south wing of the house, but I can get back here in no time."

"Thanks," Sharon said. Nothing from Ms. Spenser, nothing from Clark, the boss ran a tight ship.

Her bladder reminded her to check out the bathroom. As she settled down on the toilet seat, she realized this bathroom was laid out almost exactly like the one off the bedroom where she and Connor Shaw met. But those sessions were probably on hold for the time being. A puffy black and blue ankle was a definite turn-off.

According to Clark, everything she would likely need was already in the bedroom. She found a half dozen dresses—all her size—hanging in the closet. On the shelf above, which she could see but not quite reach she saw several pairs of jeans, probably all her size too. Next she checked out the dresser. The top two drawers were full—underwear, T-shirts, assorted tops, several pairs of sweatpants. She hadn't brought half this much stuff along when she'd first moved into the university residence hall.

She assumed that Ms. Spenser was the designated shopper when it came to women's clothing. No man, even one so talented as Connor Shaw, would be able to shop so successfully for another woman given nothing more than her sizes.

Sharon sat on the bed for a moment, wondering at

the changes in her life over the past seven months or so, beginning with launching a very successful house of ill repute, and now becoming the private property of someone else. Because, when all the trappings were stripped aside, that's what she really was—property, bought and paid for.

There was only one reasonable choice for what she would do next; she would take a nice long soak in a hot tub.

The hot bath did exactly what hot baths are supposed to do; most of Sharon's aches and pains, along with all her current concerns, flowed down the drain with the soapy water. The relaxation that followed was so complete that she practically had to crawl to the bed, where she fell into a deep, catatonic state, almost beyond sleep.

Of the three spheres of orientation—person, place and time—she remembered only one. When the bedside phone jangled softly, she awoke knowing her name but little else.

"Ms. Saluda, Mr. Shaw's physician is here to see you. Shall I send him in?"

"What? Oh, sure." For a moment Sharon felt like a character in a fairy tale, like someone who had fallen down a rabbit hole then awoke in a place far more lavish than the one she'd left behind. At least she had taken the time to pull on one of the light blue combos— stretchy cotton sweatpants and a matching top—before she collapsed on the bed. She would have preferred having time to apply a brush to her hair, but no doubt the good doctor would have seen worse.

A soft knock on the door, then Ms. Spenser entered followed by a dark-skinned man with quiet eyes.

"Ms. Saluda, this is Dr. Gupta. I'll leave you two alone now. Call me if you need anything."

Dr. Gupta extended his hand. When Sharon shook it, she noted that his skin was softer than her own.

"Mr. Shaw tells me you've had a bit of trouble with your ankle."

He pulled a chair alongside the bed while Sharon stuck out the injured foot.

"Oh, my," he said. "A nasty sprain. It's quite painful, no?"

"It feels better now. I soaked it in the tub."

"Then you've already done exactly what I was going to suggest."

He took her ankle in both of his soft hands. "I want to manipulate the ankle a bit. Tell me if I'm causing you any discomfort."

Of all the physicians Sharon had ever known, this man was by far the most gentle. His manipulation of her ankle was more like a massage, and she would have been quite content for him to continue as long as he wished.

"I've looked at the X-rays they took at the infirmary, and I quite agree with their assessment—no fracture, just a very unpleasant sprain. I'd like you to continue with the hot soaks four times a day, and I'm going to send a physical therapist over to begin some range of motion exercises. We don't want the joint to stiffen up."

"Thanks a lot. I really appreciate you seeing me like this."

"No problem. Glad to help."

So this was how the other half lived, no waiting in line, no unanswered phone calls, just first-class service when and where you wanted it. Yes, she could get used to this lifestyle, but she wouldn't. This wasn't hers. It all belonged to someone else. She was a guest, and her moment in the sun could be over before she even saw it coming.

By Monday, she could put most of her weight on the injured ankle. Ambulation was still a slow, careful process, but much improved from when she'd arrived. The physical therapist was not so gentle as Dr. Gupta had been, but her manipulation along with hot soaks in the tub seemed to move things along.

During her time at the manor, Sharon had neither seen nor heard from Connor Shaw, not directly anyway. She saw the very attentive Ms. Spenser each day, and Clark checked on her a couple of times as well. But it was time to go home.

"You're sure you can manage?" Ms. Spenser asked.

"Yes, I'm certain I can. I don't know whether Mr. Shaw expects me tomorrow evening."

"No," said Ms. Spenser. "He's still away on business. I'm sure he'll be in touch."

Sharon thanked her profusely for her kindness and even attempted a hug, which turned out to be an awkward event. Apparently, for all her outward friendliness, Ms. Spenser chose to remain apart. Sharon had only made the gesture since they were both employed by the same man, and she did so want the approval of this older woman. But therein lay the difference. Personal assistants were quite acceptable in polite society, while those who earned their money on their backs, as Sharon did, were not and never would be.

Her own apartment now seemed small and cramped, but it was home. While she liked luxury, it was unlikely she would ever become accustomed to it. She hadn't earned it, so she didn't deserve it, not really. On the other hand, if she had earned it, Ms. Spenser could kiss her ass.

By wrapping her injured ankle tightly with an elastic bandage, she could get around without crutches. Her gait was still slow and a bit clumsy, but it felt so good to be independent once again.

That evening she felt up to expanding her world, she drove over to the Faculty Club. Although she wasn't directly involved now, she still felt strong ties to the house and the girls. Chloe sat at the reception desk engaged in an animated conversation with a tall geeky guy that Sharon thought she recognized from one of her classes. She hung back out of his line of sight, but she could still pick up snippets of their conversation.

"But I want *you*." The guy leaned over Chloe. She wasn't the prettiest girl in the group, her eyes were too big for the rest of her face, cheekbones a bit too prominent, but Chloe had a way of drawing attention. She projected a kind of vulnerability that seemed to set guys off. She knew this, of course. Sharon had seen her use her talent many times.

"Not tonight," Chloe said. "I'm staying right here at the desk. But if you come back tomorrow night I'm all yours."

"I'll pay double."

"You come back tomorrow. We'll have a good time, just you and me." Her voice was like warm honey, and the magnetism with which it drew men was the stuff most perfume makers could only hope for.

When the frustrated young man had gone, Sharon emerged from the shadows.

"Sharon," Chloe said. "What happened to you?"

"Sprained my ankle. It's getting better, though."

"I'm so glad you're here. Look, we're having a hard time."

"What's the problem?" The potential for disaster in such a business always lurked in the background, and Sharon knew, sooner or later it would creep out.

"Our bookkeeping has gone all to hell. Brenda tried to do it, but she just couldn't keep up. Look at this."

Chloe opened the ledger for Sharon to see. The transition from when she had kept the books and the random entries that followed her departure were immediately apparent. She always kept two sets of books, one in case their activities ever came under scrutiny, and another that recorded specifics of who did what for whom and when.

What she thought of as her *public books* only reflected the activities and expenses of female students in an off-campus study site, sort of like a sorority without all the mystery and parties. In fact, a university administrator who didn't look too closely might even be pleased by the industry shown by a group of girls so determined to improve their academic experience as to maintain a separate facility just for study.

But the real book, the fee-for-service ledger that she always kept locked away contained the kind of information that could get them all hauled up before a very unsympathetic judge and jury. Now there it was, in plain sight, a document that could damn them all.

"Oh no," Sharon said.

"Exactly," Chloe said. "We need help."

"I'll take this ledger with me. It needs work. We should meet, all of us, so we can decide how to keep the books. This is trouble waiting to happen. If you can get the rest of the girls together on Saturday, can we meet here, say around two?" She didn't want her girls getting into a jam, because her own backside was on the line here as well. As the person who created the Faculty Club, she would be just as liable as the rest of them, should things go south.

"Done," Chloe said. "See you Saturday."

It took three evenings, evenings she'd rather have spent getting caught up on her own classwork, to transcribe all the date from the *private ledger*, which the girls had left in such disarray, into a new volume. This one, she vowed, would remain in her own possession. It was simply too dangerous to leave it floating around.

The public ledger was less troublesome. In fact, the numbers she entered on its pages were a bit slapdash, more in keeping with the kind of informal entries girls might record about their own personal expenses.

By Saturday, she had the work completed, and she had a plan as well. The Faculty Club and its history were part of her own personal history, and it would follow her wherever she went, forever. She was and would be involved, like it or not.

The only way she could protect herself, and the girls, and the Faculty Club, was to manage it all herself. This was her proposal at the Saturday meeting.

She hadn't seen them all together for weeks, and once things broke up for the summer, would she ever see them all again? Connor Shaw so filled her life that she gave little thought to the Faculty Club and those who worked there. Now she took a moment to reflect on how they had rolled the dice, taken a chance and built a business from nothing.

Of course, they were all full of questions about her new arrangement. Several of the girls had seen Connor Shaw when he had come to the house to recruit Sharon. Brenda described him as "the yummiest man she'd ever seen."

But about her new situation, Sharon could say little. As the curt Ms. Spenser had informed her, "He likes to keep his private life private." And so it would be.

"It's like the same thing as before, only with one guy," she said.

"You mean, you're still a whore?" Maggie Kirkland asked.

"Yeah, I guess I am."

"We should get t-shirts made up, advertise."

"No t-shirts. You want to get us all thrown in jail?" Sharon said.

"Just trying to get a rise out of you," Maggie said. "Been a while since I've seen you."

"Okay, since this is a business meeting, let's get to it," Sharon said. She outlined her proposal for the group. She would go back to keeping the books, and they would remain in her possession. Until they disbanded for the summer, they would continue to meet monthly for distribution of revenues. All of the records kept at the desk were to be done in pencil. "Never write down anything that can't be erased," Sharon said.

So, once again, Sharon found herself managing a whorehouse. It would require a balancing act, accommodating the demands of her regular classwork with her duties at the house, and of course, being at the beck and call of Connor Shaw. But nothing she couldn't handle, so she hoped.

Chapter Twelve

But how could she tell Connor Shaw? How would he react when she told him she had returned to her old haunts, now in a management capacity? He had taken her out of that life, bought her for himself.

Her first opportunity came with her next Tuesday night session. They hadn't been together for almost two weeks, and their reunion was a frenzied affair. As soon as the bedroom door closed, clothing flew in all directions. Nothing subtle here, they went at it like a couple of alley cats, thrashing and mewling until you couldn't tell whether they were fucking or fighting. He had her pinned beneath him for a moment, until she twisted away and got astride him, where she rode him like a rodeo cowgirl, all the while wondering if the bed could support such violence. Another reversal, and he took her from behind, her face pressed into a pillow.

This was the noisiest love-making she could remember, the type that might get police summoned to break up an assault, and come to think of it, assault wasn't far off the mark. But she gave as good as she got. No victim here, just two very satisfied customers. The smell of sex overwhelmed the subtler scent of lavender. She forgot all about her ankle as her own passion matched his, measure for measure. Not just the object of desire, now she was the instrument as well.

Afterward, the delicious afterglow, lying side by

side, panting like dogs on a hot day, in a bed so disheveled that it looked like the site of a small battle. Every nerve ending in her body was still on high alert, ready to fire off at the slightest stimulus. Connor cupped her breast in his left hand, occasionally tweaking her nipple sending electric shock waves coursing through her, shock waves that all ended up down there at her center.

"Breathe," he said.

"What?"

"Breathe. You stopped breathing."

"Oh, right, I forgot."

But she had an agenda, she just wasn't sure whether this was the right time or place, both naked, sexually sated. What if he decided to start right up again? But she couldn't wait any longer. She stared at the ceiling, afraid to look at his face, as she told him about her new duties at the Faculty Club.

He rolled up on one elbow. "So, you keep the books now."

"Yes, but it won't take much time. Once we're shut down for the summer, not much time at all."

He rolled back onto his side. "Very interesting."

She rose into a sitting position so she could see him more clearly. She could almost hear the wheels spinning inside his brain. Was he making fun of her? Was he angry? If she crossed the line, he could dismiss her, no questions asked. But no, there was that little furrow between his eyebrows, identical to the one that formed on her own face when she was deep in thought. What further interest could he possibly have in the Faculty Club?

****

"It didn't just start with Lennie, not exactly." Sharon dragged the tea bag back and forth in her cup.

"What didn't start with Lennie?" Gloria looked up from her half-eaten grilled cheese sandwich.

Their Friday lunch had become a ritual. Little by little, Sharon divulged carefully chosen bits of information about her past, things she had never told Dr. Baldwin. It was easier to reveal some items to Gloria. Her friend could relate to some elements of Sharon's past in a way that Dr. Baldwin never could. Of course, she selected these items with care, never anything incriminating that might force Gloria to make difficult choices.

"Doing it for money. When I was twelve, my dad began paying me little visits at night."

"Oh, shit," Gloria said. "How many times have I heard this story? If you took twenty hookers, asked them all how they got started in the business, half of them, probably more than half, would say what you just said. It all began with dear old dad. Did you tell your mother?"

"Yeah, but she wouldn't do anything. I think she was afraid of him."

"Same story, second verse," Gloria said. "Heard it all before."

For now, that was enough. Sharon felt unburdened, ever so slightly, and the revelation enforced the bond she felt with Gloria. Their shared experiences, along with those of girls in similar situations, bound them to one another. Even though they simply provided a service that no amount of law enforcement could ever snuff out entirely, they were set apart by the exchange of a fee for that service. Women had, and would continue, to use sex for reasons too numerous to count, but as soon as money changed hands, the act became a dark and dirty deed.

****

She didn't expect that her mother would die so soon, less than two months after her father was in the ground and with no warning at all. It was not uncommon, she knew, for grieving widows to follow their husbands to the grave, but that seemed an unlikely scenario. If anything, her mother would have looked upon his death with a sense of relief. Could she have been concealing some fatal medical condition that had finally overcome her? This seemed more likely, and if there were a serious medical issue, someone would know about it.

But her friend, Lynne Cartwright, perhaps her only friend in Jacob's Bluff, when she called to give Sharon the news, could supply no information.

"Seems like every time I call you it's for something bad," Lynne said.

"You're a good friend, Lynne, and I appreciate your keeping me in touch. God knows, I can't expect as much as the time of day from the rest of the creeps around there."

"They're just confused," Lynne said. "Your mom bad-mouthed you so much that, after a while, she sounded just plain crazy, and everybody tuned her out. To hear her talk you'd grown horns and a long spiky tail. There's a lot more to the story, but I won't bore you with that."

"What was the cause of death?" Sharon asked.

"The girl who works in Dr. Morris's office said he wrote natural causes on the death certificate. I don't know any more than that."

"I guess I should make plans to come back," Sharon said. "You know, at least take care of the house and everything."

"Maybe not," Lynne said. "I have the newspaper right here. Says somebody named Bob Hastings was named as executor of the estate. Is he family?"

"Bob Hastings?" Sharon couldn't hold back the little gasp. "No way. He's just some creep that keeps turning up at the wrong time."

"Ron Linklater is the attorney. His number is listed here, in case you want to call him."

"Thanks, maybe I will."

She'd never felt more alone in her entire life. Cut off from both her parents, now she would be denied a last look at the place she'd always known as home.

The following afternoon she called Ron Linklater, Esq. After the usual expression of condolences, which seemed a bit forced, they got down to business.

"I can't disclose any details of the will before the formal reading next week," he said.

"Of course, I just wanted to know whether there was any reason for me to be there. I'm just recovering from a surgical procedure, and travel is difficult for me."

"Oh, I hope everything turned out all right," he said.

"Yes, it just takes a while for things to get back to normal." She was surprised at how easily little white lies rolled off her tongue. But if she was right, her own little falsehoods were quite trivial in comparison to others that might have taken place. No doubt her mother's lies would have been far more colorful.

"Well, I suppose it wouldn't hurt to mention a few things. You probably know that a Mr. Bob Hastings is executor of the estate. He was your mother's choice. He says he knows you."

He knows me? You could say that. He used to fuck me for money once a week for almost six months. So, yeah, you could say he knows me.

"Mr. Hastings will handle the sale of the house and contents, and the proceeds of the sale will go to your mother's sister in Virginia. You aren't mentioned."

"I see. I have one question. What is the date of the will?"

"The will was revised two weeks before your father's death."

"Was he in good health at the time?" she asked.

"He appeared to be. They came to my office to discuss the will. Mr. Hastings was with them, I recall."

Her vexation at being summarily dismissed from her birthright had little to do with the contents of that birthright—a very modest two-bedroom house with a single bathroom (small), located at the edge of a dwindling community that seemed to slip further into obscurity with each passing year. Even if the property had been handed directly to her, Sharon's first thoughts would have been how she might get shed of it with the least amount of trouble.

No, her problem lay with that jerkoff, Bob Hastings, how he kept sticking his unwanted nose into her affairs. High time she put an end to his shenanigans.

Now he would have an inside look at the Saluda family finances. Modest as they probably were, Bob Hastings had no right to any of that information. But the time lawyer Linklater pronounced the proceedings with the will closed, Bob would know much more than Sharon did herself, and that would not do at all.

****

Two weeks had passed since she'd seen Connor. He'd told her before that, on occasion, his work would interrupt their schedule, but not to worry because he would always come back. *Always come back*, she liked the sound of that, even though she knew it wasn't true. This relationship wasn't rooted in undying love and affection. It was all about fucking, and sooner or later, the luster would dim.

But try as she might, she still worried. She tried to fill the spare time with her studies, but that wasn't enough to pacify the gnawing ache she experienced when he was away. Now she knew, or thought she knew, how an addict felt when deprived of their drug of choice.

Finally, Monday afternoon he called.

"You sound far away," she said.

"That's because I am, halfway across the Atlantic, but I want to see you tomorrow, same time."

"Perfect," she said.

"Clark will pick you up at seven."

"Shall I wear anything special?"

"No, just your beautiful self. That's more than enough."

Deep breath. "I've missed you."

He stood just inside the bedroom door, waiting for her. He wore the black silk robe, the one that hugged the contours of his chest, the musculature of his shoulders, and just below the loose tie at his waist, a protuberance that said he'd missed her too. She wanted to jump into his arms, blend into his body until they were one, but he had other ideas. He loosened the tie at his waist, allowing his erection to emerge from his now open robe. She wanted it, she wanted it now.

"Close your eyes," he said.

Oh, for the love of God, she was foaming at the mouth and down below, as well, and he was going to tease her, fan what was already smoldering into an open flame. So unfair, she wanted to be penetrated, violated, rough stuff, but they still played by Connor's rules, and she would have to play his game.

She felt the heat from his body as he moved around her. He pulled her hair away from her neck and planted tiny kisses from her ear down to her shoulder. She wanted to scream.

He unzipped her skirt, and it fell to the floor. Red panties underneath, that should push him over the edge, but it didn't, not yet. He wasn't through tormenting her. He nibbled on an earlobe, blew softly onto the back of her neck. He was in front of her again. "Eyes closed," he said.

Just strip me and fuck me, is that too much to ask?

Finally, he tugged her sweater over her head. "Eyes closed, I said. You peek again, and you're going to get a spanking."

Now you're talking. But would he? This would be something different. Did she really want to go over to the painful side? Gloria had warned her against it, but at the moment she wanted it. So, she dared him, she peeked again, with him standing right in front of her.

Nothing gentle about the way he threw her onto the bed. In fact, he growled as he tossed her. He ripped off her red panties. By now she could fill a drawer with shredded underwear. He threw his black robe aside and pulled her across his lap. He pinned her wrists with an iron grip, then clamped his leg over both of hers. *Slap. Oh shit, that hurt.* The smacks that followed were just as painful, and her ass felt like it had caught fire. But he waited between them, giving her time to fear the next blow. It worked. She dug her nails into her palms as she waited for what she knew was coming.

"Please," she said. She couldn't hold back the tears.

He hit her again.

She started to writhe, anything to escape from that avenging hand. But struggle as she might, she couldn't get away. She could cry and scream all she wanted, but she couldn't get away. He could do whatever he wanted with her.

She braced for the next slap, but it didn't come. He rested his palm on her enflamed buttock, trailed his fingers between her legs, opening her, penetrating her. He released her wrists and freed up her legs. Now she could escape. Instead, she continued to squirm on his lap, like an earthworm on hot asphalt. She ground her pelvis against his thighs. The burning in her loins was even worse than her backside, and there was only one way to put out that fire.

"What do you want me to do?" he asked.

"Fuck me."

Before he rolled her over, he kissed her burning backside. Now she would get what she so desperately needed, Connor Shaw, every inch of him, deep inside her.

"Yes," he said. "Not quite yet." He flipped her over onto her back and nestled his face between her thighs. He was still playing games, the bastard, and apparently enjoying himself.

Oh, there was plenty of action down below, just not what she expected. But with his tongue doing a little tap dance on her clit, each touch making her cry out, she was in no position to argue.

Finally, after making her mew and moan like a hungry animal he shifted his attention to her abdomen, to her chest where her breasts waited on high alert for his touch. Once again his tongue worked its magic, and her nipples were aflame. Only then did he pry apart her legs and plunge into her, what she'd wanted all along.

After a brief frenzied effort, they lay on their backs, panting, staring up at the ceiling. His right hand was draped across her hip, and his forefinger drew little circular designs in her close-cropped pubic hair. He varied the pressure of his caress, so she knew this was not random motion but all part of his design.

His light touch was just enough to keep the fire in her loins burning low. If he felt the need, he only had to turn up the temperature a notch or two, and she would be at full power, ready to do his bidding in no time at all.

But now his gentle manipulations were apparently just about giving pleasure, a quieter continuation of the ferocious act they'd completed in a simultaneous climax that seemed to shake the walls of the room.

As the heat of their passion dissipated, she became chilled. He must have sensed this because he drew the sheet from beneath them and wrapped it around her shoulders.

"Thanks," she said. "But I have to go to the bathroom." Just inside the door, she found the cozy fleece robe and wasted no time in wrapping herself inside. She bathed her face in cold water, then patted it dry. The mirror confirmed that she'd restored the color to her skin. Her backside was still crimson. When she looked closely, she could see individual finger marks on her cheeks. Had he enjoyed the spanking a little too much? Had she?

She stared for a moment longer, looking into the reflection of her own eyes. When she'd looked at her mirrored image earlier in the day it had shown all the anger and confusion brought on by the recent events in her life.

Now that slate had been wiped clean. The eyes that stared back at her showed not a hint of concern. These were eyes filled with happiness from somewhere deep inside, and she knew exactly where.

He was waiting for her by the bed. A small cart held an ice bucket with a bottle of champagne inside. That's the way it was with Connor Shaw, whatever he wanted—champagne, women—just appeared at his side.

"A celebration?" she asked.

"Every night with you is a celebration."

Their bodies were warmed by the fleece bathrobes they wore, but there were other ways to keep warm. He tugged open the loose knot that kept her robe closed, then opened his own. When he embraced her, it was all warm bare skin against warm bare skin.

She would have been more than happy to stay just as they were, pressed tightly together, letting the rest of the world go on its merry way. But he pulled away, not far away, just far enough that he could bend down to kiss her. "Champagne," he said.

She sat on the bed while he filled two glasses. She

didn't bother to close her robe. Maybe she'd get lucky again.

He raised his glass. "To you," he said, but instead of taking a sip, he trailed the cold glass across her right nipple, bringing it to an erect state of arousal.

"When I got off the plane this afternoon I felt as if I was being pulled in a dozen directions all at once, so many things that needed attention, that couldn't wait. Now, in less than an hour, you've erased all that. Do you realize how good you are for me?" The champagne glass went to the other nipple.

She ran her forefinger down his chest, across his abdomen, into the still moist matte of pubic hair. He was fully erect beneath her fingertip.

This was new territory for them, remaining in a delicious state of arousal without rushing to consummate the desire. First the spanking, now this…she liked them both, just so long as she got her reward, and the tip of that reward was peeking out at her from Connor's open bathrobe.

He sat with his eyes closed, breathing deeply.

She watched him closely, trying to stay one step ahead, to guess what his next wish would be. But he didn't move. This place where they were together, it seemed to fit him perfectly, and she had to admit, it wasn't half bad, not at all.

"Food," he said. "I'm starving, and I'll bet you are, too."

She nodded. She had something else in mind, but food would do, so long as she got dessert first. She placed both of their champagne glasses back on the tray, then pulled his robe off his shoulders. Hers followed. She pressed his shoulders back onto the bed.

Then she found him with her hand and guided him inside her, deep inside her. This time was slower but somehow more powerful. They reached the peak together, and the climax might have registered on a Richter scale.

Somehow they wound up lying face-to-face, arms and legs interlocked in a most complicated arrangement so that neither could move without the full cooperation of the other.

"Now, I'm really hungry," he said. After freeing up one arm, he reached for the phone.

She paid no attention to his conversation, just concentrated on maintaining as much physical contact with his body as possible.

"There, Ms. Spenser will have a nice snack ready for us. I asked her to set things up in the kitchen."

"The kitchen? Can't we eat here in bed?"

"You know damned well what will happen if we stay in this bed," he said.

"Yeah, I was counting on it."

Still clad in their fleece robes, they huddled at one corner of a granite-topped island in the kitchen. An improbable salad of crab, shrimp and lobster tails, and of course, more champagne.

"You must keep a chef on call all day long," she said. "This is incredible."

"Ms. Spenser takes care of everything. She's a magician."

"No argument here." Just how far did Ms. Spenser's duties go, she wondered.

Their success in consuming what had at first seemed an impossible quantity of seafood was remarkable. Connor slid off his chair, then opened the door of the massive refrigerator. "Ah, just as I expected."

"What?"

"Chocolate éclairs."

"Oh, no, I couldn't eat another bite." Even as she spoke, she felt her resistance melting.

"I'll cut one in half, some for you, some for me." He flipped a switch on the counter. "Coffee will be up in just a minute."

The éclair, creamy filling, flaky pastry shell, and a roof of dark chocolate, vanished in a flash, as did the second one.

Sharon couldn't remember having eaten so much in one sitting, and from the glazed look in Connor's eyes, she guessed that he couldn't either.

"Will you stay over tonight?" he asked.

"What?" He'd given her no warning of any such plans.

"Here, with me. We'll get you back to your apartment in plenty of time to catch your first class."

"But I have no clothes, other than what I wore."

"Not so. You have a complete wardrobe here in the guest bedroom. Remember when you stayed here after you sprained your ankle? Besides, you won't have much need for clothing."

"Well, okay then." *Better than okay, how about great?*

"Let's take our coffee up to my study. We can talk there."

"Not in the bedroom?"

"You make me crazy in the bedroom," he said. "I doubt we'd get much talking done. Besides, Ms. Spenser needs time to change the sheets."

Talk about what? In the time they'd spent together, talking had seldom been on the agenda. But something was afoot now, for sure.

He took the chair by his desk and motioned her toward a plush leather-covered chair just a few paces away.

She knew this room. During the time she waited for her sprained ankle to mend, she'd done a lot of exploring, including the study where they now sat. She only had time for a quick look around then, but the photo that caught her eye then now sat on the table next to her. Connor, along with three other men, posed by a golf cart. She'd thought she recognized one of the three then, and confirmed the identification when she'd returned to the campus. The third man was none other than the university chancellor.

"I didn't know you were a golfer," she said, pointing at the photo.

"Enthusiastic but not very proficient, I'm afraid. But I do love the game. Recognize anyone else in that photo?"

She pointed to the man standing beside Connor. "He looks familiar."

"He should. He's your university chancellor, Dr. Brendan O'Reilly."

The éclair she'd wolfed down now did a couple of back flips in her stomach. What would Chancellor O'Reilly say if he knew she was running a whorehouse at his beloved school?

"My firm handles the university endowment. The reason Dr. O'Reilly is smiling in the photo is that we are making lots of money for him. In fact, we are making a bit too much. I know that doesn't sound possible, but believe me, too much cash flow can be a problem. That's where you come in. I hope you can help me."

"I don't see how…"

"You said you keep the books for your little business enterprise, the Faculty Club."

"Yes, the girls were making a mess of them after I left, and some of this information should never see the light of day, if you know what I mean."

"So, how do you manage to do that?"

"I keep two sets of books. One just shows operating expenses, heat, utilities and such. If anybody asks to see our books, that's what I'll show them. The house, so far as anybody knows, is just a study hall for girls. And if they need to sleep over, we have beds. There's not much activity now during the summer, but I still stop over several times a week to check on the house."

"Everything's perfectly legal then," he said.

"The books on the real business I keep separate and hidden away. If anybody ever saw them we'd be in big trouble."

"What kind of cash flow are we talking about here?"

"Around two thousand dollars a night, or ten thousand a week."

"Wow, you're doing better than I thought."

"But that's split among eight girls, so about twelve-fifty a week before a share of the expenses. It's a heck of a lot more than any of the part time jobs pay."

"Ever have any trouble?"

"There was this one guy, Lennie, but somebody beat the crap out of him, and he hasn't been back since.

Most of our clients are clean-cut university types, and they don't usually cause trouble. If they do I just remind them that I have their photos and dates of service on file. If they make life hard for us I can make their nice little academic appointments go up in smoke."

He laughed. "I never realized you were such a devious woman. I suppose you have photos of me on file too?"

"No, I did some editing. So far as the Faculty Club is concerned, you don't exist."

Chapter Thirteen

He refilled their glasses, then slowly trailed the base of the chilled glass across her breasts. She gave a little gasp as, once again, both nipples sprang to attention.

"I love how they do that," he said. He set the bottle aside, then seized her right nipple between his teeth and gave a gentle tug.

Her moan sounded like agony, and that's exactly what she felt, balanced as she was on that thin wire that ran between agony and ecstasy.

He opened wide her robe and began a slow descent from her breast down to her belly. He reached behind her, grasped her buttocks, and pulled her forward so that she perched on the edge of the chair. Next, he lifted her legs and draped them over his shoulders.

She knew exactly what was coming next, but he waited, prolonging the agony that had begun at her nipple and now burned between her thighs. No more, she couldn't stand to wait any longer.

"Please," she said. "Now."

And so, he began. With his fingertips, he pried apart the lips, and his tongue darted forth, searching until he contacted the spot he sought.

It seemed weak of her to cry out so, so lacking in self-control, but as soon as his lips seized her clitoris she wailed like a soul descending into the abyss.

He took her to that place where time and space lost separation and melded like liquids in a blender. And somewhere in that whirl of sensation, the thought came to her, *I'm getting paid to do this*.

****

"There really isn't much you have to do, not much at all. We set everything up. You just sign off on the transfers when they come through, and they're deposited directly in our account," Connor said.

And just then, she would have agreed to anything. "But I don't want you to do anything you're not comfortable doing," he said.

"What are the risks?" she'd asked.

"In any kind of business endeavor, it helps to consider the balance, risks and benefits. Don't show this paper to anyone. This is the current university endowment that my company manages. We've managed it for just over a year now. Our rate of return on investment has been over twelve percent, generating a net increase of several million dollars.

"Holy cow," Sharon said.

"Yeah, impressive, I know. Now, nobody expects big returns indefinitely. There will be ups and downs, but we've made money for all our clients, every one of them."

She walked around his den, still naked, but that hardly mattered now. The magnitude of the numbers made her dizzy.

"You are doubtless wondering about your compensation," he said. He wrote a number on a slip of paper. As she moved alongside him to read it, he slipped his hand between her legs and penetrated her with his thumb.

177

Sharon's gasp had two components, the first being the thumb that now probed inside her, the second being the high six-figure sum Connor had written on the paper.

He bent her over his lap, withdrew his thumb and replaced it with two fingers, then added a third. He began a rocking movement with his hand, and despite her best attempts at concentration, the numbers she had just seen faded, then disappeared. A hell of a negotiating position she was in, lying across her boss's lap with his fingers deep inside her. It seemed that the business portion of their meeting was over and done with.

****

Sharon had never been in the building that housed Monmouth Enterprises, and had no idea what went on there. Now she was sitting at an oval table, buffed to a high shine, in the boardroom.

Connor sat directly across from her. His tie was slightly askew, another of those little shortcomings that had begun to creep into his dress code. To his right sat a man whom he had introduced as the Chief Financial Officer of Monmouth Enterprises. His tie was not askew, not by a millimeter.

The man to his left was equally flawless in a gray pinstriped suit and a dark blue tie with diagonal yellow stripes.

Connor did almost all of the talking. He introduced Sharon as an independent businesswoman who was sole owner and operator of a small enterprise on the outskirts of town. He was vague in his description, and she wondered if he hadn't already briefed the others on the nature of her business.

Connor had completed the pitch to her after she'd stayed over that night. "We've been looking for a small business to help manage our cash flow. Needless to say, it would be run by someone who has our implicit trust. The amount of cash involved requires that we have complete confidence in all our associates."

He painted the picture in broad strokes. Combined with the force of his personality, this method usually worked, she guessed. It was all too easy to get swept up in the process. How could anyone question a proposal set forth with such charm and enthusiasm? It was only when she returned to her apartment and was into her second glass of wine that she could finally admit, he had told her almost nothing.

All that she knew was that her little enterprise, the Faculty Club, would become a conduit for large sums of cash headed toward an offshore location, before doubling back to line the pockets of the investors. There was a word for money that swam in such waters…laundering.

Yes, laundering, that highly illegal system in which unclean funds, unclean because of the nefarious ways in which they were obtained, unclean in the way they had avoided the tax man, could become pure as driven snow. Money formerly hidden away in cardboard boxes, stuffed into mattresses, could now reclaim its rightful place in the financial stream. And the Faculty Club would be the first stop in that transformation.

****

"I'm not sure about this person, Gloria, that you've suggested. Her employment background is spotty," Connor said.

When he had asked Sharon for at least one other

name to list as an officer of their new sham company, Gloria was the only name that came to mind. She could have suggested one of the other girls at the Faculty Club, but she wanted to keep them out of the loop as much as possible. If one of them knew about the arrangement, they would all know in short order, and that would never do, way too risky.

"Yeah," Sharon said. "I guess stripping and prostitution don't make for much of a resumé."

Connor must have caught the implication of her remark immediately. If Gloria were disqualified because of her previous work background, where would that leave Sharon, whose work history was exactly the same?

"You are an entirely different case." He drew her close. "I trust you completely, and I can say that about very few people."

"If I have to work with someone else, I'd rather it be Gloria," she said. "I've known her for a long time, and she's never let me down."

"Okay, then, Gloria it will be. I'll keep a close eye on her, you should, too. I wish I could use someone from the office, but that would draw attention like a spotlight if anyone ever started snooping around."

"Who knows, maybe she'll refuse," Sharon said. "But I doubt it. The money is way too good."

"Just remember, she knows only what you tell her. The quarterly financials are strictly off limits. Whatever you decide to pay her, that's between the two of you. My advice is to keep it real. If you pay her too much it won't work out. I can promise you that."

"When would all this start up?" Sharon asked.

"The offshore location is already set up in the

Cayman Islands. Clearing the paperwork for your site won't take much time at all. When we have it ready, there'll be some things that need your signature. If Gloria is your financial officer, she'll have to sign too."

Sharon's first conversation with Gloria could have gone more smoothly, if she'd thought things out beforehand. She used the same approach that Connor had used, dazzling numbers for very little effort, but without his dazzling results, because Gloria didn't bite. To begin with, Connor held a great deal more leverage over Sharon than Sharon held over Gloria. Regardless of the outcome of their business discussion, Sharon could always look forward to more time in Connor's bed. She could provide no such inducement to Gloria.

So, she was forced to provide more real information than she'd planned, and Gloria sniffed it out immediately.

"You know what this sounds like, don't you?" Gloria looked her straight in the eye, as if to say, *Don't you dare lie to me*.

Sharon nodded.

"Then say it. Let me hear you say it."

"It's your basic money laundering scheme," Sharon said.

"And you know what happens to people who get caught laundering money?" Gloria asked.

"Maybe we should talk about something else. Just forget I ever brought it up," Sharon said.

"Hold on. I never said I wasn't interested. I just think we should have all our cards out on the table."

"You know most of what I know," Sharon said. "There will be financial statements, transactions, and we'll both sign off on them. Everything is done by someone else, somewhere else. We'll get a percentage of the quarterly business."

"How much are we talking about here?"

"They tell me it all depends on how much money they make each quarter, but your share should run somewhere between these two figures." Sharon had given a great deal of thought to the numbers she showed Gloria, and she kept her fingers crossed tightly as she slid the paper toward Gloria.

"Holy shit." Gloria's eyes grew wider and wider.

"I said the same thing myself, first time I saw it."

Sharon watched Gloria doing what she was sure was mental arithmetic. For sure there was more money than her friend had ever dreamed of making. Now she was probably adding up columns that had several more zeroes at the end than she had seen before.

She didn't interrupt her friend's musing. Money talked, and a lot of money spoke loudly.

"Wait," Gloria said. "What about taxes, SSI, and stuff?"

"That doesn't happen," Sharon said. "The money comes back to us in a wide circle through several countries, so it's impossible to trace. And they can't very well tax what they can't find, can they? That's the way they explained it all to me."

"Do I get to meet these financial wizards?" Gloria asked.

"I'm not sure. I don't think so. It seems like, as far as they're concerned, the less we know, the better."

"One last question, how about your girls? What happens to them?"

"Business as usual. This thing with the investment money is entirely separate. This won't involve them in any way."

About two weeks later Sharon and Gloria met for lunch. Halfway through their modest meal Sharon slid a folded newspaper over to Gloria. She placed her pen on top. "Just sign the top sheet twice, by the red marks."

Gloria turned back the corner of the paper, revealing the document that Sharon was being so careful about. "Shouldn't I read it first?" she asked.

"Sure, if you want. It's all lawyer crap. I didn't understand any of it."

"What the hell." Gloria signed the document, folded it back into the newspaper and slid it over to Sharon.

"I guess we're sort of like partners now," Sharon said.

"If I'm going to be making a lot of money, I want to upgrade my lunch. No more grilled cheese sandwiches." But she ordered another one just the same.

When the first quarterly disbursement arrived in the form of a deposit slip in her name from a bank in the Grand Cayman Islands, Sharon didn't know quite what to make of it. It didn't seem real, and even if it were, such an instrument would probably draw laughter if presented at any local bank.

"Sorry, I should have taken care of that for you," Connor said when she asked him about it. "You can have funds transferred from that bank to your own, but I wouldn't recommend it. A better idea would be to have the funds transferred through the company account. They wouldn't be so noticeable that way. However you want to do it, I'd avoid making any large transfers all at once. Don't want to do anything out of the ordinary."

Since she didn't need the money, Sharon decided to let it sit in that exotic offshore account. Just the idea sent little chills down her spine. She had an illegal account all her own. Yeah, it was small potatoes compared to what Connor and his cronies controlled, but now she felt like a team member. She was part of the food chain, a vital part if what Connor said was true.

The fact that he had chosen her for this part validated her worth. She was, and would remain, a source of physical pleasure, but now she was more. Who knew where that might lead?

****

"A beach trip? I haven't been to the beach in like, forever." She'd made a couple of trips to Myrtle Beach, South Carolina, in high school summers, but those were low-budget adventures, and often featured a group of girls sleeping in the car when there wasn't enough money for a motel room. A beach trip with Connor Shaw would be quite different, no doubt.

"We'll leave Friday afternoon and return Sunday afternoon."

"Sounds great. Which beach?"

"In the vicinity of St. Croix. It's privately owned, so it doesn't actually have a name. We'll be staying at a private home. Clark will pick you up Friday afternoon. There's a small airport just west of town."

"I should just pack beach wear. Is that okay?"

His knowing laugh sent chills down her spine. "Just bring a toothbrush. I have everything else you'll need."

"Everything?" How on earth could a man pack for

a woman, even for a couple of days, and remember everything? But then she had a full complement of clothing available in his home, and she purchased none of it. Ms. Spenser's doing, no doubt.

"Everything. I'll see you Friday."

The three days that led up to Friday seemed to crawl by. In spite of Connor's assurances that he had everything she would need, she packed a bag of her own. There were things, so many things, that a girl needed, just to get through an ordinary day, much less a weekend trip to a private home on a private beach.

Friday morning, she went through her check list one last time. Unless he planned on her wearing nothing at all, which might just be the case, there were things she couldn't do without, underwear being one of them. She stuffed a spare set into her purse.

Then she faced the biggest test of all. She set her bag by the front door, the bag full of absolute essentials, and when Clark pulled the limo in front of her apartment, she walked right past the bag. The man said he'd have everything she needed. Well, she would damned well find out, wouldn't she?

Clark drove for about twenty minutes. Sharon's poor sense of direction left her at a total loss for where they might be headed. The airfield where he stopped looked private enough. Except for the twin-engine Beechcraft idling on the single runway, it seemed deserted. He parked the car beside a concrete block building, then opened her door. "Hope you don't mind a short walk," he said.

"Not a bit." When she glanced back over her shoulder a man in a gray suit got into the limo and drove it into an unseen door in the block building. So much for deserted.

When they reached the plane a painfully thin young man waited by the stairway. His dark hair contrasted with eyes so light gray that they seemed almost colorless. He nodded at Clark who followed her up the stairway into the plane.

Connor was waiting for her just inside the doorway. She barely had both feet inside the plane when he kissed her.

"So glad you're here," he whispered.

She held up her purse. "This is all I brought, since you have everything I need."

He led her to a seat by the window. "If I've overlooked anything I can get it for you immediately."

"That sounds good. For a while I wondered if you were planning for me to walk around naked all weekend."

"That's a great idea, but not too practical, since there will be a few others coming. Perhaps on some future trip we'll plan an all bare weekend for you."

"Others?" she asked.

"Three other couples. Well, not couples, exactly. It'll be a bit like the situation at the dinner a while back. Three other men, two of them were at the same dinner. The third man will be your university chancellor."

"And the girls?"

"Someone else made those arrangements. You're the only one I'm sure of."

"So we girls will be eye candy for the weekend?"

"It will be a little more involved than that. In fact, I have something special in mind for you."

The young man who had met her at the foot of the stairway made his way back to their seats. "Captain says he's ready for take-off, so please, buckle your seatbelts."

"When are you going to tell me about my special activity?" she asked.

"When we get there and you've unpacked. You can always say no if you disapprove."

She could make a good guess as to what his special request might be. It probably wouldn't involve giving an after-dinner speech, more likely it would require removal of most or all of her clothing. But she wouldn't refuse him. If that was what he wanted, that's what he'd get.

Even though they were headed for fun in the sun, her boss was still all about business. For much of the two-hour flight he pored over files he'd brought, pausing from time to time to give her a smile. She never had time to become bored, because the Beechcraft flew low enough to give her a good view of the varying landscape beneath them. She flew so seldom that it was still a treat.

Connor stashed his folder into his briefcase. "Hang on tight," he said. "We're landing, and the runway is a bit short."

She gripped his hand tightly as they banked into a steep, rapid descent. She was very thankful that she hadn't eaten before they'd left. Nothing could be more humiliating than throwing up on your boss, and lover.

The airport did indeed appear to be a tiny affair. There were no commercial airliners to be seen, only private corporate jets like the one she was just leaving.

The thin young man with the jet black hair smiled, revealing a perfect set of teeth that seemed to sparkle in the dark confines of his face. "I hope you had a pleasant flight," he said.

Warm humid air enveloped her as soon as she was outside the plane. Even a few steps away from the aircraft the atmosphere was so different that she felt herself trying to taste it, smell it, feel it on her skin.

"Nice change, huh?" Connor said.

She squeezed his hand again. "Very nice."

Within moments Clark pulled alongside in a black limo.

"How many Clarks do you have?" she asked.

"What do you mean?"

"It seems that everywhere we stop he's right there with a limo. Hard to imagine that it's always the same guy."

"Yeah, he's remarkable. Most efficient man I've ever known. That's why he's the only one I trust driving you around."

She kissed him on the cheek. "Thanks for taking such good care of me."

While they walked, Clark loaded two bags, one much larger than the other, in the trunk.

"Is one of those for me?" she asked.

"Guess which one."

"Not the big one, surely."

"You guessed it. Like I said, everything you'll need is in there."

Clark drove them along a twisting two-lane road that ran upward through a hilly forested section. He seemed to need no instructions about their destination, so Sharon guessed he'd been there before.

The air conditioning in the limo caused her nipples to form twin points in the flimsy top she wore. She wondered if Connor had noticed. He had.

He leaned in close. "I want to bite you."

"But what about Clark?"

"He won't mind." Connor lifted her right breast and seized the nipple with his teeth. When he clamped down the mixture of pain and pleasure forced a moan from her lips.

He slipped his other hand between her knees, angling for that special place between her legs. When he reached his destination he would discover her to be wet, and ready. It mattered not whether Clark was driving, watching or standing on his head.

The car stopped. "We're here," Clark said.

"Damn," Connor said.

Sharon's breath was coming in gasps. She had reached that point of no return, where her body cried out for completion. But it was not to be, not yet.

By now the sight of yet another opulent home framed in glass no longer made her jaw drop, but she couldn't help herself. The entire first floor of the mansion gave a clear through-and-through view of the ocean beyond. It was as if the floors above were suspended rather than supported from below.

"Quite a view," Connor said.

A confirming nod was all she could manage.

"Our room is on the second floor. Clark will bring up the bags. Are you hungry?"

"Sure." Even though the heat at the junction of her thighs was beginning to dissipate, she was still in a heightened state of arousal. The dramatic vista spread before distracted her, but she was so attuned to her lover's touch that even his slightest intimate caress was enough to send her spiraling out of control. No, getting her emotional state going in high gear wasn't the problem. Winding down, now that was a problem.

Connor opened a door set off the left corner of the building. Waiting inside, a very stylish woman with platinum blonde hair pulled into a tight bun, extended her hand, Ms. Spenser once again, and she seemed to be in a more festive mood than when Sharon had last seen her.

"Ms. Saluda, what a pleasure to see you again. Is there anything I can help you with?" The way she looked at Connor suggested she would be up for just about anything.

"I think we'll change in our room, then I'd like to give Sharon a tour of the grounds. This is her first time here. Perhaps when we get back a bite to eat would be nice."

"Of course, I'll see to it." She turned to Sharon. "If there's anything I can do to make your stay more pleasant, just let me know. If you can't find me just press the intercom button on the phone by the bed."

"Thanks very much," Sharon said. Did Connor and Ms. Spenser have a history, she wondered?

She had realized some time back that being on the arm of such an incredibly attractive man as Connor Shaw placed her at the top of the pecking order and as such made her a target. Her guy was first prize and everywhere they went, every woman in the room would like to be in her shoes, or better still, her bed. At the moment the competition consisted of Ms. Spenser, but there would be others, for sure.

Their room for the weekend was split into sitting and sleeping areas. The bathroom was, of course, lavish. Of all the things that bothered Sharon when she returned to her own apartment after a stay with Connor, the sumptuous bathrooms were at the top of her list. She could easily envision spending the better part of her weekend lounging in one of the huge tubs, even bringing in a chair. There was plenty of room, and she could have her coffee there while she read the morning paper.

But reality was far less accommodating. The facilities in her own apartment were not so inviting, and she spent no more time there than was necessary. In the ongoing battle between reality and fantasy, reality always won.

Clark had left both of their bags on the bed, and Sharon was eager to see what Connor regarded as necessary for her weekend. "Shall I unpack?" she asked.

"Yeah, find something casual, and we'll tour the estate."

"There's more than just the beach?"

"Much more. I'm going back downstairs to see if anyone else has arrived. Come on down when you've changed, and we'll go for a walk."

As soon as he was gone she stripped down to bra and panties, mindful that the underwear she had on might be all she'd have for the weekend. She opened the bag and laid out its contents on the bed. A quick inventory gave her a pretty good idea of how the weekend would go.

She found two robes, one a short terrycloth garment that she would likely wear to and from the beach, and the other was a filmy silk affair with a striking floral design. When she held it up to the light it all but disappeared. Okay, then, the silk robe would definitely be for their private moments, not to leave the room.

There were two pairs of shoes, a pair of sandals and a formal-looking pair of black heels. So, there was something dress-up in the works.

The contents did not include much in the way of beach wear, only three sets of string bikini bottoms, but no tops. Surely there was some oversight. Did he expect her to parade around topless in front of total strangers and anyone else who might happen by? Sure, she'd done that back in her stripping days, but those days were over.

As she rummaged around a bit more she located a couple of tops, but they were skimpy, ending just above her rib cage, and tight, as if he'd forgotten her size. Not likely. He intended for her assets to be on full display, for one and all.

The last item puzzled her, a black strapless cocktail dress. As she examined it more closely she found that it was constructed in sections each joined by zippers. Putting it on or taking it off would be a multi-step process, each step concealing or revealing more. And she realized quickly enough that she'd be taking it off, not the other way around.

The design was ingenious. Like the strippers of old, revealing a bit more with removal of each item of apparel, this gown disappeared in sections. It would be her own choice as to the sequence.

Connor came back into the room while she was familiarizing herself with the pattern of zippers. "I see you found the gown," he said.

"You should have warned me," she said. "Something this complicated requires a bit of practice."

"I promise, you'll have all the time you need."

"But I'll be taking it off, that's the idea, right?"

"I was going to ask if you'd dance for us tomorrow night."

"You know I'll do anything you ask."

He pulled the bag to the edge of the bed. "You missed something." He handed her a velvet-covered box.

When she opened it the lights in the room glistened off the diamonds in the necklace and earrings. "Oh, my God, it's beautiful."

"All a part of the plan," he said. "When you finish your dance this is all you'll be wearing."

"A girl could do worse," she said.

"I asked Ms. Spenser to get a few more things for you. They should be in here." He pulled open the top drawer of the chest that sat beside the bed.

"I'm almost afraid to look," she said.

"Just casual wear," he said. "How about this?"

"Perfect." Tops and shorts that wouldn't set off fire alarms.

To the south side of the house she saw an extensive lounge area complete with a kidney-shaped pool and a volleyball court. The three other girls were already seated in the lounge, and Sharon almost collided with a swarthy young man bearing a tray filled with drinks. Connor seemed surprised that they'd all arrived so early, but he knew each of them by name.

Sharon recognized one of them from the dinner party they'd attended a few weeks back, but the other two, both stunning blondes, were new to her.

Connor steered Sharon away from the group. "We're going for a walk, ladies. Be back shortly."

She caught a few raised eyebrows as they walked

past, but with Connor's hand placed firmly on her lower back guiding her along, there would be no stopping for any girl talk just now.

As they made their way down to the beach she stopped to slip off her sandals. There were many things she loved about the beach, and the feeling of warm sand between her toes was one of them.

Aside from the sailboats that crept along so slowly that they seemed not to move at all, the blue surface stretched undisturbed to a horizon line so sharp that it could have been painted in. The surf rolled in, kissed the sand, then ebbed away like a fickle lover. And she was walking hand in hand with the yummiest guy on the beach.

Pure heaven, and she was about to say so to Connor when his cell phone rang.

He took a few steps away from her, listened for a moment, then barked into the phone. Gone was the gentle caressing voice, gone was the magic of the moment.

Oh shit, was her only thought. *If it seems too good to be true, it probably is.*

Connor's mood seemed to darken. She'd expected, when they got to their room, a continuation of the amorous behavior he'd begun in the car, but that did not happen. And later, as she was unpacking, she'd pranced around in front of him wearing just her bra and panties. Ordinarily this would certainly bring forth a reaction from him, but not this time.

The simple joys of waves, gentle ocean breezes seemed to pass right by him. He still wore his expensive business footwear, always buffed to a high shine.

But she knew better than to ask about what, if anything, might be bothering him. Her role was that of providing pleasure and companionship. If he wanted light conversation, she was ready for that. If he wanted no conversation at all, which seemed to be the case at the moment, she could do that as well. And their pleasure pact, no problem at all. He gave as well as he received, and seemed to enjoy doing it.

"I think I see a couple of the guys out by the pool now," he said. "I should go back, help them get squared away. Do you mind hanging out with the girls for a while? Dinner will be casual this evening, and if you get hungry before, just call Ms. Spenser."

Chapter Fourteen

She detected a distinct coolness in the way the three women greeted her. Doubtless she had been the subject of their conversation. Probably they considered her underdressed for the occasion. Her plain outfit contrasted sharply with the barely-there tops and skin-tight shorts the other women wore.

"I see you still have your hooks in Connor," Crystal, the red headed girl she'd met at dinner before said. Her British accent seemed to have faded. Had it all been fake?

"I guess," Sharon said. "Have all of you been here before?"

"I've been here twice," Crystal said, "But the others are first-timers."

"What happens during the day?" Sharon asked. "I mean, do we just sit around the pool and drink?"

"Yeah, until one of the guys decides he wants you. Of course, I don't know if Connor plans to share you. He seems pretty possessive where you're concerned."

"I see a volleyball court," one of the blondes said. "Do we have to play?"

"I'm sorry you mentioned that. My tits still hurt from last time."

The girl looked puzzled, and Sharon shared their confusion.

"I'm sure they'll want us to play, but these guys

have their own ideas about volleyball. They'll want us naked. You can wear that little bikini bottom if you want, but that's all." She cradled her breasts in her hands. "And these babies weren't meant for a lot of running around and jumping up and down. Neither are yours." She pointed at Sharon's breasts, which were just as large.

"So, that's it, nude volleyball and sunbathing? That doesn't sound so bad."

"Don't worry, hon, you'll earn your keep."

"Oh, that."

"You'll be surprised how frisky these older guys get. Must be all the fresh air."

When the late afternoon sun began to fade, they all became chilled and went inside. The men were nowhere to be seen.

"What now?" Sharon asked.

Crystal, who by virtue of her previous experience had become their unofficial hostess, said "Go to your room and get cleaned up. Put on something nice. We'll all four meet on the first floor for dinner at seven."

"What about the guys?"

"I don't know exactly what they're doing, some sort of business stuff I think. But they'll let us know when they're ready for us."

Sharon went back to her room, half expecting to find Connor waiting for her, but he wasn't there. His jacket and trousers were piled on the bed, something he rarely did. He was always so fastidious about his clothes.

She hung his things in the closet. Next item on her list, a long hot shower. She could feel sand in her hair, and that would not do.

Hot streams of water cleaned her body, but did nothing to ease her mind. Connor seemed stressed, and for a man who always seemed to have everything under control, this was a disturbing change.

The bathroom towels were the thickest and fluffiest she'd ever seen. She remembered to leave a couple for Connor so he wouldn't have to call Ms. Spenser for more. Of course, Sharon could make the call herself, but she didn't want to face that woman just now. She had the distinct impression that Spenser regarded her as a common hooker. Maybe that assessment wasn't far off the mark, but she didn't need to be reminded of it.

Besides, she'd seen the way Spenser looked at Connor. If he told her to strip she would be out of her clothes before the word was even out of his mouth.

Sharon selected a short blue dress with a tasseled cord that tied at the waist. She thought about wearing the diamond necklace and earrings that Connor had given her, but that seemed a bit over the top. She would save those for the following evening, for her performance.

She did not like the idea of running around without underwear. Connor's insistence that she didn't need it provided no reassurance at all. But he must have gotten the same message across to Ms. Spenser, because try as she might, the only underwear she had was what she had worn on the trip down. Did this limitation apply to the other women as well? Four women with at most, a single set of underwear for a long weekend trip; what genius had come up with that idea? A man, no doubt.

The four girls gathered in a small dining area on the first floor. Once again, Sharon's rather casual dress contrasted with that of the others who were arrayed in party dresses and high heels. There was all manner of jewelry on display, none as impressive as what Sharon had left in her room, but a stunning array nonetheless.

As the wine began to flow, the conversation became livelier, but not in the way Sharon expected. The other girls were not particularly forthcoming about their own personal lives, but they seemed very interested in hers. She was, after all, the apparent winner in the Connor Shaw sweepstakes, and everyone present was trying to learn how she had done it. What made her so special? Did she know some particular love-making techniques that kept him coming back for more? Outside of these little junkets, how often did she see him? How had they met in the first place? So many questions.

She remained evasive to the point of rudeness. Even though she performed the same services that the other women did she didn't consider herself one of them. And her relationship with Connor was different. He never treated her like she was just one of the girls.

"Does he get you to fuck other guys?" Crystal asked.

"How am I supposed to answer that?"

"Just yes or no. It's a simple question."

Before these questions became an issue, Ms. Spenser entered the room. She bent down and whispered into the ear of one of the blondes. Sharon heard "room three," but that was all she could make out of the brief conversation. Almost immediately the girl to whom Spenser had spoken got up and left the room.

"Well, I guess we know how she'll be spending her night," Crystal said.

But Spenser wasn't through with her rounds. She

stopped at the next chair, whispered to its occupant, and that occupant was off.

Spenser left for a moment, but then came back with a message for Crystal. As the redhead started to leave, she looked back at Sharon. "Lucky you," she said.

But at the moment Sharon wasn't feeling so lucky. She picked at her dessert, then pushed it aside. She felt like the kid who didn't get chosen for a pick-up ball game. Not that she cared about not being summoned by one of the other guys. She wanted Connor.

"Oh, shit," she said aloud. What if it had been Connor who called for one of the other girls? She left the table and ran back to her room. She hesitated at the door. If Connor was inside with one of the others she would be destroyed, completely destroyed.

Several moments and a lot of deep breathing passed before she worked up the courage to enter. There were more clothes piled on the bed, Connor's she knew. She put the errant garments on hangers, and just as she stashed them away in the closet the bathroom door opened.

Connor emerged wearing only a towel wrapped around his waist. A broad smile swept across his handsome face. "Thank God, you're here." He cradled her face in his hands, kissed her eyelids, the tip of her nose, then her lips, a kiss so long and deep it seemed his life depended on it.

"Wow," she said when he finally broke away.

"I've missed you," he said.

"But I haven't been far away."

"That just makes it worse, knowing you're so close, but I can't touch you."

"I thought you were working or something."

"I was supposed to be, but I can't concentrate when you're around. You'll be the ruin of me yet."

He untied the cord at her waist, then slipped the blue dress over her head. Since she had hidden away her only set of underwear in her purse, she wore nothing underneath. One quick tug at the towel around his waist, and he was naked too.

A velvet fog settled over them. They flowed into one another, their individual margins becoming blurred as they became one. The fog that was Connor Shaw seeped into every nook and cranny of her body, and she supposed, she did into his.

Even though he'd visited those same areas so often before, her breasts, her neck, the moistness between her thighs, each time seemed new and different. He always came up with a new twist, something she didn't expect, a bite where before there'd been a caress, magic fingers, magic tongue, crawling around her body seeking out new places to excite.

His erection ground into her abdomen until she trapped him between her legs. She slid to her knees, and took him in her hand. She traced a circular pattern around the opening of his large, almost purple penis, all the while his groans increased in volume and intensity. She took him in her mouth, but he pulled her up into his arms and eased her back onto the bed. He pried her legs apart, and rested her feet on his shoulders. He ran his fingertips up and down along the insides of her thighs, until she began to beg.

When he entered her their union was complete. They moved as a single entity. When she heard him call her name, she sought out his lips. At some point, time was no longer relevant, they reached climax together.

All was complete, and all was right with the world, for now.

She watched him drift off to sleep, all the worry lines gone from his face. Mission accomplished. She wrapped a sheet around them both and wished they could stay exactly like that forever.

When she woke the next morning, he was gone. The side of the bed where he had lain was cold. She ducked into the bathroom for a quick shower, and when she emerged the red light on the bedside phone was flashing.

Crystal's voice was mocking. "Have fun last night, did you?"

"What time is it?"

"Almost ten. Why don't you join me down by the pool? I'm having breakfast."

"Ten? You're kidding." How could she have slept so late? "What about the others?"

"I think they're still in service, if you know what I mean."

"Okay, I'll be right down."

"And dress for business. We earn our keep today." Crystal's remark probably meant that the string bikini bottoms would be the order of the day, but Sharon was damned if she would parade around naked for anybody passing by. She slipped into the required garment, such as it was, and put on the short terry cloth robe. She checked the bathroom for sunscreen but found none. That would be essential as she would be exposing certain body parts to a hot tropical sun.

Crystal sat by a table already warmed by the morning sun. She had pulled on a short t-shirt in addition to the string down below. "Smart girl." She tugged lightly on Sharon's robe. "But this will have to go when the guys come around."

"I'm famished," Sharon said. The table was laden with pitchers of juice, coffee, fruits and pastries.

"Better load up on carbs. We have the big volleyball match later on."

"So, the other two are still going at it?"

"Probably. Sometimes that happens. I barely got away myself. After we did it the guy got all morose and wanted to tell me about how his marriage was going under. Just what I needed to hear."

"How did you escape?"

"He went to sleep, and I slipped away."

"You think he'll be pissed off that you left him?"

"Nah, he won't be able to remember who he went to bed with. Now, Connor, I'm sure he'll remember. I saw him earlier this morning, and he looked happy as a clam. Sometime you're gonna have to tell me your secret."

"No secret. Things just worked out for us."

"That's nice, when it works out, I mean." She blew across the surface of her coffee. "I expect I'm getting near the end of the line here. The guys are always looking for something new, and I've been doing this for almost two years now. Can't complain, though. The money's been good, and it doesn't take me away from home that much. My mom stays with me. She has cancer, and without the extra income I don't know how I'd make ends meet."

She laughed softly. "Sorry, you didn't need to hear all that. I'm sure you've got enough problems of your own without me yammering about mine."

"No, it's okay," Sharon said. "We all have

mothers."

The two other girls ambled out to the table. Each wore a short t-shirt and string bikini bottom, and each looked a bit the worse for wear.

"Thank God, coffee." The girl poured herself a cup, grabbed a Danish and began to devour the lot. "I thought I'd never get away from that bastard," she said. "Every time I tried to slip away he'd pull me back again. He must be on some kind of medication. I've never seen a guy his age who could keep it up as long as he does."

"I could use a nice long nap," the other blonde said. "My guy only did it to me once, but then he held onto me all night, snoring into my ear. So, what's the schedule today?"

Crystal resumed her unofficial hostess routine. "The guys usually come down to the pool around noon. Remember, first sign of them, everything comes off but the bikini bottoms. And if you want to take those off too, so much the better. The guys want skin, and lots of it."

"Speaking of skin," Sharon said. "I couldn't find any sunscreen in the bathroom."

"That guy who brings the drinks should have some. He'll probably be happy to rub it on, too."

The noonday sun was nearing its zenith before the guys arrived in a group. All were shirtless, and with the exception of Connor's lean athletic build, the male physiques looked a bit past their primes. Sharon was ever so thankful that she hadn't had to suffer one of those corpulent forms rolling around on top of her all night.

The girls had already stripped down to their string

bikini bottoms and had taken turns applying liberal amounts of sunscreen to each other. Now they lay back, four glistening bodies spread across lounge chairs, eight perfect breasts pointed skyward.

Sharon kept her eyes open, safely concealed behind her sunglasses. The flip-flop of the men's sandals came closer. In a moment the perfect bodies around her, and perhaps hers as well, would be mounted, pumped and pummeled, then passed around. A classic fuck-fest that any toga-clad Roman would have joined in with glee.

But instead of slurping and slithering noises, instead of moans of pleasure, she heard only nervous laughter from the men.

"Like I'd died and gone to heaven," one man said. The others laughed but made no move on the girls.

She watched from the corner of her eye, expecting that at any moment the guys would pounce. Who in his right mind could resist the array of well-oiled flesh laid out like a buffet of carnal pleasures?

But resist they did. Instead of charging into the fray, members erect, shorts torn off and thrown to the wind, they milled about like so many junior high students at their first dance. She could almost hear them challenging one another. "You go first." "No, you go first."

The group dynamic, a stalemate so far, changed when one of the guys said, "Hey, how about some volleyball?"

This brought a soft groan from Crystal, but shortly she was on her feet, all smiles and ready to play. The net was strung up in a groomed sand lot about twenty feet from the pool. The guys dragged their chairs alongside the court, and as quiet as they had been a few minutes before, now they became a veritable chorus of catcalls, cheers and jeers.

While Sharon and the others warmed up, Ms. Spenser brought a tray of drinks for the men. She had changed into tight denim shorts and a light blue tank top. She'd also combed her hair out so that it fanned over her shoulders like a platinum halo.

Sharon teamed up with Crystal, and they squared off against the two taller blondes. Any idea she'd had about this being a leisurely match designed primarily to show naked female bodies in motion vanished during the warm-up. These girls played for keeps.

The two blondes steamrolled Sharon and her partner, winning all three matches by wide margins. At some point or another they each took a tumble, Sharon, more than once, and the sand stuck to their oiled bodies like the abrasive coating on sandpaper.

"Oh, shit," one of the blondes said after a head-over heels pratfall that drew a standing ovation from the observers. "I got sand in my…" Her voice trailed off.

"What? I didn't catch what you said." Sharon helped her to her feet.

"I got sand where you never ever want to get sand."

Most of the grit wound up on Sharon and her partner. The two blondes, the blushing victors, were much more lightly coated.

"Thanks for a great show, ladies," Connor said from the sideline. "You can shower off here before you go inside."

Right now a hot shower sounded better to Sharon than anything she could think of, anything to get rid of this damned sandy grit. She'd always figured the worst thing about nude volleyball would be putting yourself in compromising positions with nothing to shield yourself from prying eyes, but she'd been wrong. Sand was much worse by far. The embarrassment of winding up spread-eagled after a fall with your most private of private parts in full view was a momentary thing, lasting only as long as it took to close your legs and regain your feet. Sand was with you for the duration, removed only by a hot soapy shower like she and the other girls were enjoying now.

The second stage of the cleansing process began with a long soak in the tub, which Sharon began as soon as she reached her room. With luck she'd have time for a nap before dinner, and for certain she would need a bit more time to familiarize herself with the intricacies of the black cocktail dress she would be wearing, then removing.

It was a totally relaxed Sharon who finally slipped naked between the sheets. If Connor returned soon this is how she would want him to find her. Perhaps he would be inspired to a brief frolic before dinner.

But he hadn't returned by the time the bedside alarm clock told her it was six o'clock and time to dress for dinner at seven. Most of that hour would be spent applying make-up and fussing with her hair. She would probably wear it up, so that when her performance was underway she could remove a couple of hairpins, and the whole glorious mane would fall over her shoulders, all a part of the act.

There remained the small problem of how to make her body more alluring. This was never a real problem, because her truly spectacular physical assets turned heads wherever she went. But this same body had already been on display for all to see, for much of the day. How could she make it more interesting after everyone who would be at the dinner had already had a long close look at everything she had to offer?

And that's where the dress came in. Back when Sharon had begun stripping at Lennie's club, the owner had given her scant directions.

"Just watch what the other girls do, and do the same thing. And don't waste a lot of time dancing around. Get right to it. These guys want to see you naked. For that matter, so do I."

She got a bit more information from one of the other girls at Lennie's. Sandy had had classical training in dance, but realized early on that the few jobs she could find weren't going to pay the bills, so she became a stripper.

"Remember," Sandy said, "You're working for tips, so you gotta work the crowd."

"But stripping is stripping," Sharon said.

"Yeah, but you have to convince them that they're seeing something different every time. Face it, you see one naked body, you've seen them all, pretty much. I mean, there's some variation in shape and size, but the basic equipment is the same. So, it's not so much what you're showing as how you show it."

So Sharon made a point of watching Sandy's performances. The beginnings and the endings, clothes on, clothes off, were always the same, but what happened in between was different every time. And by the time Sandy finished, the crowd was foaming at the mouth.

Sharon slipped the black dress over her head. *If I'd had this back when I was dancing for a living, I could have done some real damage*. She continued her experimentation in front of the mirror. The dress had four removable panels up front. She could reveal her breasts singly or both at once. The panel covering her abdomen and the lower panel covering her pubic area could be removed partially or all at once.

The sections covering her back and buttocks required a bit of dexterity because of the location of the zippers.

After all the individual panels were removed the rest of the dress, just a framework, really, could be removed by a single clasp at the back of her neck, leaving her completely nude. Where on earth had Connor found such a garment? The man never failed to surprise her, or shock her.

The final touch, the diamond necklace and earrings completed her ensemble. And as Connor had said, "When the show's over, this is all you'll be wearing."

Seven o'clock and still no Connor, so she went down to the dining room alone. The other three girls were clustered around Ms. Spenser who, once again, wore her platinum blonde hair up in a tight bun.

"The gentlemen will be a few minutes late," Spenser said. From the corner of the table she took a stack of facemasks. "We thought it would be interesting to add a bit of intrigue to the evening, so if you'll each select one of the masks, we'll see if we can trick the gentlemen."

"You're not wearing one?" Sharon asked.

"Oh, no, that would be confusing," Spenser said.

The masks left much of their faces exposed, enough to identify them without much difficulty. But, she thought, the guys hadn't really been zeroed in on their faces for the past two days. They could probably identify their naked bodies with no trouble, but faces, perhaps not.

Spenser took Sharon's arm and led her to an open area on the other side of the room. "I hear you'll have a little surprise performance for us after dinner," Spenser whispered.

"Who told you about that?"

"Mr. Shaw, of course. I hope this area will provide enough space for you."

"There's plenty of room," Sharon said.

"Mr. Shaw will get things started, and I'll start up the music as soon as he signals me. The lights in this area operate separately, so we can darken the rest of the room while you dance."

Her knees were weak, her palms were sweaty, and for the first time in recent memory, she had stage fright.

Her stage fright was compounded by Connor's continued absence. It was almost seven-thirty before he arrived with the other men in tow. He made no apologies, gave no explanations. He took his seat beside Sharon and kissed her.

"How did you know it was me?" she asked from behind her mask.

"I could pick you out in a totally dark room," he said.

The little worry furrow was back in the middle of his forehead, and his white shirt, always so wrinkle-free, was now crisscrossed by unsightly folds. As before, she wanted to ask what might be wrong, but could not. To do so would be to violate the pact they'd made. If there was anything she should know, he would tell her when he was damned good and ready. Until then, she would wait.

Dinner was rather subdued, even as the wine flowed freely. Sharon limited her intake, because soon her time on stage would arise, and fumbling with hidden zippers would not go over well. Since she was dancing at Connor's request she wanted to be at her best.

As the meal progressed, the contrast between the two groups became more and more stark. The women, behind their masks, sparkled. Their conversation was like a pleasant background melody, always inviting, never obtrusive. Whatever they were being paid for the weekend, they were worth every penny, in Sharon's opinion.

But even their best efforts failed to spur on the males. Whatever weighed on them, fatigue was only part of it. And Connor was no more effusive than the others. There seemed to be only one way to salvage the evening…to dance like she had never danced before.

Showtime arrived all too soon. As the dessert settings were being removed, Ms. Spenser distributed black, evil-looking cigars to the men. The two blondes took cigarette cases from their bags, and soon Sharon was the only one at the table not smoking. Just as well, because shortly she would have her hands full of balky zippers.

Connor reached beneath the table and squeezed her hand. "Ready?" he asked.

She took a deep breath, then nodded.

He walked around to the clear area where Sharon would be dancing.

"We have a special after-dinner treat for you." He nodded to Ms. Spenser and the music began.

As she made her way to the area alongside Connor he lifted her chin and kissed her. It was all the inspiration she would ever need.

First rule in stripping, take control of the room. She stalked around her little dance area like a jungle animal marking its territory. Then, eye contact with her audience, not really, because she purposely blurred out faces and expressions, but they didn't know that. The edges of her little stage were only dimly lit, and she used that too, light to dark and back again, anything to blur the reality that all they were watching was a girl taking off her clothes.

A slow undulation, subtle at first, then more as she caught the rhythm. She turned her back to them, raised her arms above her head, and a wave flowed from her fingertips to her toes in one fluid motion, a trick too subtle to work at Lennie's, but just right for the small, captive audience that she held now.

Aside from the music, the room became deathly quiet. The women removed their masks. The men loosened their ties and mopped their foreheads with their napkins. She had them. They were hers.

She pulled out all the stops; every move, every nuance she'd learned at Lennie's, as well as a few she improvised right on the spot, she put to use then and there. She prowled around the little dance area, revealing, then concealing just as quickly. *Now you see it, now you don't.* She showed, then just as quickly, she covered up again. The magical dress with all its mysterious panels was perfect for the little tease she was playing out.

One by one the panels disappeared, until there was almost nothing left. The last panel, a triangle covering her pelvis, she removed by a single zipper, leaving only the framework of the magical gown. Two snaps, one at the back of her neck and one at her waist and this fell to the floor as well, leaving her triumphant in black heels, a diamond necklace, and nothing else.

The group rose as one, giving her a standing ovation. Connor swept her into his arms and kissed her long and hard. "God, Sharon, that was fantastic." His breathing was rapid and shallow. From somewhere he had retrieved the silk robe and now wrapped this around her.

Ms. Spenser had picked up the various parts of the black dress. She held them out to Sharon. "I don't know how to put this back together," she said. "That was an incredible dance."

Crystal appeared at her side. She hugged Sharon and whispered in her ear. "Where on God's green earth did you learn to dance like that? I'm beginning to see how you keep Connor coming back for more."

"It's only a dance," Sharon said.

"Yeah, like the hottest dance I've ever seen." One of the blondes leaned in close and whispered, "The guy sitting next to me, he had one hand up my skirt and the other down his pants. I thought he was going to have a heart attack. I'm glad he didn't. I don't know CPR, and I don't know if he was worth it anyway."

Connor draped a protective arm over her shoulders and led her toward the exit door. "We should go," he said.

"So early?" She wanted to stay and soak up some of the approbation generated by her dance. She'd just pulled off the performance of a lifetime, and she wanted to bask in the glow a bit longer.

The pressure of his arm around her left no room for discussion.

When they got back to the room she found the clothes she'd arrived in laid out on the bed.

"Go ahead and change," he said. He slipped behind her and unfastened the clasp of her diamond necklace. He held out his hand for the earrings. "Don't worry, you'll get them back. I promise."

He rolled the magic black dress into a ball and stuffed it into the bag on the bed. There was another bag alongside that she hadn't seen before.

"Who packed my bag?" Sharon asked.

"Ms. Spenser. We should hurry."

A soft knock on the door…Clark. He whispered something to Connor.

"Of course, she can ride back with us."

Clark gathered up the bags and was gone.

At the back door to the mansion, where they'd entered the day before, Ms. Spenser was waiting. She kept looking around her as if she expected someone to jump out and grab her.

There was a limo parked by the door, and Sharon headed for it. Connor grabbed her arm. "Not ours," he said.

The limo's tires kicked up gravel as it sped away. Clark pulled into the spot it left. Sharon and Ms. Spenser were ushered into the back seat, and Connor got into the front alongside Clark.

"What's the rush?" Sharon asked.

"Change of plans," Connor said from the front seat. "I'll tell you all about it when we get back."

Chapter Fifteen

Within minutes, the taillights of the car ahead were in view as Clark sped along the narrow road. Sharon gripped the armrest, lest she be thrown across the back seat.

The two jets sat in line on the single runway. Clark pulled alongside the second in line. Now they were all inside, waiting for takeoff. She sat close beside Connor holding his hand tightly. Clark and Ms. Spenser took up seats across the aisle. Neither looked to be surprised at the sudden change in events.

Maybe Connor would explain the abrupt change, maybe he wouldn't. In either case, she would not question his decisions or his actions.

She was still in a state of arousal after her dance. She would like nothing better than to wrap her arms around her lover and get into some serious amorous activity, but that was hardly possible with the other two sitting so close by.

A few minutes after, they were airborne, Connor drew her close. "Baby, I need you," he said. He unhooked her seat belt and drew her head down into his lap. "Please."

She could hardly believe her ears. Was he asking her to perform oral sex in front of an audience? Dancing naked was one thing, but a blowjob in plain sight? The pressure of his hand on the back of her head left no doubt. "But the others…" she whispered.

"They won't care."

Maybe they wouldn't, but she sure as hell would. Then, what choice did she have? She had signed on for the full ride, and what he was asking was just part of the job. She slid out of her seat and knelt between his legs. She unzipped him and slipped his erect member out of his trousers. There, in front of God and the other passengers, she took him in her mouth. She trailed her tongue back and forth across the base of his penis. After a very short time he became rigid, his back arched, and he discharged into her mouth. She held him there, her lips around him. She managed to look up into his face, expecting a smile of approval, but he appeared to have gone to sleep.

No point in continuing, so she put his flaccid penis back into his trousers and zipped him up once again. Now what? Her mouth was dry, and the viscous liquid that he'd deposited there resisted her efforts to swallow. She didn't want to face the other two passengers after what she'd just done in full view, so she knelt there between his legs, not knowing what to do next.

A pat on her shoulder. Ms. Spenser handed her a napkin and a chilled bottle of mineral water. An act of kindness that Sharon would not forget.

Connor slept during most of the return flight. Sharon sat beside him holding his hand. Twice he became agitated, his head rolling from side to side while his grip on her hand became painful. What demons were still chasing him in his dreams? Were they the same ones that dogged him during the day, sapping his strength so that he had so little left for her? Whatever it was, she was losing out to the competition.

If it were another woman she would know how to fight back, but nameless demons presented no target. They did their damage then crept away, unseen and unknown.

Once she caught Ms. Spenser staring at her, what looked like concern on her face. She looked as if she wanted to say something, something private that should pass between just the two of them. But the seating arrangement in the cabin made that impractical. One thing she would do in the very near future, she would get to know Ms. Spenser better, and for damned sure she would learn what to call her instead of Ms. Spenser. She'd know the woman for months now, and continuing to address her so formally seemed ridiculous.

Then, as they left the plane, she walked alongside Sharon and took her arm. "Lisa," she said. "My name is Lisa." *God, the woman was a mind reader too*?

But her smile suggested a friendly overture, one that Sharon welcomed. She gave Lisa's hand a light squeeze in return. "Thanks," she said.

****

Slipping back into a familiar routine was a welcome respite considering the chaotic weekend she'd had. The next time Connor suggested a beach trip she would call in sick.

On Wednesday evening, she dropped in at the Faculty Club, just before business hours began. Brenda was propped in one of the chairs, a textbook spread in her lap. "Looks like you got some sun," she said. "A little beach time?"

"Just a little," Sharon said. "More would have been better."

"That's always the way," Brenda said. "My dream

home would be right on the beach, waterfront, so I'd never have to take off my bathing suit, unless the right person asked me to, of course." She winked at Sharon.

"I'd think you'd get enough of that here," Sharon said.

"Yeah, I thought so too, but I like it a lot more than I expected. And it's nice getting paid for it."

"You are turning into an evil woman." Sharon laughed.

"You should know. You got me started in the first place."

"Sure, blame it on me." Sharon took the small box that contained the cash receipts for the week so far. In spite of their agreement to close down the Faculty Club for the summer, a couple of the girls still brought guys over. It would have been simpler for them to just keep what they earned for themselves, but they insisted on keeping with the old system of pooling their money and dividing it up later.

She stashed the cash in her purse and returned the steel box to its drawer in the desk.

"Things still going great between you and that amazing guy?" Brenda asked.

"Yeah, pretty much. There are ups and downs always, but the ups are so great that the downs don't matter. See you later."

Walking around with almost four thousand in cash in her purse would have been a source of concern for Sharon in the past, but by now she was so used to handling large sums, some much larger than the contents of her handbag, that the situation seemed quite ordinary. Besides, she kept her little .22 caliber handgun in her pocket when she made her collections.

Like the flimsy lock on the cash box, the little weapon wouldn't deter a real threat, but a well-aimed shot could be quite distracting.

She had at least a dozen shoe boxes stashed in the bottom of her closet. Two of those boxes contained the week's receipts from the Faculty Club. So much for security.

****

Her Friday luncheon with Gloria was now etched in stone. They simply showed up at the same diner at the same time, no planning, no arrangements to be made. Even their food choices were the same, Sharon's spinach salad and Gloria's grilled cheese sandwich. They'd both talked about upgrading their choices when the money began flowing in, but neither had made a change. Repetition in some cases might be boring, but this proved comforting. For a while she could park her brain and just be in the moment with her friend.

And her friend had a faraway look in her eyes.

"Where are you?" Sharon asked.

Gloria grinned. She smiled often enough, but grins were not her usual expression.

"Okay, out with it," Sharon said. "What's going on?"

"Have you ever been in love?" Gloria asked. "I don't mean ever, I mean more like recently."

The question caught Sharon right between the eyes. It wasn't really a question anyway. It was certainly a preliminary to something else Gloria had to say, but still the question, when Sharon thought about it, left her hanging. Love? Real romantic love? That should be an easy answer. But it wasn't.

"Like that guy you're seeing now," Gloria said.

"This isn't about me," Sharon said. "It's about you. Something has happened. You look all weird, like you've got some big secret."

"There's this guy."

"Oh my gosh, Gloria. Tell me everything." Had her friend broken one of her own rules?

"There's not that much to tell, really. And he's not really a guy. He's a client."

"Seems I remember somebody warning me about getting emotionally involved with clients."

"Like they say, there's no fool like an old fool."

"What's he like?"

"Nice, you know, comfortable. His wife died four years ago, cancer. He tried dating for a while but hated it. So, he wound up at my place. The first time we did it, you know, like a regular session. The next time we just talked. I told him he'd still have to pay, but he didn't have a problem with that."

"From the look in your eyes that must have been one hell of a talk," Sharon said.

"Not what I expected. I mean, I thought he'd want to talk about how tough life had been since his wife died, but no, he wanted to talk about me. Imagine that…me." Once again, Gloria's eyes took on that glazed appearance as if she'd gone deep inside to some special place.

"I'm happy for you, "Sharon said. "So very happy."

"Ah, it probably won't amount to anything. These things never do," Gloria said.

"There's always a first time."

They parted with a hug, first time for that too.

Have you ever been in love? That's what Gloria

had asked her, and as much as Sharon tried to ignore the question it kept popping up again. None of her previous flings deserved to be classified as real love, not like the kind you'd stake your life on. But how about Connor? Her attachment to him was deeper, more profound than she'd ever felt with any other man. But was it love? Was it real honest-to-God, no-doubt-about-it love?

She stood in front of her bathroom mirror. Do I love him? Does he love me? The mirror image wasn't any more informative than the original, in other words, no answer.

She stared for a long moment, and this time the mirror answered her. "If you have to ask the question, that's the answer."

So there, she didn't want to know, but she knew. And if Connor Shaw was only an infatuation, it was time well spent so far as she was concerned. Besides, she put little stock in that curious institution of romantic love. It seemed more like a temporary delusional state, likely to melt away after the initial period of passion was past.

At least with Connor, if the relationship ran aground, there would be no mess to clean up. They could part as friends, no worse off for the time they'd spent together. How many married couples could say that?

And passion seemed to be in short supply lately. Often their sessions seemed almost perfunctory, and she had to wonder, had her affair with Connor run its course? Either that or something else in his life was pumping him dry so that there was precious little left for her.

Sometimes he called, sometimes he didn't. And she needed those calls. The sound of his voice all soft and low summoning her to another evening of ecstasy, that's what she lived for now. The ritual, the almost ceremonial cleansing of her body, so carefully and completely, because she never knew where he might direct his caress. The careful choice of underwear, or those times she decided to go without.

All those things and more filled her Tuesday afternoons until Clark pulled the Lincoln Town Car up in front of her apartment. By then, the preparation alone would have her in a high state of anticipation, so that her lover had only to touch her to start currents of pleasure coursing through her, just a touch.

Now those sessions seemed on the wane. He no longer played her body like an instrument of desire. In fact, his contribution to their lovemaking now seemed like an afterthought. He expected her to please him. Lately that meant oral sex, after which, or sometimes during, he drifted off to sleep.

After one particularly unsatisfying episode, she left him on the bed fully clothed, snoring softly. She removed his shoes and pulled the sheet over him. Then she went to the bathroom for her usual swish of mouthwash. There was little left to do but find Clark to take her back to her apartment.

When she went out into the hallway, she found Ms. Spenser waiting for her.

"Do you have time for coffee, or a drink, perhaps?" she asked.

"Sure, I was looking for Clark, but coffee would be great."

"Good, I just made some, and it's Lisa,

remember?" She smiled as she spoke. Sharon couldn't recall seeing her smile before.

The room that Sharon thought was just Lisa's office was actually a suite of three large rooms including a bedroom and a small efficiency kitchen. "Do you live here?" Sharon asked.

"Mostly," Lisa said. "It cuts down on travel time, so when he wants me I'm right here." She waved Sharon toward a small round table for two in a nook just off the kitchen. She poured two cups and brought them over.

They sat for a moment as if unsure which one was to begin, or what that beginning might be about.

"I was at Monmouth Enterprises for just over five years before I started working for Mr. Shaw," Lisa finally said. "Sorry, I still call him Mr. Shaw. I was sort of a concierge at Monmouth. When anybody needed anything done or anything found or anything got rid of, I took care of it. You can learn a lot doing that if you keep your eyes and ears open."

Sharon wanted to contribute something to the conversation, but really it was Lisa's show. Better just sit back and listen.

"After Mr. Shaw came to Monmouth I spent most of my time doing stuff for him, so he had me assigned to him exclusively. He likes to do that with women, but you know that already. Moving me out here was his next step. I still go into the office with him several times a week. Otherwise I stay here."

The conversation slowed as Lisa seemed to be gathering her thoughts. "You're probably wondering whether Mr. Shaw and I get together, in bed, I mean. We do not. I'm gay, so that's never going to happen."

She rubbed her forehead with her fingertips as if trying to massage away a headache. "At first I was afraid he might fire me, but he never made a big issue out of it. Besides, he has plenty of other girls for that."

Sharon's fingertips tightened around her coffee cup. She could have guessed as much, a man like Connor Shaw, but that didn't mean she was glad to hear about it. "I figured there would be others," she said.

"None like you, though, not since I've known him. He's seemed happier these past few months than I've ever seen him, until the bottom started to fall out of the business, that is."

"Is that why he's been so distracted? I thought at first he was tired of me, wanted something new. I even asked him one night, but he had already gone to sleep."

"He's just tired, exhausted. He's been putting in twelve hour days for weeks now trying to keep things afloat, but it's starting to catch up to him."

Lisa stood and took a couple of steps across the small kitchen. "Are you hungry? I have a chocolate cheesecake in the fridge. I made it for Mr. Shaw, but it looks like he's done for the night."

"Chocolate cheesecake," Sharon said. "Count me in."

"While we're eating, I can give you a short history lesson," Lisa said as they attacked their slices of cheesecake. "Before Mr. Shaw came on board, Monmouth was a small company. Our list of clients wouldn't fill a single page, and they were all small accounts. When Mr. Shaw came in, things changed overnight. He brought several large clients with him, and in no time had added several more. These accounts were university endowment portfolios, big bucks, we're talking millions. He was the golden boy in university circles. People were calling him all the time."

Sharon whistled softly. The cash flow Connor Shaw handled made her little account from the Faculty Club look like a joke. Still, he'd found a use for her small operation.

"We added new stuff for the office, upgraded all our computer equipment. In less than three months we had doubled in size. Money was coming in like we'd never dreamed about."

Sharon realized she'd eaten all her cheesecake before Lisa had really gotten started. "Guess I was hungry after all," she said.

"There's plenty more," Lisa said.

"No thanks, that was quite enough." Sharon took her dish to the sink and rinsed it off.

"Well, the good times ran for about three years. Like, our Christmas parties lasted two days, big bonuses for everybody. And that little junket you just took where you did your dance, a couple of years ago there would have been fifteen, maybe twenty girls there. It was like one of those Roman orgies you read about."

"I'm not sorry I missed that," Sharon said. "But things have changed, right?"

"Yeah, a lot has happened, most of it bad. You have to have some idea of what the company was doing for any of this to make sense. First, all those glowing reports of return on investment, fifteen percent and up, never happened. It was all pure fiction. The investors got quarterly reports showing all the money they thought they were making, and they were as happy as anything. The analysts at the company kept all this investment money in house, and so long as nobody tried to withdraw any of it, the company was happy too."

"So the investment returns, that was all a sham?"

"Yes. Investments were made, but they were no more successful than average. A lot of the time they lost money. And when the economy went south last year, the investment principal started to melt away."

"Surely some people wanted to pull some funds out," Sharon said.

"Early on that was no problem. See, Mr. Shaw's strong suit was recruiting new investors. So even if somebody decided to pull out, there was always enough money coming in from new investors to pay them off, even if we hadn't made a dime on their money. So long as we had new cash coming in from new groups, we were sitting pretty."

"I got it now," Sharon said. "A Ponzi scheme."

"That's about it, and now that the economy is in trouble, we're in trouble too…big trouble."

"Do you know about the money he's funneling through the little business I have at the university?"

"I do. The term for that is money laundering, but you probably know that too. They're trying to divert enough money to an offshore account so that if things go under here they won't be left with nothing at all. It will remain hidden from anybody trying to seize our assets."

"Do you have anything stronger than coffee?" Sharon asked.

"Of course. Name your poison."

Lisa came back to the table with a bottle of single-malt scotch and a couple of glasses. She held the bottle up for Sharon's inspection.

"Yeah," Sharon said. "That should do the trick."

After a few moments of silent sipping, Sharon asked, "Isn't it a little risky for you to be telling me all this?"

"Maybe, but things could go bad in a hurry. I don't want you to get hurt in the process."

"I appreciate that, but what about you?"

"I've got a little nest egg set aside, just in case. You should do that too. I know you have some of the offshore business, but all that sounds a little shaky to me. I wouldn't want my savings sitting in some empty building that doesn't even have a name."

"This is all starting to sound very serious. I'm going to need another one." She pushed her empty glass over to Lisa.

She had a closet stuffed full of new clothes, more expensive jewelry than she would probably ever use, and a large lump of cash sitting in a bank in the Grand Cayman Islands, as well as access to a much larger lump. She didn't want to lose it. But there was more to consider. "People get thrown in jail for this sort of thing, don't they?"

"The biggest problem will be the fraudulent quarterly reports. The feds really get upset over those. But they would be after the big boys, not you and me."

"Big boys meaning Connor?"

"I'm afraid so."

"Any advice for me?" Sharon asked.

"Yes, pray that the economy picks up, and have a back-up plan, a secret Swiss bank account or something. Here's my private number. If I can help with anything at all." She slid a slip of paper across the table.

When Sharon reached for it their fingertips touched. Neither of them moved, neither of them breathed. "So, you're gay," Sharon said.

"Yes." Lisa's voice was a husky whisper.

"I never did it with another woman."

"If you ever want to give it a try, let me know." Lisa edged around the table and kissed Sharon. Their tongues darted back and forth like little electric wands, setting off sparks each time they touched.

So unlike kissing a man, Sharon thought. The difference between being dominated vs. sharing a kiss between equal partners. She liked it both ways, but Lisa's kiss raised new possibilities, new areas she would like to explore. She rested her right hand on Lisa's chest, trailed her thumb across an erect and very firm nipple. "Do you have time now?"

"Oh, God, yes."

Sharon woke to the sound of a shower running. As the details of the room came into focus, she realized that she wasn't in Connor's bed, but she wasn't in her own either. Lisa. She was in Lisa's bed. Last night, for the first time in her life she'd made love to a woman, the woman in whose bed she now lay. The woman who, while lacking some of the basic equipment that Connor possessed, made up for it in the skilled application of what she had.

And her skin, so soft and velvety, so unlike any man's skin. Simply running her fingertips, her tongue, over Lisa's body brought her new delights, unlike any she'd known before. And the sweet smell of lavender that hung about in Connor's bedroom, Lisa seemed to be its epicenter. Everywhere that Sharon ran her lips, her nose, over Lisa's body, and she missed very few, if any spots, there was lavender, her new favorite.

On those rare occasions when Sharon had thought about love making between two females she just didn't get it. What could possibly be so great about an act without a penis to share? Now she knew.

She ran her fingertips down her belly to the light thatch of hair between her legs. There was always a bit of tenderness there after Connor had been pumping away at her the night before. No tenderness now. Now that same area tingled, as if remembering the electric pleasure of the night before.

Sharon was in the act of reviving some of that pleasure as she ran her forefinger back and forth in the furrow between her labia when Lisa emerged from the bathroom wrapped in a towel, her wet hair wrapped in a smaller version.

"Ah, you're awake," Lisa said. She knelt on the bed beside Sharon. "I hope I didn't disappoint you last night."

"Umm, I was just thinking about that." She pulled apart the edges of the towel exposing Lisa's body still warm and rosy from her shower. She raised herself up on one elbow so that she could grasp Lisa's left nipple with her lips.

Lisa tossed the towel aside and stretched out beside Sharon. "You mustn't get me started again," she said. "Mr. Shaw called an early morning meeting, and I have to be there."

"Just a quick one?" Sharon asked.

"It won't be a quick one, and you know it." She lay alongside Sharon and cupped her right breast in her palm. "You are so beautiful."

"If you want me again, I'm all yours." Sharon drew

her thigh up along Lisa' hip. She pulled her head down and kissed her. Kissing Lisa was rapidly becoming one of her favorite things to do, right up there with kissing Connor.

"You know I want you, but when the boss calls, I gotta jump," Lisa said.

"Does he know I'm here with you?"

"No, he left over an hour ago. Believe me, he was in such a fog he wouldn't have noticed if I'd had a dozen girls in here."

"Please, tell me you never do that."

"You know better." Lisa still held Sharon's breast, and the nipple jutted out like a pencil eraser.

"Come on," Sharon said. "Just five minutes. You'll still have plenty of time to get to the office."

"You are the worst." Lisa laughed as she dove between Sharon's outstretched thighs.

Chapter Sixteen

Without a lot of effort, Sharon figured out that the clinical course of most Ponzi operations was wedded to the economy. Good news from Wall Street meant smiles all around, Monmouth Enterprises in particular. When the economy was bounding along, they could continue sending out their fraudulent economic reports showing high gains on investment, and no one would be the wiser. Happy investors were much more likely to leave their money where it was, safe in the capable hands of the Monmouth investment team.

Very clever, but it didn't take a genius with a degree in economics to spot the holes in such an operation. The more she thought about it the more she was convinced it would all come tumbling down. It had to. It was just a matter of time.

The bigger question concerned the fate of the perpetrators. Sharon was, of course, a part of the operation, a small part, but when things went south, she was very likely to go with it. Her own mandated penance would not be so great as that of the major players, but she was in no mood for any penance at all. If she had to cut a deal to keep her head out of the noose, then that deal would surely be cut.

That left Connor. Her only knowledge of his involvement had come from her conversations with Lisa, usually in Lisa's bed.

"I don't know how to help him," Sharon said. She was covered in a sheen of perspiration after she and Lisa had gone from a head-to-head position to a head-to-toe pose, winding up joined at the hip, their legs entwined like some complex sailor's knot. The room reeked of sex, slightly acrid, Sharon loved it.

When she was with Lisa, her orgasms came in little bunches. Unlike the explosion when Connor ejaculated inside her, these were smaller events, but their number and their persistence continued as long as Lisa worked her magic with her fingers and tongue. Sharon tried to keep track of the places on her body that Lisa visited and what she did when she got there, but all her good intentions were lost in the rapture that her new lover created.

Without warning, Lisa started on her again, penetrating, nipping, tugging gently on those secret parts that caused Sharon to writhe around like a cat in heat. The noises that escaped from her were also like those of a feline in the throes of estrogen overdrive.

"I'm sorry," Lisa said after several minutes of thrashing around. "I couldn't stop myself. You started to say something about Mr. Shaw."

"I did?" The beauty of girl-on-girl sex, they could stop for a quick break, then pick up again right where they left off.

"Yes, about how you couldn't help him."

Sharon took a few deep breaths, trying to calm herself. "You've seen how he is. He doesn't even resemble the same guy I was seeing here a couple of weeks ago. And the sex is lousy now. He squeezes my tits, I suck his dick, and he goes to sleep. If I couldn't come here to you, I would be one very unsatisfied lady."

"I hear you. I'm just as concerned about him as you are. And as best I can tell, he's the only one busting his ass to keep this operation afloat."

"I'm afraid for him," Sharon said. "Really afraid."

"I still have half a bottle of scotch in the kitchen. How about I grab that."

"Maybe I'll grab something too." Sharon grabbed a breast.

"Hey, that's not going to help us help Mr. Shaw." She rolled on top of Sharon, her knees almost up to Sharon's armpits.

Sharon pried Lisa's knees farther apart. Then she reached behind and pulled her buttocks forward.

"I know what you're up to." She leaned over Sharon, whose tongue was beginning to find its mark. "Oh, yes." Lisa began rocking back and forth.

They both froze at the sound of Connor's voice. "What the hell is going on here?"

With her face wedged between Lisa's thighs, Sharon managed to turn her head only slightly. That was enough to see the mixture of outrage and betrayal that flashed from Connor's face.

Lisa didn't move, or perhaps couldn't move, until Sharon pushed her gently to one side. They both sat watching Connor. Neither said anything, because there was nothing to say.

Finally, Lisa spoke up. "All my fault. This was all my fault."

"No," Sharon said. "It was just as much me as you."

"You cheated," he said as he turned to leave.

Sharon managed to squirm from beneath Lisa and

ran to him, grabbing his arm. "No, not like this."

"Let go," he said.

But she didn't let go, and by now Lisa had clamped onto his other arm. "Even if you drag us, you'll still have to explain why you have two naked women hanging onto you. Please, come back, and let's talk."

He let them lead him back to the bed. He was still wearing his rumpled shirt and tie, and his trousers. Sharon had removed his shoes before she left him.'

Sharon pulled off his tie and began unbuttoning his shirt. "This is about you," she said.

"What does the two of you fucking have to do with me?"

"A lot more than you think." She removed his shirt.

While Sharon was busy above, Lisa was working below undoing his trousers. She pulled them off and draped them over a chair beside the bed.

"First time I've see you naked," he said to Lisa. "You're beautiful. You both are."

"Only one problem," Sharon said. "We're naked and you aren't, not yet." She pulled his undershirt over his head while Lisa removed his briefs.

"You two can strip a guy in nothing flat," he said.

They pulled him into the center of the bed and lay down on either side of him. "Now, let's talk," Sharon said.

"Talk? Are you kidding me?" His penis was beginning its vertical ascent.

"We'll take care of that in a minute," Sharon said. "First things first. We're both very concerned about you."

"You can't go on like this, running yourself into the ground. We want to help you, but we don't know what to do," Lisa said.

Connor's erection began to ebb. He locked his fingers behind his head and stretched out full length on the bed. "There's really nothing you can do. Unfortunately, there's not much I can do either. Everything depends on the market now. We're holding all the cash we're likely to get, and it won't cover us if there's a substantial withdrawal of funds."

"We both know about the funds in the Grand Caymans," Sharon said. "Can't you use that in an emergency?"

"It would just prolong the inevitable, and bringing that out would just get us in deeper. Besides, I'm not sure it's even enough to cover us, and the other partners in the firm would never agree to it anyway."

Not enough? How could that possibly be true? After the first transfer of funds to the Grand Caymans Sharon had received a communication from the bank's president addressing her, not by name, but as president of the Faculty Club.

When Connor had first approached her about passing funds through the Faculty Club, Sharon had assumed that the amounts would be substantial. Even so, she was shocked when she saw the huge sums that were being passed along. She had thought that Connor was aware of the magnitude of these transfers, but now she began to wonder. Did he know that there were millions stashed away in the offshore bank? Had his partners in crime at Monmouth fed him false information, in addition to the phony reports they were sending out to their investors?

Lisa had been quiet so far. Now she spoke up. "We can't solve the problem tonight, but we can certainly give you a break from your troubles."

"What do you have in mind?" he asked.

"A good night's sleep, then a good breakfast in the morning. That's just to start with," she said.

"I've had trouble sleeping lately," he said.

"Not tonight, you won't." Lisa winked at Sharon who ran her fingertip across his abdomen, stopping at his semi-erect penis. She slid her palm beneath it and caressed its soft underside. In no time at all he was fully erect and open for business.

Sharon wasted no time as she threw her leg across him and guided his shaft between her legs. "It's been awhile," she said as she began a gentle rocking motion.

Connor drew Lisa to him and began kissing her. From Sharon's vantage point it appeared they were going at it like a pair of high school kids in a back seat. Yeah, her guy would sleep well tonight, for sure.

It didn't take long. Connor, who she knew could sustain an erection almost indefinitely, swelled inside her, and his forceful ejaculation sent little shock waves through her body. His forearm muscles tensed as he remained locked onto Lisa. And then it was just a matter of tucking him in for the night.

Sharon and Lisa sat at the small kitchen table where Lisa poured two glasses of scotch. "It hasn't been very long since we were right here drinking scotch," Sharon said.

Lisa clinked her glass against Sharon's. "Between the two of us I think we did him in."

"Yeah, you two seemed to be enjoying yourselves. For a girl who claims to be gay, you were hot and heavy into some good old heterosexual kissing."

"Sometimes I wonder about myself," Lisa said.

"Have you tried it the other way?" Sharon asked.

"Not for a long time." She swirled her scotch and stared into the bottom of the glass. "I had a bad experience when I was twelve. Over the course of a whole summer, my two cousins took turns at me. After that I swore nobody would ever shove a dick in me again."

"Bastards," Sharon said. She thought about sharing her own experience with Lisa, but there seemed no point in doing it. Dragging up old demons just made things worse, often as not.

"So, I don't know for sure that I'm really gay so much as just afraid. But I do love getting it on with you. Speaking of which, should we put on some clothes?"

"Not yet, I like looking at you. Connor was right, you are beautiful. You know, there are toys you can use, just to see if you like it. Have you ever tried one?"

A nervous laugh. "I could try, I guess." Lisa looked dubious. "But I have no idea where to get one of those things."

"I know where. Next time I come over I'll bring a couple, and you can try them out."

"Not too big though, huh? It's been a long time since anything bigger than a couple of fingers has been in there."

"I think we can do better than fingers. I know we can." She pushed her glass around with her forefinger.

"A little more?" Lisa held up the bottle.

"Just a bit." After Lisa had topped off her glass Sharon said, "Any thoughts on what Monmouth is doing to our guy?"

"I'm not over there as much as I'd like. Mr. Shaw has me spend most of my time here. And I don't think they trust me since I work strictly for him. Whenever I enter a room conversations stop. A couple of times Mr. Shaw asked me to sit in on meetings while he was away, but the others asked me to leave."

"Why are they being such pricks?" Sharon said.

"From what little I know these things can only end up in a few ways. If the investors want to start taking their money out, and discover that most of it has disappeared, the whole thing crashes. Law enforcement comes in and a lot of people can wind up in jail.

"There's another scenario where a few of the inside people take the money and run. The folks they leave behind are left holding the bag, and that bag will be empty."

"What are you thinking?" Sharon asked.

"This is only a guess, but I wonder if a few of the Monmouth executives might be planning to scoop up the money in the Grand Caymans and head for the hills."

"Leaving Connor with his dick in his hand and nothing else."

"That's one way of putting it."

****

Her first threesome. Not bad at all. A guy who could play her body like a well-tuned instrument, with a range of tempo and pitch she would never have thought possible, and a woman who could, with a slight variation in equipment, do much the same thing.

But her little triangle was not without risk. Connor stood to lose and lose big if Lisa's assessment of his partners at Monmouth was correct. And Lisa would be cut loose if the money pit dried up, as would Sharon herself.

So her problem was pretty straightforward; how could she protect her friends and herself if the good ship Monmouth went down?

****

After her Wednesday morning accounting class, Sharon took her coffee to a bench beneath an oak tree. She spread out the contents of her book bag over the bench to discourage anyone who might decide to join her. This was her private time, and company was not welcome.

But the tall slender woman with close-cropped black hair was not deterred. She sat on the last available space, crossed her legs and leaned back as if she intended to stay a while. All this on the one bench that Sharon had come to regard as her own personal property.

"Nice day," the woman said.

Sharon didn't respond. Maybe this interloper would take the hint and leave.

"It's Sharon, right?" The woman turned her head slightly toward Sharon, but did not change her position at all.

"Huh?"

"Your name, Sharon Saluda, right?"

When Sharon didn't respond the woman laid a small leather case between them and opened it. The visible contents included a gold shield identifying her as a detective, and a photo ID. The detective had a name, Diane Merkel.

Sharon gathered up her books and stuffed them into her book bag.

"Wouldn't try running off if I was you," Merkel said. "See the guy over there reading a newspaper?

He's with me, and I'm pretty fast myself. So, I thought we could talk a bit, just you and me, without having to get all physical."

"What do you want?" Sharon clutched her book bag close to her chest.

"I'll cut through the preliminaries. We know all about your arrangement with Connor Shaw, and just so you know, we have enough to arrest you as a common prostitute.

"But we know from past experience that taking one hooker off the streets doesn't accomplish much. Before we get one booked, there are two more ready to fill her spot. Of course, how the university might regard one of their students moonlighting as a whore is something else you'll have to consider."

Sharon knew what was coming next and knew as well the less she said, the better, without appearing to be intentionally difficult.

"We're interested in something bigger than rounding up a few hookers, and you know what I'm talking about…Monmouth Enterprises."

"Mr. Shaw works for Monmouth. He told me that, and that's all I know."

"You must know some other people there. You've been seeing Connor Shaw for what, a couple of months now?"

"He never talks about business."

"You just fuck and leave, huh?"

Sharon said nothing. The bitch was trying to get a rise out of her.

"Let's talk about the little beach trip you took a few weeks back. I know what your primary purpose was there, but you must have talked to some of the men."

Sharon shook her head. "No talking."

The detective laughed out loud, drawing glances from students passing by. "Just fucking, no talking. That must have been quite a trip." She shifted so that she was facing Sharon. "Look, you might not be the primary target here, but that doesn't mean you won't get hurt. Your best bet is to cooperate, to help us."

"What do you want me to do?" No way she was going to help this woman, but she was playing for time.

"I want you to wear a wire, see if you can get him to say anything about Monmouth or the people who work there."

This time it was Sharon's turn to laugh.

"What's funny?" the detective asked.

"A wire? Most of the time I'm with him I'm naked. There's no place to hide it."

"Oh, yeah. God, what a life. Okay, but this doesn't end here. Here's my card. I'll be in touch. If you help us, we can help you. Otherwise you're on your own, and pretty girls don't fare too well in prison. You might not have much choice about who you fuck, or how."

Sharon watched the detective walk away. In spite of her casual dress she didn't blend in, not a student, not faculty. She could have been no less conspicuous with COP printed on the back of her jacket. The guy standing beside the tree followed her out. He didn't blend in either.

In their short conversation, the detective hadn't mentioned the Faculty Club. Had it slipped past her, since she was so focused on Monmouth and the big money? This had been, after all, Sharon's greatest fear, that the long arm of the law would come crashing down on her illegitimate enterprise, but apparently that had escaped notice. So much the better.

It took some time for her breathing to return to normal, for her hands to stop shaking. After her talk with Lisa, she'd realized that she must do something or Connor could go right down the criminal drain, emerging many years later as an impoverished old man, the prime years of his life spent behind bars. There had been no sense of urgency in that discussion; now there was. And if Detective Merkel was on the level, Sharon had her own ass to cover as well.

The cops wouldn't wait long. If they were asking her to eavesdrop on Connor's conversation they would be asking others as well. They would probe and probe until they had a soft spot. Then, in all likelihood, it would be too late. Connor would be working away in an almost empty building, while his former partners basked on beaches safely out of reach of U.S. law enforcement. The cops would make an example of him, make him pay for everyone.

She called Lisa's private number from a pay phone.

"Sure, come on over about six. I'll fix dinner for us. You like Italian?" Lisa asked.

"Yeah."

"Good, because I fix a mean lasagna. You want me to send Clark over to get you?"

"Could you, please? I know it sounds stupid, but I'm still not sure how to find your place. Clark takes a different route every time."

****

The aroma of garlic enveloped Sharon as she made her way toward Lisa's kitchen.

"I can't cook this when Mr. Shaw is around. He

hates the smell of garlic." Lisa poured wine for both of them.

Sharon told her about the visit from the detective. "I don't know how long they've been snooping around, or who they might have been talking to in the first place. Nobody at the Faculty Club knows anything about Monmouth, and I don't think the detective knows about the Faculty Club, so those two are completely separate, so far as I know."

"I remember an assistant at Monmouth they fired about six months back. She was embezzling funds. She got a couple of years in jail and a big fine."

"So she might have been pissed off enough to rat on the company," Sharon said.

"Must have been her. I can't think of anybody else."

"It seems like they're still putting their case together if they're trying to intimidate me. Otherwise they could just swoop in and grab everybody in sight."

"Help me set the table. We can talk while we eat."

As serious as their topic for discussion was, the lasagna won out, and for most of the meal there was eating but little talking.

"This is delicious," Sharon said when she came up for air.

"There's lots more," Lisa said.

"Not for me. Here, I'll help you clean up."

Later they continued their discussion over coffee.

"Could be," Sharon said, "That the best move would be to take off before the other guys at Monmouth do. You know, take the money and run."

"The problem with that is Mr. Shaw. He would never go for it. He would never shaft his partners like that, even though they might very well stick it to him."

"Well, there's a pot full of money sitting out there in the Grand Caymans, and somebody's going to take it. Might as well be us," Sharon said. "We could at least keep it away from the cops, and it will be there for Connor when he needs it."

"That's the reason they cooked up the laundering scheme in the first place. The trouble is, even if you have the money stashed away you can never bring it back into the country. There's close to fifteen million in that account, and that much money gets a lot of attention," Lisa said.

"What if we didn't bring it back? What if we just moved it to an account somewhere else, like one of those secret Swiss bank accounts you mentioned? But I don't know how that works or how to do the transfer." They were talking about shifting millions around like it was play money in a Monopoly game. And the idea of a Swiss bank account had just popped into her head moments before. This was crazy stuff, absolutely crazy. She was in way over her head, but her alternatives were limited.

"I might be able to work that out through the office, or at least get it started. You can finish it up with your own computer. If you pull this off, you'll be a very wealthy lady."

"But that's not the point," Sharon said. "The idea is to save Connor, if we can. I know we won't be able to get him off clean, but if they can't find the money the cops can't prove very much, can they?"

"If he has a good lawyer, he might get off with a shorter sentence," Lisa said. "Or if he's lucky, maybe he can stay out of jail altogether."

"And we can be his safety net when he gets out. You are okay with this, aren't you?"

"Yes. I wish things could go on as they are now, but I know that's not going to happen. I'm thinking too, that if we do this, put all the money in a Swiss account, we'd better be prepared to leave town fast, at least you should. All hell is going to break loose when we pull the plug. This whole investment pyramid is going to crash like a ton of bricks."

"My only question is whether we should inform Mr. Shaw, let him make his own decisions."

"You said yourself he would never go for a deal like this, and for all the wrong reasons."

"I guess I'd better see about opening a new bank account for you. I'll need a little information from you, and I should have an account number by Thursday. You'll be the only one who knows the magic number. The next step will be the big switch."

Chapter Seventeen

Sharon spent the next two days covering her tracks. She couldn't risk just leaving town; she would have to leave the country. This would have to be a quick move, the quicker the better. If Detective Merkel got wind of it she'd be toast.

She met with Gloria on Wednesday morning.

"I just heard about some big changes in the works," Sharon said. "The money supply is probably going to dry up. Might be safer to withdraw the money you have in that offshore account and deposit it in a U.S. bank."

"I was thinking about doing that anyway," Gloria said. She flashed her engagement ring in Sharon's face.

"Holy cow, what's this?"

"Yeah, we're going to do it. I planned to use that money as down payment on a house."

Gloria, it appeared, was taking care of herself quite nicely. No worry there. That left the Faculty Club and its girls to consider. From her conversation with the detective, law enforcement wasn't even aware of the illicit activities going on there. If they had known, surely they would have used that information to intimidate her.

As it was, the detective seemed well informed of the sex-for-money deal Sharon had with Connor Shaw, but not about the nightly exchanges at the Faculty Club. She would let the Club make its own way. She had built in all the safeguards she could think of, so maybe they would emerge unscathed from the crisis that she was about to unleash.

Lisa called her Wednesday afternoon. A bank of dark gray clouds that hung in the west that morning had, by now, crept forward and taken over every patch of blue sky, not so very different from the dark clouds that were creeping into her own life.

"What's up, Lisa?"

"I have something for you. We'd best get together so I can explain it."

That something was Sharon's own new Swiss bank account.

"It's simpler than I thought," Lisa said. "Once you have the account number you can transfer everything electronically."

Simplicity didn't make it any easier, though. If and when she pushed the right series of buttons, the repercussions would spread outward like a great wave, washing right up to the doors of Monmouth Enterprises.

"What if I make just a small transfer first, see if it works," Sharon said.

"There is a minimum transaction," Lisa said.

"Okay, then, I'll start with one million dollars." She gasped when she said it, as casually as if she'd been discussing a car payment. "As big as the account is in the Grand Caymans, this much won't be noticed."

She made the necessary contacts with the offshore bank authorizing transfer of funds to her new account number. "Do you think it worked?" she asked.

"Let's wait a few minutes to check," Lisa said. "I might have to break out a bottle of bubbly to toast your success."

"It's really our success," Sharon said.

Well into her second glass, the champagne did what champagne always did with Sharon. Everything she did, said or heard became extremely funny. Lisa's reaction was a bit more subdued, but she joined in the fun as well, laughing right along.

"We just moved a million dollars." Sharon giggled like she'd never stop. "Or at least I think we did."

"Maybe we should wait until tomorrow before we push any more buttons," Lisa said. "Neither of us is in condition to do something like that just now."

Sure, part of it was the champagne, but a lot of it had to do with a sudden release of the tension both had been holding in for several days. Nothing either of them had ever done or would ever do again would have such profound consequences for as many people as the course that lay before them.

"And I think you should stay with me tonight," Lisa said.

Sharon agreed. Neither of them got much sleep, but that was part of the plan. When she woke the next morning Lisa was gone. She'd left coffee for Sharon, so after her morning cup of fortification, Sharon went back to her apartment to finish off her preparations.

She wished she had more time to think things over, but a call from Lisa forced her hand.

"I think they're getting ready to do something," Lisa said.

"Who?"

"The guys here at the office. They've been in the boardroom all morning with the door closed. Even their executive secretary has been banned."

"Where is Connor?"

"Mr. Shaw is out of town. He'll never know what hit him. You have to act, now. Do you have a plan?"

"Yeah, like, get the hell out of town," Sharon said.

"Where will you go?"

"Antigua."

"Why Antigua? Have you been there before?"

"No, but then I've never been anywhere before. My second cousin went there on her honeymoon. She raved about the place. So, it's Antigua, unless you know of a better place."

"Actually, that's a great choice, so long as you leave soon."

So she did. Moving a million dollars around had scared the hell out of her. Redirecting fifteen million and change left her catatonic. Her fingers and toes went numb. She had to remind herself to breathe. Now all she had to do was await confirmation of the transfer to her new account.

In the meantime, she finished her preparation for a quick exit. She had sold her car the week before. She would leave most of her clothing behind. Where she was headed, the island of Antigua, she would have no use for boots and winter jackets. She packed her jewelry away in a shiny aluminum case, burgundy colored, and only death could cause her to release her grip.

Clark would pick her up for a last ride to the airfield. She wasn't sure what angle Lisa had used to get him to agree with this, because most of his marching orders came straight from Connor Shaw. With Lisa's help, she had chartered a private Cessna for the trip to Antigua. She had enough cash in hand to see her through several weeks if she was careful with her spending. And if she wasn't, she had a new Swiss bank account, all her own.

She placed one of her bags by the door. Then she looked around the room, so many things she was seeing for the last time. She had barely gotten over the shock of being homeless; now she would be without a country as well. Would she truly be able to give up all this, just walk away, or would she be tempted to sneak back into the country from time to time?

No, she mustn't entertain such thoughts. When she left it had to be a permanent solution. No doubt, a number of people would want to know her whereabouts and whether her disappearance had anything to do with the missing millions. She had chosen her destination carefully so as to minimize the risk of extradition to the U.S. No reason to make things easy for them by coming back of her own accord.

The knock on the door she assumed was Clark, which was why she opened up without first checking to see who it was.

"Hello, Sharon. Remember me? Mind if I come in for a couple of minutes?" The detective looked at her from behind dark glasses.

Sharon opened the door farther to let the detective in.

"Surprised to see me?" Detective Merkel asked. "I was hoping you'd call, but since you didn't, I thought I'd pay you a visit." She looked back at Sharon's bag sitting by the door. "Going someplace?"

"A friend is sick, cancer. I'm going to stay with her for a while, help out with the kids."

"That's good of you. Where does this friend live?"

"Back in my hometown, Jacob's Bluff. It's not far,

about a forty-minute drive."

"The folks back in Jacob's Bluff, do they know how you make your living?"

"No."

"Anything new over at Monmouth that you want to tell me about?"

"I told you before, I see Connor Shaw, but I don't know anything about what goes on at Monmouth," Sharon said.

"Too bad, we could be a big help to one another if you were more cooperative. And someday you'll need a friend, remember that."

The detective let herself out, leaving Sharon standing in the middle of the room. Any questions she had about leaving were resolved immediately. By the time Clark pulled the Town Car out front, she had all three of her bags by the door.

She hadn't seen Connor in five days, and now it might be years before she saw him again. She had no chance to plead her case, to tell him why she had to do what she'd done. Her only hope was that Lisa could convince him that this grand theft had been pulled off with his best interests at heart.

Clark drove her to the same airfield where she had boarded private jets with Connor before. Now a twin-engine Cessna awaited her and all her worldly belongings.

"Maybe I'll see you again sometime," she said to Clark as he loaded her bags onto the plane.

"Maybe." He looked as if he wanted to say more, but whatever it was he finally kept it to himself. Why wasn't she surprised?

A few minutes later she was airborne, and a new

life lay ahead of her. All that she had known before was disappearing beneath her. She would have to create a new identity for herself. Sharon Saluda, student, manager of a whorehouse, wouldn't fit anymore. But she could play it however she wished. Time and money, those two precious commodities, were hers in abundance.

****

Airsickness was the worst. The Cessna flew through two thunderstorms, buffeted by updrafts in between. If she ever left the island, it would be by boat. She almost kissed the ground when she crawled off the plane.

She found a cart and wheeled her bags into the terminal, large for such a small island. Inside was a Tower of Babel. She'd never heard so many different languages spoken at one time, but then her experience with international travel ranked somewhere between slim and none. The information desk was in the hands of a petite, dark-skinned beauty with shoulder-length jet-black hair. She looked Sharon up and down as if she were ready to provide more than just information.

Another time Sharon might have tuned into this apparent invitation and tried to set up a rendezvous, but the episode of vomiting she'd undergone in flight pushed sex way down on her priority list. At this moment, a hot bath and a nice long nap filled the first two spots, then, maybe a walk on the wild side, but not just yet.

"Welcome to Antigua. How can I help you?" The beauty's smile radiated heat.

"Everything," Sharon said. She didn't mean everything, not yet, but it just popped out.

The beauty's smile turned up a notch. "There's lots to do here. What kind of things are you interested in?"

"Lots of sun, lying on the beach, nothing too ambitious." She tried to make her plans sound casual, not like she was running for her life after she'd just absconded with millions.

"No problem there." The beauty spread a map out on the counter. "All of these beaches are lovely. You can't miss with any of them. If you want to get more active, there's snorkeling, sailing, scuba diving, all within easy reach. It's a small island, fourteen miles long by eleven miles wide, so you're never far from anything." She pushed a small stack of brochures across to Sharon.

Almost as an afterthought Sharon asked about real estate.

"Oh, that's great. You might be staying with us long term." The beauty seemed to find this possibility exciting. So did Sharon.

She got information about the best hotel on the island, and the name of a real estate outfit. The beauty at the desk gave her a map and circled an area on the northern tip of the island. "This is the best place to live. It's called Bougainvillea, just like the flower."

"Where do you live?" Sharon asked.

The beauty tapped the point of her pen in the center of the circle she'd drawn and smiled. "My name is Angela."

"Then we might be neighbors," Sharon said. "Are you here every day?"

"Yes, and here is my phone number in case you have any questions." She sealed the deal with a wink and a smile that left open every possibility.

The exchange of information and brochures had included a lot of touching, arms, hands, and everywhere that Angela's fingertips made contact left a tingling in Sharon's skin. As soon as she recovered from her flight, Angela would get another visit, and they would probably exchange much more than information.

The oceanfront hotel, an adult only lodging, "In case you don't like a lot of kids running around," was a welcome sight. The entire ocean-side was glass, giving a stunning view of blue water, interrupted only by a pool complex that would be her first destination. Quiet efficiency seemed the order of the day, from the young man who took care of her bags to another smiling, dark-skinned beauty behind the desk. God, did they clone them down here? Everything moved in an orderly fashion. Yes, she might stay here for a while.

Her second floor room featured a small balcony that looked out over the pool area. "Well, you're not in Kansas anymore," she said as she watched the little parade of skimpy bikinis, several thongs, around the pool, a long oval structure with an abundance of shaded sitting areas. No complete nudity, but about as close as they could get and still claim to be legally dressed. So long as the ladies' three magical areas remained covered, even just barely, everything else was on display. She almost wished she'd brought that suit she'd worn at Connor's beach trip. She would fit right in.

She had picked Friday as her escape date, holding onto hope that her thievery at Monmouth wouldn't be discovered until the following Monday. She promised to call Lisa from a pay phone for an update.

"You won't believe it," Lisa said. "Your timing

was perfect. If you had waited one more day, the rats would have left town with all the money."

"Wow, so they left today too," Sharon said.

"Yes, but I don't think they know yet that the golden egg they expect to find in the Grand Caymans isn't there anymore."

"They are going to be so pissed off. Are you going to be safe?"

"I'm going back to Mr. Shaw's house now, and I'll have Clark to protect me."

"So Connor doesn't know yet either."

"I don't think so. I don't know how I'm going to keep a straight face when I see him. Maybe I should just come clean, tell him everything. I mean, the deed is done now. He can't stop it even if he wants to."

"Maybe not," Sharon said. "Better let this play out on its own. He'll find out soon enough that the others have taken off and left him behind. This way he'll be angry with his partners instead of us."

"Okay, how's your hotel?" Lisa asked.

"Delicious. When can you come for a visit? I miss you."

"I'd love to right now, but I'm plenty busy around here. The worst is yet to come. I'll keep you posted."

Alone in a new country, for the first time ever Sharon found herself without attachments of any sort. She had no family ties left, no educational commitments, and her home town was off-limits permanently. Lisa and Connor were out of sight, if not out of her mind for the time being.

Since her own disappearance coincided with the disappearance of a huge sum of cash from the company account in the Grand Caymans, someone at Monmouth would, without doubt, put the two together immediately. She had done just what the Monmouth crew was planning to do, only she'd done it first. She could only imagine how angry they would be when they discovered that the pot of gold in the Caymans was empty. And it wouldn't be long before Detective Merkel and her associates figured things out, if they hadn't already. But if local law enforcement wanted her, they'd have to come and get her.

Connor remained a huge question mark. In spite of her good intentions he could wind up hating her. Her actions had brought down his little empire. Sure, his house of cards was going to collapse one way or the other, but now he could lay the blame at her feet. In which case resurrecting their relationship might be impossible.

For the time being she would have to depend on Lisa to be her eyes and ears. Sharon knew that her friend would not be able to keep the truth from Connor very long. And when he found out, which he surely would, she could only guess what his reaction might be.

She looked out once again at the pool. The clear blue water looked ever so cool and inviting, and tucking into one of the many poolside lounge chairs with the late afternoon sun caressing her skin seemed just the thing to push aside some of the anxiety that kept her insides churning. She dug out her own swimwear, a white bikini that, while a bit more conservative than the outfits some of the women wore, still showed enough of her assets to turn heads. Not that she was trying to attract attention, but old habits die hard. She put it on, then did a few turns in front of the mirror. "Yeah, that should do it," she said.

The sun and the gentle onshore breeze worked their magic, and soon she was in a better place.

"Can I bring you something to drink?"

The voice seemed to come from far away, and Sharon had to climb out of her state of deep relaxation before she could focus properly.

"Sorry, I didn't mean to wake you."

Another swarthy young man, another radiant smile. "Our barman makes a wonderful rum punch."

"That sounds good," she said. As he scurried off, she sat up and looked around her. She'd never realized how very fair her own skin was until she checked out the deeply tanned specimens that strolled around her.

As if he'd read her mind, when her waiter returned with her rum punch, he'd added a bottle of sunscreen. "You might need this," he said. "Even in the afternoon, the sun is still strong."

At the moment, she was feeling quite good about her choice of hideouts. She would, however, have to invest in more beachwear, because it looked as if she would be spending a lot of time in a bikini.

On Monday, at their arranged time, Sharon called Lisa using a prepaid phone she'd purchased at the airport. "Where are you?" she asked.

"I'm at the house. Mr. Shaw told me to stay away from the office. I know he's trying to protect me."

"So you don't know what's going on."

"No. The thing that really scares me, he took Clark in with him this morning, like he was expecting trouble."

"How did he seem when you talked to him? You did talk to him, didn't you?"

"It wasn't so much what he said, just the way he

looked at me, like he knew everything we'd done."

Sharon struggled with her breathing. "We did the right thing, remember that."

"Easy for you to say, but I'm scared, Sharon, really scared."

"You want to come down here, stay with me?" The more she considered it, the more Sharon liked the idea.

"No, he needs me. I have to be here for him."

Sharon could only imagine the chaos that swirled around Monmouth Enterprises with Connor Shaw at its center. For sure Lisa would help all she could, but with the amount of money at stake things were apt to get brutal. And if he needed heavy artillery, there was always Clark.

Tuesday morning, clear and bright, as was every morning since she'd arrived, she took a private charter boat trip around the island. She slathered on sunscreen before boarding the van that took her to the marina, and covered up her bathing suit with a flimsy top. To that she had added a broad-brimmed hat.

Her tour boat, an open cockpit inboard, was driven by a young woman about Sharon's age. "Hi, I'm Janey," she said. "I guess you were expecting a guy. People are always surprised when I turn up, but I've done this hundreds of times, so don't worry. I won't get lost."

"I'm Sharon. No worry at all. It will be nice to have another female to talk to."

"My husband and I split up two years ago. He went back to the 'States, and left me the boat, and not much else. Are you married?"

"No. So, you're like a permanent resident now?"

"Yeah, love it here. We're on the eastern side of

the island. I usually head south from here, go into a few of the bays, check out the sights. I like to stop for lunch around a place called Nelson's Dockyard, if that's okay with you."

"Sounds good," Sharon said, "so long as I'm not seasick."

"No problem, I go slow."

Each beach seemed lovelier than the last, and each of the bays was full of yachts, lavish floating palaces of the type that Connor and his friends would have. True to her word, Janey puttered along at a very leisurely pace. She dodged a few jet skis, but otherwise the trip was pleasantly uneventful. "Nelson's Dockyard," she said after an hour or so. She pulled alongside a wooden dock below several stone monuments.

"So, who was Nelson?" Sharon asked.

"I don't know, some British navy guy, I think. I'm not really into history stuff."

She had a delicious shrimp cocktail for lunch, along with another tumbler of rum punch. "I could get to like this drink," she said.

Just past two o'clock Janet pulled back into the marina. "Be careful of your skin," she said. "You're fair, like me, and it's real easy to burn."

Janey gave her a hug when they parted company. "If you ever want to get together, let me know. There are lots of places here where you can have a good time, and I've been to most of them."

Sharon thanked her, tipped her rather lavishly, and took the van back to her hotel. It was so easy, too easy, to forget the turmoil she'd left behind, but this was probably the reason most people came to Antigua, to get away from it all, if only for a while.

Tuesday afternoon she called Lisa again. Her friend mumbled her words like someone who was sleep-deprived. "It's started now, all the investors want their money, but there's no money to give them. Your name came up. They wanted the financial records from that little house you managed, the Faculty Club."

"They won't find anything," Sharon said. "I shredded everything before I left." But how had they found out about the Faculty Club? Only Connor had that information. Surely he wouldn't have given her up.

"The way they're going at one another, I'm afraid things might turn violent. I'm glad Clark's around, just in case."

The run, that's what they all feared, that day when an investor tried to withdraw his funds but could not because there were no funds left to withdraw. And in the time it took for that enraged investor to dial up his lawyer, everybody knew. It would begin to resemble one of the old-fashioned bank failures, depositors lined up in the streets, pounding on doors, demanding their money.

But the Monmouth depositors didn't take to the streets and didn't pound on doors. They had squads of attorneys to handle that chore, and by the end of the day, they had Monmouth sewn up so tight that not even a paper clip could be taken off the premises.

Chapter Eighteen

Having grown up inland, water sports, snorkeling in particular, was never a focal point of Sharon's life, but the brochures about island activities she accumulated made it sound easy, even for poor swimmers, and a great opportunity to see a part of the world she'd never even glimpsed. So, she signed up for Wednesday morning. Since this should involve real activity, she opted for a swimsuit slightly more substantial than her bikinis, which provided minimal coverage dry and might desert her entirely underwater.

The hotel van took her to a harbor where she boarded the dive boat. The other participants, three couples, left Sharon as the odd woman out, not exactly an enviable situation owing to the looks she got from the other females in the group. Apparently they each regarded her as a threat, but looking over the less-than-optimal males they accompanied, they had nothing to fear. None of them were even close to Connor Shaw standards, but then, few men were.

Properly outfitted with her swim mask, snorkel, and long fins on her feet, she plunged overboard. So this was what she'd been missing, easy as pie so far, just like they told her.

The views were everything the dive group promised and more. They passed over several old shipwrecks, which she found less interesting, but the fishery was fabulous. She'd never dreamed they came in so many colors, so many patterns, solitary fish, fish in groups, every imaginable combination. The dive master made them aware of the occasional visiting shark, but when the first one cruised by her heart raced. For a moment, she froze, unable to move, but neither the first shark nor those that followed showed even a passing interest in any of the swimmers.

After an hour or so, the dive master herded them all back into the boat. An exhilarated Sharon promised herself another session. Maybe she would even try a real dive, one with oxygen tanks, the whole bit.

****

She called Lisa most evenings. The events at Monmouth had made national news, so she could get some details from the newspapers and evening TV.

Some of the background information was new to her, how Monmouth had been in Connor's family for two generations. She understood now his anguish over seeing a long-standing family business die on his watch. That fact raised the same old questions, had she done the right thing when she pulled the plug that got Monmouth circling the drain? Might not Connor with his energy and personal magnetism be able to right the ship so that it survived in name, at least?

From Lisa's reports, he was putting forth an extraordinary effort to salvage what could be saved, but without funds his options were limited.

"I could just cry," Lisa said. "Except for Mr. Shaw it's like every man for himself. I mean, they're all blaming him for what's happened, and he's accepting full responsibility. That's not fair. I know he's made some mistakes, but all the shenanigans with the money, that was his partners."

Sharon let her friend ventilate. Each time was a variation on the same theme, how unfair it was and how Connor was being such a saint, protecting everyone else while the noose tightened around his own neck. Was it just loyalty that forced him to stand up and take the hit? Was there something else?

"What if I give it back?" Sharon said. "I took the money to try and save him. I can give it all back for the same reason. It was never really mine to begin with."

"I don't think so. I considered that too, but I think it would make him look even more guilty. I mean, you were his girl."

"I was his whore. I'll say it if you won't."

"That's not what I meant. If you return the money now it will look like he planned the whole thing. His partners would walk away clean, and he would go away for a long time."

****

Time on her hands, time and money, a risky combination for an attractive young stunner like Sharon. How long would she be alone? She really had no idea. So much depended on Connor's fate. If he got a short sentence, she could ride it out, find ways to amuse herself until he was free. When things got sorted out at Monmouth, Lisa would probably join her, and Sharon counted on taking up where they'd left off before…in bed. But for all her skill, Lisa could not provide what Connor gave her, that rhythmic thrust building in vigor and tempo until the explosion inside that left her limp, mewing like a hungry kitten.

Now she would have to make new arrangements for herself. Whether Lisa or Connor or both of them were part of her new life remained to be seen. All she could do at the moment was to monitor the situation she'd left behind through Lisa.

"Nothing new to report," Lisa said. "They have an army of accountants going over the books trying to follow the money trail. And there's a Detective Merkel, I think it is, asking about you. She knows you've left town, but that's about all."

"How are you holding up?" Sharon asked.

"Okay, with the help of my vodka bottle. I think about you a lot, lying out there in the sun, not a care in the world."

"It's not like that, Lisa. I'm just as worried as you are. In some ways, being out of town makes it even harder. I can't do anything to help out." Well, not entirely true, since she did spend a lot of time doing just what Lisa said, lying in the sun. So much so that when she stripped off her bikini the small regions of coverage stood out in sharp white contrast to the rest of her tanned body.

But that wasn't the whole story, was it? She began to think of the contents of the Swiss account, some of it, at least, as her own. She was, in her fantasies, rich, filthy rich. No, the money wasn't exactly free and clear. She designated some of it to provide a golden parachute for Connor when he emerged from his current trials. And Lisa might lay claim on some of it too.

For now, control of that fortune was in her own hands, and she found the thought a bit overwhelming. Now she commanded a sum so staggering that even considering it left her dizzy.

Connor, on the other hand, had seemed to treat wealth like a comfortable old shoe, smooth and easy, without a hitch. The type of attitude you could manage if you'd come from money. Perhaps in time she could attain a similar level of comfort with extreme wealth, but it would require a lot of practice.

****

At the end of her first week in Antigua, the first clouds since she'd been there rolled in leaving an overcast sky, but little threat of rain. She took a taxi to the capital city of St. John and walked about enjoying the little shops and sights. After lunch in an open-air café, she began to formalize plans she'd been considering the past few days, plans for a lengthy stay.

The island provided the usual institutions to service its more or less permanent residents. It had a post office, a small brick affair with two windows for customers, both run by a single attendant. The island bank, First Union, was a bit more substantial, also brick but with four customer windows.

The air inside the bank smelled of bananas slightly past their prime, but the tellers were prompt and efficient. Sharon inquired about opening an account and was directed to the desk of a swarthy young man with oiled hair. He looked to be about her age.

"I am Mr. Suarez. How can I be of assistance?"

"I'd like to open an account here, but I don't yet have a permanent address," she said.

"That will not be a problem. A number of our long-term customers are transient, seasonal, actually." He gave her a clipboard with an application attached. He also gave her his own pen, warm from being carried in his breast pocket, and offered the use of his own desk.

A bit later Sharon left in possession of a new account including a checkbook. Her permanent checks, he assured her, would be available in a week. Her next task for the day, already past noon and steaming, was to make plans for a more sustainable abode than her current hotel accommodations. As comfortable and convenient as her room was, she already found it too confining. She wanted a place with a view of the ocean, and with her financial resources that wasn't at all farfetched.

"Real estate? Then you'll be leaving us soon, Ms. Saluda?" The hotel concierge asked when Sharon inquired about agencies.

"I just want to look around a bit, see what's available," Sharon said.

"Interested in any one particular area?"

"I hear the southwest part of the island is nice. An area called Bougainvillea."

"Yes, indeed, it's lovely there. Quiet, the beach is pristine. There's an agency, Island Realty that handles a lot of properties there. I have their phone number right here."

Sharon made an appointment with an agent, Louise Beeson—the name didn't sound local and neither did the accent—for an afternoon tour. Promptly at two o'clock, a dark blue Ford Focus with Island Realty in white letters on the front doors, pulled into the parking circle in front of the hotel.

A bleached blonde with lipstick on her teeth extended her hand. "Ms. Saluda? I'm Louise Beeson."

"North Carolina, right?" Sharon said.

"Right you are. Oh, God, is it that obvious?"

"Only because I'm from western North Carolina," Sharon said. "I've heard it before, lots of times."

"What an amazing coincidence," Louise said. "But

you don't have much of an accent yourself. What brings you to this part of the world?"

"My mother's sister died and left most of her estate to me. And I was just getting over a bad breakup, so this seemed like a great opportunity to turn my life around."

"You couldn't have picked a better location," Louise said. They drove around for about fifteen minutes, never exceeding thirty miles an hour, the speed limit for the entire island, as Sharon kept reminding herself. Louise stopped at a pinnacle overlooking a wide span of beach. Two multicolored umbrellas were stuck in the sand, but otherwise the beach appeared deserted.

"But there's no one around," Sharon said.

"That's the beauty of this area," Louise said. "It's about as private as you can get."

The drop down to the beach was sheer at first, then leveled off into a gentler slope. Louise pointed out rooflines in the foliage that Sharon hadn't noticed before.

"Even the waterfront homes are tucked back into the trees, so you don't see them at first. Of course, they're more pricey."

"Are there any for sale?"

"A couple, yes, but like I say, they're pricey. Unless, of course, your aunt left you a great big pot of money." Louise laughed as if she saw the possibility of a fat commission.

"If you don't mind, I'd like to look at some houses," Sharon said. Wasting time dickering about prices with people like Louise was one thing she didn't have to put up with, not anymore.

"Okay, then. I have three properties on the water, and two that are a bit farther up the hill. Even with those, the walk down to the beach is only a few minutes."

Sharon's only yardstick for luxury homes was the time she'd spent in Connor's mansion, and even then her exploration had been far from complete. For now, she would be better off blending into something a bit more modest, rather than standing out as the most expensive home in the area. Besides, she was alone. What the hell would she do with a lot of unused space?

The first house, a mini-hotel with seven bedrooms spread over seven thousand square feet of floor space, she rejected after a cursory inspection. She didn't know enough people to fill up all that space.

The second showing was more like a dollhouse, smaller with gingerbread cutouts above all the windows. Nothing wrong with the size or the floor plan, just a little too cute. She wasn't into cute.

The third house made her jaw drop. It was set farther back up the hill with a sheer drop at the western corner of the lot, ensuring complete privacy on that side. The front of the house reminded her of a smaller version of the beach house Connor had taken her to, along with all the other girls as playmates for his friends. It had three bedrooms, each with its own bathroom, and all the rooms were very spacious. Almost all the area facing the ocean was tinted glass, you could see out, but no one could see in. The furnishings were lean and functional, no unnecessary bulk or clutter. It was made for her.

"How much?" Sharon asked. There was no dickering about the price, in the high six figures, so, as soon as the paperwork was complete, Sharon was ready to move in.

"Quickest sale ever," the real estate agent said. "Easiest too."

Sharon was on a roll. She deposited her belongings in a bedroom of her new abode, admired the stunning view for a moment, then continued shopping. She topped off her spending later that day with a new red Miata convertible. A girl had to have a way to get around, after all.

At day's end she sat on her patio watching a waxing gibbous moon rise over a gentle sea. The only food in her new home was two quarts of dark rum and three bottles of white wine, but that would certainly get her through the night. She raised her glass to the rising moon. Spending money wasn't nearly as difficult as she thought it would be. Maybe she could get used to this after all.

Her last thought as she drifted off to sleep in a spacious round bed that would do nicely for play as well as sleep, was that she had forgotten to call Lisa for an update on happenings at Monmouth. But that could wait until tomorrow.

No goddam coffee, a house with top-of-the-line kitchen appliances but no coffee. Would it have been too much trouble for Island Realty to include a five-dollar bag of coffee in the deal?

She brushed her teeth, ran a brush through her hair and stomped out of the house, barely dressed but with all vital parts covered. She had things to do, a phone call to Lisa among them, but nothing was happening until she had coffee running through her system. At least the Miata had a full tank of gas. She set off in search of a Starbucks or a reasonable facsimile.

She circled around the small shopping area on the northern tip, not far from her house. The shops, while few in number, were decidedly upscale, and one of them featured the large green sign that promised quick relief from her misery. And since her new car had an automatic transmission, she could drink her brew as she drove, taking in the sights along the way.

Next stop, a Whole Foods store diagonally across from Starbucks. Her kitchen and pantry were bare; she needed everything, and that's exactly what she got, everything. She crammed all she could into the Miata's small trunk and wedged the rest into the miniscule backseat.

After she had unloaded and packed away all her purchases, she called Lisa.

"You're in the newspapers," Lisa said. "Second page."

"Oh, great." There were several possible ways that she might become newsworthy, none of them good.

"It's a rather long article. I'll e-mail it all to you, but it says that the higher-ups at Monmouth are pointing the finger at you for bringing down the company. They're accusing you of embezzling company funds. It goes on, nothing good. You can read for yourself."

"I can't say I'm too surprised. When you think about it, that's the logical conclusion. Have you talked with Connor about it?"

"Yes, for a few minutes. He won't say it, but I believe he thinks we made the wrong choice. Anything they pin on you rubs off on him too."

"To begin with, it was my choice, not yours, not

Connor's. So don't get yourself in a jam over this. And anything they want to do to me they'll have to do it by remote control, because I'm not coming back," Sharon said.

"That's what Mr. Shaw advised too, lay low and don't do anything to attract attention. That's very important, he says."

"I hear you." Would a new house and a new red sports car attract attention? Very likely, but she'd made her decision and planned to stay right where she was. "They can't make me come back, can they?"

"Extradite you, you mean. I asked Mr. Shaw about that too. He said it's possible, but he doesn't think it's likely. He says extradition is very complicated and can take a long time. And if the officials where you are now decide not to give you up, they just don't do it."

"Okay," Sharon said. "I still wish you could come here and stay with me. Every time I think about you I get all itchy, and you know exactly what I'm talking about." She didn't tell Lisa about her new purchases. It hardly seemed fair that she was having the time of her life while her friends were left behind to face the music. Whenever she got the chance, she would make it up to them, both of them, preferably at the same time, in the same bed.

"Yeah, me too," Lisa said, her voice husky. "Once we get this mess all cleaned up I'm all yours."

Sharon couldn't recall ever being the subject of a newspaper article, let alone one that filled most of the page. Of course, it wasn't all about her, but there were many, many fingers pointing in her direction.

And you could take your pick about the grievance you wanted to address. She was a thief, an embezzler, a whore in her own right, as well as a madam who ran a house of her own. She came off as the very essence of evil, a girl who would do anything for money. If she wore a scarlet letter for each of her major sins, there would barely be enough space on her clothing for all of them. Of course, with the clothing she usually wore now, there was little enough space to begin with.

Staying under the radar didn't mean she had to go all monastic either, not that she would be able to anyway. She still had needs. Some people dampened their sexual urges by strenuous exercise, but what was the point? Why beat yourself up when there was such a pleasurable alternative to be had? And what better place to look for some action than Angela at the airport?

She spent a lot of time getting ready, all of which might be wasted since she didn't know if Angela was working that day, what time she might get off, or if what she had taken as an invitation was really that. What if Angela was just being friendly, nothing more? Wouldn't she feel foolish then?

But those unanswered questions didn't slow her down. It was fun getting dressed up as if she were going out on a date, which was what she hoped for. Besides that, she'd bought several new outfits and had no intention of leaving them hanging in the closet.

She stood naked in front of her bathroom mirror staring at the three small white triangles that had been covered by her bikini. Some nude sunbathing was in order for sure, and her new house had a private deck that would do nicely.

She applied an odorless deodorant. Then a light application, above and below the waist, of a scent called Musk, which might, from the effect it had when she first sniffed it, have been extracted from the scent glands of a feline in heat.

She snipped the sales tags off a new bra and underpants. When she slipped them on, wispy, light pink, she smiled at her reflection. Anyone who got this far would certainly pause, taken in by the flimsy boundary between near nudity and the real thing. Then they would continue on toward the goal. Stopping to enjoy the view, delicious as it might be, could only last for a moment. Patience and lust were not compatible.

Pink shorts, very short and very snug, a light pink pullover top that stopped several inches above her navel, and she was dressed for business. What kind of business? That would depend on Angela. And yeah, she was far from inconspicuous, but sometimes a girl just had to do what she had to do to get someone's attention.

She had two sheltered parking spaces in the back of her house, so she'd left the top down on the Miata. The day's oppressive heat was just a memory now, so she drove along the narrow two-lane gravel road that meandered, first upward, a rather steep climb for the better part of a mile, then back down again, just as steep. The few houses she saw resembled her own, very large and spacious with a glass front drawing in the ocean view.

The ascent ended up in a level space that sat above all the surrounding area. She pulled the Miata off the road and got out to take in the panorama. A full three hundred and sixty degrees of ocean view lay before her. The view made her gasp. She had seen broad expanses of blue water from the air, but never with her feet on solid ground.

Apparently others enjoyed this promontory as well.

Beer cans, candy wrappers and a few condoms lay scattered about. Her initial surge of anger gave way to speculation; what would it be like to do it up here with the wide world of ocean spread out below and nothing but stars above. She planned to find out at her first opportunity.

The road followed a downward trajectory back toward civilization, and about twenty minutes later to the airport and Angela, if she was lucky.

Sharon pulled her car into the short-term parking lot. She thought about making a quick restroom stop to check things out that might have been mussed in the drive over, hair and such. But the leers she drew from the parking lot attendant to the baggage handlers, to the two pilots, one of whom walked slam into a bench while ogling her, said things must look pretty good.

She saw Angela before Angela saw her. She took a few minutes to spy on the young beauty. Most of the people who approached her desk were men. From the way Angela smiled and shook her head Sharon could easily guess at the kind of questions they were asking her. Shortly she would be asking her the same thing.

How had it happened that she had never before been attracted to a woman? Lisa had been her first girl-on-girl encounter, but as pleasant as that had been and as much as she looked forward to renewing those activities, this raw, visceral feeling she had for Angela was something new. The way her white teeth flashed in the caramel of her skin, all framed in that glossy black halo of hair. So far she'd worn her hair pinned up every time Sharon had seen her, but soon, very soon, Sharon would take out those pins and watch that black mass come tumbling down.

Enough, she couldn't wait any longer. The tingling in her lower half was becoming unbearable. She took a deep breath, squared her shoulders and began the short trek to the desk where Angela sat, pointing out something on a local map to a man who risked dislocation in his cervical spine trying to get a better look down her blouse. Fool, that's what buttons are for.

After the man left, map in one hand, rubbing the back of his neck with the other, Sharon took his place in front of Angela. "Hi, remember me?"

"Sharon, thank goodness, I was about to give up on you."

"It took me a little while to get settled in."

"Are you still at the hotel?" Angela asked.

"No, now I'm a home owner."

"Wow, so fast. You didn't waste any time."

"I figured the quicker I got all of that taken care of, the quicker I could get back to see you."

For a moment, they stood smiling at each other, both on the same wavelength, both thinking the same thing. Sharon slipped her hand across the desk as if pointing at the map. Their fingertips met, and Angela intertwined her fingers with Sharon's.

"What time do you get off work?" Sharon asked.

"Five minutes. Shall we go to my place then?"

"Sounds good, if I can wait that long." She squeezed Angela's hand.

"I am so glad to see you."

"I was watching the guys who came up to your desk. You know, you really should wear something more low cut, so they wouldn't have to go through all those contortions to look down your shirt."

"I know. Isn't it fun? If it weren't for the lechers

I'd be bored out of my mind." She winked at Sharon. "You, on the other hand, won't have any trouble at all. I promise."

"I can hardly wait."

Chapter Nineteen

A short time later, Sharon followed Angela's dark blue Chevy Nova to a small house with a front porch that extended the length of the house. It wasn't half as large as Sharon's own, but it looked far more cozy.

Angela trotted back and gawked at Sharon's red Miata. "Wow, a new house and a new red convertible. You really do move fast."

"Now I'm ready for a bit of fun," Sharon said.

Angela linked arms with her. "Come with me."

Inside was open, airy. The ceiling fans kept the air moving. Sharon spotted a pair of shoes, definitely a man's, and large too, beside the rattan sofa.

"Oh, yeah, those belong to Roger. I should have told you, I have a boyfriend. Sometimes we like to experiment, if you're interested. Otherwise, just you and me."

"Since it's our first time, maybe just the two of us," Sharon said. "Then I'd be happy to participate in your experiments."

Sharon kissed her on the cheek, but that little peck quickly evolved into a mouth-to-mouth, tongue-to-tongue full bore lip-lock that left them both gasping for air.

Angela laughed, a soft musical laugh that sounded like wind chimes in a light breeze. "I haven't even taken my shoes off yet."

"I'll take them off for you."

"How about I get us both a glass of wine." A few moments later Angela brought chilled glasses of white wine with moisture condensing on the outside. She clinked her glass against Sharon's. "Welcome to my home."

"I'm going to have to kiss you again," Sharon said.

Again, the musical laugh. "I'm looking forward to it."

They chatted, sipped wine, kissed, chatted some more. They both knew what was coming, and chatting was simply a way to prolong that delicious state of anticipation. But all chatting ceased when Angela stood and began to unbutton her blouse. "I need to pop into the shower for a moment, get rid of that airport grunge. When you've finished your wine, the bedroom is right through there."

Sharon strolled around the living area, wine glass in hand. Indeed, sitting still was impossible. Her hormones were in overdrive. The prospect of grappling with this dusky beauty with the one-hundred-watt smile had her drooling. She looked for family photos, mementos, anything that might provide information about this girl with whom she would soon be so intimately linked. So far, all she knew was that Angela worked at an information desk at the airport, and she was, as was Sharon herself, bisexual.

The perfect logic in it all, being a switch-hitter, was remarkable. With a few alterations in technique, being able to go both ways practically doubled her sexual opportunities. And she'd just begun to scratch the surface. The very thought that, even six months ago she would have passed up the chance at a bedroom romp with Angela, what a terrible waste.

Not much the wiser about her hostess, Sharon finished her wine in a single gulp, and placed the empty glass on the table by the sofa. She paused at the bedroom doorway, the anticipation, she was practically salivating.

A few moments later Angela walked in wrapped in a white towel. The hot water had added a flush to her dark skin leaving her the color of burnished copper. "Ah, much better," Angela said.

"Oh, yes," Sharon said in a whisper.

"Oh my God, look at you," Angela said, her eyes wide and her lips curved into a wicked grin.

While she waited, Sharon had stripped down to her filmy bra and panties. She thought about taking everything off, but she'd rather let Angela finished the job for her.

Angela dropped her towel on the floor.

"Oh," Sharon said, but the word came out as a gasp. Before her stood a body that could, without too great a stretch of the imagination, start world wars, make time stand still. And in no time at all she would be touching, tasting every inch of it.

"Sweetheart, you are gorgeous," Angela said. She wrapped her arms around Sharon and began kissing her. Her hands crept around Sharon's shoulders and unhooked the clasp on her bra. She dropped slowly to her knees, trailing kisses across Sharon's breasts, her belly.

She slipped down Sharon's panties, so slowly that Sharon began to moan. She ran her fingertips up the backs of her legs and teased them apart. Then her tongue began exploring the soft fleece between

Sharon's legs.

"I'm going to fall," Sharon said. And indeed she would have had Angela not risen and helped her onto the bed.

"I'm glad it's just the two of us," Angela said. She pushed Sharon's shoulders back onto the bed and began again with the kisses, soft little pecks on her forehead, her eyelids, the tip of her nose, her cheeks, then lips. She nibbled and tugged at Sharon's lips, her tongue darting in and out. She only moved when Sharon's moaning went beyond pleasure to something more like a wail, even with Angela's tongue in her mouth. Angela moved on and continued her trek down Sharon's trembling body.

Each of Sharon's breasts received equal attention. While Angela's fingertips were teasing one, her lips were on the other. Then she reversed it. Sharon's nipples were on fire, and Angela wasn't letting up, not even a little bit.

All so reminiscent of the first time Connor had taken her to places she'd never been before. Now Angela had brought her back to the same edge where her control was slipping away, and there was nothing she could do about it, or wanted to.

Angela went on in a southerly direction ending up with her nose buried in Sharon's fleece. She sniffed about, not entirely unlike a dog on a hunt. Sharon remembered the musky scent she had applied to her body, in particular to the area where Angela was inhaling so deeply. She would make a point of keeping a good supply of the fragrance on hand, for special occasions.

Angela parted the lips just below the fleece with

her fingertips, and her tongue darted inside, magical, as if it could see exactly where it wanted to go, what it wanted to touch. Sharon had marveled at the skill with which Connor employed his own tongue, but Angela's talent was beyond compare.

Could there possibly be too much of a good thing? Was there a point at which pleasure became too intense to bear and became more like agony? This thought floated through Sharon's barely conscious brain as she lay, eyes squeezed shut, fists clenched, legs spread, breathing in tiny gasps while Angela's tongue continued its assault down below. One thing was clear, she had to do something before she began babbling and drooling like someone demented.

She slowly rotated her body so that her own face was buried in Angela's thick black mesh. This time she parted those swollen lips and let her own tongue invade. She must have found her mark quickly, because Angela unleashed a moan much louder than any Sharon had uttered. The gush of fluids that followed confirmed that she had hit her target.

How much time? She didn't know, and it didn't matter. What did matter was that her energy reserves were ebbing. She was like a wind-up toy that needed a few fresh turns of the key. She loosened her grip on Angela's buttocks.

Angela laughed softly. "Enough. I can't take any more. You're too much for me."

They pushed up from their upside-down positions, and their faces, wet and gleaming, met in the middle. Angela ran a fingertip along Sharon's slippery cheek, then popped it into her mouth. "Umm," she said. "Tasty."

Wanting more than what she could get on the tip of her finger, Sharon ran her tongue along Angela's cheek then made a circle around her mouth. "You taste good too."

More wine, much more wine. And more loving, much more of that too. Sometime in the wee hours of the morning they lay in each other's arms, satiated and glowing. This was a new place for Sharon, a state of fulfillment where there was no more to give, no more to receive. From the look on Angela's face, eyes closed beneath her long black lashes, lips slightly parted, she must have felt the same.

They had done it all. Every orifice had been invaded and thoroughly explored. Every sensory spot, and some that Sharon hadn't even realized were sensory spots, had been teased and tantalized to the point that more touching felt like an electrode placed on the skin, nipple, genital area. And even while Angela sucked and nibbled on her clitoris, two voices rose in Sharon, one asking for more of the same, and the other begging for a reprieve.

When Sharon got up for a trip to the bathroom she stumbled and fell to her knees.

"You'd better stay with me tonight," Angela said.

"I should get back," Sharon said.

"You're in no condition to drive."

"I'll go slow." Somewhere between dressed and naked she must have taken off her clothes, but where were they now?

"Everything is on the chair," Angela said.

It all looked the same to Sharon, every piece looked as if a strong wind would blow it to shreds. "I can't remember what's mine," she said.

"Just pick whatever you like. I'm pretty sure we'll be swapping underwear again."

A clothed but very wobbly Sharon looked down at her Miata. Since the top was down she was able to tumble into the seat, none of the contortions that she usually had to endure to get in the otherwise small opening. "Go slow," she reminded herself. And she did. But even creeping along she had several close calls. Two of them occurred when she stopped at houses that looked somewhat like hers, but weren't. She only realized her mistake when her key didn't fit. Drunken guests, she learned, were not welcome at three o'clock in the morning, or any other time, for that matter.

The third house was the charm, her key fit, home sweet home. The bedroom would be her last stop for the night. She stripped off her shorts and top and realized that she must have left her bra at Angela's. Ah, Angela, why hadn't she stayed there? Now she would be all alone in a huge bed. No problem, she was asleep before her head hit the pillow.

The chirping bedside clock said eleven. She sat up but lay back down when the room started spinning. A few more tries and she was able to get around the room, supporting herself on the bed. She made it to the bathroom leaning on the wall or anything else she could grab onto. If she was going to spend much more time with Angela, she'd better install handrails.

Coffee, if anything, could brush away the cobwebs that seemed to have engulfed her brain. But coffee meant a trip to the kitchen, something that seemed far away at the moment. Slow and careful had got her home the night before, and that's how she would proceed now.

She caught a glimpse of herself in the mirror atop her dresser. Her hair was a tousled mess, no surprise there, and as usual, she was nearly naked. "Come on, girl," she said to her reflection. True, there was no one around to see her, but she was out in the big wide world now, all alone. A bit more caution was in order, but she would think about that later.

She passed the sitting area on her way to the kitchen. The TV set was on, the sound turned very low. How could she have forgotten that? Now she couldn't find the damned remote control. She fumbled through the pile of CDs by the TV set, but no remote.

It was all like a big practical joke, now the lamp behind her went on, and the TV volume went up. What the hell? She whirled around, and there he sat, Clark, just as taciturn as ever.

He turned off the lamp. "You should put on some clothes."

Naked, in front of Clark, probably the last man on the planet she would want to see her naked. She dashed out of the room, tripped and sprawled onto the bedroom floor. Thank God for thick carpets.

She picked up the shorts she'd left by the bed the night before, but tight, brief and revealing was not what she wanted just now. In the bottom drawer of her dresser she found something more appropriate, a gray sweatshirt and pants, both baggy. She gave each a sniff test, but came up empty. Perhaps all that alcohol the night before had interrupted her sense of smell.

Once she'd put on the outfit, she glanced at herself in the mirror. Perfect, she was about as attractive as dog food. Good thing Angela couldn't see her now.

Clark was right where she'd left him. "How did

you get in here?" She had to shout above the noise of the TV. "What the hell are you doing in my house?"

Clark pressed his forefinger to his lips. Then he patted the sofa cushion next to him, close to him.

A guy who scared the pants off her, now he wanted her to snuggle up next to him. No way. She sat at the opposite end of the sofa.

His low voice and the noisy TV made it impossible for her to hear him. "I can't hear you. Turn down the TV."

He shook his head and patted the sofa cushion again. When she didn't move, he grabbed her arm and pulled her over next to him.

"Ouch, damn you, that hurt. And if you touch me again I'll scratch your eyes out." Brave talk, but she knew better. If he grabbed her again she would probably faint dead away. She rubbed her arm and grimaced as if in great pain. He hadn't hurt her, but he didn't know that, and she had to score points any way she could. "How did you get in here?" When she'd asked him before he hadn't answered. Probably wouldn't this time either.

"You left your doors unlocked." He spoke close to her ear. "And promise me one thing. Promise that you won't drive drunk on that narrow road again. Scared the hell out of me. I almost pulled you over and took away your keys."

"You followed me home last night?" This was beginning to get creepy. On the other hand, the little speech that Clark had just made was the longest he'd spoken to her, ever.

He nodded. This was more like it, good old non-verbal Clark.

"Why are you here?" she asked.

"Because I couldn't stand by and watch any longer."

"What? Watch what?"

"What they've been doing to you. And there are other reasons, maybe if we get out of this you'll learn about them too," he said.

"I don't know what the hell you're talking about. You're not making sense."

"Look, this is going to be hard for you, and it won't be easy for me either. Could you make coffee?"

Of course, coffee. How could she have forgotten coffee, the one thing that had clarified more murky situations than any other? If anything could restore her equilibrium, it was coffee. "I'll be right back."

By the time the brew was ready, Clark had moved into her breakfast nook. It was the only room so far that had normal-sized windows. "Thanks," Clark said. "I really need this. You will too." For the first time she noticed the dark circles beneath his eyes.

"How come you aren't whispering anymore?"

"I've already finished sweeping in here. It's a smaller room, didn't take much time."

"Sweeping? You're telling me you vacuumed in here?"

"No, no, I was looking for bugs, listening devices." He took two small objects from his jacket pocket. Held in the palm of his hand, they were just slightly larger than pencil erasers. "I found these in the TV room. That's why I spoke so softly, I don't know for sure if I got all of them."

Through no conscious effort, her hands flew to her face and covered her eyes. "No. Who would do this, and why?"

"This is the hard part. Are you ready for it?"

"Yes, but wait. How do I know I can trust you?"

"You can't. Just hear me out, then decide." He took a long drag from his cup, then pushed his chair away from the table, like he was going to make some big announcement. "First off, your friends, Connor and Lisa are not your friends. They've been setting you up. It's been going on for months."

"Now I know you're lying. They would never do anything of the sort."

"Listen, then make your choices. I must say their little scheme is very clever. For a while they had me fooled too. He's planned the Monmouth crash for a long time. Then you came along and made the perfect fall guy, or girl. All that stuff about Lisa being gay, not getting it on with Connor, all a big lie. He had you in his bed one night a week. The other six he had Lisa. That's what tipped me off. These little bugs, I planted one in his bedroom."

"I think I'm gonna be sick."

She curled into a ball, arms wrapped around her knees, her back to Clark. If she was expecting him to comfort her, she was in for a long wait, but she knew that. "Go on," she said.

"Your new friend, Angela, she isn't your friend either."

"You are definitely wrong about her. She's the best thing that's happened to me since I got here. Besides, she couldn't possibly be part of some big plot. She doesn't even know where I live."

"Oh, she knows, all right. She's been here several times. They knew which house you'd pick, even before you bought it. And that guy, who wears the shoes you saw under her sofa…"

"Roger," she said.

"His name isn't Roger. It's Boris. Just hope you don't ever meet him."

"You've been in her house."

"Of course."

"And you've been in my house before, too?"

"Yeah, and before I forget, those tinted windows that you can't see through from the outside, there are at least two types of goggles available almost anywhere, that let you see right through them, like they weren't there."

"So, people can see me any time I walk in front of a window, whether I'm wearing anything or not?"

"Yeah, some nights you've drawn a crowd."

"God, what is this, see Sharon naked week? Maybe I should put up a billboard so people won't have to go to all the trouble of peeking in my windows," she said. "I guess you've seen me too."

"Yep."

"This sucks, really sucks." She buried her face in the cradle she'd made on the table with her forearms. "You've ruined my life."

"I hope I'll be able to save it, but the people we're up against are good. Just think about the neat little knot they have around your neck. All this juicy information in the newspapers, those reporters didn't have to look very far. It was all fed right to them, carefully planned, every bit of it. They even have some quotes from the girls you ran at the Faculty Club, how you more or less forced them into prostitution, and how they're so glad it's over at last.

"And there are a few tidbits from your old pal, Bob Hastings, says he's a friend of the family and how it's almost better your parents are deceased, because finding out about you would crush them."

"That son of a bitch. I'd scratch his eyes out if I could."

"You probably won't get the chance. He's served his purpose, part of the smear campaign, so most likely he disappeared. He would be a loose end, and Connor and his buddies aren't ones to leave loose ends lying around."

"Lisa?"

"The same. She's made you look like scum, and it was all part of the plan. She's still in the game, though. I guess she's too valuable to kill off just yet. I have to say, this is the most clever bit of work I've seen in years."

"Lucky me. But Connor can't be too happy with the situation, especially if he doesn't get his money back," she said.

"Don't worry about Connor. He's been skimming off Monmouth money for many years. Plus, he had a lot of family money. Even without what you have stashed away, he's still a very wealthy man."

"Then why is he after me?"

"That's the thing about money, no matter how much you have, it's never enough. And believe me, he wants what you have, and he'll do anything to get it."

"Anything? Like what?"

"Like I say, the man will do anything. Look what he's already done to you. See, he won't send in the feds, because then he'll lose the money himself. He'll send somebody like me."

"What if I just run like hell?" she asked. Her voice had become tremulous, but there was nothing she could do about it.

"If it was me looking for you, I'd find you, no problem. And you don't want to know what happens then."

"Tell me anyway. I have to know what I'm up against."

"If you're on your own, his boys will find you. After a little time with them, you'll give Connor Shaw anything he wants, anything. But that won't be enough. You're the only person who can hurt him, so you'll disappear. There will be no trace of you left. Your red Miata will be parked in another garage. Your house will have new owners. You will vanish into thin air. Of course, after spending time with Connor's goons that will probably be a relief."

She buried her face in her hands. "No," she whispered. Now she knew, all of it stuff she didn't want to know. "Here I thought I was safe, nobody knew where I was. But now I learn I'm being watched all the time. The people I thought I could trust, I can't. And they've bugged my house, probably one of those damned bugs in the bathroom so they can hear me tinkle."

"I'll check that."

"Okay, if I believe what you're saying, and I'm not sure I do, what's in this for you? Why are you helping me? I'm sure Connor pays you well, but you're throwing that away. I don't get it," she said.

"Like I said, I don't like what they're doing to you. I have other reasons, but explaining them would take too long, and time is not your friend, mine either."

"What do I do now? If they know exactly where I am, how can I get away? Where would I even go?"

"First, we kill off the old Sharon."

"What's that supposed to mean?"

"I'm good at making people disappear too. You'll start with a new passport, a new driver's license, a new birth certificate and a new name, Shannon Sullivan. I thought we should keep your old initials in case you have anything monogrammed."

"I don't get to pick my new name?"

"No, the documents have already been made out."

"How? Oh, never mind." She was learning not to question Clark, what he did or how he did it. The very thought of what could have happened if Connor had sent Clark after her made her teeth chatter. By now, she might have been hustled down to the bay for a boat ride, one way. So, she trusted him, not because she wanted to, but because she had to.

"What about the money?" she asked.

"Keep it right where it is. That's your insurance policy. The money stays, you go away."

"Okay, so just tell me what to do, and I'll do it."

"First, wash your hair."

"What? I hardly think this is the time for a shampoo."

"A little dye job, that's what I had in mind. You'll be a nice auburn color, at least that's what it says on the box. Since we're going someplace where people with red hair don't stand out, you'll blend right in. Make sure you dry it thoroughly."

About twenty minutes later, she emerged from the bathroom. She'd taken a long, appreciative look at her new hair. "You know, I sort of like it this color. I might keep it."

"Not for long." He tossed her a blonde wig.

"I don't get it. No sooner do I dye my hair than you give me an ugly wig, a completely different color."

"Just put it on. I'll explain later. Your clothes are on the bed."

Arranged on the bed lay a pair of baggy jeans, a plaid flannel shirt and a padded belt that increased her waistline by several inches. He'd topped off the outfit with a pair of scuffed sneakers. He'd also left her a leather bag that looked as if it had been dragged along a highway for several miles.

"One more thing," he said. "Do you have any more durable underwear? That stuff in your dresser doesn't look like it will hold up very well."

"You went through my underwear? Who gave you permission to do that?" So far she'd gone along with his program without fighting back, but this was a step too far. He knew too much about her, intimate things that no man had a right to know without her consent. Her underwear? For God's sake.

"Or we can just buy something later."

"We? We will most certainly not buy my underwear. I can take care of that myself."

"Just doing my job."

"If you're so damned clever, how am I going to get this on the plane?" From the shelf in her closet she took down a bundle of oily rags, her .22 caliber pistol.

"How the hell did you get that here in the first place?" he asked.

"I have a few tricks of my own, but I don't think they'll work next time. I've heard airport security is real picky about what they allow on board."

"Damn right they are. Better give that to me."

"You'll give it back?"

"Yeah, you ever fired this thing?"

"You bet, and I'm a pretty good shot, used to be at least."

"Too small to do much damage," he said.

"So far I've only shot at tin cans and rats. It'll do the job on a rat, small ones, at least."

"Finish getting ready. Five minutes, then we go."

After she'd changed, she took one last look in the mirror. A short while ago she'd fallen in love with her new auburn tresses. Now it was all covered up by a frumpy blonde wig. She hadn't bothered with makeup, no point. No amount of makeup would make her look good in what she was wearing. Frumpy was the order of the day.

The padded belt seemed to add about twenty-five pounds. Her bust line merged straight into her waistline. Any man that took a second look at her now would have to be one desperate sonofabitch.

Out in the hallway, Clark took her bag and leaned in close. "No talking above a whisper. We'll go out the front entrance. They'll be watching the back."

"Wait, my case." The little burgundy aluminum case that held her jewelry, a nonnegotiable item.

"We don't have room for that."

"I'm not leaving without it."

"Women," he muttered. "Give it to me."

She asked no more questions, simply followed along behind him like an obedient dog.

Clark's vehicle was parked in a turnoff about one hundred yards up the road. It was a far cry from the limo in which he had driven her to those weekly trysts with Connor. His chariot was scuffed and dented, fore and aft. The driver's side window had a crack running from its base to the top.

When she reached for the door Clark stopped her. "Put these on," he said. He gave her a pair of clear latex gloves like the ones he was wearing himself. "They might dust this car for fingerprints."

The inside smelled like old, very old, leather, not unpleasant but just a bit more pungent than she would have liked. "I liked your limo better," she said.

It was the first time she'd ever heard Clark laugh. She wasn't even sure he could. "Yeah, the limo, me too, I guess."

The car sounded like an angry beast when he started it up. Now she knew why he'd parked so far away. "Is this thing safe?" she asked.

"It'll outrun anything we'll come up against."

"Where are we going, I mean, when we leave here?"

"A quick stopover in London, then on to Ireland."

London, Ireland, and she'd barely gotten settled into her new house. "Wait," she said. "I can't do this. I can't just run off and leave everything behind." She buried her face in her latex-clad hands. This was insane, what she was about to do. But according to Clark's rules, how could she not obey? If he was giving her a straight story, her life depended on it.

He explained that they would arrive at the airport together, but would have no further contact, not even a nod of recognition, until after they'd landed at Heathrow. Why all the cloak and dagger bit? He made it sound like the hounds of hell were nipping at their heels.

But the last chance she would have to question him passed in total silence. As they pulled into the paved road, he gave her an envelope. "Everything you'll need is in there, new passport, new U.S. driver's license, birth certificate, everything. And remember, from now until further notice, you are Shannon Sullivan. If anybody calls you Sharon, ignore them, but keep an eye on them. Chances are they're following you.

She entered the terminal first. Catching a glimpse of herself in one of the glass doors gave her a shock. *That can't be me, that homeless person.* At least she wouldn't have to fend off any annoying seatmates. More likely anyone seated next to her would request another seat.

Clark sat several rows in front of her. She made a mental note of his location and didn't look at him again. The man had told her what to do, and she did it.

She hadn't thought to bring anything to read, crossword puzzles, nothing. From her window seat she had a brief view of the countryside, then only blue water.

With nothing to occupy her mind, questions began popping up again. In only a few hours her life had been turned upside down. She had walked away from an oceanfront house and a red sports car. She was leaving a place that was warm and humid year-round, a place where she could splash in the ocean whenever she wanted, and she was headed for a place that was probably humid, but cold as well. No frolicking in the ocean where she was going. The switch sounded crazy.

Then there was her mystery man, Clark, the instrument of her undoing. Even though she'd been acquainted with him for almost five months, all she knew about him could be written on the back of a postcard, with space left over. But he knew stuff about her, about her arrangement with Connor. A common whore, that's how he would probably have classified her. Then why the hell was he trying to save her?

Everything he'd told her could just as well be a big fat lie. Other than the newspapers he'd given her, she had no way of verifying anything he'd said. And those little bugs that he claimed were listening devices he'd found in her house, he could have bought them at any audio store. How would she have known the difference?

Eventually the sheer monotony of the flight got to her, and she dozed off. She woke with a lurch. Where was she? When the cobwebs cleared, and she recognized her surroundings, she checked her watch. Clark had given her a cheap knock-off with a scuffed band and Gucci printed on its case in letters almost too small to read. "Does Gucci make watches?" she'd asked him.

"Don't know," he'd said. "All part of the disguise."

The effects of her marathon session with Angela, including the alcohol, still lingered. The fake timepiece indicated that almost three hours had passed since she'd slipped into sleep mode. When she looked up she saw the man two rows up and across the aisle staring at her. He was the one person on the flight who looked even less attractive than Sharon thought of herself, bald, close-set eyes almost hidden beneath bushy brows, and a big nose. His massive biceps looked as if they would split the seams of his jacket if he flexed.

Salvation, a voice from the cockpit, "Prepare for landing."

In case the beast who'd been staring at her had mischief in mind, her first priority would be to locate Clark and keep close to him, but she lost sight of him as soon as she walked into the terminal. Chasing after any man with white hair and a black jacket proved hopeless. She could only go where the crowds propelled her, so like being swept along by a torrent with no visible banks on either side.

After several moments of being pushed and pummeled, she finally worked her way out to the margin of the throng. At last, a wall. She flattened herself against it, resigning herself to having lost Clark indefinitely, if not forever. Why in hell had she ever left the safety of her own house?

There was no way he could find her now, but he did. As usual, he materialized out of thin air. She seldom saw him coming or going, then there he was.

She didn't know whether to punch him or hug him, so she hugged him. It seemed like the safer move. "I'm so glad to see you," she whispered into his neck. It was a flagrant violation of his set of rules, but she had to have some kind of friendly contact.

With Clark leading the way, parting the throng like Moses on the sea, they made their way to a quieter nook.

"Our flight is delayed," he said. "We have a couple of hours to kill."

"I wish you wouldn't use that word," she said. They sat together on a padded bench while she caught her breath. "There was a man on the plane, a big ugly brute, he kept staring at me."

"Yeah, I know him. He won't be any trouble."

"How do you know that? I mean, he was really

big," she said.

"He knows we're together, so he won't bother you. Besides, his business doesn't involve us. But that doesn't mean you can let your guard down. I screw up sometimes, everybody does."

She felt him slip a small bundle into her jacket pocket. From the weight of it she knew that she was once again in possession of her .22.

"Keep this with you, but don't use it unless you absolutely have to. The Brits get their panties in a bunch if somebody gets shot around here. Not like the U.S."

"How did you get it past security?" she asked.

"Don't ask."

She nodded. The crowds that had engulfed her earlier had thinned out. "I need to find a bathroom," she said.

"I won't be here when you get back, but I won't be far away. Are you hungry?" he asked.

"Sure, always."

"There's a coffee shop just up the street that way. The hike will give you a chance to stretch your legs." He gave her another envelope with folding money and a plastic bag filled with coins. "Enough to get you through a couple of days."

"I have to go right now," she said.

"Okay, we'll meet back here later, same spot," he said.

Chapter Twenty

The stroll down to the coffee shop was so much more pleasant than playing bumper cars, without cars, in the airport. Now a bright day and an empty bladder, and nobody shoving her around, things could be worse. Even the scruffy sneakers, while not up to par in the style category, were comfortable. After all the craziness of the last ten hours, her spirits were comfortable too. Yeah, things could be worse, even though her future was one big muddle.

The aroma inside the eatery was a mouth-watering blend of baked goods, bringing back memories of a family bakery in the tiny town of Jacob's Bluff, where she'd grown up. Some afternoons after school she wandered in to peer at the delights in the glass case up front. Most of all she went for the smell, intoxicating. She would close her eyes and let the aroma lift her up to a place where she had an unlimited supply of donuts, cupcakes, apple-filled pastries with big granules of sugar on the outside and the scent of cinnamon from inside. Yes, when she grew up she would run her very own bakery. Instead, she wound up running a whorehouse. And now she was just plain running…for her life.

"What'll it be, dear?" The matronly lady behind the counter smiled at her.

"Coffee and one, no, two of those beautiful

cupcakes."

"Made 'em myself this morning," said Matron. "You just have a seat, and I'll bring it over to you."

Pure heaven, from the first bite. Okay, so cupcakes weren't on anybody's list of healthy foods, but somehow that made it all the sweeter. The first one disappeared in a twinkle. She leaned back, took a long look at the second culprit sitting there so smug in its little white foil wrapper. For a second she thought of saving it for Clark, but he didn't seem like a cupcake guy, so she attacked it with vigor.

"I see someone was hungry." Matron stood by Sharon's shoulder, coffee pot in her hand.

"Oh, yes, they were so delicious. I couldn't help myself."

"Glad you enjoyed them, dear. More coffee?"

"No, thanks, I should be getting back." Sharon emptied the plastic bag of coins on the table. "I don't know anything about the money here, so if you'll just take what you need."

"You should get someone to show you, dear. Some folks will be bound to cheat you. Now, I'll just take two of these and one of these. You put your money away where it's safe."

"I will, and thank you." For a stranger in a strange land she was doing pretty well. Clark would be proud when she told him about her little adventure. She wasn't completely helpless after all. She patted her jacket pocket to make sure the .22 was still there, then picked up her bag and ventured back out into the street.

For a country with a reputation for dreary weather, London seemed to be doing its best to impress her. Blue skies in all directions, at least where her vision wasn't obstructed by tall buildings. Even the people in the streets seemed caught up in the general good will. Might she convince Clark to stay here for a couple of days, some sightseeing, shopping, a nice dinner, or two?

With her head in the clouds and her feet several inches off the ground she paid no mind to the man who approached on her right, not until he seized her elbow between his thumb and forefinger. When he squeezed, she was sure he was going to separate the bones and tear apart whatever held them together. The pain made her knees buckle.

Another man, black leather jacket, black turtleneck, jeans and heavy shoes, grabbed her left arm, and between them they hustled her into a white van waiting at the curb.

"No noise." The man who still held her right elbow gave it an extra squeeze. She didn't scream, but she did wet her pants a little.

Perhaps it would have been to her advantage to try to keep track of the trip, but she didn't. She couldn't. She went into shutdown mode. She knew how this would end; Clark had told her.

Only once did she react, when the man who controlled her elbow applied pressure. Her head jerked back, and she whimpered.

"Still hurts, does it? Good, lots more where that came from. Gonna be a long day for you, sweetheart."

One more squeeze for good measure. One more whimper.

They dragged her out of the van, then half-carried her toward a cinder block building and through a rusted metal door. Somehow she still had her scruffy bag by its handle, like she'd bonded to it by some weird symbiotic process.

The man on her left reached across and seized her breast. "Holy shit, Lucius, get a feel of these things."

Lucius did just that. Suddenly the pain from her elbow was transferred to her breast, which Lucius squeezed as if he were trying to crush it. He located her nipple through the flannel shirt and gave it a vicious twist. She dropped to her knees, but they pulled her right back up again.

Lucius gave her breast one more slap. "Oh, yeah, we're gonna have some fun tonight."

Another steel door, this time leading into a room brightly lit by a single bulb swinging from the ceiling. The light blinded her, but she could hear voices in the shadows. The men who dragged her in left her standing there and walked to the other side of the room.

"We'll take over from here." She thought it was Lucius speaking. "Hello there, Clark, long time no see. Too bad this will be the last time. I've got a lot to settle up with you so don't expect to get off easily. I'll hear you beg to die before this is over." He gave Clark a punch in the chest that slammed him against the wall.

Sharon could, by squinting, get a glimpse of Clark. His hands were cuffed in front of him. Any hopes she had for a last minute rescue were dashed right then and there.

Another voice, no mistaking this one, her old friend and bedmate, Connor Shaw.

"Sharon, surprised to see me?"

She knew that suit, too, gray, pin stripes. She'd helped him take it off several times. She could even make an educated guess about his underwear. Those memories still made her tingle in the damnedest places, and all this from the man who aimed to kill her very soon.

She had held out hope that Clark had painted far too grim a picture, perhaps they were just trying to frighten her. But now she knew, it was worse than he'd described, much worse. And it would all end right here, in a grubby little room in a grubby little building.

Connor took a step forward, and the bottom half of his face came into view, that confident smile that she'd seen so often, just before he'd buried his face between her thighs. So many delicious memories, now going up in flames.

"How did you get here so fast?" she asked.

"The Concorde is a very fast plane, expensive, but fast."

Keep him talking. He loved the sound of his own voice almost as much as he loved money, or screwing her. It wouldn't buy her much time, but knowing that her own life would likely end within the next hour, every minute became precious.

"How did you find us?" she asked.

"Not that it makes much difference, but that diamond bracelet that I gave you last month has a tiny GPS transmitter in the clasp. It's complicated, and I don't understand it. Clark probably would, but he can't help you now."

Lisa stepped out of the shadows beside him. "Sharon, darling, I must say you've looked better. Where on earth did you get those ridiculous clothes? You look like a clown."

"But we both remember what she looks like underneath. Maybe once we have our business completed we can all have a look. You boys would like that I'll bet," Connor said.

Connor's goons responded with grunts, their mouths twisted into hideous grins.

The pin-striped suit advanced another step. Big confident smile, like he was king of the world.

Her hand slipped to her side and brushed against the .22 in her pocket. She pulled it out and pointed it at Connor.

He responded with a great, roaring laugh. "What in hell is that, a toy? You're going to shoot me? No, you won't shoot me. You can't."

But she did, two small round holes in his forehead, no more than an inch apart. No thought at all, just point and shoot, like shooting at tin cans. The shots were no louder than someone clapping their hands. Connor stood for a moment, wavering as if the message of death from his brain hadn't reached his body yet. Then he crumpled like a puppet whose strings had been cut.

A moment of silence, disbelief, then Lisa came at her, screeching and clawing. Sharon pushed the barrel underneath her jaw and fired one round directly into her brain. Lisa dropped immediately.

Sharon turned the gun toward the goons who held Clark. "It's all over now," she said. I have three bullets left. You can leave or one of you gets two rounds in the head, and the other gets one in the eye. Your choice. At this point I'd as soon shoot you as not."

Both men extended their hands in front of them and edged toward the door.

"Wait," she said. "Take the cuffs off Clark."

A moment later the goons were gone, and Clark was at her side. If he hadn't caught her she would have landed on the floor, right alongside Connor and Lisa.

When he took the gun from her hand he had to pry her fingertips off the grip. "We have to go, right now," he said.

"What about them?" she asked.

"Leave them where they are. Let's go."

She walked like someone between the states of inebriation and passing out. Clark held one of her arms across his shoulders and his other around her waist. Without his support she would never have gotten out of the room.

"Wait, my bag," she said.

"I got it."

"How will we get out of here?"

"The assholes forgot about my cell phone. Either that or they figured dead men don't make calls, so why bother?"

When their taxi arrived Clark had to lift her onto the seat. Her shakes were coming on with a vengeance.

"She okay?" the driver asked.

"Yeah, just had a bit of a fright, that's all."

Somehow Clark managed to get them on their flight to Dublin. With Sharon barely coherent he had to do all the talking. On board he abandoned their plan for separate seats, because Sharon had a death grip on his hands and refused to let go.

"I'm so very sorry," he said in a low voice. "You never should have had to go through that. All my fault."

Later she would have almost no recollection of the flight. She spent the entire trip with her head nestled on Clark's shoulder. The only way she could prevent her hands from shaking was to hold onto him for all she was worth. Even after landing, it required a lot of coaxing before she would release him.

The air outside the terminal revived her somewhat.

"I have a car here," Clark said. "If you'll wait here I'll go get it."

"No," she said, almost shouting. "You're not leaving me."

Even a simple thing like walking across a parking lot now required an act of courage, courage that she did not possess. Her world consisted only of Clark, and she clung to his arm as if, should she let go, she would fall off the end of the earth. Past and future didn't exist anymore. Living in the moment was all she could handle, and that moment was Clark.

The light blue Toyota Camry was a substantial upgrade from the vehicle Clark had driven away from her house in Antigua. He drove past the attendant in the parking booth with only a wave.

"You don't have to pay?" she asked.

"Not here."

"Why not?"

"A cousin, I think. Sometimes I'm not sure myself who is and who isn't."

Cousins? Who on earth was this man? Her hands hurt, and she realized that she'd kept them balled into fists ever since they'd left that horrid little room. Now, being in an enclosed space with Clark, she opened her hands and saw that she'd driven her fingernails into her palms. So much horror, so fast, would she ever feel safe again? "Where are we going?" she asked.

"South." Not much information, but perhaps he thought that was all she could handle at the moment. Off to the west she followed a mountain range that reminded her of home, a home to which she could never return.

"Wicklow Mountains," he said, as if he was reading her mind.

An hour or so after they left Dublin, Clark turned off the main road onto a narrow track that often barely had room for a single vehicle, let alone two. She could say very little about the trip, because much of the time she'd kept her eyes closed. What she couldn't see couldn't hurt her, or so she pretended.

Now, at a slower pace, she took more notice of her surroundings. The green countryside reminded her of home too, except for the virtual absence of trees. Then there were those odd lumps that looked like sections of logs stacked in field after field. "What are those?"

"Peat. It's cut out of the bogs and left to dry. Folks use it for heating, cooking, just about anything that requires an open flame."

"And what happened to all the trees?" she asked. She didn't care, not really, but focusing on something else took her mind away from her near-death experience, and the fact that she'd just killed two people.

"Mostly cut away, not profitable enough," he said. "People live off the land do better with crops, livestock, sheep, pigs and such."

She gazed out at gently rolling hills of farmland, all so very green. Ordinarily a road trip in a new place would keep her peering out the window. Instead, a heavy drowsiness descended upon her. She fought it for a while; she'd had a long nap earlier, but then drifted off to sleep.

She woke with a jolt, amidst the disorientation that follows a deep slumber. There was Clark, who might very well have been carved out of stone, so fixed were his features. She thought about speaking to him, but decided against it.

The sun was only a few degrees above the horizon now, and shadows from barns they passed spread across their path as if trying to entrap them. It took so little to set her off now, and strange shadows in a strange place sent a shudder through her. She inched closer to Clark. He patted her knee, just a pat, but it was enough to chase all the goblins back to wherever they'd come from.

A light flickered in the distance, becoming several beams streaming through several windows.

"Almost there," he said.

"Almost where?"

"My home. We'll be staying here a while."

He pulled up to a cobblestone house with a thatched roof like nothing she'd ever seen before. There were four windows across the front, all well-lit. A short distance, on the other side of the road, sat another stone house, only about half the size of the one where Clark had parked.

He took her bag from the back seat. "Come on inside," he said.

She had no idea what to expect, but even so, she was impressed with how neat and tidy the front rooms were. The furnishings, while far from luxurious, looked warm and comfortable. In spite of having been there only a few minutes, she felt a sense of home.

"Your room is in back." He carried her bag, and she followed along.

Once again, cozy and comfortable was the order of the day, like the room had been waiting for her to come along. A double window spread across the wall opposite the spacious bed. The curtains were considerably more frilly than she would have expected from Clark, and the sprightly floral print could not have been his idea. The dressing table that filled one corner of the room sealed the deal, this was a woman's room.

"Bathroom's right here." He opened one door. "Closet's here." Another door. "I know you don't have much stuff yet, but that will change."

"Who usually stays here?"

"Sometimes Maureen, my little sister. We call her Mo. She's off somewhere now. Girl never stays put very long."

"What's she like, Maureen?"

"Like all little sisters, a pain in the butt."

"What an awful way to talk about your sister."

"You haven't met her yet."

And there it was, a rare Clark smile. She could count all of them she'd seen on the fingers of one hand. "But you like her, I can tell."

"When she's not around, yeah." He sat on the bed and motioned for her to sit beside him. "Now, here's the deal. This will be your room for as long as you want to stay here."

"You won't be with me?"

"I'll be right across the hall. I'll leave my door open, so if you need anything, anything at all, yell and I'll be here in no time."

"You promise?"

"I do. Look, I know my promises aren't worth much right now. I let you down in London. I should have seen that coming. I should have pulled that trigger, not you. I can't tell you how sorry I am about that."

She leaned her head on his shoulder. "What's done is done. We can't change it. I shot and killed two people. I'll have to live with that." She didn't mention that she'd shared a bed with both of them, but probably he already knew.

"Not like you had much choice. Besides, you saved both of us."

So far, during the whole ordeal, she hadn't shed a tear. She'd left London as dry-eyed as when she'd arrived. Now all that changed as all the grief and fear and god-knows-what else came surging out in a gush of liquids. She couldn't talk. She could barely breathe. She was drowning.

Clark wrapped an arm around her shoulders and squeezed until it hurt, and she wanted him to squeeze harder still. Of course, that didn't stop the flood. Nothing could. Like a force of nature, it ran its course completely, then it ended, leaving her a sniffling, whimpering child-like figure with a red runny nose and matching red eyes.

She burbled out what was intended to be "I'm sorry," but it triggered another cloudburst. This one, in comparison to its predecessor, was just a shower.

"Will you eat something?" Clark asked.

"I can't."

"Maybe you need rest more than anything." He opened a dresser drawer and retrieved a garment that he held up for her. "I guess this is a nightgown. Mo left some things behind in case you needed them. Put this on and go wash your face and brush your teeth and climb into bed. I'll be back in about fifteen minutes."

"You aren't leaving?"

"I'll be right outside your door."

The last thing she saw before she drifted off again was her little burgundy case sitting on the dresser. How on earth had he managed that? She hadn't laid eyes on it since they left Antigua. The man must be a magician.

Later, climbing back from the deep sleep into which she had fallen was like escaping from an underwater trap. She fought to get to the surface, and when she broke through she found herself in yet another strange place. The soft cry that escaped her lips meant nothing, but in an instant Clark was at her side, his hands gripping her shoulders.

"I'm sorry," she said. "I'm fine. I just woke with a start. You must think I'm a complete idiot."

His grip on her shoulders tightened. "Nobody just walks away from what you've been through, nobody. You have to give yourself plenty of time and plenty of space. You don't have to do anything, go anywhere until you're damned well ready. If you want to spend the whole day in the house watching your toenails grow, that will be just fine."

For the first time, perhaps, she became aware of Clark as a man. Initially there had been her fear of him, and that combined with what she was sure was his total contempt for her and what she did—she was Connor's whore, after all—placed a wall between them. Only in the past day and a half had they interacted on a human level.

How quickly her feelings for him changed. Still, she remained wary. She'd been burned before. Connor had been a shooting star, set her aflame. But in the end he was a false god. Aside from his jackhammer penis and his magical tongue there was little else. It would be a long time before she made that mistake again.

And it was a perfectly ridiculous time to be entertaining such feelings. Why, less than twenty-four hours earlier, she had shot and killed two people. Not strangers, mind you, but two people she had trusted and with whom she had shared the most scintillating sexual experiences of her life. Both dead now, by her own hand, and had she not pulled the trigger, a gruesome death would have been her own fate. Clark's too.

****

The curtains in her bedroom did little to reduce the intensity of the morning sunlight, which caught her squarely in the face. If she was going to spend more time in this bedroom she would have to find sturdier coverings for her windows. She glanced at her wrist where her watch should have been, but wasn't. Since she couldn't remember taking it off, it was probably still in London, and on someone else's wrist.

Sounds from the front of the house, easily identifiable as pots and pans, glassware and tableware became audible; time for breakfast. She ran into the bathroom and splashed water on her face, hung the nightgown on the hook by the door, then put on the jeans and the thoroughly wrinkled flannel shirt she'd worn during their dash through London. The shirt still reeked of her own fear. If it weren't for the shocking effect it would have on Clark's family, she might have thrown off the shirt and gone out in her bra. He'd seen her in less.

"Good morning." Clark stood beside a round table in a small nook just off the kitchen, a cup of coffee in his hand. "Were you able to get back to sleep last night?"

"Oh, yes. I feel a hundred percent better today."

"Then we'll start you off with a good breakfast. I put in the oven to keep it warm."

She hadn't paid much attention to the kitchen the night before. A warm, safe bed had been the first item on her agenda. Now she was struck by the feeling she had when she had walked into the compact room, yes, there was that word again…cozy, like home.

The aroma from the oven that Clark had just opened set her salivary glands into overdrive, even before she saw the cast iron skillet mounded with food…bacon, eggs, potatoes, grilled tomatoes. On a smaller plate he had buttered toast made from thick slices of bread that no doubt had been baked on the premises.

"Oh, that looks wonderful," Sharon said, and she meant it. "What's that?"

"What's what?"

"The black things."

"Those are sausages. They're called blood pudding, but obviously they're not really a pudding."

"They're made of blood?"

"Yeah, inside the casing, the sausage part is made from cooked blood. Ma mixes in some grain. Blood pudding has been around forever."

"Where do you get the blood? No, don't answer that."

He began loading two plates with food. The only thing she could remember as comparable were some of the Thanksgiving dinners that her grandmother prepared.

"Aren't the others coming?" she asked.

"Nope, just the two of us."

"But there's plenty of food for a half dozen

313

people."

He pulled out a chair for her. "It's Ma's way. I guess she tries to make the world a better place by feeding it. And I can tell you, nobody, whether they drove up in a nice car, or walked up with everything they owned strapped to their backs, ever left her house with an empty stomach."

The hint of accent that she'd heard before in the few words he'd spoken to her now became more and more apparent.

"When do I get to meet this amazing lady?"

"Soon as you're up to it."

"Where is she?"

"The little house on the hill to the west. Here, you can see it through the window"

"But it's so tiny." She thought about the huge house on the ocean that she'd bought in Antigua. The entire stone house he showed her would easily fit in one of the mansion's bedrooms.

"That's why I built this house. Back when Da was still alive I wanted them to have a more comfortable place, more conveniences, but when he died, Ma refused to move. Said the little place had been good enough for generations of Clarks before her, and there she stayed. Gets her water from a pump out back. You remember those peat logs you saw in the fields? There's a stack of them on the far side of the house. That's how she cooks and keeps the place warm."

"She lives there by herself?" Sharon asked.

"No, Mo is with her now. She's the one I've been trying to keep away as long as possible. When she gets the chance she'll be all over you like fleas on a dog. Most inquisitive human I've ever seen."

314

"You make her sound like a monster."

"I guess, to another woman, her behavior might seem normal."

"Oh, so now I'm a monster too?" Did he have a sense of humor? She'd soon find out.

"See, that's the hard part about talking to women. They're always twisting your words around."

"Please, don't go all cranky on me now. It's too early in the day." Perhaps she saw the glimmer of a smile.

"I suppose if I've survived Mo and Ma, I can survive you too. Now, shut up and eat."

And she did, with gusto. Her last meal had been the three bottles of wine she'd shared with Angela the night before Clark had appeared and carried her away. Ah, Angela, bedroom skills like hers and a body to go with it were a rare combination. But this same delicious Angela had betrayed her, so there would be no repeat performance in her future.

It seemed no time at all had passed since she cleaned her plate, and Clark had ladled out a second helping for her.

"Slow down a bit," he said. "Too much food might upset your stomach."

"You're right," she said. "I should stop right here. Shall I put the leftovers in the fridge?"

"No, I'll take them out back. A farmer lives over the next rise, feeds it to his pigs. Then when he butchers them late in the fall, we get pork tenderloin and a few other choice bits."

"Including blood pudding?"

"That too. You should try it."

"I'll pass." The very thought of it almost pushed

her agitated stomach over the edge.

When Clark returned with the empty skillet she had located the dishwashing detergent under the sink and was halfway through the dirty dishes.

"What are you going to do with me today?" she asked.

"Well, Ma is dying to meet you, but of course, that will include Mo. We can try for a while if you feel up to it."

"I am definitely up for it, and I'll bet your sister is a lovely person, in spite of all the terrible things you've said about her." She stacked the last of the dishes in the rack. "Oh, wait, am I Sharon or Shannon?"

"Using your real name will be less complicated. Mo will worm it out of you anyway. And you should know, around here people call me Seamus."

"Okay, then, Seamus." She stopped at the doorway ahead of him. "Oh my gosh, everything is so green, everywhere, green."

A girl about her own height, and Sharon guessed, about her own age, leapt from the doorway of the little stone house where Seamus had said his mother lived. She ran down the path toward them, her auburn locks blowing in the breeze that had just sprung up.

"Sharon, hi, I'm Mo." She ran right past Seamus and latched onto Sharon. "I'm so glad you're here, and safe."

Mo already knew her real name. Sharon glanced at Seamus, then back at Mo. "But how did you know I was coming?" Only the night before, she and Seamus had crept out the back door of her Antigua house like a pair of thieves, and it bothered her that her arrival seemed to have been expected.

"Oh, big brother told us a few days ago," Mo said. "He was all hush-hush about it, like he was expecting an attack by aliens from outer space. Did you have a good breakfast? That's the first thing Ma will ask."

"I had an outstanding breakfast, thank you." Sharon patted a distended abdomen. If she weren't very careful, her waistline would begin to suffer. And now she had a new question to ponder, the mixed signals she'd gotten from Mo and Seamus. How had Seamus known they would become fugitives together, even before she did?

But she would have to think this through later, because Mo, with a tight grip on her arm, was leading her to the door of the small house where a diminutive lady with white hair fashioned into a tight bun, waited. Ma, had to be. Without doubt, this was the primal force that held the Clark family together. Sharon expected a larger woman, but this small lady with smile lines radiating out from her eyes seemed, like her son, Seamus, to possess the strength to do whatever she set her mind to.

But above the warm smile she directed at Sharon, there seemed to lurk some deep concern. Even her hug seemed a bit forced, a bit desperate. Something else to ponder at a later date.

The inside of the Clark ancestral home was more spacious than she would have thought. The room where she now stood obviously doubled as a dining room and sitting area, all grouped around a fireplace with a rod running across the top from which hung several pots and a kettle. It looked for all the world like one of the old pioneer cabins preserved in the Smoky Mountains National Park in North Carolina.

A pot on the small stove that sat in a far corner of the room gave off coffee smells. The aroma was mouth-watering, but Sharon had to wonder, after that huge breakfast, where would she put it? She would have to find out quickly, because cups and a cinnamon cake appeared on the table.

"Thank you for that delicious breakfast, Mrs. Clark," she said.

"No Mrs. Clark around here," Mo said. "You'll have to call her Ma, like the rest of us do."

Lots of small talk, at which Mo seemed quite adept, but those dreaded questions for Sharon about her origins, family, how she'd met Seamus, did not appear. Presumably she had Seamus to thank for that.

"Seamus isn't staying?" Sharon asked as he ducked out the door.

"No, he isn't much for chit-chat, particularly the way we girls carry on," Mo said. "I'm sure he'll be back shortly."

Sharon knew as much already, that Seamus was a man of few words, very few. And now she knew a bit more. As she studied Ma, she thought that, if one set aside gender, age and physical size, Ma and her son had been chiseled from the same block of granite.

Chapter Twenty-One

A bit later in the morning, that same son came to her rescue. "Thought you might do with a walk about," he said. "Beautiful day outside, and you need a chance to work off that breakfast."

Sharon jumped up, not too quickly, she hoped. "The master calls," she said.

Mo came forth with a belly laugh, probably audible at some distance. Ma shook her head, almost imperceptibly, and to that added a faint glimmer of a smile that somehow carried more weight than Mo's raucous contribution.

"You might need a light jacket," he said. "Kind of windy out by the cliffs."

"They seem a long way off," she said.

"Maybe a couple of miles, no more."

They headed off due east into the morning sun. Without thinking she linked her arm with his. It seemed the right thing to do, and he didn't seem to mind at all.

About three hundred yards out he took a path that ran more northeast. They stopped on a little rise that gave a panoramic view of the countryside, not because of its great height, but because it stood taller than any of the flat land around it.

Sharon, when she was able to catch her breath, said, "We haven't passed a single soul since we left."

"Not many souls around here. A couple of farms

off to the north there. Daugherty is the closest. He raises sheep."

"What are those areas set off with the stone walls?" She pointed to a patchwork system of walls about waist high, all interconnected.

"That's how he rotates the grazing areas. Sheep will strip a place down to bare ground in no time, so Daugherty takes down part of the wall and herds the sheep into the next area. O'Flaherty is the next farm up. Hard to see much of his spread from here."

"Seems like a lot of trouble, taking down walls all the time. Are they friendly?" she asked.

"Yeah, and they know about you, so they won't be a problem."

"Exactly what do they know about me?" There it was again, that feeling that her coming had been announced and discussed well in advance, a feeling that raised more questions than answers.

"That you're a close friend of mine. That's all they need to know."

How? When? He'd laid the groundwork for her before she even knew she would arrive. It was all so fast, almost too fast, and trying to pry answers from this taciturn man would be next to impossible. She could probably learn some things from Mo, but did she really want to get into private areas with the sister yet, until she knew her better?

They crossed over onto an adjoining path that headed more easterly. An onshore breeze brought the aroma of ocean directly into their faces. The shape of the coastline, if a sheer vertical cliff could be called a coastline, became more distinct.

She stopped and pulled him off the path. She

released his arm but held onto his hand. "I'm thinking you're just like your Ma, right?"

"Some people have made that comparison, yeah. But there's no way I can match up to her. When Mo and I were growing up, she was the only thing that kept this family together. She was already up working when I got up in the morning, and still working long after I went to bed. Never complained, not even once."

They resumed their trek toward the sea. Now she held his arm with her own, and his hand with her free hand. It made for an awkward walk, but that didn't matter. He was her lifeline now, and clinging to him made perfect sense.

Soon she could see the edge, where land ended and free space began.

"Look up to the north, where the shoreline curves around, that's what the cliffs below us are like."

Even in the mountain areas where she'd grown up she'd never seen such a stark drop going on for mile after mile, like some gigantic cleaver had chopped into the land mass leaving a vertical drop down to the sea. She clung even more tightly to Seamus. "That's what the little fence is for, to keep people from falling over the edge?"

"No, that's to keep the livestock from tumbling over. People are supposed to know better. And that brings us to Clark's first rule; never walk too far east or you're in for a nasty fall."

"Over the edge and right into the sea," she said.

"More likely onto the rocks. You only reach water if you bounce. Most people don't bounce."

"That's gruesome. I guess there are more rules."

"Yeah, no ten-mile hikes, especially after dark.

You might fall into a bog where we couldn't find you for years."

Too much, she thought, too damned much. "Look at me," she said. When he kept his face turned away toward the north she moved around in front of him and took his face in both hands. The shy smile that he seemed so desperate to hide was clearly visible. "So, that's it, you were just having a little joke at my expense."

"Not completely. Part of it is true."

"And the other part?" she asked.

"Just for fun."

"I'm going to remember that," she said.

He took off his jacket and spread it over the grass. "Want to sit for a while?"

"Yes, if you're sure I won't fall over the edge onto the rocks and maybe bounce into the sea, or maybe a bog."

"I'll hold onto you," he said. He grabbed her waist and pulled her down beside him.

She was nestled close to him, and soon her head was resting on his shoulder. "I thought you were going to keep me from falling. Well, you're not doing a very good job of it." She pulled his arm around her shoulders. "There, that's better.

"This feels like a good thinking place." She snuggled deeper into his armpit. Right now it was the safest place she could think of, and the only place she felt welcome.

"You have all the time you need, right here."

"I want somebody to tell me what I should do, where I should be. With all the craziness I feel like I'm lost in space. There are no signposts that say, 'Sharon go here, do this.'"

"Nobody around here can do that, and if they do, they're feeding you a line."

"Not even you?"

"Especially not me."

"What's that supposed to mean?" she asked.

"When you want things for other people, you box them in, influence their decisions. You can't make your choices based on what you think I want."

"You're not much help, you know?"

"I'm trying to help by staying out of your way."

True, perhaps, but she didn't want him out of the way. She wanted him squarely in her way. She could see no other way out of the mess she was in.

The shadows they cast had lengthened, and the onshore breeze had lessened. "Time to go, you think?" he asked.

Not until that moment did she realize how closely she was pressed into his body. Was this something she had done herself, or had he drawn her in. Either way, she liked the result, and was reluctant to give it up.

He stood and pulled her to her feet. "Long walk back," he said. "Don't want to do it in the dark. Remember the bogs."

"What a terrible thing to say." She punched him in the ribs, which seemed to have about the same effect as if she'd punched one of the stone walls surrounding the nearby pastures. "Just for that I should make you carry me back."

"Walk, woman." He smacked her on the backside.

"Ouch. You know, I've a good mind to have a talk with your Ma when we get back, let her know what a brute her son has become."

"No, no, don't do that. She's real sensitive about my behavior. And believe me, when she comes after you with her broom, it hurts."

Sharon laughed at the thought. "So now I know how to keep you in line, go tell your Ma."

The walk back was even more awkward than that earlier as they struggled along wrapped together like a couple of infatuated teenagers.

That night she opened the little burgundy case where she'd stashed her jewelry. She still had no idea how Seamus had managed to save it, but everything was there, jewelry from a man she'd shot. Ill-gotten gains all, but stuff that she wouldn't give up without a fight.

When she woke the next morning Seamus was gone. She hadn't heard him leave, but when had she ever? Usually he didn't arrive so much as he materialized, same when he left, he simply vanished.

Snuggling with him at the cliffs was an unexpected bonus. She could still feel the warmth of his arm around her, but the experience had also left her in a state of arousal. Several times during the night she'd thought of creeping into his bed. If her old techniques from the Faculty Club weren't too rusty, she could have him fired up before he even had a chance to resist.

No, she would let things develop at their own pace with Seamus. She would be patient and let him make the first real move, if and when he wanted to. But her patience was limited, and if he didn't soon take those first steps she might have to.

She dressed and walked back to the little house to see Ma. The clothes she put on were looking threadbare and barely passed the sniff test. She wondered whether

Seamus had noticed the day before during their walk. New clothes were very near the top of her list, but she had no idea where or when she might go shopping.

Ma had a pot of coffee on the stove and a plate of scrambled eggs and bacon on the table. She motioned for Sharon to take a seat.

Sharon, once again faced with a breakfast large enough to feed four or more, had stopped asking about the other diners; this was hers and hers alone. "Thank you," she said. "Won't you join me?"

A little nod of her head, that inscrutable smile, and Ma took a seat across from her.

The aroma of the breakfast sitting in front of her demanded attention…now. "Delicious," she said as she dug in. And that was the only word she could muster for several minutes.

"Seamus left early," she said when she raised her head for a short break.

A nod, a smile, that was all.

The other questions she wanted to ask, where did he go, when would he be back, were better left unsaid, she guessed. So she let them slide. This would take even more getting used to, a man who came and went with no explanation at all. Could she change him? Should she?

"I guess I'll go for another hike out by the cliffs," Sharon said.

Ma's eyes opened wider. "By yourself?"

"Sure, I don't think I'll get lost. Just walk east, then west to get back."

"But you be careful out there."

"I will. Seamus told me to look out for the bogs, but I didn't see any yesterday. Is there something else I should know?"

A shake of her head, then Ma looked away. "Just be careful."

The day was glorious, like the first of all days, blues, greens so bright they seemed lit up by some unseen power source. An occasional puffy white cloud crept across the sky as if it knew it shouldn't be there. And Sharon was going for a walk.

Except for not having Seamus at her side, her trek was much like the day before. There was a special feeling, being out in the countryside. Once when she'd attended a church camp in the mountains of North Carolina, she'd wandered off alone. Apparently missing girls were a big deal for the folks who ran the camp, as she found out later that they'd mobilized half the county to find her. But the hour or so that she'd spent by herself still burned in her memory. She noticed things she'd never noticed before, heard things, smelled them.

The magic returned now. About a mile into her walk she stopped, raised her arms above her head and ran around in circles like a possessed person. Nobody in sight in any direction, except for the car parked south of her. She'd seen no vehicle the day before. Oh well, if they'd come to watch her, let them watch. She'd been watched before, and this time she was fully clothed.

Just before noon she arrived at what now could become her favorite place. She could almost see the imprint of where she and Seamus had sat the day before. She settled into that same spot, inhaled deeply a few times and closed her eyes.

Maybe this was the place. Maybe here, even if she couldn't come up with any definitive answers, she could at least begin working through the terrible muddle that was now her life. She had a place where she could live safely, and according to Seamus, all the time she needed to make her decisions. But that didn't mean an indefinite period of waffling about.

Her questions were, of course, the same that had annoyed people for as long as there have been choices. Where shall I go? What shall I do? These had been the subject of many late night discussions among Sharon and her college classmates, questions that remained unanswered.

To that basic list of queries, she could add a few more, one involving millions stashed in a secret Swiss bank. She'd set thoughts of the money aside. Yes, it could open doors for her, but too many doors. Having too many options was almost as bad as having only a few. At the moment she had no use for huge sums of cash. She had no plans for it.

Moreover, her self-image needed some serious repairs. According to the press reports back in the U.S., she was now one of the most despicable women on the planet. And that was before she'd killed two people. Her self-esteem needed a boost so that she could look in a mirror without being overwhelmed by guilt.

Patience, that's what Seamus had advised. To that he'd added that the answers would come, but in their own good time.

Late afternoon, when she returned, Seamus's car was parked by the house. He was sitting inside with a cup of coffee in his grasp, and that far away unreadable look in his eyes.

"You're back," he said. "You've been spending more time out by the cliffs."

"A good place to think through some things," she said.

"You are keeping your eyes open, aren't you?"

"I won't fall over the edge," she said. "Not since you told me about the rocks."

"It's not just that. Keep your eyes open. You see anything weird or suspicious, let me know."

"Okay, but what am I looking for?" She thought for a moment of telling him about the car she'd seen, but decided against it. Probably just some sightseers. Not everything had to be part of a plot.

"Anything you haven't seen before, that's what I want to hear about. Now, come sit. Coffee?"

"Absolutely."

"What were you thinking about out there, if it's not too personal?"

She stuck her nose just above the rim of her cup and inhaled deeply. "About how I'm hiding out here like some desperado. You have to understand, this isn't me. I'm used to a very quiet life. Most people would say I'm as dull as dishwater. Okay," she looked at him closely. "If you start laughing I will kick you where it hurts."

"Sorry."

"It's just that crazy stuff happens to me. I don't like it. I want my old life back."

"How do you plan to do that?"

"I don't know, dammit. I just don't know. I can't go back home, probably never. I realize that."

"Unless you're there already."

"What's that supposed to mean?" she asked.

"Nothing, just talk."

Yeah, right, just talk. He was holding back on her,

something big, and her patience would wear thin, very soon. How could she be home in a place she'd never been before?

The next morning Seamus was already up and gone before she'd had her first cup of coffee with Ma.

"Another hike today?" Ma asked.

"I think so, maybe a different direction, though." Once again she caught that glimmer of what she thought to be concern in Ma's eyes. "Don't worry, I'll watch my step."

But she hardly watched where she was going, because she was quickly lost in thought. There were so many unanswered coincidences that she'd not considered before, and now they screamed at her. To start with there was Connor's first appearance at the Faculty Club, when he'd asked for her full time. How had he even known about the Club? He wasn't faculty at the college. And how had he known about her? Her little house of ill repute had only been in operation for a few months when he showed up, hardly enough time to establish a wide following, and she could only hope that her own reputation hadn't drawn him there. Becoming a famous prostitute was hardly the line of work in which she'd hoped to excel.

When she'd made her dash to Antigua, it seemed that everybody she met knew she was coming. If Seamus was to be believed, her bedmate, Angela not only knew about Sharon's arrival, but had even toured her house in Sharon's absence. It was all part of a plan, and she'd followed along without a clue.

Seamus had apparently known about her movements, as had the bad dudes Connor had sent to get her. Same when they caught her in London, Connor,

Lisa and the goons were already there waiting for her.

She seemed to be a step behind, everywhere she went, as if she'd been asleep for a week or so and was just catching up to everybody else. When she and Seamus arrived at his home in Ireland, Mo and Ma were waiting. Sharon herself was the only one surprised.

The only one who could answer the questions floating around in her head was Seamus, and he owed her a very large explanation. And that crack about being home now, what the hell did that mean?

This time her walk carried her to the cliffs, but by a different route. She discovered a cobblestone path, almost covered over by grass. A short distance to the north from where she stopped sat a low rectangle of stones…a foundation now in ruins? What little remained in place above the stone foundation appeared charred, as if the whole thing had been burned to the ground.

This place felt different, as if she'd been directed here, beckoned by some force she'd not known before.

The ruined foundation, if that's what it was, sat a bit higher than the land around it, and the view in all directions was breathtaking, even with the cloud cover that had rolled in. She walked around it, kicking at a few of the stones. What could it be? Why did she feel she'd been there before? Yes, indeed, Seamus had a lot of explaining to do.

She got caught in a cold rain about halfway back and arrived at the house soaked to the skin. Seamus seemed highly agitated, which seemed odd, not like she had never been caught in the rain before.

"You should have told me where you were going,"

he said. "I have people out looking for you."

"I'm sorry. You weren't here when I left."

He ushered her in by the fireplace, then wrapped her in a blanket. "Warm up a bit, then go change into some dry clothes."

"These are all I have," she said.

"You can find something in the closet. Mo never uses them."

She found jeans and a sweatshirt in the closet. The jeans were tight, but at least the sweatshirt was stretchy enough that she didn't feel like she was on display. Still, new clothes moved to the top of her list.

Seamus had dinner on the table when she returned. "You know, there's really not much to do except hike when you're not here," she said. "I found what must have been the foundation of an old house out by the cliffs. Have you seen it?"

"You found it," he said. He looked at her, brow furrowed like she'd done something wrong.

"So, it was a house. Who lived there?" she asked.

"That's a talk for another time, but I'll tell you soon, I promise. Now, eat."

Chapter Twenty-Two

Seamus was gone again the next morning, but returned in the late afternoon. Just in time, too. With nothing to read, no TV, no one to talk to, the solitude was getting to her. He must have known.

"Time for a trip to O'Reilly's pub," he said. "It's just a small place. Don't expect too much. They have Guinness and a bit of dancing. That's about it."

"Dancing? You're taking me dancing?"

"I'm taking you to a place where some people dance. But first we have to get you prettied up. I can't be seen escorting a scruffy woman. Bad for my reputation."

"You are really asking for a kick. You just get me the rest of my things from my house in Antigua, and I'll put on a show that will leave them talking for years."

He reddened. She caught it just before he turned his face away. Well, well, the tough guy had the same basic instincts as any other male. Maybe he'd even seen some of the strip routine she'd performed for Connor and his friends at the beach house. The memory of that performance made her blush too. If she ever did that number again it would be for an audience of one, only one.

"Remember, it's a family style place."

"Maybe I can borrow some clothes from Mo. We're about the same size." Everywhere except the bust, that is. Mo was flat, while Sharon packed enough for both of them. Several times she'd caught Mo staring at her breasts, but only silicone would ever bring her up to Sharon's league.

"Don't know why that woman has so many clothes, or where she gets the money to pay for them. She has them stashed in half a dozen places. Doubt she even knows where most of the stuff is," he said.

"I'll see what I can find. Then you can check me out, see if I'm up to your standards."

All of Mo's t-shirts were too small in the most obvious places. Whatever Sharon picked would be returned stretched out front and center. If Mo hadn't felt inadequate before, she certainly would when she saw how Sharon deformed her wardrobe. A green cardigan provided a bit of modesty, and so long as she remembered not to take it off, she would probably not create an uproar.

She found a pair of Mo's jeans that fit perfectly, but all her shoes were too small. Sharon was stuck with the grungy sneakers she'd worn when they'd fled Antigua.

She walked back into the kitchen and did a little pirouette in front of Seamus. From the look in his eyes she knew that he approved.

"That'll do," he said. "We can go now."

"Wait just a minute," she said. "I have standards too, you know." She motioned with her finger, directing him to perform the same maneuver she'd just done for him.

"What, you're going to inspect me?"

"What's fair is fair. You checked me out, now I'm going to see about you."

"That's ridiculous. This is the same thing I always wear."

"And that is part of the problem. Suppose sometime you want to take me out to a nice restaurant. You'll have to do better than that. And you certainly can't borrow clothes from Mo."

She scored a direct hit, the blush, the shy smile, she got them both. Now, press onward.

"When I go shopping I'm taking you along. You need some new duds too."

"That's not going to happen. We're going to O'Reilly's pub. I've been there hundreds of times, and this is what I always wear. If I go in wearing something different, especially something you'd pick out, they'll all think I've gone round the bend."

"Okay, I'll let you off this time, but very soon…shopping, you and me."

"This must be the scenic route, huh?" she asked. In the twenty minutes since they'd set out, Seamus had driven them along paths that scarcely resembled a road. Twice he'd had to stop to open gates that confined herds of sheep.

"Short cut," he said.

Soon after, almost appearing from thin air, sat a small cluster of buildings, five in number. They all appeared to be constructed from the same materials, lumber and stone.

"Groceries right there." Seamus pointed to the first building they passed on the right.

"Small," she said.

"No supermarkets around here. Dentist is right there. He does a bit of veterinary work on the side, so don't expect too much. O'Reilly's is the last place on the left."

The sign above the pub was small and unlit. Still, cars were parked alongside the road as far down as she could see. Apparently O'Reilly's drew a crowd. She heard music, laughter and a buzz of conversation when Seamus opened the door. But as soon as they walked in the music stopped, along with the laughter. This might be a good time to run away, she thought.

"Seamus." His name rose as from a single voice. Any hope she had for a fast getaway disappeared as the people in the room crowded around them. "Seamus." They pounded on his back, lined up to shake his hand, all vying for the privilege of buying his first beer.

And Sharon herself got tagged with the label of honored guest. They introduced themselves, hats in hands. Some even bowed, as if she were visiting royalty. Her own hand was taken up ever so gently in hands that felt powerful enough to crush stones.

A hefty man, as tall as Seamus but much larger in girth, wrapped Seamus in a bear hug and lifted him off the floor. For sure, if she got the same hug it would break ribs and damage internal organs.

"Thought you'd forgotten all about us," said the bear hugger, his brawny arms still wrapped around Seamus.

"Not likely," Seamus said. "Now, if you'll put me down I'd like to breathe again." He put his hand on Sharon's arm. "This is my good friend, Sharon."

She tensed up, anticipating a full frontal assault, but the man Seamus introduced took her hand gently, as if he were cradling a child's.

"I'm O'Reilly, Miss. So glad to meet you. If you need anything, anything at all, just snap your fingers and I'll be right there. But this fella here," he slapped a meaty paw on Seamus's shoulder, "I plan to ignore him completely, because he ran off and forgot about us."

"I'm afraid that was all my fault," she said.

O'Reilly laughed. "I guess any time spent in the service of a beautiful lady should count as an excused absence. All is forgiven then."

"In that case, how about a couple of Guinness," Seamus said. "And tell Will to crank up that fiddle."

O'Reilly led them to a corner table. A moment later a winsome young girl, flaming red hair, milky white skin and green eyes arrived with bottles of Guinness, glasses and a dish overflowing with snacks.

"Hi, Lauren," Seamus said. "How've you been?"

"Great, Mr. Clark. So good to see you again."

"This is my friend, Sharon," Seamus said.

"You must be Maureen O'Hara's great granddaughter," Sharon said. "But you must have heard that comparison hundreds of times."

"A few," Lauren said. Her smile revealed a sparkling set of teeth. "Mr. O'Reilly says I'm to take orders from you," she said to Sharon. "And I'm to ignore Mr. Clark." Her laugh was like wind chimes.

"What an absolutely beautiful girl," Sharon said. "If all the girls here are as pretty as she is, I'd just as well pack up and move on."

"You'll do fine," Seamus said. "As soon as we get you some new shoes."

Just as Sharon polished off her first Guinness, several couples began dancing in the small open area. "You said you were going to take me dancing. I don't know that dance, but it doesn't look too complicated."

"Dancing? That's what you want?" he asked.

"That's right, and you promised to teach me."

"I don't remember that, but if it's dancing lessons you want I'll set you up with an expert." Before she could protest, Seamus waved to a tall, gaunt man with a shock of white hair standing at the end of the bar. "Clem," he said. "We need your services."

Clem's craggy face broke into the wall-to-wall grin that seemed to be the order of the evening at O'Reilly's.

"Clem, this is my friend, Sharon, and she needs a dance lesson," Seamus said.

"Then what she needs is a lively young fella like myself. We'll have you dancing a jig in no time."

Some new ventures gave her pause could she do it or couldn't she? But dancing wasn't one of them. The only difference this time was that she'd be keeping her clothes on. In only a few moments she had mastered the basics and added a few new ones of her own.

"You're a natural," Clem said. "If anything, you should give me lessons."

"You're a great teacher, Clem," She added a smile that made the tips of his ears turn red.

A few more turns around the floor, and Clem obviously needed a break.

"Time for a beer?" she asked.

But they were intercepted on the way to the bar.

"Clem, you've monopolized this beautiful lady all evening." He took Sharon's arm. "I'm Charlie."

Charlie was not as tall as Clem, but fuller in the shoulders. He, too, flashed a one hundred-watt grin, straight from a face that looked as if it might have been hewn from the stones atop the fences. Damn, beautiful girls and great-looking guys. Must be something in the water, or the Guinness.

The little band struck up a livelier tune, and Charlie proved up to the task. The tightly packed room was getting warmer, and she wished she could peel off the stifling cardigan, but the t-shirt she had on underneath was too tight to begin with, and the layer of perspiration she'd worked up would have it plastered to her skin. Taking off the outer sweater would probably set off the fire alarms.

After Charlie there was another younger buck whose name she didn't catch and wouldn't have remembered anyway. Then another.

By now she was gasping and sweating profusely. "Enough," she said. "I need a break." She found Clem back at his station at the end of the bar. "Can I buy you a beer, for that dance lesson?" she asked.

"Oh, no," Clem said. "Ladies do not buy beer in O'Reilly's. House rules. But I'll be happy to buy you one, and maybe one for myself. Besides, you didn't need any lessons. Like I said before, you're a natural."

She kissed him on the cheek, and predictably, his ears turned red, but it didn't matter, because she was happier than she'd been in a long while, really happy.

She'd been watching Seamus out of the corner of her eye. Ever since she left the table there was a steady stream of men approaching him. They leaned in close when they talked with him, but they didn't linger. Others were waiting.

"Who are all those men waiting to talk to Seamus?" she asked Clem.

"Business," he said. "Poor fella can't get away from it."

"What kind of business?"

"Just business."

Her questions, and there were many, were cut short when the lights in the room lowered, and two bright overhead lights lit up the far end of the room. Four young girls, maybe ten to twelve years of age, three brunettes and one platinum blonde, marched in unison onto the platform under the lights. Their dresses matched perfectly, black tights, patent leather shoes with gold buckles, dark green skirts with gold trim, and white blouses with gold-trimmed collars and wristbands. All topped off by dark green hair ribbons that matched their skirts. Their bodies were those of youth, but their faces showed a mature focus. Not fun and games this, but serious business.

With their entrance, everyone in the room, including Sharon, inhaled deeply. That communal breath was held until the band struck up a lively tune, and the young girls began a series of rapid, intricate maneuvers, the gold buckles on their shoes flashing in the overhead lights. Aside from a few moves in which they danced in a circle, arms entwined overhead, those arms remained fixed at their sides.

Now Sharon knew where those ear-to-ear smiles came from; she was wearing one herself.

"Irish step dancing," Clem whispered in her ear.

No conversations, no laughter, all eyes on the dancers. These were hometown girls, their own girls. And this was what hometown was all about, belonging, something she wanted so desperately for herself.

"My granddaughter, the one on the right," again, Clem whispering in her ear.

As if she'd heard him, impossible, of course, the platinum blonde smiled at Clem, who, at the moment, was likely the happiest man on the planet. Sharon used a napkin to blot the tears from his cheeks.

Sometime later, the lights in the big room went up again. The dancers took their bows then skipped off the stage. The room erupted in applause.

"So beautiful," Sharon said. "I've never seen anything so beautiful."

"They're champions," Clem said. "Tour all over the country."

Sharon looked for Seamus, and he still sat as their table. But instead of watching where the dancers must reappear for their encore, he was watching her. How long had that been going on?

She made her way back to the table, along the way, declining several offers to dance. "Do you have time for me now? Looked like you were very busy."

"Just old friends is all. You seemed to be having a good time."

"I've had a great time." She edged a bit closer to him. "So, Clem taught me a bit. Now when are you going to ask me to dance?"

"Soon, I think."

"When?" She held his gaze. She sat too close for him to turn away without being obvious.

"Real soon. I'm a bit rusty myself," he said.

"When?"

"God, woman, you'd drive a man to drink."

"You're right, if that's what it takes. Now, when?"

"When you've had a little more practice," he said.

"Ooh, that was low. I'm keeping score, you know, all these little digs you think you're getting away with. I'm remembering all of them, and you'll pay."

As quickly as their bottles of Guinness were emptied, fresh ones appeared on the table. She could only hope that Seamus was keeping count, because on her last trip to the bathroom she'd lurched into several tables.

Seamus must have noticed. "It might be time to take you home," he said.

Stars glowed in the clear night sky, and the shock of the cool evening air on her moist skin cleared a few of the cobwebs from her brain. "Thanks for bringing me here. I really needed this."

"Kind of warm inside," he said. "I expect you're sorry you wore that sweater."

Yeah, she was sorry. She could hardly wait until they got into the car before she peeled off the cardigan. She'd been right about the sweat-soaked t-shirt. It clung to her like a second skin.

"Now I see why you wore it."

She clutched the cardigan to her chest. "It's all I could find. Mo is a lot smaller than I am."

"She certainly is."

"Don't you start," she said. "I did the best I could." Why, then, was she becoming all modest in front of a man who had seen her completely naked before? Was the ground shifting just a little? New rules of engagement?

They rode in silence for a short time, Seamus maneuvering along a road that she could not see. A three-quarter moon rose behind them in a sky already lit by countless stars. Stars, stars, she'd never seen so many. But there were no other lights around them, only moonlight.

The question crept out of some place in her subconscious mind. "Who are you?" she asked him.

"Just Seamus, same as always. That's a weird thing

to ask."

"What was all that stuff back there at the pub? All those men, it was like they were paying homage to you. Know what it reminded me of? The Godfather, did you ever see that movie?"

"Sure, I saw it, but you got it all wrong. Those fellows were just old friends and neighbors. Godfather indeed." He laughed loudly, a bit too loudly.

"Cousins?"

"Some of them, yeah."

And that was as far as she would get, tonight, anyway. This most secretive man was far beyond any techniques of coercion that she knew of, and any attempt at extracting information from him would drive him away and build a wall between them. And she definitely did not want a wall or anything else separating them.

The moonlight bathed the countryside, almost commanding silence. She obeyed the command, and so did Seamus, although she thought it was probably easier for him.

They didn't speak until they entered the house, where, just before they each went to their own rooms, she grabbed his arm, spun him around and kissed him on the cheek. "Thanks for taking me to the pub, and you still have to dance with me."

"I know."

"Don't say it like that. It's not as if I were asking you to walk off a cliff."

Again, "I know." But this time he took her by the shoulders and kissed her, not on the cheek, but full on the lips. Then he walked into his room, leaving her standing there, dumbstruck.

All those times when she thought he might kiss her, hoped he would, he hadn't. Now, right out of the blue, he'd planted one on her, then walked away without a word. And it wasn't even the most skilled kiss she'd ever received, still it had left her with blurred vision, weak knees, short of breath.

But if the guy thought he was calling the shots, that everything would happen when and where he wanted, he had another think coming. She had a few tricks of her own.

Chapter Twenty-Three

There was never any doubt as to whether Mo was around, or not. Like Seamus, she appeared, then disappeared for no apparent reason, except with noise.

On this occasion her target clearly was Sharon. She marched into the kitchen where Sharon was enjoying a quiet cup of coffee, and poured one for herself. "You must be going bat shit crazy out here by yourself, nothing going on," Mo said.

"I don't mind," Sharon said, and indeed, she didn't. Whether Seamus was orchestrating her mix of alone time, she wasn't sure. But as far as she was concerned, it was having the best possible effect. It was as if something she had lacked before was creeping inside her, filling up empty spaces, almost a feeling, crazy as it was, of coming home.

"Maybe when you're as old as Ma this sort of life might suit you, but you're way too young to be dying a slow death out here in the sticks. And if you're counting on Seamus to take care of you, forget about it. Mostly, he takes care of himself. He's never around when you want him and always underfoot when you don't need him. Best just do what you want when you want."

Sharon wasn't quite sure where this was going, but whatever, it was making her uncomfortable.

"I mean, has he taken you anywhere since you got

here?" Mo asked.

"We went to O'Reilly's pub. I had a really good time," Sharon said.

"He took you to O'Reilly's? Just like him to do that. O'Reilly's is an old folks' home. You need some place livelier, and I know plenty of spots that will do."

"It was lively enough for me." This from a girl who'd earned her tuition payments stripping. She got up to rinse out her cup. "So, what do you have in mind?"

"Something different, that's for sure. Seamus, he tries, but he doesn't understand women. No man does, really. But I know exactly what you need to pick you up, retail therapy, I call it. To other people it's just shopping," Mo said.

"Seamus mentioned that he might take me."

"Oh, no. He'll have you dressed like an old lady. He's such a control freak. Believe me, you don't want to go shopping with him," Mo said.

"I don't think of him like that."

"You don't know him like I do. You should see him when he doesn't get his way. Which is exactly why we should just take off, nobody will know."

"But that seems sort of mean, running off without telling him."

"All the more reason we should just go. See, the worst thing in the world is for a man to take a woman for granted. And they all do unless you do something to make them sit up and take notice. Now, where are your shoes?"

Sharon, who was barefoot, and liking it, dragged her scruffy old sneakers from under the bed.

"Oh, sweet Jesus, this is all you have? Absolutely

not, this will not do. Shoes are first on the list."

Mo almost dragged her out to the car, a glistening black BMW convertible, parked on the east side of the house, out of sight from her Ma's little place.

"Nice wheels," Sharon said.

Mo patted the polished dash. "It belongs to a friend. Be a long time before I can afford something like this. You think you'll be getting a car soon, or maybe you don't plan to stay that long?"

"Haven't decided yet."

"I know the girl who owns the shop where I'm taking you. They have everything you'll need, and believe me, you'll look a hell of a lot sharper than if Seamus took you shopping."

She took a longer look at Mo's outfit, white see-through top with a black bra underneath, a skirt so short it almost shouted "Look at me." And stiletto pumps. A hell of a lot of good she would get from footwear like that out on the farm.

Mo tore off across the countryside, while Sharon maintained a death grip on the door handle. Either she was fearless or crazy, but her driving definitely did not fit the conditions. Even on the main road she still drove like a fury, slowing only when they entered a small town that reminded Sharon of the shopping area that surrounded Pisgah College.

Eventually Mo pulled to a stop in front of a shop, Erin's, according to the small sign above the door. Sharon said a simple prayer of thanks at having survived the drive, far too fast for the twisting, narrow paths that Mo had followed.

Music blasted from speakers in the four corners of the large room. The sales staff, none of who appeared to be over sixteen, darted about like objects in a pinball game. The atmosphere was high energy, bordering on chaos.

A moment after they'd entered, while Sharon was still in a state of confusion, a young woman about Mo's age embraced her and kissed Mo on the cheek.

"Erin, this is my new friend, Sharon. As you can see, she needs outfitting from top to bottom, inside and out."

Erin shook Sharon's hand then walked slowly around her, like an inspection tour. "Oh, yes, we can do wonderful things with you. I won't even ask where you got those awful things you're wearing, but they can go right in the trash bin before you leave."

Erin snapped her fingers, and a waif-like girl appeared at Sharon's side. "The works, Eileen."

As Eileen led Sharon off to battle Mo grabbed her free arm. "Do you have any money?" she asked.

"Yes, I have some."

"I hope it's a lot. Things are pricey here," Mo said. "I should know."

"No, really, I'll be fine."

"Wow, next time I need a loan I'll look you up."

When Mo disappeared, Eileen was the default winner in the tug-of-war game with Sharon in the middle. With one glance at Sharon's sneakers she announced that shoes would be their first stop. She set out a selection in front of Sharon ranging from low heels to higher heels to ridiculous stilettos, similar to those that Mo wore.

Sharon tried on the low heels, but after her time in sneakers even they felt a bit awkward for her.

Eileen urged her to try on the next set of heels.

Sharon resisted at first, but Eileen was determined. "A girl has to have a nice set of heels, you know, just in case."

The heels would be useless, but there seemed to no point in battling Eileen, so into the large shopping bag they went. Sharon's own contribution was a pair of walking shoes, quite suitable for her hikes out to the cliffs.

Underwear was diagonally across from shoes, and that's where Eileen headed next. "You're going to love some of the new things we have in."

Sharon wandered among the displays, among the semi-transparent items too sheer to hold back a gentle breeze. In truth, she'd left nicer items behind in the Antigua house. But she planned no more erotic dances and had little interest in the flimsy garments that Eileen kept thrusting at her.

"Look at this." Eileen shoved a diaphanous bra against Sharon's chest. "It's supportive but not too confining, you know, you can still have, you know, movement."

"Jiggle, you mean," Sharon said.

Eileen reddened. "Yes, that too." This was obviously not a consideration for Eileen who was perfectly flat in front.

Another compromise. Sharon's selections were serviceable; Eileen's more effective at causing traffic accidents.

Progressing from inside out, they were now amidst the outerwear that Erin felt would best suit her clientele, including some of the briefest skirts that Sharon ever seen. Even during her campus days, she hadn't seen anything so skimpy, except on cheerleaders. She could have guessed as much, looking around at the pencil-thin salesgirls who could only pull it off because they had such tiny asses, leaving almost no curvature between their waists and knees.

It seemed centuries ago, not just a few months, since she had paraded around in nothing at all in front of a room full of howling, drunken men. Now she was concerned over a few inches in skirt length. "You've come a long way, girl," she said to herself.

Then Mo was right in front of her holding up a swath of red fabric that resembled a skirt, must have been. "Look what I found. It's perfect for you." She held up the garment to Sharon's waist. "Oh, yeah."

"Uh, Mo, where would I wear something like this?"

"No problem," Mo said. "I know plenty of places. See, you don't know what young people wear around here. Seamus keeps you around old fogies. Sometimes I think he's afraid to let you out, you know, have a little fun. Now, here, try this one on. I picked out a few other things for you, too."

Mo's skirt selections had two things in common; sitting down would be a challenge, and bending over was out of the question.

The tug-of-war resumed, and in the end, Sharon had enough serviceable clothing to get by, as well as a few outfits that Mo had selected, including the red skirt.

"I guess that should do it," Sharon said.

"Not quite. It's time for your grand entrance into our local scene." She held out the red skirt and a black top that was predictably snug. "We're meeting a couple of guys for lunch and drinks."

"Mo, I can't wear that. What will people think?"

"They'll think you're a knockout. Now, please, please, please, just for me." She half-guided, half-pushed Sharon toward a changing room.

Just this once, she thought. Then the red skirt and the stiletto heels would go into the bottom of the closet never to see the light of day again.

God, how things change. Only a few weeks ago she wouldn't have minded the red skirt, no problem. She might have compounded the effect with a pair of flimsy underpants, or none at all.

Now she stood in front of the mirror tugging the hemline down in front, in back and both sides, none of which improved its coverage. Fortunately, she'd bought a pair of black tights that made her feel a bit less bare.

"Oh, what have you done?" Mo asked. "Those horrid black stockings."

"Either this or I go back and change into jeans."

Mo sighed deeply, as if her entire project had been laid in ruins. She held up her hands in apparent exasperation. "Seamus has really done a number on you. Come on, let's go meet the guys."

Such a relief to finally be outside again, away from the frenetic activity of the shop. The black tights helped a little, perhaps, but Sharon still drew stares from every male that passed, and a few of the females as well.

Mo, from all appearances, couldn't be happier, as if she had rescued Sharon from a life of drudgery, transforming her into a budding rose.

As they turned the corner Sharon thought she glimpsed a familiar and unsettling face, Bob Hastings? But that couldn't be. There was no way he could have followed her here.

"What's the matter, Sharon? You look like you've

seen a ghost." Mo clutched her arm.

"Oh, nothing, just hungry, I think." When she looked back he was gone. Perhaps he'd never been there in the first place, just unpleasant memories coming back to haunt her.

Mo led her across the street, then to a building with a large neon cocktail glass including a luminous green olive that kept bouncing up and down. The windows were tinted, presumably so the patrons inside could see out, but those passing by could not see in. This was how Sharon thought the floor-to-ceiling windows in her Antigua house were supposed to work, until Seamus informed her of how easily affordable night vision goggles rendered her windows completely transparent.

"Here we are," said Mo, and she opened the door.

Any hope Sharon had of being able to hide behind Mo vanished as Mo pushed her front and center. This definitely wasn't O'Reilly's pub. It wasn't a pub at all, just an upscale bar with the same cowboys she'd been fighting off for years. She hadn't created much of a stir at O'Reilly's, but here she was clearly the main attraction.

The guys sitting in a corner booth waved them over, and Mo tugged Sharon along to their table. When one of the guys stood up Mo maneuvered Sharon in between them. Same old squeeze play she'd learned to avoid long before. Now the only way she could escape would be to crawl over or under the table.

The game, she assumed, would be much the same as in times past, keep her wedged in between them, keep refilling her glass until her eyes crossed, and she would do anything they wanted.

"Do they serve food here?" Sharon asked Mo.

One of the guys pushed a bowl of peanuts in front of her. "Here you go," he said as if he'd just given her a juicy steak with all the trimmings.

"Sharon, haven't seen you around before. Where have you been hiding?"

She felt hands on both her thighs at once and had to drive her fingernails into their wrists before they'd let go. Yeah, Mo had really set her up, like fresh meat in front of a pack of wolves.

"Seamus keeps her shut away out at the farm. Poor thing didn't have any decent clothes to wear until I took her shopping today," Mo said.

Instantly the two bodies pressing against Sharon's hips stiffened and inched away. The temperature in the room dropped a few degrees, then a few more. Was it just the mention of Seamus that had caused this seismic change?

"Damn," Michael said. "I forgot about that guy I was supposed to meet. He really gets pissed if I'm late."

"I should be going too," Danny said.

Then they were gone, with only the fingerprints pressed into Sharon's thighs to say they'd ever been there.

"Guess they didn't like me much," Sharon said.

"No, it's that damned Seamus. I should have known better. Every time somebody mentions his name all the fun gets sucked out of the room."

The drive back ended when Mo stopped some fifty yards from the house. "Do you mind?" she asked. "If Seamus is around I'd rather not get into it with him right now."

"I thought you two were friendly," Sharon said.

"We could be if he didn't strut around like he was

king of the county or something."

"Thanks for taking me shopping, Mo. I really appreciate it."

Sharon was barely out of the car before Mo began pulling away. She wished there were a back door to the cabin so she could change out of what she now thought of as her streetwalker outfit before Seamus saw it.

No chance. She had to walk right past him in the brightly lit kitchen.

"Don't tell me, been shopping with Mo, right?" he asked. Then he turned back to his newspaper. "Supper's in the oven."

Not even a look? Her red skirt ensemble might not do for a hike out to the cliffs, but she looked damned good, and she knew it. No way she was going to let him off this easy.

She set her shopping bag on the floor and did a slow twirl for him. He was still half hidden by his newspaper, so she pulled it from his hand and tossed it onto the table. Then she did another twirl, slower than the first. "Do you like it?" she asked. She stopped with her hips cocked and her right toe pointed at him.

"Oh, yes, very nice." He reached for his newspaper, but she pushed it away.

"Nice? Just nice? After all the time we spent picking this out, all you can say is nice?"

They were all there, the signs she knew so well in the male aroused. Him trying not to look but not able to stop himself. Nervously tapping his fingertips on the table. If she could run her fingertips beneath the collar of his shirt she certainly would have touched moist skin, becoming moister.

"Well?" she asked. She increased his discomfort by

taking a step closer.

"Uh, really nice, lovely."

Not much better but probably all she would get from this taciturn man. She bent forward and kissed him on the cheek. "Thanks."

It was a bit unfair, what she had just done. But a girl had to put what God had given her to good use. Besides, if he wanted more all he had to do was walk down the hall into her room.

****

She didn't expect to find him waiting for her the next morning, and indeed, he was nowhere to be found. The usual extravagant breakfast was waiting for her in the oven, though. The large meal demanded a nice brisk walk. She grabbed a rain slicker from the hanger on the wall and set off. This time she gave no thought to where she might go, but her feet let her know soon enough. It seemed as if she was drawn along the same path she'd followed earlier, back toward the old ruined foundation, that place that held secrets that Seamus hadn't shared with her yet.

Her new hiking shoes proved quite comfortable, and fortunately had a rubberized outside, which came in handy because the grass was still quite wet, and soon to become wetter. As she figured, if she waited for perfect weather she'd never go anywhere, so, in spite of a dismal gray cloud cover she'd plunged ahead. Only the slicker saved her from a drenching.

As she neared the old foundation, she discovered an almost hidden cobblestone path that she'd missed the last time. Grass had crept over the stones until they were barely visible. How long had they been here? Who had put them out in the first place? More questions that

Seamus would have to answer.

For her part, she felt a stirring, vague at first but becoming stronger the closer she got to the foundation. If she hadn't known better she would have thought that she belonged there, and it wasn't a bad feeling at all. Belonging somewhere, one of her prime needs at the moment, because with the doors to her past now closed, she needed a real home. Seamus belonged, for sure. Even when he wasn't around, he was still close by; she could feel his presence.

She leaned into the wind. Even now in late June, the gusts off the sea made her teeth chatter. She walked the perimeter of the foundation. It seemed a foolish thing to stand there buffeted by the wind, but her impulse to stay was far, far stronger than her impulse to leave.

The foundation was set back at least three hundred feet from the cliff edge, far enough that a casual stroll wouldn't have the walker falling over. Even farther back, it seemed to her, might be safer, but the view from where it stood was fantastic

Time passed, how long? She knew not. Her jeans were soaked at the knees, but that had happened shortly after she'd knelt. The sun had descended, and she was thoroughly chilled. She was aware of tears coming down her face, and that they'd been falling for a while.

A soft rustle in the grass behind her. A hand on her shoulder, gently…Seamus. He knelt beside her and wrapped his arm around her shoulders. "Gets to you, doesn't it?" he said. "You have to be careful, though. Even out here, not everything is true."

She twisted in his arms so that she could look directly into his face. "But you are, aren't you? True?"

"That's what you're looking for. I wish I had a better answer for you, but you'll have to decide that one for yourself. It's as much a matter of choice as fact."

She laid her head against his shoulder. "How did you find me?"

"It wasn't hard. I figured you'd come back here."

"And just how did you know that?"

"For you, this is an important place. That's all I'm going to say now, but it's no surprise that you'd come here again. We'd best be heading back. You're cold and wet, and probably hungry too."

"And it's a long walk," she said.

"We're going to ride."

Not until that moment did she realize he'd ridden his horse. The noise of the wind must have masked his approach. Seamus vaulted into the saddle, then held out his hand for her. "Put your foot in the stirrup, and I'll pull you up."

With Sharon seated in front, they began the ride back home. The rain had fallen off to a steady drizzle, and a glimmer of late afternoon sunlight fought its way through the cloud cover.

It wasn't something she'd planned, or even thought about; she just did it. Somehow through twisting and squirming and almost falling off the horse in the process, she managed to get her right leg swung over to where her left had been, and vice versa. This new arrangement put her face to face with Seamus who did not seem amused.

"What on earth are you doing?" he asked.

"I like to look at you when we talk." Then, to make matters worse, she wrapped her legs around his waist. From any distance at all they must have looked like a single large body with two heads.

"I can't see where we're going," he said.

"I expect the horse knows the way. Your job is to make sure we don't fall off." Now, in addition to clasping him with her legs she wrapped her arms around his neck. Never one to pass up such an opportunity, she kissed him.

"What's that for?"

"That's for coming to get me. You saved me a long walk home."

"I think we'd better get you a horse of your own. But you can still kiss me if you feel so inclined."

"Good, glad to hear that." She kissed him again, longer, harder, the kind of kiss that usually required the close proximity of a bed.

The horse stopped, and she heard a voice, full of mirth, just short of outright laughter.

"I never thought I'd ever see it done on horseback. Is this one of the new tricks you learned in the States, Cousin?"

"Oh, shit." Seamus pulled away from her. "And in front of the biggest mouth in County Wicklow."

"Well, ain't you gonna introduce me to your friend?" The man rode a dappled mare that seemed quite skittish compared to Seamus's own mount.

"This reprobate is my cousin, William. We don't use his last name, because his family won't claim him," Seamus said.

"All true," William said. He flashed a wicked grin at Sharon. "And I can tell you a few tales about the man you're riding with. If anybody but me saw you like this with him, your reputation would suffer for sure." He tipped his hat and rode away to the north.

"Another one of your cousins," Sharon said. "I never saw anyone with so many cousins. Are you really related to all of them?"

"Some are, some aren't, some I'm not sure about."

"Are you going to tell me about it, or is this another one of your secrets?"

"No secret, and there's not much to tell. Some years back, around the time of 'the troubles,' I'm sure you've heard of them, that's when it got started."

"I didn't know you were involved in all that."

"Everybody was in one way or another. Even after things settled down there were hard feelings, and some things were done that should not have been. The cousins were never an official organization, just a bunch of neighbors who looked out after one another."

"Is that how everybody seemed to know about me even before I got here?" she asked.

"That's part of it, yeah. Strangers, in particular, people want to know where they're from and what they're doing here. So I spread the word that you were my special friend."

"Under your protection, you mean."

"Not quite so dramatic. Just wanted to make sure people made you feel welcome, that's all."

"Okay, then, even if I buy that part, how did you know I'd be here ahead of time? Mo and your Ma acted like they were expecting me. How could they have known?"

"That's how the system works, we share information, the sooner the better."

"It's spooky, if you ask me. Ever since I left my home I've felt like I was followed, first to Antigua, then London, then here."

"You were, and not all of them had your best interests at heart. You needed a few friendly faces along the way."

"Are you going to tell me how you got involved? When you were driving me back and forth to meet Connor I always thought you had a pretty low opinion of me. Prostitutes are far down on anybody's list."

"Don't call yourself that. Sometimes you do what you have to do. How I got involved is a long story, and I will tell you. I promise. But we're close to home now, and I don't want to get halfway into it. I want you to hear the whole story, all at once."

"You're scaring me," she said.

"I'm sure, but it will all be a lot clearer soon."

They ate their meal in silence. Seamus seemed wrapped in his own thoughts as she was in hers. He had stocked the small refrigerator with Guinness the day before, and they'd each consumed a couple of bottles with their meal. But even that smooth, dark beverage, the mainstay of every pub in the region, failed to loosen their tongues.

She had planted a couple of vigorous kisses on Seamus earlier, but since they'd arrived home he showed no inclination to continue that sort of activity. Did that mean he wanted no further amorous contact with her? Too much too soon? Would the time ever be right?

"Lost your appetite?" he asked.

"That huge breakfast seems to last me all day." No, it wasn't the food, it was the mound of questions that piled up around her that caused her to push her potatoes and sausages around her plate instead of eating them.

And the biggest question was Seamus himself. Any

other man who failed to return her affections would simply be scratched off her list. There were other fish in the sea, lots of them. But there was a depth to her feelings for him that she hadn't experienced before.

Not even Connor, with whom she'd shared some of the most scintillating sexual episodes she ever expected to have, created this kind of emotion. And in the end, she'd shot him. She would never shoot Seamus, never. Besides, it would take something far more powerful than a .22 caliber bullet to bring him down.

Later, as she washed the dishes, she wondered whether there would ever come a time when she and Seamus would sit together for an after dinner chat, like normal couples. Or would the quiet man remain uncommunicative leaving her to fend for herself?

"I think I'll turn in early," she said. "That big walk wore me out." All she wanted now was to lie in bed with his strong arms wrapped around her, but that seemed about as likely as an earthquake. Okay, then, she would wait. What else could she do?

Chapter Twenty-Four

Sharon took her morning coffee outside and sat on a rough bench facing the morning sun. Somewhere in the shuffle, she'd lost track of time. She knew it was late June, and that the day of the week was Thursday, but that was about it. It seemed all too easy to let the world slip by, since everything else seemed so far away. But this was a temporary respite. Reality would come creeping back before long.

She was becoming a bit tired of spending her mornings alone, and most of her evenings as well. If this was how things were going to be, she might as well pack up and leave. She didn't need the frenetic social life that Mo seemed to crave, but she'd taken no vow of silence either.

And Seamus, as important as he was to her, was mostly absent. She'd wondered during her time with Connor how it might be to be married to him. Most likely he would chase her around the bedroom a few nights a week, but otherwise she would spend little time with him. So far, that was how things had been with Seamus, except that he didn't chase her around the bedroom, even when she wanted him to.

God, she knew so little about the man. Where did he go? What did he do? Was he a violent man, someone to be feared? The world in which he moved, one with people who would kill to get and keep what they wanted, was surely a place where violence was always a possibility. People like Connor Shaw might do business with a smile and a handshake, but they enforced their deals through other men who could inflict severe physical damage. Seamus, she guessed, would do what had to be done all by himself, with his own capable hands.

And where did he fit into this big, expensive picture? Was he just an enforcer? Who gave him his marching orders, or maybe he was the man who gave the orders in the first place. The memory of their first trip to O'Reilly's pub, the men, the "cousins" all lined up at Seamus's table. They did everything but kneel and kiss his ring.

And why had he chosen to rescue her, to become her protector? Coming to her aid had placed him at great risk. What had moved him to put himself in jeopardy to save a prostitute? This was the biggest question of all, the one that kept her from packing up and moving out.

Mo came by in the early afternoon. The noonday sun forced Sharon to seek refuge in the cool interior of the stone house. Times past, she might have donned a bikini and enjoyed the heat, but that sort of display seemed inappropriate in her current surroundings. Jeans and a t-shirt had become her go-to casual attire.

On the other hand, Mo didn't seem to share her inhibitions. The white shorts she wore appeared to have been applied with a paintbrush, and her yellow top was no more spacious.

"Wow," Sharon said. "You'll stop traffic in that outfit."

"No traffic to stop, not around here anyway." She

paced around the living room as if she'd overdone her morning coffee quotient.

"The reason I came, Seamus wants to see you."

The idea of Seamus sending Mo to fetch her, especially dressed as she was, seemed no more likely than if he'd sent a horse-drawn carriage with red velvet seats.

"It's about a half hour drive," Mo said. "He would have come himself, but he was tied up with some guys. You know how he is."

"Why didn't he mention this before?" Sharon asked.

"Who knows? I never can figure the guy out." Mo resumed pacing. She stopped each time she passed one of the front windows.

"Were you expecting someone else?" Sharon asked.

"Oh, no. Say, we'd best get going. Don't want to keep the master waiting. You know how he gets."

This was so wrong, but she couldn't come up with any graceful way to refuse. "Let me get my purse."

Mo was driving a black Lexus sedan. She pulled away from the house as if it was on fire.

"What happened to the little BMW convertible?" Sharon asked.

"Time for a change," Mo said.

"Aren't you driving a little fast for roads like these?"

"Faster than Seamus, you mean. He drives like an old lady."

Sharon clung to the edges of her seat.

After a few narrow misses, one involving a small flock of sheep that scattered in all directions and left an angry farmer shaking his fist at them, Mo turned onto the Interstate.

"Where are we going?" Sharon asked.

"South, toward Waterford."

Something more specific would have been nice, but Sharon asked no more questions. At the speed Mo was blasting along she didn't dare distract her.

Mo took an exit off the four lane, and after a few more turns was back on narrow roadways like those Seamus had driven over, still driving much too fast.

Sharon still had all sorts of questions about their destination and why they were going there, but she probably wouldn't get a straight answer out of Mo, so she didn't ask. For damned sure, the Seamus story was bogus.

The Lexus slid to a stop in loose gravel in front of a solitary stone house flanked on each side by evergreens that almost hid it from the road. Another black Lexus with tinted windows and an older model Mercedes, were parked out front.

"Who's here?" Sharon asked.

"Just some friends. Seamus is with them."

Like hell, Sharon thought, like hell.

Mo opened the front door with a key. She held it open, and when Sharon hesitated, Mo grabbed her arm and pulled her inside.

"Easy," Sharon said. "Stop dragging me around."

"We're already late," Mo said.

"Late for what?"

"They're all in here waiting for you." She led Sharon down a short hallway. She opened a door on the left and pushed Sharon through.

A stocky man who Sharon thought she recognized

but couldn't place, stood off to the left beside an unmade bed. But the other guy, standing relaxed, arms folded across his chest, she recognized immediately.

"Bob Hastings?" It couldn't be. "What are you doing here?"

"Hello, Sharon. I've sure missed our sessions back at the house. We're both tired of fucking Mo. I mean, she's okay but she just can't do it like you do."

"Oh, no," she said, shaking her head.

"You remember my friend, Lou, don't you, that little threesome we were going to have before you chased us away? He's been talking about it ever since."

"Oh, yeah, the girl with the great tits," Lou said.

She flattened herself against the wall. Mo had the door blocked. She might be able to get past Mo, but the other two would be on her in a second. "I want to leave," she said.

"Not happening," Bob said. "We got unfinished business, you and me. First let's get some names straight. I'm Bob Hennessey, not Hastings. And you are Sharon Sullivan, not Saluda."

"That's not true," she said. "Sullivan is just a name Seamus made up for me while I'm here."

"Tricky one, that Seamus, giving you back your family name without telling you," he said.

"You're lying. I've seen my birth certificate. I'm Sharon Saluda, and I was born in Jacob's Bluff, North Carolina. I don't care what you say, that's the truth."

"I've seen that birth certificate in your family papers, and it's a fake. Not only is the name wrong, but you were born a half hour's drive north of here. Something else Seamus didn't tell you, I'm guessing."

"How did you find this out?" Sharon asked. She

didn't believe him, but it would be good to know where he got his information.

"You helped me, when you pissed off your ma, and she named me executor of her estate."

"There was no estate. That house wasn't worth anything."

"I don't give a shit about the house. I wanted information. It took me some time to dig it all out, and without access to your family documents I never would have. Your ma owned a lot of land just north of here, and if you were still in the picture, it would all be yours."

"I am still in the picture. I'm right here."

"Not for long. See, as executor, all of that comes right to me, if you disappear."

"What do you mean, disappear?" she asked.

"Oh, you'll find out soon enough. You won't be the first person who fell over the cliffs. Easy to do if you're not careful."

"I'm leaving," Mo said. "You don't need me for any of this."

"No, you're not. You're gonna help us undress Ms. Sullivan. In fact, you two might put on a little show for us."

"That wasn't part of the deal," Mo said.

"What deal?" Sharon asked.

"Your buddy, Mo, owes me money. We let her work off some of it in bed, but she's still in to me for big bucks. Delivering you was going to clear up her debt, save us from having to break her legs. A shame to have to do that, they're pretty legs."

"I did what you wanted," Mo said. "Now I want to go."

"You're staying until we're finished. Then you'll be just as guilty as anybody else. Help you remember to keep your mouth shut. Otherwise we'll have two bodies to dump instead of one."

"Don't do this, whatever you're planning," Sharon said. "I've got money, all the money from Monmouth. I'll give you the account numbers if you'll just let me walk out of here."

"What do you think, Lou?" Bob asked.

Lou ground his fist into his palm. "What I think is, I can persuade her to give us the account numbers, and we'll get all the family land too. Of course, it might get a little bloody. You want to fuck her first or after I'm through?"

"If you're going to mess her up I want to do her first. No reason we can't do her again while you're working on her. Be just like old times, huh, Sharon?"

"No, please, don't do it," Sharon said.

"Mo, do your thing."

Mo stood facing Sharon. "Please, don't fight me. The sooner we finish the better for you." She reached for the top of Sharon's shirt.

"Touch me and I'll scratch your eyes out."

"Hot damn," Lou said. "Cat fight."

The door splintered and flew off its hinges, knocking Mo to the floor.

Seamus charged in and took Lou out with a single punch to the head. The man fell to the floor not far from Mo and didn't move again. The two large men who came in behind Seamus grabbed Bob as he bolted for the door. Poor Bob looked like a child suspended between them, kicking and squirming with no real hope of escape.

"You know what to do with him," Seamus said as the men dragged Bob outside. In a moment they came back for the unconscious Lou and dragged him out as well.

Mo lunged for Seamus's feet and wrapped her arms around his legs. "Seamus, please, don't hurt me. I'm your sister."

"Seamus, let her go," Sharon said.

"Family business," he said. He grabbed one of Mo's arms and yanked her to her feet. He pulled a roll of bills from his pocket, peeled off several and shoved them into her hand. "You've got until sundown to get out of the country. If you ever come back, you know what will happen."

Mo lurched through the door and was gone.

Seamus wrapped an arm around Sharon's shoulder and led her out to his car. The other vehicles that had been there earlier were gone now.

Except for the annoying whine of the four-cylinder engine and the noise of tires bumping along a primitive roadway, the interior of the car was silent. The rays from the late afternoon sun, with no cloud cover to impede them, bored through the left side windows.

The shakes didn't hit her until they'd drive a couple of miles. Then her body was no longer her own. She wailed, she cried, she convulsed as if electrodes were driven into her arms and legs. Seamus pulled off the road and wrapped her in an embrace so tight that it was painful. But that pain was all that kept her from spinning out of control.

"No more," she said. "Please, no more. When does it all end?"

"That's the last of them," he said.

He dragged her out of the car, then carried her across the road and up a gentle rise. He set her down facing the setting sun.

"Why?" she asked. "Why do all these people want to kill me?"

"You know part of it. I'll tell you the rest later. But it's over now. I swear to God, it's over."

It took some time before her sobs subsided and she breathed normally again. All the while she clung to him like a raft in a stormy sea.

"What about Mo? She can't come back home, ever?" Sharon asked.

"No."

"Does your poor Ma know?"

"She's been expecting it."

Sharon felt like she'd been living in a bubble with the lights off. So much happening around her, and everyone in on it but her.

"I'm really pissed at you," she said.

"I know. We'll talk tonight."

"It may be too late for that. I'm tired of being treated like somebody's prize idiot. Maybe the only thing I'm good for is fucking. That's what everybody seems to think."

They said no more until Seamus pulled the car in front of the house. Sharon got out and headed toward her bedroom. Her only alternative now seemed to pack up her things and get out, leave this lunacy behind her. Surely there was somewhere she could go and live a normal life. She'd hoped for more, much more, but she would settle for less, just as long as it wasn't crazy.

"I'll be out here at the table," Seamus said. "If you want to talk. If not, I'll understand."

What was there to talk about? Her life recently had turned out to be one big fat joke. Talking wasn't going to make that any better. She dragged her suitcase out of the closet and packed enough clothes to last for a few days. Tomorrow she would ask Seamus to drive her to the airport.

From the time her head hit the pillow until the rising sun warmed her face was a complete blank. Her pillow was wet; sometime during the night she must have had a crying spell, but she didn't remember it. Her body had gone into shut-down mode, closing off everything; that's the way she figured it. She lay for a time watching sunbeams form shifting patterns on her bedroom wall.

Her bag, along with her little burgundy case, sat by the door, packed and ready to go. Her plans extended only as far as the ticket counter at the airport. Then and there she would decide where to go. Maybe back to Antigua, maybe somewhere else.

Showered and dressed, her room straight and tidy, she picked up her bag and headed off to the kitchen for her final confrontation with Seamus. But Seamus wasn't there. Instead, Ma sat at the table, a coffee mug cradled in her hands. "You should eat," she said.

"I'm not hungry, maybe just some coffee."

Ma returned from the stove with a coffee mug and a plate laden with her standard breakfast fare, as usual, enough to feed a family of four. "You should eat," she said again.

What the hell, her last breakfast in this house. Sharon dug in.

Sometime later she stared down at an empty plate. Where had it all gone? She couldn't possibly have…

Ma was smiling now. "Good," she said.

"Where is Seamus?" Sharon asked.

"He went for a walk. He'll be back soon."

"Maybe I should just call a cab."

"No need. He'll take you wherever you want to go." Ma took Sharon's plate to the sink and rinsed it off. She brought over the battered coffee pot and refilled their cups. "I knew your mother," she said.

Her mother? Impossible. The door behind which she had shut away all unpleasant things swung open, and what she had hoped not to face for a long time now closed around her like so much dead fish, reeking and impossible to ignore. "Tell me, everything," she said.

"You were such a tiny thing back then."

"Back when? What happened?" Sharon asked.

"There were some old feuds, nobody could remember how they started. Our generation, your mother's and mine, were the last to be caught up in it. There was a raid. Your father was shot dead right by the front door of your house. They burned the house.

"They knew it was coming, your mom and dad. Your ma ran with you and one small bag. She stayed with us for a couple of days, then caught a ride to the coast. That's how you got to America.

"That seemed to be the end of it, but it wasn't. I didn't hear from your Ma until last year. She said someone named Bob Hastings had come to visit her, said he was a classmate of yours, but she guessed who he really was, Hennessey, not Hastings. That's when I asked Seamus to go and look after you, until we knew for sure."

"But I wasn't on good terms with my parents, neither one of them," Sharon said.

"I know. She told me in her letter." She took an envelope from the pocket of her apron and passed it over to Sharon.

Sharon took the thick envelope with trembling hands. This missive would be the final communication from her mother. Would it be a scathing indictment of her daughter, or some resolution to those difficult final years? The thought of her mother racing away carrying a baby Sharon in her arms put a lump in her throat that she would never be able to swallow.

"Do people here know who I am?" Sharon asked, as if she knew herself.

"Some do, yes. Others can probably guess. The older ones will recognize you immediately, because you look just like your mother as a younger woman."

Then the tears came, and there was nothing she could do to stop them. The things she would want to say to her mother, and now never could. That reconciliation would never happen. She was starting over, a rebirth, and that was not an easy process. Getting to know herself would be as close as she would ever come to knowing her own mother.

But there was still the matter of Bob Hastings, Hennessey, whatever. It had been a punch in the gut to learn that he had been named executor of her mother's estate.

"I don't understand why, if she was afraid of Bob Hastings, why she made him executor of her estate," Sharon said.

"Probably he threatened her, said he would do something bad to you if she didn't go along. Maybe she was just trying to protect you from all that had happened so long ago. I don't know. I do know Seamus was a lot more worked up about that man Connor Shaw."

Sharon's stomach knotted up. The last thing she wanted this woman to ever know was about her arrangement with Connor Shaw. Having been the man's whore was nothing to be proud of. "How did he ever find out about me and Connor Shaw?"

"Seamus can answer that a lot better than I can, if you'll give him a chance. And I do hope you'll give him a chance."

She reached across and took Sharon's hand between hers. Small hands with bulging knuckles, two fingers on the left hand deformed as if they'd been broken and never set properly, hands that had known hard work and hardship, lots of it. It seemed to Sharon that she could read the woman more through her hands than her words. She could feel pain and joy and a lifetime of struggle in the hands that held hers.

Ma stood as she released Sharon's hand. She walked around the table and kissed her cheek. "Welcome home," she said. Then she was gone. Sharon realized she'd just had the longest conversation she'd ever had or would have with this quiet woman, mother of an even quieter son.

Welcome home, in that brief conversation Ma had flipped her world upside down. She wasn't who she thought she was. She wasn't even born where she thought she'd been born. In short, who the hell was she? All she knew was that where she stood now felt like home, felt like where she belonged. But that only made the craziness worse. She couldn't very well become another person in the space of a few hours. It just couldn't happen.

So many unanswered questions, and near the top of the list sat Seamus. She had feelings for him, strong feelings, but they were confused feelings. And that confusion was compounded by not having any idea of how he felt about her. There had been moments, those few times when he'd kissed her, when a definite spark had flared. But he never followed through. The next day he would be as closed and distant as ever.

With Connor she had taken the plunge immediately, no questions asked. She'd known very little about him, but the intense pleasure he'd given her more than made up for her lack of information. And in the end he'd turned on her, used her body and soul.

The difference, it seemed to her, was trust, knowing that if things really went bad, she could count on him to stand by her. And trust took time. The circumstances under which he'd known her longest—Connor's whore—hardly inspired confidence.

If she wanted Seamus's trust, which she most definitely did, she would have to be patient, and earn it. But there was no time for that now.

She didn't wait long before she took off. She had to return once more to that burned out hull where, according to Seamus, she'd been born. If there were answers to be had, that's where she'd find them. Mother Nature seemed to think she was following the right path and encouraged her with blue skies and a gentle breeze to block the heat of the early afternoon sun. So green, everywhere she looked, so bright that it practically glowed.

No leisurely stroll this time. She walked with a purpose. As she hiked along, the fog in her brain lifted, and some things cleared up for her. By the time the old foundation came into view she had a plan. She walked around the perimeter of that foundation, many of the stones still charred from that fire so many years before. An opening faced the sea. This, she thought, must have been a door. What a magnificent vista her parents would have enjoyed through the front windows of this house that had now lain in ruins for twenty years.

Had her mother really fled for her life that night with room for only Sharon and a small bag in her arms? Had her own father fallen in the spot where she now stood? Did his blood seep into the ground beneath her?

She found a flat stone and sat, her legs drawn up and her chin resting on her knees. This was it. This was the place. No more running. A new Sullivan had come home to claim her birthright. When had she made this decision? She really couldn't say.

Seamus rode toward her on the same black gelding he'd ridden before, but this time he led a palomino mare, all saddled up and ready to go.

"Whose horse?" she asked.

"Yours if you like her. She's very gentle." He dismounted and walked over beside her.

"Your mother told me a lot about my history, stuff I never dreamed of. I still don't know which end is up, who I am or anything."

"Yeah, that must have been quite a shock."

"You never told me any of this," she said. "You left me hanging like a complete fool."

"It wasn't time, and you weren't ready."

"Shouldn't that be my decision?"

"You're right, but you know pretty much everything now," he said.

"Not yet. I'm just starting. What happened, back

when my dad was killed?"

"Old feuds, most of them started so long ago nobody remembers why. But that's all over now, I promise."

"Does everybody around here know who I am?" She'd asked Ma the same question, but that didn't matter now.

"Some do, some don't. You have lots of friends you don't even know about."

"And I guess I have a lot of cousins, just like you," she said.

"Probably more than me." He laughed.

"Oh, God, please tell me we aren't cousins, you and me."

"Not that I know of. Maybe back a few centuries ago we were related. It's a small island after all."

"I feel like I'm starting over. I don't know anything or anybody."

"That's true, in a way. Now, mount up," he said. "If you're going to stay here you'll have to learn to ride a horse. You are staying, aren't you?"

"Yes, I am." The mare nuzzled Sharon's chest.

"Here, give her this. It's what she's looking for." He tossed her an apple.

The mare took the apple from Sharon's open palm. She didn't flinch at all when Sharon climbed aboard.

"You'll need to get started on your house soon. The summer months are going fast. And you'll need a barn for your horses."

"You have to stop doing that," she said.

"Stop what?"

"Knowing what I'm going to do before I know it myself. And I'm still not going to eat blood sausage, not ever."

That got her a big booming Seamus laugh, one like she hadn't heard before. "Come on, woman, I'm going to show you around your new home."

So that's how it would be, then. It still pissed her off , how he'd planned everything out, but he'd left her lots of room as well, room to discover her own identity, room to grow and establish herself as the rightful heir to the land over which they rode.

Yes, it was all coming together now, his distance, his resistance to her overtures. First she had to become who she really was, not just the high-priced call girl he'd known before. She had to become Sharon Sullivan, a girl whose roots grew deep into the soil where her own father's blood had been spilled.

Then they could come together as kindred spirits, as parts of a whole.

"I'm onto you," she said. "I know what you're up to."

He turned in his saddle and smiled, and that was all.

Bastard, his smile said more than most people could get out in a long speech. Fine for now, she thought. *But someday, Mr. Seamus Clark, we'll do it my way, and I'll make you howl at the moon. Someday.*

Mike Owens

About the Author

Mike Owens lives in coastal Virginia with his wife, Marilyn. He claims to bleed Tar Heel Blue, having received both his undergraduate and medical degrees from the University of North Carolina. He topped off the educational effort with an MFA in creative writing from Old Dominion University—a darker shade of blue.

Earlier writing themes, both fiction and non-fiction, involved the often contentious interface between medical science and biomedical ethics, but it's fiction from now one, a lot more fun.

This biographical note would not be complete without mention of the contribution of Molly, his highly critical Weimaraner, who is now editor-in-chief in doggy heaven. God bless.

~*~

Visit Mike at

http://www.mikeowens42.com

~*~

To chat with Mike Owens and other Wild Rose Press authors of erotic romance, join us at

www.groups.yahoo.com/group/thewilderroses.

Also Available
A War Like Ours
By Saffron A. Kent
http://a.co/f86FssN

A liar…

Three weeks ago, James Maxwell's wife died in a car accident, but he hasn't been able to tell his five-year old daughter the heartbreaking truth behind her mother's death. Instead, he packs them up and leaves for a summer resort in upstate New York to spend a few peaceful weeks and to gradually break the news. But a spirited and outspoken maid at the resort has figured out his secret.

A hater…

After witnessing her mother's violent death at the hands of her stepfather, Madison Smith has turned aimless and bitter toward the world—men, in particular. Her dead-end job at the local resort and her convenient girlfriend are barely keep Madison from falling apart. When she meets James, however, she's driven to protect his child from the darkness she sees inside him.

A forbidden kiss…

But Madison doesn't expect to find that very darkness irresistible. Drowning in guilt and memories, James doesn't expect to be drawn to the sharp-witted woman who has made his life miserable. When their tempers flare, a brutal kiss triggers a need that blurs the lines of hate and desire. As their lust spins out of control, they must decide if their attraction is worth fighting for or if love is the real enemy.

Also Read

One Hard Ride
By M.M. Bordeaux
http://a.co/eLskCjN

Amanda Sloane's passion has been solely focused on becoming a well-respected, NYC art appraiser. With that appetite sated, she can no longer ignore her body's carnal desires.

Tasked with authenticating an uncataloged Randell painting that could be worth millions, she meets a trio of Texas ranch hands who take her on an erotic ride imagined only in her deepest fantasy. Between ranch owners, Jake and Justin Morgan, and their ranch foreman, Luke, the cowboys ignite in Amanda a raging fire of uninhibited sexuality.

For years, the Morgan brothers have fought off their greedy cousin's attempts to take their ranch, including poison and sabotage. Now, Jake is counting on the elegant and sophisticated art appraiser to authenticate his grandaddy's painting to stave off foreclosure on the family ranch. Awakening the big city vixen's sexual hunger has his body ablaze with need and his heart yearning for love.

Can Amanda give up the intoxicating pleasure of her sexual awakening? Or is Jake's love unconditional enough to encourage her to continue her erotic odyssey?

Thank you for purchasing this
publication of The Wild Rose Press, Inc.
If you enjoyed the story, we would appreciate
your letting others know by leaving a review.
For other wonderful stories, please visit our
on-line bookstore at www.wilderroses.com.

For questions or more
information contact us at
info@thewildrosepress.com.

The Wild Rose Press, Inc.
www.thewilderroses.com

Stay current with The Wild Rose Press, Inc.
Like us on Facebook
https://www.facebook.com/TheWildRosePress
And Follow us on Twitter
https://twitter.com/WildRosePress